W9-BRT-934

RANDOM HOUSE LARGE PRINT

The
Fourth
Hand

The Fourth Hand

A NOVEL

John Irving

RANDOM HOUSE
LARGE PRINT

EASTON PUBLIC LIBRARY
P.O. BOX 2
EASTON, CT 06612

The Fourth Hand is a work of fiction. Other than those well-known individuals and news events referred to for purposes incidental to the plot, all names, places, characters, and events are the product of the author's imagination, and any resemblance to actual events, locales, or persons, living or dead, is entirely coincidental. To the extent that real persons and reported events are mentioned in the novel, the author has included such references without the knowledge or cooperation of the individuals involved.

Copyright © 2001 by Garp Enterprises, Ltd.

All rights reserved under International and Pan-American Copyright Conventions.
Published in the United States of America by Random House Large Print in association with Random House, New York.
Distributed by Random House, Inc., New York.

Library of Congress Cataloging-in-Publication Data
Irving, John, 1942–
The fourth hand / by John Irving.
p.   cm.
ISBN 0-375-43121-7
1. Transplantation of organs, tissues, etc.—Fiction.   2. Donation of organs, tissues, etc.—Fiction.   3. Television journalists—Fiction.
4. Transplant surgeons—Fiction.   5. Hand—Surgery—Fiction.
6. Large type books.   I. Title.
PS3559.R8 F68 2001
813'.54—dc21   00-054694

Random House Web Address: *www.randomlargeprint.com*

FIRST LARGE PRINT EDITION

10   9   8   7   6   5   4   3   2   1

This Large Print edition published in accord with the standards of the N.A.V.H.

37777002131159

For

Richard Gladstein

and

Lasse Hallström

"... a person who is looking for something doesn't travel very fast."

—the telephone repairman in

E. B. White's *Stuart Little*

CONTENTS

x • Contents

The
Fourth
Hand

The Lion Guy

*I*MAGINE A YOUNG MAN on his way to a less-than-thirty-second event—the loss of his left hand, long before he reached middle age.

As a schoolboy, he was a promising student, a fair-minded and likable kid, without being terribly original. Those classmates who could remember the future hand recipient from his elementary-school days would never have described him as daring. Later, in high school, his success with girls notwithstanding, he was rarely a bold boy, certainly not a reckless one. While he was irrefutably good-looking, what his former girlfriends would recall as most appealing about him was that he deferred to them.

Throughout college, no one would have predicted that fame was his destiny. "He was so unchallenging," an ex-girlfriend said.

Another young woman, who'd known him briefly in graduate school, agreed. "He didn't have the confidence of someone who was going to do anything special" was how she put it.

He wore a perpetual but dismaying smile—the look of someone who knows he's met you before but can't recall the exact occasion. He might have been in the act of guessing whether the previous meeting was at a funeral or in a brothel, which would explain why, in his smile, there was an unsettling combination of grief and embarrassment.

He'd had an affair with his thesis adviser; she was either a reflection of or a reason for his lack of direction as a graduate student. Later—she was a divorcée with a nearly grown daughter—she would assert: "You could never rely on someone that good-looking. He was also a classic underachiever—he wasn't as hopeless as you first thought. You wanted to help him. You wanted to change him. You *definitely* wanted to have sex with him."

In her eyes, there would suddenly be a kind of light that hadn't been there; it arrived and departed like a change of color at the day's end, as if there were no distance too great for this light to travel. In noting "his vulnerability to scorn," she emphasized "how touching that was."

But what about his decision to undergo hand-transplant surgery? Wouldn't only an adventurer or an idealist run the risk necessary to acquire a new hand?

No one who knew him would ever say he was an

adventurer or an idealist, but surely he'd been idealistic once. When he was a boy, he must have had dreams; even if his goals were private, unexpressed, he'd had goals.

His thesis adviser, who was comfortable in the role of expert, attached some significance to the loss of his parents when he was still a college student. But his parents had amply provided for him; in spite of their deaths, he was financially secure. He could have stayed in college until he had tenure—he could have gone to graduate school for the rest of his life. Yet, although he'd always been a successful student, he never struck any of his teachers as exceptionally motivated. He was not an initiator—he just took what was offered.

He had all the earmarks of someone who would come to terms with the loss of a hand by making the best of his limitations. Everyone who knew him had him pegged as a guy who would eventually be content one-handed.

Besides, he was a television journalist. For what he did, wasn't one hand enough?

But he believed a new hand was what he wanted, and he'd alertly understood everything that could go medically wrong with the transplant. What he failed to realize explained why he had never before been much of an experimenter; he lacked the imagination to entertain the disquieting idea that the new hand would not be entirely his. After all, it had been someone else's hand to begin with.

How fitting that he was a television journalist. Most television journalists are pretty smart—in the sense of being mentally quick, of having an instinct to cut to the chase. There's no procrastination on TV. A guy who decides to have hand-transplant surgery doesn't dither around, does he?

Anyway, his name was Patrick Wallingford and he would, without hesitation, have traded his fame for a new left hand. At the time of the accident, Patrick was moving up in the world of television journalism. He'd worked for two of the three major networks, where he repeatedly complained about the evil influence of ratings on the news. How many times had it happened that some CEO more familiar with the men's room than the control room made a "marketing decision" that compromised a story? (In Wallingford's opinion, the news executives had completely caved in to the marketing mavens.)

To put it plainly, Patrick believed that the networks' financial expectations of their news divisions were killing the news. Why should news shows be expected to make as much money as what the networks called entertainment? Why should there be any pressure on a news division even to make a profit? News wasn't what happened in Hollywood; news wasn't the World Series or the Super Bowl. News (by which Wallingford meant *real* news—that is, in-depth coverage) shouldn't have to compete for ratings with comedies or so-called dramas.

Patrick Wallingford was still working for one of

the major networks when the Berlin Wall fell in November 1989. Patrick was thrilled to be in Germany on such a historic occasion, but the pieces he filed from Berlin were continually edited down— sometimes to half the length he felt they deserved. A CEO in the New York newsroom said to Wallingford: "Any news in the foreign-policy category is worth shit."

When this same network's overseas bureaus began closing, Patrick made the move that other TV journalists have made. He went to work for an all-news network; it was not a very good network, but at least it was a twenty-four-hour international news channel.

Was Wallingford naïve enough to think that an all-news network wouldn't keep an eye on *its* ratings? In fact, the international channel was overfond of minute-by-minute ratings that could pinpoint when the attention of the television audience waxed or waned.

Yet there was cautious consensus among Wallingford's colleagues in the media that he seemed destined to be an anchor. He was inarguably handsome— the sharp features of his face were perfect for television—and he'd paid his dues as a field reporter. Funnily enough, the enmity of Wallingford's wife was chief among his costs.

She was his ex-wife now. He blamed the travel, but his then-wife's assertion was that other women were the problem. In truth, Patrick *was* drawn to first-time sexual encounters, and he would remain drawn to them, whether he traveled or not.

Just prior to Patrick's accident, there'd been a paternity suit against him. Although the case was dismissed—a DNA test was negative—the mere allegation of his paternity raised the rancor of Wallingford's wife. Beyond her then-husband's flagrant infidelity, she had an additional reason to be upset. Although she'd long wanted to have children, Patrick had steadfastly refused. (Again he blamed the travel.)

Now Wallingford's ex-wife—her name was Marilyn—was wont to say that she wished her ex-husband had lost more than his left hand. She'd quickly remarried, had got pregnant, had had a child; then she'd divorced again. Marilyn would also say that the pain of childbirth—notwithstanding how long she'd looked forward to having a child—was greater than the pain Patrick had experienced in losing his left hand.

Patrick Wallingford was not an angry man; a usually even-tempered disposition was as much his trademark as his drop-dead good looks. Yet the pain of losing his left hand was Wallingford's most fiercely guarded possession. It infuriated him that his ex-wife trivialized his pain by declaring it less than hers in "merely," as he was wont to say, giving birth.

Nor was Wallingford always even-tempered in response to his ex-wife's proclamation that he was an addicted womanizer. In Patrick's opinion, he had never womanized. This meant that Wallingford didn't seduce women; he simply allowed himself to be seduced. He never called them—they called him. He was the boy equivalent of the girl who couldn't say no—emphasis, his ex-wife would say, on *boy*. (Patrick had been in his late twenties, going on thirty, when his then-wife divorced him, but, according to Marilyn, he was permanently a boy.)

The anchor chair, for which he'd seemed destined, still eluded him. And after the accident, Wallingford's prospects dimmed. Some CEO cited "the squeamish factor." Who wants to watch their morning or their evening news telecast by some loser-victim type who's had his hand chomped off by a hungry lion? It may have been a less-than-thirty-second event— the entire story ran only three minutes—but no one with a television set had missed it. For a couple of weeks, it was on the tube repeatedly, worldwide.

Wallingford was in India. His all-news network, which, because of its penchant for the catastrophic, was often referred to by the snobs in the media elite as "Disaster International," or the "calamity channel," had sent him to the site of an Indian circus in Gujarat. (No sensible news network would have sent a field reporter from New York to a circus in India.)

The Great Ganesh Circus was performing in Junagadh, and one of their trapeze artists, a young woman, had fallen. She was renowned for "flying"— as the work of such aerialists is called—without a safety net, and while she was not killed in the fall, which was from a height of eighty feet, her husband/ trainer had been killed when he attempted to catch her. Although her plummeting body killed him, he managed to break her fall.

The Indian government instantly declared no more flying without a net, and the Great Ganesh, among other small circuses in India, protested the ruling. For years, a certain government minister—an over-zealous animal-rights activist—had been trying to ban the use of animals in Indian circuses, and for this reason the circuses were sensitive to government interference of any kind. Besides—as the excitable ringmaster of the Great Ganesh Circus told Patrick Wallingford, on-camera—the audiences packed the tent every afternoon and night *because* the trapeze artists didn't use a net.

What Wallingford had noticed was that the nets themselves were in shocking disrepair. From where Patrick stood on the dry, hard-packed earth—on the "floor" of the tent, looking up—he saw that the pattern of holes was ragged and torn. The damaged net resembled a colossal spiderweb that had been wrecked by a panicked bird. It was doubtful that the net could support the weight of a falling child, much less that of an adult.

Many of the performers *were* children, and these mostly girls. Their parents had sold them to the circus so they could have a better (meaning a safer) life. Yet the element of risk in the Great Ganesh was huge. The excitable ringmaster had told the truth: the audiences packed the tent every afternoon and night to see accidents happen. And often the victims of these accidents were children. As performers, they were talented amateurs—good little athletes—but they were spottily trained.

Why most of the children were girls was a subject any good journalist would have been interested in, and Wallingford—whether or not one believed his ex-wife's assessment of his character—was a good journalist. His intelligence lay chiefly in his powers of observation, and television had taught him the importance of quickly jumping ahead to what might go wrong.

The jumping-ahead part was both what was brilliant about and what was wrong with television. TV was driven by crises, not causes. What chiefly disappointed Patrick about his field assignments for the all-news network was how common it was to miss or ignore a more important story. For example, the majority of the child performers in an Indian circus were girls because their parents had not wanted them to become prostitutes; at worst, the boys not sold to a circus would become beggars. (Or they would starve.)

But that wasn't the story Patrick Wallingford had been sent to India to report. A trapeze artist, a grown woman hurtling downward from eighty feet, had landed in her husband's arms and killed him. The Indian government had intervened—the result being that every circus in India was protesting the ruling that their aerialists now had to use a net. Even the recently widowed trapeze artist, the woman who'd fallen, joined in the protest.

Wallingford had interviewed her in the hospital, where she was recovering from a broken hip and some nonspecific damage to her spleen; she told him that flying without a safety net was what made the flying special. Certainly she would mourn her late husband, but her husband had been an aerialist, too—he'd also fallen and had survived his fall. Yet possibly, his widow implied, he'd not *really* escaped that first mistake; her falling on him had conceivably signified the true conclusion of the earlier, unfinished episode.

Now *that* was interesting, Wallingford thought, but his news editor, who was cordially despised by everyone, was disappointed in the interview. And all the people in the newsroom in New York thought that the widowed trapeze artist had seemed "too calm"; they preferred their disaster victims to be hysterical.

Furthermore, the recovering aerialist had said her late husband was now "in the arms of the goddess he believed in"—an enticing phrase. What she meant was that her husband had believed in Durga, the Goddess of Destruction. Most of the trapeze artists believed in Durga—the goddess is generally depicted as having ten arms. The widow explained: "Durga's arms are meant to catch and hold you, if you ever fall."

That was interesting to Wallingford, too, but not to

the people in the newsroom in New York; they said they were "sick of religion." Patrick's news editor informed him that they had run too many religious stories lately. What a dick, Wallingford thought. It didn't help that the news editor's name was Dick.

He'd sent Patrick back to the Great Ganesh Circus to acquire "additional local color." Dick had further reasoned that the ringmaster was more outspoken than the trapeze artist.

Patrick had protested. "Something about the child performers would make a better story," he said. But apparently they were also "sick of children" in New York.

"Just get more of the ringmaster," Dick advised Wallingford.

In tandem with the ringmaster's excitement, the lions in their cage—the lions were the background for the last interview—grew restless and loud. In television terms, the piece that Wallingford was filing from India was the intended "kicker," the show-ender. The lions would make the story an even better kicker if they roared loudly enough.

It was meat day, and the Muslims who brought the meat had been delayed. The television truck and the camera and sound equipment—as well as the cameraman and the female sound technician—had intimidated them. The Muslim meat wallahs had been frozen in their tracks by so much unfamiliar technology. But primarily it was the sight of the female sound technician that had halted them.

A tall blonde in tight blue jeans, she wore headphones and a tool belt with what must have struck the
meat wallahs as an assortment of male-looking ac-
cessories: either pliers or a pair of wire cutters, a
bunch of clamps and cables, and what might have
been a battery-tester. She was also wearing a T-shirt
without a bra.

Wallingford knew that she was German because
he'd slept with her the night before. She'd told him
about the first trip she took to Goa—she was on vacation, traveling with another German girl, and
they'd both decided that they never wanted to live
anywhere but India.

The other girl got sick and went home, but Monika
had found a way to stay in India. That was her
name—"Monika with a *k*," she'd told him. "Sound
technicians can live anywhere," she had declared.
"Anywhere there's sound."

"You might like to try living in New York,"
Patrick had suggested. "There's a lot of sound there,
and you can drink the water." Unthinkingly, he'd
added: "German girls are very popular in New York
right now."

"Why 'right now'?" she'd asked.

This was symptomatic of the trouble Patrick
Wallingford got into with women; that he said things
for no reason was not unlike the way he acquiesced
to the advances women made to him. There'd been
no reason for saying "German girls are very popular
in New York right now," except to keep talking. It

was his feeble acquiescence to women, his tacit as-
sent to their advances, that had infuriated Wallingford's wife, who'd just happened to call him in his
hotel room when he was fucking Monika with a *k*.

There was a ten-and-a-half-hour time difference
between Junagadh and New York, but Patrick pretended he didn't know whether India was ten and a
half hours ahead or behind. All he ever said when his
wife called was, "What time is it there, honey?"

"You're fucking someone, aren't you?" his wife
asked.

"No, Marilyn, I am *not,*" he lied. Under him, the
German girl held still. Wallingford tried to hold himself still, too, but holding still in the act of lovemaking is arguably more difficult for a man.

"I just thought you'd like to know the results
of your paternity test," Marilyn said. This helped
Patrick to hold still. "Well, it's negative—you're not
the father. I guess you dodged that bullet, didn't
you?"

All Wallingford could think of saying was: "That
was improper—that they gave you the results of my
blood test. It was *my* blood test."

Under him, Monika with a *k* went rigid; where
she'd been warm, she felt cool. "*What* blood test?"
she whispered in Patrick's ear.

But Wallingford was wearing a condom—the German sound technician was protected from most
things, if not everything. (Patrick always wore a condom, even with his wife.)

"Who is she this time?" Marilyn hollered into the phone. "Who are you fucking at this very minute?"

Two things were clear to Wallingford: that his marriage could not be saved and that he didn't want to save it. As always, with women, Patrick acquiesced. "Who *is* she?" his wife screamed again, but Wallingford wouldn't answer her. Instead he held the mouthpiece of the phone to the German girl's lips.

Patrick needed to move a wisp of the girl's blond hair away from her ear before he whispered into it. "Just tell her your name."

"Monika . . . with a *k*," the German girl said into the phone.

Wallingford hung up, doubting that Marilyn would call back—she didn't. But after that, he had a lot to say to Monika with a *k;* they hadn't had the best night's sleep.

In the morning, at the Great Ganesh, the way everything had started out seemed a little anticlimactic. The ringmaster's repeated complaints about the Indian government were not nearly so sympathetic as the fallen trapeze artist's description of the ten-armed goddess in whom all the aerialists believed.

Were they deaf and blind in the newsroom in New York? That widow in her hospital bed had been great stuff! And Wallingford still wanted to tell the story of the *context* of the trapeze artist falling without a safety net. The child performers were the context, those children who'd been sold to the circus.

What if the trapeze artist herself had been sold to the circus as a child? What if her late husband had been rescued from a no-future childhood, only to meet his fate—his wife falling into his arms from eighty feet—under the big top? *That* would have been interesting.

Instead, Patrick was interviewing the repetitive ringmaster in front of the lions' cage—this commonplace circus image being what New York had meant by "additional local color."

No wonder the interview seemed anticlimactic compared to Wallingford's night with the German sound technician. Monika with a *k,* in her T-shirt without a bra, was making a noticeable impression on the Muslim meat wallahs, who had taken offense at the German girl's clothes, or lack thereof. In their fear, their curiosity, their moral outrage, they would have given a better and truer depiction of additional local color than the tiresome ringmaster.

Near the lions' cage, but appearing either too afraid or too dumbfounded or too offended to come any closer, the Muslims stood as if in shock. Their wooden carts were piled high with the sweet-smelling meat, which was a source of infinite disgust to the largely vegetarian (Hindu) community of the circus. Naturally the lions could smell the meat, too, and were vexed at the delay.

When the lions began roaring, the cameraman zoomed in on them, and Patrick Wallingford—recognizing a moment of genuine spontaneity—

extended his microphone to within reach of their cage. He got a better kicker than he'd bargained for.

A paw flicked out; a claw caught Wallingford's left wrist. He dropped the microphone. In less than two seconds, his left arm, up to his elbow, had been snatched inside the cage. His left shoulder was slammed against the bars; his left hand, including an inch or more above his wrist, was in a lion's mouth.

In the ensuing hullabaloo, two other lions competed with the first for Patrick's wrist and hand. The lion tamer, who was never far from his lions, intervened; he struck them in their faces with a shovel. Wallingford retained consciousness long enough to recognize the shovel—it was used principally as a lion pooper-scooper. (He'd seen it in action only minutes before.)

Patrick passed out somewhere in the vicinity of the meat carts, not far from where Monika with a *k* had sympathetically fainted. But the German girl had fainted *in* one of the meat carts, to the considerable consternation of the meat wallahs; and when she came to, she discovered that her tool belt had been stolen while she'd lain unconscious in the wet meat.

The German sound technician further claimed that, while she was passed out, someone had fondled her breasts—she had fingerprint bruises on both breasts to prove it. But there were no handprints among the bloodstains on her T-shirt. (The bloodstains were from the meat.) It was more likely that the bruises on her breasts were the result of her night-long lovemaking with Patrick Wallingford. Whoever had been bold enough to swipe her tool belt had probably lacked the courage to touch her breasts. No one had touched her headphones.

Wallingford, in turn, had been dragged away from the lions' cage without realizing that his left hand and wrist were gone; yet he was aware that the lions were still fighting over something. At the same moment that the sweet smell of the mutton reached him, he realized that the Muslims were transfixed by his dangling left arm. (The force of the lion's pull had separated his shoulder.) And when he looked, he saw that his watch was missing. He was not that sorry to have lost it—it had been a gift from his wife. Of course there was nothing to keep the watch from slipping off; his left hand and the big joint of his left wrist were missing, too.

Not finding a familiar face among the Muslim meat wallahs, Wallingford had doubtless hoped to locate Monika with a *k,* stricken but no less adoring. Unfortunately, the German girl was flat on her back in one of the mutton carts, her face turned away.

Patrick took some bitter consolation from seeing, if not the face, at least the profile of his unfazed cameraman, who had never wavered from his foremost responsibility. The determined professional had moved in close to the lions' cage, where the lions were caught in the act of not very agreeably sharing what little remained of Patrick's wrist and hand. Talk about a good kicker!

For the next week or more, Wallingford watched and rewatched the footage of his hand being taken from him and consumed. It puzzled him that the attack reminded him of something mystifying his thesis adviser had said to him when she was breaking off their affair: "It's been flattering, for a while, to be with a man who can so thoroughly lose himself in a woman. On the other hand, there's so little *you* in you that I suspect you could lose yourself in *any* woman." Just what on earth she could have meant by that, or why the eating of his hand had caused him to recall the complaining woman's remarks, he didn't know.

But what chiefly distressed Wallingford, in the less-than-thirty seconds it took a lion to dispose of his wrist and hand, was that the arresting images of himself were not pictures of Patrick Wallingford as he had ever looked before. He'd had no previous experience with abject terror. The worst of the pain came later.

In India, for reasons that were never clear, the government minister who was an activist for animal rights used the hand-eating episode to further the crusade against the abuse of circus animals. How eating his hand had abused the lions, Wallingford never knew.

What concerned him was that the world had seen

him scream and writhe in pain and fear; he'd wet his pants on-camera, not that a single television viewer had truly seen him do *that*. (He'd been wearing dark pants.) Nevertheless, he was an object of pity for millions, before whom he'd been publicly disfigured.

Even five years later, whenever Wallingford remembered or dreamed about the episode, the effect of the painkiller was foremost in his mind. The drug was not available in the United States—at least that was what the Indian doctor had told him. Wallingford had been trying to find out what it was ever since.

Whatever its name, the drug had elevated Patrick's consciousness of his pain while at the same time leaving him utterly detached from the pain itself; it had made him feel like an indifferent observer of someone else. And in elevating his consciousness, the drug did far more than relieve his pain.

The doctor who'd prescribed the medication, which came in the form of a cobalt-blue capsule—"Take only one, Mr. Wallingford, every twelve hours"—was a Parsi who treated him after the lion attack in Junagadh. "It's for the best dream you'll ever have, but it's also for pain," Dr. Chothia added. "Don't ever take two. Americans are always taking pills in twos. Not this one."

"What's it called? I presume it has a name." Wallingford was suspicious of it.

"After you take one, you won't remember what

it's called," Dr. Chothia told him cheerfully. "And you won't hear its name in America—your FDA guys will never approve it!"

"Why?" Wallingford asked. He still hadn't taken the first capsule.

"Go on—take it! You'll see," the Parsi said. "There's nothing better."

Despite his pain, Patrick didn't want to go off on some drug-induced trip.

"Before I take it, I want to know why the FDA will never approve it," he said.

"Because it's too much fun!" Dr. Chothia cried. "Your FDA guys don't like fun. Now take it, before I spoil your fun by giving you some other medication!"

The pill had put Patrick to sleep—or was it sleep? Surely his awareness was too heightened for sleep. But how could he have known he was in a state of prescience? How can anyone identify a dream of the future?

Wallingford was floating above a small, dark lake. There had to have been some kind of plane, or Wallingford couldn't have been there, but in the dream he never saw or heard the plane. He was simply descending, drawing closer to the little lake, which was surrounded by dark-green trees, fir trees and pines. Lots of white pines.

There were hardly any rock outcroppings. It didn't look like Maine, where Wallingford had gone to summer camp as a child. It didn't look like Ontario, either; Patrick's parents had once rented a cottage in Georgian Bay, Lake Huron. But the lake in the dream was no place he'd ever been.

Here and there a dock protruded into the water, and sometimes a small boat was tied to the dock. Wallingford saw a boathouse, too, but it was the feeling of the dock against his bare back, the roughness of its planks through a towel, that was the first physical sensation in the dream. As with the plane, he couldn't see the towel; he could only feel something between his skin and the dock.

The sun had just gone down. Wallingford had seen no sunset, but he could tell that the heat of the sun was still warming the dock. Except for Patrick's near-perfect view of the dark lake and the darker trees, the dream was all feeling.

He felt the water, too, but never that he was in it. Instead he had the feeling that he'd just come out of the water. His body was drying off on the dock, yet he still felt chilled.

Then a woman's voice—like no other woman's voice Wallingford had ever heard, like the sexiest voice in the world—said: "My bathing suit feels so *cold.* I'm going to take it off. Don't you want to take yours off, too?"

From that point on, in the dream, Patrick was aware of his erection, and he heard a voice that sounded a lot like his own, saying "yes"—he wanted to take off his wet bathing suit, too.

There was additionally the soft sound of the water

lapping against the dock, and dripping from the wet bathing suits between the planks, returning to the lake.

He and the woman were naked now. Her skin was at first wet and cold, and then warm against his skin; her breath was hot against his throat, and he could smell her wet hair. Moreover, the smell of sunlight had been absorbed by her taut shoulders, and there was something that tasted like the lake on Patrick's tongue, which traced the contours of the woman's ear.

Of course Wallingford was inside her, too—having never-ending sex on the dock at the lovely, dark lake. And when he woke up, eight hours later, he discovered that he'd had a wet dream; yet he still had the hugest hard-on he'd ever had.

The pain from his missing hand was gone. The pain would come back about ten hours after he'd taken the first of the cobalt-blue capsules. The two hours Patrick had to wait before he could take a second capsule were an eternity to him; in that miserable interim, all he could talk to Dr. Chothia about was the pill.

"What's in it?" Wallingford asked the mirthful Parsi.

"It was developed as a cure for impotence," Dr. Chothia told him, "but it didn't work."

"It works, all right," Wallingford argued.

"Well . . . apparently not for impotence," the Parsi repeated. "For pain, yes—but that was an accidental discovery. Please remember what I said, Mr. Wallingford. Don't ever take two."

"I'd like to take three or four," Patrick replied, but the Parsi was not his usual mirthful self on this subject.

"No, you *wouldn't* like to—believe me," Dr. Chothia warned him.

Swallowing only one capsule at a time, and at the proper twelve-hour intervals, Wallingford had ingested two more of the cobalt-blue painkillers while he was still in India, and Dr. Chothia had given him one more to take on the plane. Patrick had pointed out to the Parsi that the plane would be more than twelve hours in getting back to New York, but the doctor would give him nothing stronger than Tylenol with codeine for when the last of the wet-dream pills wore off.

Wallingford would have exactly the same dream four times—the last time on the flight from Frankfurt to New York. He'd taken the Tylenol with codeine on the first part of the long trip, from Bombay to Frankfurt, because (despite the pain) he'd wanted to save the best for last.

The flight attendant winked at Wallingford when she woke him up from his blue-capsule dream, just before the plane landed in New York. "If that was pain you were in, I'd like to be in pain with you," she whispered. "Nobody ever said 'yes' that many times to me!"

Although she gave Patrick her phone number, he

didn't call her. Wallingford wouldn't have sex as good as the sex in the blue-capsule dream for five years. It would take Patrick longer than that to understand that the cobalt-blue capsule Dr. Chothia had given him was more than a painkiller and a sex pill—it was, more important, a *prescience* pill.

Yet the pill's primary benefit was that it prevented him from dreaming more than once a month about the look in the lion's eyes when the beast had taken hold of his hand. The lion's huge, wrinkled forehead; his tawny, arched eyebrows; the flies buzzing in his mane; the great cat's rectangular, blood-spattered snout, which was scarred with claw marks—these details were not as ingrained in Wallingford's memory, in the stuff of his dreams, as the lion's yellow-brown eyes, in which he'd recognized a vacant kind of sadness. He would never forget those eyes—their dispassionate scrutiny of Patrick's face, their scholarly detachment.

Regardless of what Wallingford remembered or dreamed about, what viewers of the aptly nicknamed Disaster International network would remember *and* dream about was the footage of the hand-eating episode itself—every heart-stopping second of it.

The calamity channel, which was routinely ridiculed for its proclivity for bizarre deaths and stupid accidents, had created just such an accident while reporting just such a death, thereby enhancing its reputation in an unprecedented way. And this time the disaster had happened to a journalist! (Don't think that wasn't part of the popularity of the less-than-thirty-second amputation.)

In general, adults identified with the hand, if not with the unfortunate reporter. Children tended to sympathize with the lion. Of course there were warnings concerning the children. After all, entire kindergarten classes had come unglued. Second-graders—at last learning to read with comprehension and fluency—regressed to a preliterate, strictly visual state of mind.

Parents with children in elementary school at the time will always remember the messages sent home to them, messages such as: "We strongly recommend that you do not let your children watch TV until that business with the lion guy is no longer being shown."

Patrick's former thesis adviser was traveling with her only daughter when her ex-lover's hand-consuming accident was first televised.

The daughter had managed to get pregnant in her senior year in boarding school; while not exactly an original feat, this was nonetheless unexpected at an all-girls' school. The daughter's subsequent abortion had traumatized her and resulted in a leave of absence from her studies. The distraught girl, whose charmless boyfriend had dumped her before she knew she was carrying his child, would need to repeat her senior year.

Her mother was also having a hard time. She'd still been in her thirties when she'd seduced Wallingford, who was more than ten years her junior but the best-looking boy among her graduate students. Now in her early forties, she was going through her second divorce, the arbitration of which had been made more difficult by the unwelcome revelation that she'd recently slept with another of her students— her first-ever undergraduate.

He was a beautiful boy—sadly the *only* boy in her ill-advised course on the metaphysical poets, which was ill advised because she should have known that such "a race of writers," as Samuel Johnson had called them when he first nicknamed them the "metaphysical poets," would mostly be of interest to young women.

She was ill advised, too, in admitting the boy to this all-girl class; he was underprepared for it. But he'd come to her office and recited Andrew Marvell's "To His Coy Mistress," flubbing only the couplet "My vegetable love should grow / Vaster than empires, and more slow."

He'd said "groan" instead of "grow," and she could almost hear him groaning as he delivered the next lines.

An hundred years should go to praise
Thine eyes, and on thy forehead gaze;
Two hundred to adore each breast;
But thirty thousand to the rest

Oh, my, she'd thought, knowing they were *her* breasts, and the rest, that he was thinking of. So she'd let him in.

When the girls in the class flirted with him, she felt the need to protect him. At first she told herself she just wanted to mother him. When she dumped him—no less ceremoniously than her pregnant daughter had been dumped by her unnamed boyfriend—the boy dropped her course and called his mother.

The boy's mother, who was on the board of trustees at another university, wrote the dean of faculty: "Isn't sleeping with one's students in the 'moral turpitude' department?" Her question had resulted in Patrick's onetime thesis adviser and lover taking a semester's leave of absence of her own.

The unplanned sabbatical, her second divorce, her daughter's not dissimilar disgrace . . . well, mercy, what was Wallingford's old thesis adviser to do?

Her soon-to-be second ex-husband had reluctantly agreed not to cancel her credit cards for one more month. He would deeply regret this. She spontaneously took her out-of-school daughter to Paris, where they moved into a suite at the Hôtel Le Bristol; it was far too expensive for her, but she'd received a postcard of it once and had always wanted to go there. The postcard had been from her first ex-husband—he'd stayed there with his second wife and had sent her the card just to rub it in.

Le Bristol was on the rue du Faubourg Saint Honoré, surrounded by elegant shopping of the kind not even an adventuress could afford. Once they were there, she and her daughter didn't dare go anywhere or do anything. The extravagance of the hotel itself was more than they could handle. They felt under-dressed in the lobby and in the bar, where they sat mesmerized by the people who were clearly more at ease about simply being in Le Bristol than they were. Yet they wouldn't admit it had been a bad idea to come—at least not their first night.

There was quite a nice, modestly priced bistro very near them, on one of the smaller streets, but it was a rainy, dark evening and they wanted to go to bed early—they were yielding to jet lag. They planned on an early dinner at the hotel and would let the real Paris begin for them the next day, but the hotel restaurant was very popular. A table wouldn't be available for them until after nine o'clock, when they hoped to be fast asleep.

They'd come all this way to make recompense for how they'd both been unjustly injured, or so they believed; in truth, they were victims of the dissatis-factions of the flesh, in which their own myriad dis-contents had played a principal part. Unearned or deserved, Le Bristol was to be their reward. Now they were forced to retreat to their suite, relegated to room service.

There was nothing inelegant about room service at Le Bristol—it was simply not a night in Paris of the kind they had imagined. Both mother and daughter, uncharacteristically, tried to make the best of it.

"I never dreamed I'd spend my first night in Paris in a hotel room with my *mother*!" the daughter ex-claimed; she tried to laugh about it.

"At least I won't get you pregnant," her mother re-marked. They both tried to laugh about that, too.

Wallingford's old thesis adviser began the litany of the disappointing men in her life. The daughter had heard some of the list before, but she was developing a list of her own, albeit thus far vastly shorter than her mother's. They drank two half-bottles of wine from the mini-bar before the red Bordeaux they'd ordered with their dinner was delivered, and they drank that, too. Then they called room service and asked for a second bottle.

The wine loosened their tongues—maybe more than was either appropriate or seemly in a mother-daughter conversation. That her wayward daughter could easily have got herself pregnant with any number of careless boys before she encountered the lout who'd done the job was a bitter pill for any mother to swallow—even in Paris. That Patrick Wallingford's former thesis adviser was an inveterate sexual aggressor grew evident, even to her daughter; that her mother's sexual taste had led her to dally with ever-younger men, which eventually included a teenager, was possibly more than any daughter cared to know.

At a welcome lull in her mother's nonstop confessions—the middle-aged admirer of the meta-physical poets was signing for the second bottle of Bordeaux while brazenly flirting with the room-service waiter—the daughter sought some relief from this unwanted intimacy by turning on the tele-vision. As befitted a recently and stylishly renovated hotel, Le Bristol offered a multitude of satellite-TV channels—in English and other languages, as well as in French—and, as luck would have it, the inebriated mother had no sooner closed the door behind the room-service waiter than she turned to face the room, her daughter, and the TV, where she saw her ex-lover lose his left hand to a lion. Just like that!

Of course she screamed, which made her daughter scream. The second bottle of Bordeaux would have slipped out of the mother's grasp, had she not gripped the neck of the bottle tightly. (She might have been imagining that the bottle was one of her own hands, disappearing down a lion's throat.)

The hand-eating episode was over before the mother could reiterate the tortured tale of her relationship with the now-maimed television journalist. It would be an hour until the international news channel aired the incident again, although every fifteen minutes there were what the network called "bumpers," telling of the upcoming item—each promo in a ten- or fifteen-second installment. The lions fighting over some remaining and indistinguishable tidbit in their cage; the handless arm dangling from Patrick's separated shoulder; the stunned expression on Wallingford's face shortly before he fainted; a hasty view of a braless, headphone-wearing blond woman, who appeared to be sleeping in what looked like meat.

Mother and daughter sat up a second hour to watch the whole episode again. This time the mother remarked of the braless blonde, "I'll bet he was fucking her."

They went on like that, through the second bottle of Bordeaux. Their third watching of the complete event prompted cries of lascivious glee—as if Wallingford's punishment, as they thought of it, was what should have happened to every man they had ever known.

"Only it shouldn't have been his hand," the mother said.

"Yeah, right," the daughter replied.

But after this third viewing of the grisly event, only a sullen silence greeted the final swallowing of the body parts, and the mother found herself looking away from Patrick's face as he was about to swoon.

"The poor bastard," the daughter said under her breath. "I'm going to bed."

"I think I'll see it one more time," her mother answered.

The daughter lay sleeplessly in the bedroom, with the flickering light coming from under the door to the living room of the suite. Her mother, who had turned the volume off, could be heard crying.

The daughter dutifully went to join her mother on the living-room couch. They kept the TV sound off; holding hands, they watched the terrifying but stimulating footage again. The hungry lions were immaterial—the subject of the maiming was *men*.

"Why do we need them if we hate them?" the daughter tiredly asked.

"We hate them *because* we need them," the mother answered, her speech slurred.

There was Wallingford's stricken face. He dropped to his knees, his forearm spurting blood. His handsomeness was overwhelmed by his pain, but such was Wallingford's effect on women that a drunken, jet-lagged mother and her scarcely less damaged daughter felt their arms ache. They were actually reaching out to him as he fell.

Patrick Wallingford initiated nothing, yet he inspired sexual unrest and unnatural longing—even as he was caught in the act of feeding a lion his left hand. He was a magnet to women of all ages and types; even lying unconscious, he was a danger to the female sex.

As often happens in families, the daughter said aloud what the mother had also observed but was keeping to herself. "Look at the lionesses," the daughter said.

Not one lioness had touched his hand. There was a measure of longing in the sadness in their eyes; even after Wallingford fainted, the lionesses continued to watch him. It almost seemed that the lionesses were smitten, too.

CHAPTER TWO

The Former Midfielder

THE BOSTON TEAM was headed by Dr. Nicholas M. Zajac, a hand surgeon with Schatzman, Gingeleskie, Mengerink & Associates—the leading center for hand care in Massachusetts. Dr. Zajac was also an assistant clinical professor of surgery at Harvard. It was his idea to initiate a search for potential hand donors and recipients on the Internet (www.needahand.com).

Dr. Zajac was a half-generation older than Patrick Wallingford. That both Deerfield and Amherst were all-boys' institutions when he'd attended them is insufficient explanation for the single-sex attitude that accompanied his presence as strongly as his bad choice in aftershave.

No one from his Deerfield days, or from his four years at Amherst, remembered him. He'd played var-

sity lacrosse, in both prep school and college—he
was actually a starter—but not even his coaches remembered him. It is exceedingly rare to remain that
anonymous on athletic teams; yet Nick Zajac had
spent his youth and young manhood in an uncannily
unmemorable but successful pursuit of excellence,
with no friends and not one sexual experience.

In medical school, another med student, with
whom the future Dr. Zajac shared a female cadaver,
would forever remember him for his outraged shock
at the sight of the body. "That she was long dead
wasn't the problem," the lab partner would recall.
"What got to Nick was that the cadaver was a
woman, clearly his first."

Another first would be Zajac's wife. He was one of
those overgrateful men who married the first woman
who had sex with him. Both he and his wife would
regret it.

The female cadaver had something to do with Dr.
Zajac's decision to specialize in hands. According to
the former lab partner, the cadaver's hands were the
only parts of her that Zajac could stand to examine.

Clearly we need to know more about Dr. Zajac.
His thinness was compulsive; he couldn't be thin
enough. A marathoner, a bird-watcher, a seed-eater—
a habit he had acquired from his observation of
finches—the doctor was preternaturally drawn to
birds and to people who were famous. He became a
hand surgeon to the stars.

Mostly they were sports stars, injured athletes,

such as the Boston Red Sox pitcher with a torn anterior radio-ulnar ligament on his throwing hand. The pitcher was later traded to the Toronto Blue Jays for two infielders who never panned out and a designated hitter whose principal talent was hitting his wife. Zajac operated on the designated hitter, too. In attempting to lock herself in the car, the slugger's wife had shut the car door on his hand—the most extensive damage occurring to the second proximal phalanx and the third metacarpal.

A surprising number of sports-star injuries happened away from the field or the court or the ice—like that goalie for the Boston Bruins, since retired, who slashed his superficial transverse ligament, left hand, by gripping a wineglass too tightly against his wedding ring. And there was that frequently penalized linebacker for the New England Patriots who severed a digital artery and some digital nerves by trying to open an oyster with a Swiss Army knife. They were risk-taking jocks—an accident-prone bunch—but they were famous. For a time, Dr. Zajac worshiped them; their signed photographs, radiating physical superiority, looked down from his office walls.

Yet even the on-the-job injuries to sports stars were often unnecessary, including a center for the Boston Celtics who attempted a backward slam dunk after the time on the shot clock had expired. He simply lost control of the ball and made a mess of his palmar fascia against the rim.

Never mind—Dr. Zajac loved them all. And not only the athletes.

Rock singers seemed prone to hotel-room injuries of two kinds. Foremost was what Zajac categorized as "room-service outrage"; this led to stab wounds, scalding coffee and tea injuries, and a host of unplanned confrontations with inanimate objects. A close second to these were the innumerable mishaps in wet bathrooms, to which not only rock stars but also movie stars were inclined.

Movie stars had accidents in restaurants, too, mostly upon leaving them. From a hand surgeon's point of view, striking a photographer was preferable to striking a photographer's camera. For the hand's sake, any expression of hostility toward something made of metal, glass, wood, stone, or plastic was a mistake. Yet, among the famous, violence toward *things* was the leading source of the injuries the doctor saw.

When Dr. Zajac reviewed the docile visages of his renowned patients, it was with the realization that their success and seeming contentment were only public masks.

All this may have preoccupied Zajac, but the doctor's colleagues at Schatzman, Gingeleskie, Mengerink & Associates were preoccupied with *him.* While they never called Dr. Zajac a star-fucker to his face, they knew what he was and felt superior to him—if only in this regard. As a surgeon, he was the best of them, and they knew this, too; it bothered them.

If, at Schatzman, Gingeleskie, Mengerink & Associates, they refrained from comment on Zajac's fame-fucking, they did permit themselves to admonish their superstar colleague for his thinness. It was commonly believed that Zajac's marriage had failed because he'd grown thinner than his wife, yet no one at Schatzman, Gingeleskie, Mengerink & Associates had been able to persuade Dr. Zajac to feed himself to save his marriage; they were not likely to have any success at convincing him to fatten himself up now that he was divorced.

It was principally his love of birds that drove Zajac's neighbors nuts. For reasons that were incomprehensible even to the area's ornithologists, Dr. Zajac was convinced that the abundance of dogshit in Greater Boston had a deleterious effect on the city's bird life.

There was a picture of Zajac that all his colleagues savored, although only one of them had seen the actual image. On a Sunday morning in his snow-covered yard on Brattle Street, the renowned hand surgeon—in knee-high boots, his red flannel bathrobe, and a preposterous New England Patriots ski hat, a brown paper bag in one hand, a child-size lacrosse stick in the other—was searching his yard for dog turds. Although Dr. Zajac didn't own a dog, he had several inconsiderate neighbors, and Brattle

Street was one of the most popular dog-walking routes in Cambridge.

The lacrosse stick had been intended for Zajac's only child, an unathletic son who visited him every third weekend. The troubled boy, disturbed by his parents' divorce, was an underweight six-year-old, an obdurate noneater—quite possibly at the urging of his mother, whose uncomplicated mission was to drive Zajac crazy.

The ex-wife, whose name was Hildred, spoke dismissively on this subject. "Why should the kid eat? His father doesn't. He sees his father starving himself, so he starves himself, too!" Therefore, in the divorce settlement, Zajac was permitted to see his son only once every three weeks, and for no longer than a weekend at a time. And Massachusetts has what they call no-fault divorce! (What Wallingford called his favorite oxymoron.)

In fact, Dr. Zajac agonized over his beloved child's eating disorder and sought both medical and practical solutions to his son's condition. (Hildred would barely acknowledge that her starved-looking son had a problem.) The boy's name was Rudy; and on the weekends when he visited his father, he was often treated to the spectacle of Dr. Zajac force-feeding himself copious amounts of food, which Zajac would later vomit up in private, disciplined silence. But with or without his father's example, Rudy hardly ate at all.

One pediatric gastroenterologist called for exploratory surgery to rule out any possible diseases of the colon. Another prescribed a syrup, an indigestible sugar that worked as a diuretic. A third suggested Rudy would outgrow the problem; it was the only gastroenterological advice that both Dr. Zajac and his ex-wife could accept.

Meanwhile, Zajac's former live-in housekeeper had quit—she could not bear to see the quantity of food that was thrown away every third Monday. Because Irma, the new live-in housekeeper, took offense at the word "housekeeper," Zajac had been careful to call her his "assistant," although the young woman's principal responsibilities were cleaning the house and doing the laundry. Maybe it was her obligatory daily retrieval of the dog turds from the yard that broke her spirit—the ignominy of the brown paper bag, her clumsiness with the child's lacrosse stick, the menial nature of the task.

Irma was a homely, sturdily built girl in her late twenties, and she'd not anticipated that working for a "medical doctor," as Irma called Zajac, would include such demeaning labor as combating the shitting habits of the Brattle Street dogs.

It further hurt her feelings that Dr. Zajac thought she was a new immigrant for whom English was a second language. English was Irma's first and only language, but the confusion came from what little Zajac could understand from overhearing her unhappy voice on the telephone.

Irma had her own phone in her bedroom off the

kitchen, and she was often talking at length to her mother or to one of her sisters late at night when Zajac was raiding the refrigerator. (The scalpel-thin surgeon limited his snacks to raw carrots, which he kept in a bowl of melting ice in the fridge.)

To Zajac, it seemed that Irma was speaking a foreign language. Doubtless some interference to his hearing was caused by his constant chomping on raw carrots and the maddening trill of the caged songbirds throughout the house, but the primary reason for Zajac's mistaken assumption was that Irma was always hysterically crying when she spoke to her mother or sisters. She was recounting to them how humiliating it was to be consistently undervalued by Dr. Zajac.

Irma could cook, but the doctor rarely ate regular meals. She could sew, but Zajac assigned the repair of his office and hospital clothing to his dry-cleaning service; what chiefly remained of his other laundry were the besweated clothes he ran in. Zajac ran in the morning (sometimes in the dark) before breakfast, and he ran again (often in the dark) at the end of the day.

He was one of those thin men in their advancing forties who run along the banks of the Charles, as if they are eternally engaged in a fitness competition with all the students who also run and walk in the vicinity of Memorial Drive. In snow, in sleet, in slush, in summer heat—even in thunderstorms—the wispy hand surgeon ran and ran. At five-eleven, Dr. Zajac weighed only 135 pounds.

Irma, who was five-six and weighed about 150, was convinced that she hated him. It was the litany of how Zajac had offended her that Irma sang, sobbing into the phone at night, but the hand surgeon, over-hearing her, thought: Czech? Polish? Lithuanian?

When Dr. Zajac asked her where she was from, Irma indignantly answered, "Boston!" Good for her! Zajac concluded. There is no patriotism like that of the grateful European immigrant. Thus Dr. Zajac would congratulate her on how good her English was, "considering," and Irma would weep her heart out on the phone at night.

Irma refrained from comment on the food the doctor bought every third Friday, nor did Dr. Zajac explain his instructions, every third Monday, to throw it all away. The food would simply be collected on the kitchen table—an entire chicken, a whole ham, fruits and vegetables, and melting ice cream—with a type-written note: DISPOSE OF. That was all.

It must be connected to his abhorrence of dogshit, Irma imagined. With mythic simplicity, she assumed that the doctor had a dispose-of obsession. She didn't know the half of it. Even on his morning and evening runs, Zajac carried a lacrosse stick, a grown-up one, which he held as if he were cradling an imaginary ball.

There were many lacrosse sticks in the Zajac

household. In addition to Rudy's, which was relatively toylike in appearance, there were numerous
adult-size ones, in varying degrees of overuse and
disrepair. There was even a battered wooden stick
that dated from the doctor's Deerfield days. Weapon-
like in its appearance, because of its broken and
retied rawhide strings, it was wrapped in dirty adhe-
sive tape and caked with mud. But in Dr. Zajac's
skilled hands, the old stick came alive with the nervous energy of his agitated youth, when the neuras-
thenic hand surgeon had been an underweight but
intensely accomplished midfielder.

When the doctor ran along the banks of the
Charles, the outmoded wooden lacrosse stick conveyed the readiness of a soldier's rifle. More than
one rower in Cambridge had experienced a dog turd
or two whizzing across the stern of his scull, and one
of Zajac's medical-school students—formerly the
coxswain of a Harvard eight-oared racing shell—
claimed to have adroitly ducked a dog turd aimed at
his head.

Dr. Zajac denied trying to hit the coxswain. His
only intention was to rid Memorial Drive of a no-
table excess of dogshit, which he scooped up in
his lacrosse stick and flicked into the Charles River.
But the former coxswain and med-school student
had kept an eye out for the crazed midfielder after
their memorable first encounter, and there were other
oarsmen and coxswains who swore they'd seen

Zajac expertly cradle a turd in his old lacrosse stick and fire it at them.

It's a matter of record that the former Deerfield midfielder scored two goals against a previously undefeated Andover team, and three goals against Exeter *twice*. (If none of Zajac's teammates remembered him, some of his opponents did. The Exeter goalie said it most succinctly: "Nick Zajac had a wicked fucking shot.")

Dr. Zajac's colleagues at Schatzman, Gingeleskie, Mengerink & Associates had also heard him decry the "utter silliness of participating in a sport while facing backward," thereby documenting Zajac's contempt for rowers. But so what? Aren't eccentricities fairly common among overachievers?

The house on Brattle Street resounded with warblers, like a woodland glen. The dining-room bay windows were spray-painted with big black *X*'s to prevent birds from crashing into them, which gave Zajac's home an aura of perpetual vandalism. A wren with a broken wing lay recovering in its own cage in the kitchen, where not long before a cedar waxwing with a broken neck had died—to Irma's accumulating sorrows.

Sweeping up the birdseed that was scattered under the songbirds' cages was one of Irma's never-ending chores; despite her efforts, the sound of birdseed crunching underfoot would have made the house an unwise choice for burglars. Rudy, however, liked the

birds—the undernourished boy's mother had heretofore refused to get him a pet of any kind—and Zajac
would have lived in an aviary if he thought it would
make Rudy happy, or get him to eat.

But Hildred was so steadfastly conniving in tor-
menting her ex-husband that it was insufficiently sat-
isfying for her to have reduced Zajac's time with
their son to a mere two days and three nights every
month. And so, thinking she'd found a way to further
poison their time together, she finally got Rudy a
dog.

"You'll have to keep it at your father's, though,"
she told the six-year-old. "It can't stay here."

The mutt, which came from some humane-society
sort of place, was generously referred to as "part
Lab." Would that be the black part? Zajac wondered.
The dog was a spayed female, about two years old,
with an anxious, craven face and a squatter, bulkier
body than that of a Labrador retriever. There was
something houndlike about the way her upper lips
were floppy and overhung her lower jaw; her forehead, which was more brown than black, was wrinkled by a constant frown. The dog walked with her
nose to the ground, often stepping on her ears, and
with her stout tail twitching like a pointer's. (Hildred
had got her in the hope that the abandoned mutt was
a bird dog.)

"Medea will be put to death if we don't keep her,
Dad," Rudy solemnly told his father.

"Medea," Zajac repeated.

In veterinary terms, Medea suffered from "dietary indiscretion"; she ate sticks, shoes, rocks, paper, metal, plastic, tennis balls, children's toys, and her own feces. (Her so-called dietary indiscretion was definitely part Lab.) Her zeal for eating dogshit, not only her own, was what had prompted her former family to abandon her.

Hildred had outdone herself in finding a dog on death row with habits that seemed certain to make her ex-husband insane, or more insane. That Medea was named for a classical sorceress who killed her own children was too perfect. Had the voracious part-Lab had puppies, she would have eaten them.

What a horror it was for Hildred to discover that Dr. Zajac *loved* the dog. Medea searched for dogshit as assiduously as *he* did—they were kindred souls— and now Rudy had a dog to play with, which made him happier to see his father.

Dr. Nicholas M. Zajac may have been a hand surgeon to the stars, but he was first and foremost a divorced dad. It would be initially her tragedy and then her triumph that Irma was moved by Dr. Zajac's love for his son. Her own father had left her mother before she was born, and he'd not troubled himself to have any relationship with Irma or her sisters.

One Monday morning after Rudy had gone back to his mother, Irma began her workday by attempting to clean the boy's room. For the three weeks that he was gone, the six-year-old's room was kept as tidy as a shrine; in practice, it *was* a shrine, and Zajac could often be found sitting worshipfully there. The morose dog was also drawn to Rudy's room. Medea appeared to miss Rudy as much as Zajac did.

This morning, however, Irma was surprised to find Dr. Zajac asleep, naked, in his departed son's bed. The doctor's legs overhung the foot of the bed, and he had flung the bedcovers off; no doubt the heat of the sixty-pound dog was sufficient. Medea lay chest-to-chest with the hand surgeon, her muzzle at his throat, a paw caressing the sleeping doctor's bare shoulder.

Irma stared. She'd never before had such an uninterrupted look at a naked man. The former midfielder was more puzzled than insulted that women were not drawn to his superb fitness, but while he was by no means an unattractive man, his utter craziness was as visible as his skeleton. (This was less apparent when Zajac was asleep.)

The transplant-driven surgeon was both mocked and envied by his colleagues. He ran obsessively, he ate almost nothing, he was a bird nut newly enamored of the dietary indiscretion of an exceedingly neurotic dog. He was also driven by the unchecked agony he felt for a son he hardly ever saw. Yet what Irma now perceived in Dr. Zajac overrode all this. She suddenly recognized the heroic love he bore for the child, a love shared by both man and dog. (In her newfound weakness, Irma was also moved by Medea.)

Irma had never met Rudy. She didn't work weekends. What she knew was only what she could glean from photographs, of which there were an increasing number after each of the blessed son's visits. While Irma had sensed that Rudy's room was a shrine, she was unprepared to see Zajac and Medea in their embrace in the little boy's bed. Oh, she thought, to be loved like that!

That instant, that very second, Irma fell in love with Dr. Zajac's obvious capacity for love— notwithstanding that the good doctor had evinced no discernible capacity for loving *her.* On the spot, Irma became Zajac's slave—not that he would soon notice it.

At that life-changing moment, Medea opened her self-pitying eyes and raised her heavy head, a string of drool suspended from her overhanging lip. To Irma, who had an unrestrained enthusiasm for finding omens in the most commonplace occurrences, the dog's slobber was the haunting color of a pearl.

Irma could tell that Dr. Zajac was about to wake up, too. The doctor had a boner as big around as his wrist, as long as . . . well, let's just say that, for such a scrawny guy, Zajac had quite a schlong. Irma thereupon decided that she wanted to be thin.

It was a reaction no less sudden than the discovery of her love for Dr. Zajac. The awkward girl, who was nearly twenty years younger than the divorced doctor, was scarcely able to stagger into the hall before Zajac woke up. To alert the doctor that she was nearby, she called the dog. Halfheartedly, Medea made her way out of Rudy's room; to the depressed dog's bewilderment, which quickly gave way to fawning, Irma began to shower her with affection.

Everything has a purpose, the simple girl was thinking. She remembered her earlier unhappiness and knew that the dog was her road to Dr. Zajac's heart.

"Come here, sweetie-pie, come with me," Zajac heard his housekeeper/assistant saying. "We're gonna eat only what's *good* for us today!"

As has been noted, Zajac's colleagues were woefully beneath his surgical skills; they would have envied and despised him even more if they hadn't been able to feel they had certain advantages over him in other areas. It cheered and encouraged them that their intrepid leader was crippled by love for his unhappy, wasting-away son. And wasn't it wonderful that, for the love of Rudy, Boston's best hand surgeon lived night and day with a shit-eating dog?

It was both cruel and uncharitable of Dr. Zajac's inferiors to celebrate the unhappiness of Zajac's six-year-old, nor was it accurate of the good hand surgeon's colleagues to deem the boy "wasting-away." Rudy was crammed full of vitamins and orange juice; he drank fruit smoothies (mostly frozen strawberries and mashed bananas) and managed to eat an apple or a pear every day. He ate scrambled eggs and toast; he would eat cucumbers, if only with ketchup. He drank no milk, he ate no meat or fish or cheese, but at times he exhibited a cautious interest in yogurt, if there were no lumps in it.

Rudy *was* underweight, but with even a small amount of regular exercise or any healthy adjustment in his diet, Rudy would have been as normal-looking as any little boy. He was an exceptionally sweet child—not only the proverbial "good kid" but a model of fairness and goodwill. Rudy had simply been fucked up by his mother, who had nearly succeeded in poisoning Rudy's feelings for his father. After all, Hildred had three weeks to work on the vulnerable six-year-old; every third weekend, Zajac had scarcely more than forty-eight hours to counteract Hildred's evil influence. And because Hildred was well aware of Dr. Zajac's idolatry of strenuous exercise, she forbade Rudy to play soccer or go ice-skating after school—the kid was hooked on videos instead.

Hildred, who in her years with Zajac had half killed herself to stay thin, now embraced plumpness. She called this being "more of a woman," the very thought of which made her ex-husband gag.

But what was most cruel was the way Rudy's mother had all but convinced the child that his father didn't love him. Hildred was happy to point out to Zajac that the boy invariably returned from his weekends with his father depressed; that this was because Hildred *grilled* Rudy upon his return would never have occurred to her.

"Was there a woman around? Did you meet a woman?" she would begin. (There was only Medea, and all the birds.)

When you don't see your kid for weeks at a time, the desire to bestow gifts is so tempting; yet when Zajac bought things for Rudy, Hildred would tell the boy that his father was bribing him. Or else her conversation with the child would unfold along these lines: "What did he buy you? *Roller skates!* A lot of use you'll get out of them—he must want you to crack your head open! And I suppose he didn't let you watch a single movie. Honestly, he has to entertain you for just two days and three nights—you'd expect him to be on his best behavior. You'd think he'd try a little harder!"

But the problem, of course, was that Zajac tried too hard. For the first twenty-four hours they were together, his frenetic energy overwhelmed the boy.

Medea would be as frantic to see Rudy as Zajac was, but the child was listless—at least in comparison to the frenzied dog—and despite the evidence, everywhere, of what affectionate preparations the hand surgeon had undertaken to show his son a good time, Rudy seemed downright hostile to his father. He had been primed to be sensitive to examples of his father's lack of love for him; finding none, he began their every weekend together confused.

There was one game Rudy liked, even on those miserable Friday nights when Dr. Zajac felt he'd been reduced to the painful task of trying to make small talk with his only child. Zajac clung with fatherly pride to the fact that the game was of his own invention.

Six-year-olds love repetition, and the game Dr. Zajac had invented might well have been called "Repetition Plus," although neither father nor son bothered to name the game. At the onset of their weekends together, it was the only game they played.

They took turns hiding a stove timer, unfailingly set for one minute, and they always hid it in the living room. To say they "hid it" is not quite correct, for the game's only rule was that the stove timer had to remain visible. It could not be tucked under a cushion or stowed away in a drawer. (Or buried under a mound of birdseed in the cage with the purple finches.) It had to be in plain sight; but because it was small and beige, the stove timer was hard to see, especially in Dr. Zajac's living room, which, like the rest of the old house on Brattle Street, had been hastily—Hildred would say "tastelessly"—refurnished. (Hildred had taken all the good furniture with her.) The living room was cluttered with mismatched curtains and upholstery; it was as if three or four generations of Zajacs had lived and perished there, and nothing had ever been thrown away.

The condition of the room made it fairly easy to hide an innocuous stove timer right out in the open. Rudy only occasionally found the timer within one minute, before the beeper would sound, and Zajac, even if he spotted the stove timer in ten seconds, would *never* locate the thing before the minute was up—much to his son's delight. Hence Zajac feigned frustration while Rudy laughed.

A breakthrough beyond the simple pleasure of the stove-timer game took both father and son by surprise. It was called reading—the truly inexhaustible pleasure of reading aloud—and the books that Dr. Zajac decided to read to Rudy were the two books Zajac himself had loved most as a child. They were *Stuart Little* and *Charlotte's Web,* both by E. B. White.

Rudy was so impressed by Wilbur, the pig in *Charlotte's Web,* that he wanted to rename Medea and call her Wilbur instead.

"That's a boy's name," Zajac pointed out, "and Medea is a girl. But I suppose it would be all right. You could rename her Charlotte, if you like—Charlotte is a girl's name, you know."

"But Charlotte dies," Rudy argued. (The eponymous Charlotte is a spider.) "I'm already afraid that Medea will die."

"Medea won't die for a long time, Rudy," Zajac assured his son.

"Mommy says you might kill her, because of the way you lose your temper."

"I promise I won't kill Medea, Rudy," Zajac said. "I won't lose my temper with her." (This was typical of how little Hildred had ever understood him; that he lost his temper at dogshit didn't mean he was angry at dogs!)

"Tell me again why they named her Medea," the boy said.

It was hard to relate the Greek legend to a six-year-old—just try describing what a sorceress is. But the part about Medea assisting her husband, Jason, in obtaining the Golden Fleece was easier to explain than the part about what Medea does to her own children. Why *would* anyone name a dog Medea? Dr. Zajac wondered.

In the six months since he'd been divorced, Zajac had read more than a dozen books by child psychiatrists about the troubles children have after a divorce. A great emphasis was put on the parents' having a sense of humor, which was not the hand surgeon's strongest point.

Zajac's indulgence in mischief overcame him only in those moments when he was cradling a dog turd in a lacrosse stick. However, in addition to his having been a midfielder at Deerfield, Dr. Zajac had sung in some kind of glee club there. Although his only singing now was in the shower, he felt a spontaneous outpouring of humor whenever he was taking a shower with Rudy. Taking a shower with his father was another item on the small but growing list of things Rudy liked to do with his dad.

Suddenly, to the tune of "I Am the River," which Rudy had learned to sing in kindergarten—the boy, as many only children do, liked to sing—Dr. Nicholas M. Zajac burst into song.

> *I am Medea*
> *and I eat my poo.*
> *In an-tiq-ui-ty*
> *I killed my kids, too!*

"What?" Rudy said. "Sing that again!" (They'd already discussed antiquity.)

When his father sang the song again, Rudy dissolved into laughter. Scatological humor is the best stuff for six-year-olds.

"Don't sing this around your mother," Rudy's father warned him. Thus they had a secret, another step in creating a bond between them.

Over time, two copies of *Stuart Little* made their way home with Rudy, but Hildred would not read it to the boy; worse, she threw away both copies of the book. It wasn't until Rudy caught her throwing away *Charlotte's Web* that he told his father, which became another bond between them.

Every weekend they were together, Zajac read all of either *Stuart Little* or *Charlotte's Web* to Rudy. The little boy never tired of them. He cried every time Charlotte died; he laughed every time Stuart crashed the dentist's invisible car. And, like Stuart, when Rudy was thirsty, he told his father that he had "a ruinous thirst." (The first time, naturally, Rudy had to ask his father what "ruinous" meant.)

Meanwhile, although Dr. Zajac had made much headway in contradicting Hildred's message to Rudy—the boy was increasingly convinced that his father *did* love him—the hand surgeon's small-minded colleagues were nonetheless convincing themselves that they were superior to Zajac *because of* the alleged unhappiness and undernourishment of Zajac's six-year-old son.

At first Dr. Zajac's colleagues felt superior to him because of Irma, too. They regarded her as a clear loser's choice among housekeepers; but when Irma began to transform herself, they soon noticed her, long before Zajac himself showed any signs of sharing their interest.

His failure to be aware of Irma's transformation was further proof of Dr. Zajac's being a madman of the unseeing variety. The girl had dropped twenty pounds; she'd joined a gym. She ran three miles a day—she was no mere jogger, either. If her new wardrobe was lacking in taste, it quite consciously showed off her body. Irma would never be beautiful, but she was *built*. Hildred would start the rumor that her ex-husband was dating a stripper. (Divorced women in their forties are not known for their charitableness toward well-built women in their twenties.)

Irma, don't forget, was in love. What did she care? One night she tiptoed, naked, through the dark upstairs hall. She'd rationalized that if Zajac had not gone to bed, and if he happened to see her without her clothes on, she would tell him she was a sleepwalker and that some force had drawn her to his room. Irma longed for Dr. Zajac to see her naked—by accident, of course—because she had developed more than a terrific body; she'd also developed a stalwart confidence in it.

But tiptoeing past the doctor's closed bedroom door, Irma was halted by the baffling conviction that she'd overheard Dr. Zajac praying. Prayer struck

Irma, who was not religious, as a suspiciously unscientific activity for a hand surgeon. She listened at the doctor's door a little longer and was relieved to hear that Zajac *wasn't* praying—he was just reading *Stuart Little* aloud to himself in a prayerful voice.

" 'At suppertime he took his ax, felled a dandelion, opened a can of deviled ham, and had a light supper of ham and dandelion milk,' " Dr. Zajac read from *Stuart Little*.

Irma was shaken by her love for him, but the mere mention of deviled ham made her feel ill. She tiptoed back to her bedroom off the kitchen, pausing to munch some raw carrots out of the bowl of melting ice in the fridge.

When would the lonely man ever notice her?

Irma ate a lot of nuts and dried fruit; she ate fresh fruit, too, and mounds of raw vegetables. She could concoct a mean steamed fish with gingerroot and black beans, which made such an impression on Dr. Zajac that the doctor startled Irma (and everyone who knew him) by hosting an impromptu dinner party for his medical-school students.

Zajac imagined that one of his Harvard boys might ask Irma out; she seemed lonely to him, as did most of the boys. Little did the doctor know that Irma had eyes only for him. Once Irma had been introduced to his young male med students as his "assistant"—and because she was so obviously a piece of ass—they assumed he was already banging her and abandoned all hope. (Zajac's female med students probably thought that Irma was every bit as desperate-looking as Zajac.)

No matter. Everyone loved the steamed fish with gingerroot and black beans, and Irma had other recipes. She treated Medea's dog food with meat tenderizer, because she'd read in a magazine at her dentist's office that meat tenderizer made a dog's poo unappetizing, even to a dog. But Medea seemed to find the tenderizer enhancing.

Dr. Zajac sprinkled the birdseed in the outdoor birdfeeder with red pepper flakes; he'd told Irma that this made the birdseed inedible to squirrels. Afterward, Irma tried sprinkling Medea's dog turds with red pepper flakes, too. While this was visually interesting, especially against the new-fallen snow, the dog found the pepper off-putting only initially.

And drawing even greater attention to the dogshit in his yard did *not* please Zajac. He had a far simpler, albeit more athletic method of preventing Medea from eating her own shit. He got to her turds first, with his lacrosse stick. He usually deposited the turds in the ubiquitous brown paper bag, although on occasion Irma had seen him take a shot at a squirrel in a tree clear across Brattle Street. Dr. Zajac missed the squirrel every time, but the gesture went straight to Irma's heart.

While it was too soon to say if the girl Hildred had named "Nick's stripper" would ever find her way into Zajac's heart, there was another area of concern at Schatzman, Gingeleskie, Mengerink & Associates: it was only a matter of time before Dr. Zajac, although he was still in his forties, would have to be included in the *title* of Boston's foremost surgical associates in hand treatment. Soon it would have to be Schatzman, Gingeleskie, Mengerink, *Zajac* & Associates.

Don't think this didn't gall the eponymous Schatzman, even though he was retired. Don't think it didn't rile the surviving Gingeleskie brother, too. In the old days, when the other Gingeleskie was alive, they were Schatzman, Gingeleskie & Gingeleskie—this being before Mengerink's time. (Dr. Zajac said privately that he doubted Dr. Mengerink could cure a hangnail.) As for Mengerink, he'd had an affair with Hildred when she was still married to Zajac; yet he despised Zajac for getting a divorce, even though the divorce had been Hildred's idea.

Unbeknownst to Dr. Zajac, his ex-wife was on a mission to drive Dr. Mengerink crazy, too. It seemed the cruelest of fates, to Mengerink, that Zajac's name was soon destined to follow his on the venerable surgical associates' letterhead and nameplate. But if Dr. Zajac pulled off the country's first hand transplant, they would all be lucky if they weren't renamed *Zajac,* Schatzman, Gingeleskie, Mengerink & Associates. (Worse things could happen. No doubt Harvard would soon make Zajac an associate professor.)

And now Dr. Zajac's housekeeper/assistant had transformed herself into an instant erection machine, although Zajac himself was too screwed up to realize it. Even old Schatzman, retired, had observed the changes in Irma. And Mengerink, who'd had to change his home phone number twice to discourage Zajac's ex-wife from calling him—Mengerink had noticed Irma, too. As for Gingeleskie, he said: "Even the *other* Gingeleskie could pick Irma out of a crowd," referring, of course, to his dead brother.

From the grave, a *corpse* couldn't miss seeing what had happened to the housekeeper/assistant-turned-sexpot. She looked like a stripper with a day job as a personal trainer. How had Zajac missed the transformation? No wonder such a man had managed to pass through prep school and college un-remembered.

Yet when Dr. Zajac went shopping on the Inter-net for potential hand donors and recipients, no one at Schatzman, Gingeleskie, Mengerink & Associates called him crass or said that they thought www .needahand.com was a tad crude. Despite his shit-eating dog, his obsession with fame, his wasting-away thinness, and his problem-ridden son—and, on top of everything, his inconceivable obliviousness to his cheeks-of-steel "assistant"—in the pioneer territory of hand-transplant surgery, Dr. Nicholas M. Zajac re-mained the man in charge.

That Boston's most brilliant hand surgeon was reputed to be a sexless jerk was a matter of no account to his only son. What does a six-year-old boy care about his father's professional or sexual acumen, especially when he is beginning to see for himself that his father loves him?

As for what launched the newfound affection between Rudy and his complicated father, credit must be spread around. Some acknowledgment is due a dumb dog who ate her own poo, as well as that long-ago single-sex glee club at Deerfield, where Zajac first got the mistaken idea he could sing. (After the spontaneous opening verse of "I Am Medea," both father and son would compose many more verses, all of them too childishly scatological to record here.) And there were also, of course, the stove-timer game and E. B. White.

In addition, we should put in a word for the value of mischief in father-son relations. The former midfielder had first developed an instinct for mischief by cradling and then whizzing dog turds into the Charles River with a lacrosse stick. If Zajac had initially failed to interest Rudy in lacrosse, the good doctor would eventually turn his son's attention to the finer points of the sport while walking Medea along the banks of the historic Charles.

Picture this: there is the turd-hunting dog, dragging Dr. Zajac after her while she strains against her leash. (In Cambridge, of course, there is a leash law; all dogs must be leashed.) And there, running abreast of the eager part-Lab—yes, actually *running*, actually *getting some exercise*!—is six-year-old Rudy Zajac, his child-size lacrosse stick held low to the ground in front of him.

Picking up a dog turd in a lacrosse stick, especially on the run, is a lot harder than picking up a lacrosse ball. (Dog turds come in varying sizes and are, on occasion, entangled with grass, or they have been stepped on.) Nevertheless, Rudy had been well coached. And Medea's determination, her powerful lunges against the leash, gave the boy precisely what was needed in the process of mastering any sport— especially "dog-turd lacrosse," as both father and son called it. Medea provided Rudy with competition.

Any amateur can cradle a dog turd in a lacrosse stick, but try doing it under the pressure of a shit-eating dog; in any sport, pressure is as fundamental a teacher as a good coach. Besides, Medea outweighed Rudy by a good ten pounds and could easily knock the boy down.

"Keep your back to her—attaboy!" Zajac would yell. "Cradle, cradle—keep cradling! Always know where the river is!"

The river was their goal—the historic Charles. Rudy had two good shots, which his father had taught him. There was the standard over-the-shoulder shot (either a long lob or a fairly flat trajectory) and there was the sidearm shot, which was low to the water and best for *skipping* the dog turds, which Rudy preferred. The risk with the sidearm shot was that the lacrosse stick passed low to the ground;

Medea could block a sidearm shot and eat it in a hurry.

"Midriver, midriver!" the former midfielder would be coaching. Or else he would shout: "Aim for under the bridge!"

"But there's a boat, Dad."

"Aim for the boat, then," Zajac would say, more quietly, aware that his relations with the oarsmen were already strained.

The resulting shouts and cries of the outraged oarsmen gave a certain edge to the rigors of competition. Dr. Zajac was especially engaged by the high-pitched yelps the coxswains made into their megaphones, although nowadays one had to be careful—some of the coxswains were girls.

Zajac disapproved of girls in sculls or in the larger racing shells, no matter whether the girls were rowers or coxswains. (This was surely another hallmark prejudice of his single-sex education.)

As for Dr. Zajac's modest contribution to the ongoing pollution of the Charles River . . . well, let's be fair. Zajac had never been an advocate of environmental correctness. In his hopelessly old-fashioned opinion, a lot worse than dogshit was dumped into the Charles on a daily basis. Furthermore, the dogshit that little Rudy Zajac and his father were responsible for throwing into the Charles River was for a good cause, that of solidifying the love between a divorced father and his son.

Irma deserves some credit, too, despite being a prosaic girl who would one day watch the lions-eating-the-hand episode on video with Dr. Zajac and say, "I never knew lions could eat somethin' so *quick.*"

Dr. Nicholas M. Zajac, who knew next to everything there was to know about hands, couldn't watch the footage without exclaiming: "Oh, God, my God—there it goes! Sweet Jesus, it's *gone*! It's all gone!"

Of course it didn't hurt the chances of Patrick Wallingford, Dr. Zajac's first choice among the would-be hand recipients, that Wallingford was *famous;* a television audience estimated in the millions had witnessed the frightening accident. Thousands of children and uncounted adults were *still* suffering nightmares, although Wallingford had lost his hand more than five years ago and the televised footage of the accident itself was less than thirty seconds long.

"Thirty seconds is a long time to be engaged in losing your hand, if it's your hand," Patrick had said.

People meeting Wallingford, especially for the first time, would never fail to comment on his boyish charm. Women would remark on his eyes. Whereas Wallingford had formerly been envied by men, the way in which he was maimed had put an end to that; not even men, the gender more prone to envy, could be jealous of him anymore. Now men *and* women found him irresistible.

Dr. Zajac hadn't needed the Internet to find Patrick Wallingford, who had been the first choice of the Boston surgical team from the start. More interesting was that www.needahand.com had turned up a surprising candidate in the field of potential donors. (What Zajac meant by a donor was a fresh cadaver.) This donor was not only alive—he wasn't even dying!

His wife wrote Schatzman, Gingeleskie, Mengerink & Associates from Wisconsin. "My husband has got the idea that he wants to leave his left hand to Patrick Wallingford—you know, the lion guy," Mrs. Otto Clausen wrote.

Her letter caught Dr. Zajac in the middle of a bad day with the dog. Medea had ingested a sizable section of lawn hose and had required stomach surgery. The miserable dog should have spent the weekend recovering at the vet's, but it was one of those weekends when young Rudy visited his father; the six-year-old divorce survivor might have reverted to his former inconsolable self without Medea's company. Even a drugged dog was better than no dog. There would be no dog-turd lacrosse for the weekend, but it would be a challenge to prevent Medea from eating her stitches, and there was always the reliable stove-timer game and the more reliable genius of E. B. White. It would certainly be a good time to devote some constructive reinforcement to Rudy's ever-experimental diet.

In short, the hand surgeon was a trifle distracted. If there was something disingenuous about the charm of Mrs. Otto Clausen's letter, Zajac didn't catch it. His eagerness for the media possibilities overrode all else, and the Wisconsin couple's unabashed choice of Patrick Wallingford as a worthy recipient of Otto Clausen's hand would make a good story.

Zajac didn't find it at all odd that Mrs. Clausen, instead of Otto himself, had written to offer her husband's hand. All Otto had done was sign a brief statement; his wife had composed the accompanying letter.

Mrs. Clausen hailed from Appleton, and she proudly mentioned that Otto was already registered with the Wisconsin Organ Donor Affiliates. "But this hand business is a little different—I mean different from organs," she observed.

Hands were indeed different from organs, Dr. Zajac knew. But Otto Clausen was only thirty-nine and in no apparent proximity to death's door. Zajac believed that a fresh cadaver with a suitable donor hand would show up long before Otto's.

As for Patrick Wallingford, his desire and need for a new left hand might possibly have put him at the top of Dr. Zajac's list of wannabe recipients even if he hadn't been famous. Zajac was not a thoroughly unsympathetic man. But he was also among the millions who'd taped the three-minute lion story. To Dr. Zajac, the footage was a combination of a hand surgeon's favorite horror film and the precursor of his future fame.

It suffices to say that Patrick Wallingford and Dr. Nicholas M. Zajac were on a collision course, which didn't bode well from the start.

CHAPTER THREE

Before Meeting Mrs. Clausen

*T*RY BEING AN ANCHOR who hides the evidence of his missing hand under the news desk—see what that gets you. The earliest letters of protest were from amputees. What was Patrick Wallingford ashamed of?

Even two-handed people complained. "Be a man, Patrick," one woman wrote. "Show us."

When he had problems with his first prosthesis, wearers of artificial limbs criticized him for using it incorrectly. He was equally clumsy with an array of other prosthetic devices, but his wife was divorcing him—he had no time to practice.

Marilyn simply couldn't get over how he'd "behaved." In this case, she didn't mean the other women—she was referring to how Patrick had behaved with the lion. "You looked so . . . unmanly," Marilyn told him, adding that her husband's physical attractiveness had always been "of an inoffensive kind, tantamount to blandness." What she really meant was that nothing about his body had revolted her, until now. (In sickness and in health, but not in missing pieces, Wallingford concluded.)

Patrick and Marilyn had lived in Manhattan in an apartment on East Sixty-second Street between Park and Lexington avenues; naturally it was Marilyn's apartment now. Only the night doorman of Wallingford's former building had not rejected him, and the night doorman was so confused that his own name was unclear to him. Sometimes it was Vlad or Vlade; at other times, it was Lewis. Even when he was Lewis, his accent remained an indecipherable mixture of Long Island with something Slavic.

"Where are you from, Vlade?" Wallingford had asked him.

"It's Lewis. Nassau County," Vlad had replied.

Another time, Wallingford said, "So, Lewis . . . where *were* you from?"

"Nassau County. It's Vlad, Mr. O'Neill."

Only the doorman mistook Patrick Wallingford for Paul O'Neill, who became a right fielder for the New York Yankees in 1993. (They were both tall, dark, and handsome in that jutting-chin fashion, but that was as far as the resemblance went.)

The confused doorman had unusually unshakable beliefs; he first mistook Patrick for Paul O'Neill when O'Neill was a relatively unknown and unrecognized player for the Cincinnati Reds.

"I guess I look a little like Paul O'Neill," Wallingford admitted to Vlad or Vlade or Lewis, "but I'm Patrick Wallingford. I'm a television journalist."

Since Vlad or Vlade or Lewis was the night doorman, it was always dark and often late when he encountered Patrick. "Don't worry, Mr. O'Neill," the doorman whispered conspiratorially. "I won't tell anybody."

Thus the night doorman assumed that Paul O'Neill, who played professional baseball in Ohio, was having an affair with Patrick Wallingford's wife in New York. At least this was as close as Wallingford could come to understanding what the poor man thought.

One night when Patrick came home—this was when he had two hands, and long before his divorce—Vlad or Vlade or Lewis was watching an extra-inning ball game from Cincinnati, where the Mets were playing the Reds.

"Now look here, Lewis," Wallingford said to the startled doorman, who kept a small black-and-white TV in the coatroom off the lobby. "There are the Reds—they're in *Cincinnati*! Yet here I am, right beside you. I'm not playing tonight, am I?"

"Don't worry, Mr. O'Neill," the doorman said sympathetically. "I won't tell anybody."

But after he lost his hand, Patrick Wallingford was more famous than Paul O'Neill. Furthermore, it was his left hand that Patrick had lost, and Paul O'Neill bats left and throws left. As Vlad or Vlade or Lewis would know, O'Neill became the American League batting champion in 1994; he hit .359 in what was only his second season with the Yanks, and he was a great right fielder.

"They're gonna retire Number Twenty-One one day, Mr. O'Neill," the doorman stubbornly assured Patrick Wallingford. "You can count on it."

After Patrick's left hand was gone, his single return visit to the apartment on East Sixty-second Street was for the purpose of collecting his clothes and books and what divorce lawyers call personal effects. Of course it was clear to everyone in the building, even to the doorman, that Wallingford was moving out.

"Don't worry, Mr. O'Neill," the doorman told Patrick. "The things they can do in rehab today . . . well, you wouldn't believe. It's too bad it wasn't your right hand—you bein' a lefty is gonna make it tough—but they'll come up with somethin', I know they will."

"Thank you, Vlade," Patrick said.

The one-handed journalist felt weak and disoriented in his old apartment. The day he moved out, Marilyn had already begun to rearrange the furniture. Wallingford kept turning to look over his shoulder to see what was behind him; it was just a couch that had been moved from somewhere else in the apartment, but to Patrick the unfamiliarly placed shape took on the characteristics of an advancing lion.

"I think the hittin' will be less of a problem than the throw to the plate from right field," the three-named doorman was saying. "You'll have to choke up on the bat, shorten your swing, lay off the long ball—I don't mean forever, just till you're used to the new hand."

But there was no new hand that Wallingford could get used to; the prosthetic devices defeated him. The ongoing abuse by his ex-wife would defeat Patrick, too.

"You were never sexy, not to me," Marilyn lied. (So she was guilty of wishful thinking—so what?) "And now . . . well, missing a hand . . . you're nothing but a helpless *cripple*!"

The twenty-four-hour news network didn't give Wallingford long to prove himself as an anchor. Even on the reputed disaster channel, Patrick failed to be an anchor of note. He moved quickly from early morning to midmorning to late night, and finally to a predawn slot, where Wallingford imagined that only night workers and insomniacs ever saw him.

His television image was too repressed for a man who'd lost his left hand to the king of beasts. One wanted to see more defiance in his expression, which instead radiated an enfeebled humility, an air of wary acceptance. While he'd never been a bad man, only a bad husband, Patrick's one-handedness came across as self-pitying, and it marked him as the silent-martyr type.

While looking wounded hardly hurt Wallingford

with women, now there were *only* other women in his life. And by the time Patrick's divorce was settled, his producers felt they had given him adequate opportunity as an anchor to protect themselves from any later charges that they'd discriminated against the handicapped; they returned him to the less visible role of a field reporter. Worse, the one-handed journalist became the interviewer of choice for various freaks and zanies; that the twenty-four-hour international channel already had a reputation for captured acts of mauling and mutilation only underscored Patrick's image as a man irreversibly damaged.

On TV, of course, the news was catastrophe-driven. Why *wouldn't* the network assign Wallingford to the tabloid sleaze, the beneath-the-news stories? Without fail, they gave him the smirking, salacious tidbits—the marriage that lasted less than a day, including one that didn't make it through the honeymoon; the husband who, after eight years of marriage, discovered that his wife was a man.

Patrick Wallingford was the all-news network's disaster man, the field reporter on the scene of the worst (meaning the most bizarre) accidents. He covered a collision between a tourist bus and a bicycle rickshaw in Bangkok—the two fatalities were both Thai prostitutes, riding to work in the rickshaw. Wallingford interviewed their families and their former clients; it was disquietingly hard to tell which was which, but each of the interviewees felt compelled to stare at the stump or the prosthesis at the end of the reporter's left arm.

They always eyed the stump or the prosthesis. He hated them both—and the Internet, too. To him, the Internet chiefly served to encourage the inherent laziness of his profession—an overreliance on secondary sources and other shortcuts. Journalists had always borrowed from other journalists, but now it was too easy.

His angry ex-wife, who was also a journalist, was a case in point. Marilyn prided herself in writing "profiles" of only the most literary authors and the most serious actors and actresses. (It went without saying that print journalism was superior to television.) Yet in truth, Patrick's ex-wife prepared for her interviews with writers *not* by reading their books— some of which were admittedly too long—but by reading their previous interviews. Nor did Marilyn make the effort to see every film that the actors and actresses among her interviewees had been in; shamelessly, she read the *reviews* of their movies instead.

Given his Internet prejudice, Wallingford never saw the publicity campaign on www.needahand.com; he'd never heard of Schatzman, Gingeleskie, Mengerink & Associates until Dr. Zajac called him. Zajac already knew about Patrick's mishaps with several different prosthetic devices, not just the one in SoHo, which received a fair amount of attention: the shutting of his artificial hand in the taxi's rear door; the cabbie blithely driving on for a block or so. The doctor also knew about the embarrassing entanglement with the seat belt on that flight to Berlin, where Wallingford was rushing to interview a deranged man who'd been arrested for detonating a dog near the Potsdamer Platz. (In an avowed protest against the new dome on the Reichstag, the fiend had attached an explosive device to the dog's collar.)

Patrick Wallingford had become *the* TV journalist for stray acts of God and random nonsense. People called out to him from passing taxis—"Hey, lion guy!" Bicycle messengers hailed him, first spitting the whistles from their mouths—"Yo, disaster man!"

Worse, Patrick had so little liking for his job that he'd lost all sympathy for the victims and their families; when he interviewed them, this lack of sympathy showed.

Therefore, in lieu of being fired—since he was injured on the job, he might have sued—Wallingford was so further marginalized that his next field assignment lacked even disaster potential. Patrick was being sent to Japan to cover a conference sponsored by a consortium of Japanese newspapers. He was surprised by the topic of the conference, too—it was called "The Future of Women," which certainly didn't have the sound of a disaster.

But the idea of Patrick Wallingford's attending the conference . . . well, the women in the newsroom in New York were all atingle about *that*.

"You'll get laid a lot, Pat," one of the women teased him. "A lot *more,* I mean."

"How could Patrick possibly get laid *more?*" another of the women asked, and that set them all off again.

"I've heard that women in Japan are treated like shit," one of the women remarked. "And the men go off to Bangkok and behave abominably."

"All men behave abominably in Bangkok," said a woman who'd been there.

"Have you been to Bangkok, Pat?" the first of the women asked. She knew perfectly well that he'd been there—he had been there with her. She was just reminding him of something that everyone in the newsroom knew.

"Have you ever been to Japan, Patrick?" one of the other women asked, when the tittering died down.

"No, never," Wallingford replied. "I've never slept with a Japanese woman, either."

They called him a pig for saying that, although most of them meant this affectionately. Then they dispersed, leaving him with Mary, one of the youngest of the New York newsroom women. (And one of the few Patrick *hadn't* yet slept with.)

When Mary saw they were alone together, she touched his left forearm, very lightly, just above his missing hand. Only women ever touched him there.

"They're just teasing, you know," she told him. "Most of them would take off for Tokyo with you tomorrow, if you asked them."

Patrick had thought about sleeping with Mary before, but one thing or another had always intervened. "Would *you* take off for Tokyo with me tomorrow, if I asked you?"

"I'm married," Mary said.

"I know," Patrick replied.

"I'm expecting a baby," Mary told him; then she burst into tears. She ran after the other New York newsroom women, leaving Wallingford alone with his thoughts, which were that it was always better to let the woman make the first pass. At that moment, the phone call came from Dr. Zajac.

Zajac's manners, when introducing himself, were (in a word) surgical. "The first hand I get my hands on, you can have," Dr. Zajac announced. "If you really want it."

"Why wouldn't I want it? I mean if it's healthy . . ."

"Of *course* it will be healthy!" Zajac replied. "Would I give you an *un*healthy hand?"

"When?" Patrick asked.

"You can't rush finding the perfect hand," Zajac informed him.

"I don't think I'd be happy with a woman's hand, or an old man's," Patrick thought out loud.

"Finding the right hand is my job," Dr. Zajac said.

"It's a *left* hand," Wallingford reminded him.

"Of course it is! I mean the right *donor.*"

"Okay, but no strings attached," Patrick said.

"Strings?" Zajac asked, perplexed. What on earth

could the reporter have meant? What possible strings could be attached to a donor hand?

But Wallingford was leaving for Japan, and he'd just learned he was supposed to deliver a speech on the opening day of the conference; he hadn't written the speech, which he was thinking about but would put off doing until he was on the plane.

Patrick didn't give a second thought to the curiousness of his own comment—"no strings attached." It was a typical disaster-man remark, a lion-guy reflex—just another dumb thing to say, solely for the sake of saying something. (Not unlike "German girls are very popular in New York right now.")

And Zajac was happy—the matter had been left in his hands, so to speak.

CHAPTER FOUR

A Japanese Interlude

*I*S THERE SOMETHING cursed about Asia and me? Wallingford would wonder later. First he'd lost his hand in India; and now, what about Japan?

The trip to Tokyo had gone wrong even *before* the start, if you count Patrick's insensitive proposition to Mary. Wallingford himself counted it as the start. He'd hit on a young woman who was newly married and pregnant, a girl whose last name he could never remember. Worse, she'd had a look about her that haunted him; it was more than an unmistakable prettiness, although Mary had that, too. Her look indicated a capacity for damage greater than gossip, a ferocity not easily held in check, a potential for some mayhem yet to be defined.

Then, on the plane to Tokyo, Patrick struggled with his speech. Here he was, divorced, for good reason—and feeling like a failed sexual predator, because of pregnant Mary—and he was supposed to address the subject of "The Future of Women," in notoriously keep-women-in-their-place Japan.

Not only was Wallingford not accustomed to writing speeches; he was not used to speaking without reading the script off the TelePrompTer. (Usually someone else had written the script.) But maybe if he looked over the list of participants in the conference—they were all women—he might find some flattering things to say about them, and this flattery might suffice for his opening remarks.

It was a blow to him to discover that he had no firsthand knowledge of the accomplishments of any of the women participating in the conference; alas, he knew who only one of the women was, and the most flattering thing he could think of saying about her was that he thought he'd like to sleep with her, although he'd seen her only on television.

Patrick liked German women. Witness that braless sound technician on the TV crew in Gujarat, that blonde who'd fainted in the meat cart, the enterprising Monika with a *k*. But the German woman who was a participant in the Tokyo conference was a Barbara, spelled the usual way, and she was, like Wallingford, a television journalist. Unlike Wallingford, she was more successful than she was famous.

Barbara Frei anchored the morning news for ZDF. She had a resonant, professional-sounding voice, a wary smile, and a thin-lipped mouth. She had shoulder-length dirty-blond hair, adroitly tucked behind her ears. Her face was beautiful and sleek, with high cheekbones; in Wallingford's world, it was a face made for television.

On TV, Barbara Frei wore nothing but rather mannish suits in either black or navy blue, and she never wore a blouse or a shirt of any kind under the wide-open collar of the suit jacket. She had wonderful collarbones, which she quite justifiably liked to show. She preferred small stud earrings—often emeralds or rubies—Patrick could tell; he was knowledgeable about women's jewelry.

But while the prospect of meeting Barbara Frei in Tokyo gave Wallingford an unrealistic sexual ambition for his time in Japan, neither she nor any of the conference's other participants could be of any help in writing his speech.

There was a Russian film director, a woman named Ludmilla Slovaboda. (The spelling only approximates Patrick's phonetic guess at how one *might* pronounce her last name. Let's call her Ludmilla.) Wallingford had never seen her films.

There was a Danish novelist, a woman named Bodille or Bodile or Bodil Jensen; her first name was spelled three different ways in the printed material that Patrick's Japanese hosts had sent. However her name was spelled, Wallingford presumed one said "bode *eel*"—accent on the *eel*—but he wasn't sure.

There was an English economist with the boring name of Jane Brown. There was a Chinese geneticist, a Korean doctor of infectious diseases, a Dutch bacteriologist, and a woman from Ghana whose field was alternately described as "food-shortage management" or "world-hunger relief." There was no hope of Wallingford's pronouncing any of their names correctly; he wouldn't even try.

The list of participants went on and on, all highly accomplished professional women—with the probable exception of an American author and self-described radical feminist whom Wallingford had never heard of, and a lopsided number of participants from Japan who seemed to represent the arts.

Patrick was uncomfortable around female poets and sculptors. It was probably not correct to call them poetesses and sculptresses, although this is how Wallingford thought of them. (In Patrick's mind, most artists were frauds; they were peddling something unreal, something made up.)

So what would his welcoming speech be? He wasn't entirely at a loss—he'd not lived in New York for nothing. Wallingford had suffered through his share of black-tie occasions; he knew what bullshitters most masters of ceremonies were—he knew how to bullshit, too. Therefore, Patrick decided his opening remarks should be nothing more or less than the fashionable and news-savvy blather of a master of ceremonies—the insincere, self-deprecating humor of someone who appears at ease while making a joke of himself. Boy, was he wrong.

How about this for an opening line? "I feel inse-

cure addressing such a distinguished group as your-
selves, given that my principal and, by comparison,
lowly accomplishment was to illegally feed my left
hand to a lion in India five years ago."

Surely that would break the ice. It had been good
for a laugh at the last speech Wallingford had given,
which was not really a speech but a toast at a dinner
honoring Olympic athletes at the New York Athletic
Club. The women in Tokyo would prove a tougher
audience.

That the airline lost Wallingford's checked luggage, an overstuffed garment bag, seemed to set a
tone. The official for the airline told him: "Your luggage is on the way to the Philippines—back tomorrow!"

"You already know that my bag is going to the
Philippines?"

"Most luridly, sir," the official said, or so Patrick
thought; he'd really said, "Most assuredly, sir," but
Wallingford had misheard him. (Patrick had a childish and offensive habit of mocking foreign accents,
which was almost as unlikable as his compulsion to
laugh when someone tripped or fell down.) For the
sake of clarification, the airline official added: "The
lost luggage on that flight from New York *always*
goes to the Philippines."

" '*Always*'?" Wallingford asked.

"Always back tomorrow, too," the official replied.

There then followed the ride in the helicopter from

the airport to the rooftop of his Tokyo hotel. Walling-ford's Japanese hosts had arranged for the chopper.

"Ah, Tokyo at twilight—what can compare to it?" said a stern-looking woman seated next to Patrick on the helicopter. He hadn't noticed that she'd also been on the plane from New York—probably because she'd been wearing an unflattering pair of tortoise-shell glasses and Wallingford had given her no more than a passing look. (She was the American author and self-described radical feminist, of course.)

"You're being facetious, I trust," Patrick said to her.

"I'm always facetious, Mr. Wallingford," the woman replied. She introduced herself with a short, firm handshake. "I'm Evelyn Arbuthnot. I recognized you by your hand—the other one."

"Did they send your luggage to the Philippines, too?" Patrick asked Ms. Arbuthnot.

"Look at me, Mr. Wallingford," she instructed him. "I'm strictly a carry-on person. Airlines don't lose my luggage."

Perhaps he'd underestimated Evelyn Arbuthnot's abilities; maybe he should try to find, and even read, one of her books.

But below them was Tokyo. He could see that there were heliports on the rooftops of many hotels and office buildings, and that other helicopters were hovering to land. It was as if there were a military in-vasion of the huge, hazy city, which, in the twilight, was tinged by an array of improbable colors, from pink to blood-red, in the fading sunset. To Wallingford, the rooftop helipads looked like bull's-eyes; he tried to guess which bull's-eye their helicopter was aiming at.

"Japan," Evelyn Arbuthnot said despairingly.

"You don't like Japan?" Patrick asked her.

"I don't 'like' anyplace," she told Wallingford, "but the man-woman thing is especially onerous here."

"Oh," Patrick replied.

"You haven't been here before, have you?" she asked him. While he was still shaking his head, she told him: "You shouldn't have come, disaster man."

"Why did *you* come?" Wallingford asked her.

She was kind of growing on him with every negative word she spoke. He began to like her face, which was square with a high forehead and a broad jaw— her short gray hair sat on her head like a no-nonsense helmet. Her body was squat and sturdy-looking, and not at all revealed; she wore black jeans and a man's untucked denim shirt, which looked soft from a lot of laundering. Judging by what Wallingford could see, which was not much, she seemed to be small-breasted—she didn't bother to wear a bra. She had on a sensible, if dirty, pair of running shoes, which she rested on a large gym bag that only partially fit beneath her seat; the bag had a shoulder strap and looked heavy.

Ms. Arbuthnot appeared to be a woman in her late

forties or early fifties who traveled with more books than clothes. She wore no makeup and no nail polish, and no rings or other jewelry. She had small fingers and very clean, small hands, and her nails were bitten to the quick.

"Why did *I* come here?" she asked, repeating Patrick's question. "I go where I'm invited, wherever it is, both because I'm not invited to many places and because I have a message. But *you* don't have a message, do you, Mr. Wallingford? I can't imagine what you would ever come to Tokyo for, least of all for a conference on 'The Future of Women.' Since when is 'The Future of Women' *news*? Or the lion guy's kind of news, anyway," she added.

The helicopter was landing now. Wallingford, watching the enlarging bull's-eye, was speechless.

"Why did *I* come here?" Patrick asked, repeating Ms. Arbuthnot's question. He was just trying to buy a little time while he thought of an answer.

"I'll tell you why, Mr. Wallingford." Evelyn Arbuthnot put her small but surprisingly strong hands on his knees and gave him a good squeeze. "You came here because you knew you'd meet a lot of *women*—isn't that right?"

So she was one of those people who disliked journalists, or Patrick Wallingford in particular. Wallingford was sensitive to both dislikes, which were common. He wanted to say that he had come to Tokyo because he was a fucking field reporter and he'd been given a fucking field assignment, but he held his tongue. He had that popular weakness of wanting to win over people who disliked him; as a consequence, he had numerous friends. None of them were close, and very few of them were male. (He'd slept with too many women to make close friendships with men.)

The helicopter bumped down; a door opened. A fast-moving bellman, who'd been standing on the rooftop, rushed forward with a luggage cart. There was no bag to take, except Evelyn Arbuthnot's gym bag, which she preferred to carry herself.

"No bag? No luggage?" the eager bellman asked Wallingford, who was still thinking of how to answer Ms. Arbuthnot.

"My bag was mistakenly sent to the Philippines," Patrick informed the bellman. He spoke unnecessarily slowly.

"Oh, no problem. Back tomorrow!" the bellman said.

"Ms. Arbuthnot," Wallingford managed to say, a little stiffly, "I assure you that I don't have to come to Tokyo, or this conference, to meet women. I can meet women anywhere in the world."

"Oh, I'll bet you can." Evelyn Arbuthnot seemed less than pleased at the idea. "And I'll bet you *have*—everywhere, all the time. One after another."

Bitch! Patrick decided, and he'd just been beginning to like her. He'd been feeling a lot like an asshole lately, and Ms. Arbuthnot had clearly got the better of him; yet Patrick Wallingford generally thought of himself as a nice guy.

Fearing that his lost garment bag would not come back from the Philippines in time for his opening remarks at the "Future of Women" conference, Wallingford sent the clothes he'd worn on the plane to the hotel laundry service, which promised to return them overnight. Patrick hoped so. The problem then was that he had nothing to wear. He'd not anticipated that his Japanese hosts (fellow journalists, all) would keep calling him in his hotel room, inviting him for drinks and dinner.

He told them he was tired; he said he wasn't hungry. They were polite about it, but Wallingford could tell he'd disappointed them. No doubt they couldn't wait to see the no-hand—the other one, as Evelyn Arbuthnot had put it.

Wallingford was looking distrustfully at the room-service menu when Ms. Arbuthnot called. "What are you doing for dinner?" she asked. "Or are you just doing room service?"

"Hasn't anyone asked you out?" Patrick inquired. "They keep inviting me, but I can't go because I sent the clothes I was wearing to the laundry service—in case my bag isn't back from the Philippines tomorrow."

"Nobody's asked me out," Ms. Arbuthnot told him. "But I'm not famous—I'm not even a journalist. Nobody ever asks me out."

Wallingford could believe this, but all he said was: "Well, I'd invite you to join me in my room, but I have nothing to wear except a towel."

"Call housekeeping," Evelyn Arbuthnot advised him. "Tell them you want a robe. Men don't know how to sit in towels." She gave him her room number and told him to call her back when he had the robe. Meanwhile she'd have a look at the room-service menu.

But when Wallingford called housekeeping, a woman's voice said, "Solly, no lobes." Or so Wallingford misheard. And when he called back Ms. Arbuthnot and reported what housekeeping had told him, she surprised him again.

"No lobe, no loom service."

Patrick thought she was kidding. "Don't worry—I'll keep my knees tight together. Or I'll try wearing *two* towels."

"It's not you, it's me—it's my fault," Evelyn said. "I'm just disappointed in myself for being attracted to you." Then she said, "Solly," and hung up the phone. At least housekeeping, in lieu of the robe, sent him a complimentary toothbrush and a small tube of toothpaste.

There's not a lot of trouble you can get into in Tokyo when you're wearing just a towel; yet Wallingford would find a way. Not having much of an appetite, he called something listed in the hotel directory as MASSAGE THERAPY instead of room service. Big mistake.

"Two women," said the voice answering for the massage therapist. It was a man's voice, and to Patrick it sounded like he said, "Two lemons"; yet he thought he'd understood what the man had said.

"No, no—not 'two women,' just one man. I'm a man, alone," Wallingford explained.

"Two lemons," the man on the phone confidently replied.

"Whatever," Wallingford answered. "Is it shiatsu?"

"It's two lemons or nothing," the man said more aggressively.

"Okay, okay," Patrick conceded. He opened a beer from the mini-bar while he waited in his towel. Before long, two women came to his door.

One of them carried the table with the hole cut in one end of it for Wallingford's face; it resembled an execution device, and the woman who carried it had hands that Dr. Zajac would have said resembled the hands of a famous tight end. The other woman carried some pillows and towels—she had forearms like Popeye's.

"Hi," Wallingford said.

They looked at him warily, their eyes on his towel.

"Shiatsu?" Patrick asked them.

"There are two of us," one of the women told him.

"Yes, there certainly are," Wallingford said, but he didn't know why. Was it to make the massage go faster? Maybe it was to double the cost of the massage.

When his face was in the hole, he stared at the bare feet of the woman who was grinding her elbow into his neck; the other woman was grinding her elbow (or was it her knee?) into his spine, in the area of his lower back. Patrick gathered his courage and asked the women outright: "Why are there two of you?"

To Wallingford's surprise, the muscular massage therapists giggled like little girls.

"So we won't get raped," one of the women said.

"Two lemons, no lape," Wallingford heard the other woman say.

Their thumbs and their elbows, or their knees, were getting to him now—the women were digging pretty deep—but what really offended Wallingford was the concept that someone could be so morally reprehensible as to *rape* a massage therapist. (Patrick's experiences with women had all been of a fairly limited kind: the women had wanted him.)

When the massage therapists left, Wallingford was limp. He could barely manage to walk to the bathroom to pee and brush his teeth before falling into bed. He saw that he'd left his unfinished beer on the night table, where it would stink in the morning, but he was too tired to get up. He lay as if rubberized. In the morning, he awoke in the exact same position in which he'd fallen asleep—on his stomach with both arms at his sides, like a soldier, and with the right side of his face pressed into the pillow, looking at his left shoulder.

Not until Wallingford got up to answer the door—

it was just his breakfast—did he realize that he couldn't move his head. His neck felt locked; he looked permanently to the left. That he could face only left would present him with a problem at the podium, where he soon had to make his opening remarks to the conference. And before that he had to eat his breakfast while facing his left shoulder. Compounding the difficulty of brushing his teeth with his right (and only) hand, the complimentary toothbrush was a trifle short—given the degree to which he faced left.

At least his luggage was back from its journey to the Philippines, which was a good thing because the laundry service called to apologize for "misplacing" his only other clothes.

"Not losing, merely misplacing!" shouted a man on the verge of hysteria. "Solly!"

When Wallingford opened his garment bag, which he managed by looking over his left shoulder, he discovered that the bag and all his clothes smelled strongly of urine. He called the airline to complain.

"Were you just in the Philippines?" the official for the airline asked.

"No, but my *bag* was," Wallingford replied.

"Oh, that explains it!" the official cried happily. "Those drug-sniffing dogs that they have there— sometimes they piss on the suitcases!" Naturally this sounded to Patrick like "piff on the sweet cheeses," but he got the idea. Filipino dogs had urinated on his clothes!

"Why?"

"We don't know," the airline official told him. "It just happens. The dogs have to go, I guess."

Stupefied, Wallingford searched his clothes for a shirt and a pair of pants that were, relatively speaking, not permeated with dog piss. He reluctantly sent the rest of his clothes to the hotel laundry service, admonishing the man on the phone not to lose *these* clothes—they were his last.

"Others *not* losing!" the man shouted. "Merely misplacing!" (This time he didn't even say "Solly!")

Given how he knew he smelled, Patrick was not pleased to share a taxi to the conference with Evelyn Arbuthnot—especially as he was forced, by the crick in his neck, to ride in the taxi with his face turned rudely away from her.

"I don't blame you for being angry with me, but isn't it rather childish not to look at me?" she asked. She kept sniffing all around, as if she suspected there were a dog in the cab.

Wallingford told her everything: the two-lemon massage ("the two-woman mauling," he called it); his one-way neck; the dog-peeing episode.

"I could listen to your stories for hours," Ms. Arbuthnot told him. He didn't need to see her to know she was being facetious.

Then came his speech, which he delivered standing sideways at the podium, looking down his left arm at his stump, which was more visible to him than the hard-to-read pages. With his left side to the audience, Patrick's amputation was more apparent, prompting one wag in the Japanese press to describe Wallingford as "milking his missing hand." (In the Western media, his missing hand was often referred to as his "no-hand" or his "nonhand.") More generous Japanese journalists attending Patrick's opening remarks—his male hosts, for the most part—called his left-facing oratorical method "provocative" and "incredibly cool."

The speech itself was a flop with the highly accomplished women who were the conference's participants. They had not come to Tokyo to talk about "The Future of Women" and then hear recycled master-of-ceremonies jokes from a man.

"Was that what you were writing on the plane yesterday? Or *trying* to write, I should say," Evelyn Arbuthnot remarked. "Jesus, we *should* have had room service together. If the subject of your speech had come up, I might have spared you that embarrassment."

As before, Wallingford was rendered speechless in her company.

The hall in which he'd spoken was made of steel, in tones of ultramodern gray. That was roughly how Evelyn Arbuthnot struck Patrick, too—"made of steel, in tones of ultramodern gray."

The other women shunned him afterward; Wallingford knew that it wasn't only the dog pee.

Even his German colleague in the world of television journalism, the beautiful Barbara Frei, wouldn't speak to him. Most journalists meeting Wallingford for the first time would at least offer him some commiseration about the lion business, but the aloof Ms. Frei made it clear that she didn't want to meet him.

Only the Danish novelist, Bodille or Bodile or Bodil Jensen, seemed to look at Patrick with a flicker of pity in her darting green eyes. She was pretty in a kind of bereft or disturbed way, as if there'd recently been a suicide or a murder of someone close to her—possibly her lover or her husband.

Wallingford attempted to approach Ms. Jensen, but Ms. Arbuthnot cut him off. "I saw her first," Evelyn told Patrick, making a beeline for Bodille or Bodile or Bodil Jensen.

This damaged Wallingford's failing self-confidence further. Was that what Ms. Arbuthnot had meant by being disappointed in herself for being attracted to him? Was Evelyn Arbuthnot a lesbian?

Not all that eager to meet anyone while smelling wretchedly of dog piss, Wallingford returned to the hotel to await his clean clothes. He left his two-man television crew to film whatever was interesting in the rest of the speeches that first day, including a panel discussion on rape.

When Patrick got back to his hotel room, the hotel management had sent him flowers—in further apology for "misplacing" his clothes—and there were two massage therapists, two *different* women, waiting for him. The hotel had also sent him a complimentary massage. "Solly about the crick in your neck," one of the new women told Patrick.

This sounded something like "click in your knack," but Wallingford understood what she'd meant. He was doomed to have another two-woman mauling.

But these two women managed to cure the crick in his neck, and while they were still engaged in turning him to jelly, the hotel laundry service returned his clean clothes—*all* his clothes. Perhaps this marked a turn for the better in his Japanese experience, Patrick imagined.

Given the loss of his left hand in India, even though it had happened five years before—given that Filipino dogs had pissed on his clothes, and that he'd needed a second massage to correct the damage done by the first; given that he'd not known Evelyn Arbuthnot was a lesbian, and given his dreadfully insensitive speech; given that he knew nothing about Japan, and arguably even less about the future of women, which he never, not even now, thought about—Wallingford should have been wise enough not to imagine that his Japanese experience was about to take a turn for the *better.*

Anyone meeting Patrick Wallingford in Japan would have known in an instant that he was precisely the kind of penis-brain who would casually put his hand too close to a lion's cage. (And if the lion had had an accent, Wallingford would have mocked it.) In retrospect, Patrick himself would rank his time in

Japan as an even lower point in his life than the hand-eating episode in India.

To be fair, Wallingford wasn't the only man who missed the panel discussion on rape. The English economist, whose name (Jane Brown) Patrick had thought was boring, turned out to be anything but. She threw a fit at the rape panel and insisted that no men should be present for the discussion, declaring that for women to discuss rape honestly with one another was tantamount to being naked.

That much the cameraman and the sound technician for the twenty-four-hour international channel managed to get on film before the English economist, to make her point, began to take off her clothes. Thereupon the cameraman, who was Japanese, respectfully stopped filming.

It's debatable that watching Jane Brown take off her clothes would have been all that watchable for most television viewers. To describe Ms. Brown as matronly would be a kindness—she needed only to *start* taking off her clothes to empty the hall of what few men were there. There were almost no men attending the "Future of Women" conference, only the two guys in Patrick Wallingford's TV crew, the Japanese journalists who were the conference's unhappy-looking hosts, and, of course, Patrick himself.

The hosts would have been offended if they'd heard about the long-distance request of the New York news editor, who wanted no more footage of the conference itself. Instead of more of the women's conference, what Dick said he now wanted was "something to contrast to it"—something to undermine it, in other words.

This was pure Dick, Wallingford thought. When the news editor asked for "related material," what he really meant was something so *un*related to the women's conference that it could make a mockery of the very idea of the future of women.

"I hear there's a child-porn industry in Tokyo," Dick told Patrick. "Child prostitutes, too. All this is relatively new, I'm told. It's just emerging—dare I say *budding*?"

"What about it?" Wallingford asked. He knew this was pure Dick, too. The news editor had never been interested in "The Future of Women." The Japanese hosts had wanted Wallingford—the lion-guy video had record sales in Japan—and Dick had taken advantage of the invitation to have disaster man dig up some dirt in Tokyo.

"Of course you'll have to be careful how you do it," Dick went on, warning Patrick that there would be "aspersions of racism" cast against the network if they did anything that appeared to be "slanted against the Japanese."

"You get it?" Dick had asked Wallingford over the phone. "*Slanted* against the Japanese . . ."

Wallingford sighed. Then he suggested, as always, that there was a deeper, more complex story. The "Future of Women" conference was conducted over a four-day period, but only in the daylight hours.

Nothing was scheduled at night, not even dinner parties. Patrick wondered why.

A young Japanese woman who wanted Wallingford to autograph her Mickey Mouse T-shirt seemed surprised that he hadn't guessed the reason. There were no conference-related activities in the evening because women were "supposed to" spend the nighttime at home with their families. If they'd tried to have a women's conference in Japan at night, not many women could have come.

Wasn't this interesting? Wallingford asked Dick, but the New York news editor told him to forget it. Although the young Japanese woman looked fantastic on-camera, Mickey Mouse T-shirts weren't allowed on the all-news network, which had once been involved in a dispute with the Walt Disney Company.

In the end, Wallingford was instructed to stick to individual interviews with the women who were the conference's participants. Patrick could tell that Dick was pulling out on the piece.

"Just see if one or two of these broads will open up to you," was how Dick left it.

Naturally Wallingford began by trying to arrange a one-on-one interview with Barbara Frei, the German television journalist. He approached her in the hotel bar. She seemed to be alone; the idea that she might be waiting for someone never crossed Patrick's mind. The ZDF anchor was every bit as beautiful as she appeared on the small screen, but she politely declined to be interviewed.

"I know your network, of course," Ms. Frei began tactfully. "I don't think it likely that they will give serious coverage to this conference. Do you?" Case closed. "I'm sorry about your hand, Mr. Wallingford," Barbara Frei said. "That was truly awful—I'm very sorry."

"Thank you," Patrick replied. The woman was both sincere and classy. Wallingford's twenty-four-hour international channel was not Ms. Frei's, or anyone else's, idea of serious TV journalism; compared to Barbara Frei, Patrick Wallingford wasn't serious, either, and both Ms. Frei and Mr. Wallingford knew it.

The hotel bar was full of businessmen, as hotel bars tend to be. "Look—it's the lion guy!" Wallingford heard one of them say.

"Disaster man!" another businessman called out.

"Won't you have a drink?" Barbara Frei asked Patrick pityingly.

"Well . . . all right." An immense and unfamiliar depression was weighing on him, and as soon as his beer arrived, there also arrived at the bar the man whom Ms. Frei had been waiting for—her husband.

Wallingford knew him. He was Peter Frei, a well-respected journalist at ZDF, although Peter Frei did cultural programs and his wife did what they called hard news.

"Peter's a little tired," Ms. Frei said, affectionately rubbing her husband's shoulders and the back of his neck. "He's been training for a trip to Mount Everest."

"For a piece you're doing, I suppose," Patrick said enviously.

"Yes, but I have to climb a bit of the mountain to do it properly."

"You're going to climb Mount Everest?" Wallingford asked Peter Frei. He was an extremely fit-looking man—they were a very attractive couple.

"Oh, everyone climbs a bit of Everest now," Mr. Frei replied modestly. "That's what's wrong with it—the place has been overrun by amateurs like me!" His beautiful wife laughed fondly and went on rubbing her husband's neck and shoulders. Wallingford, who was barely able to drink his beer, found them as likable a couple as any he'd known.

When they said good-bye, Barbara Frei touched Patrick's left forearm in the usual place. "You might try interviewing that woman from Ghana," she suggested helpfully. "She's awfully nice and smart, and she's got more to say than I have. I mean she's more of a person with a cause than I am." (This meant, Wallingford knew, that the woman from Ghana would talk to anyone.)

"That's a good idea—thank you."

"Sorry about the hand," Peter Frei told Patrick. "That's a terrible thing. I think half the world remembers where they were and what they were doing when they saw it."

"Yes," Wallingford answered. He'd had only one beer, but he would scarcely remember leaving the hotel bar; he went off full of self-disgust, looking for the African woman as if she were a lifeboat and he a drowning man. He was.

It was an unkind irony that the starvation expert from Ghana was extremely fat. Wallingford worried that Dick would exploit her obesity in an unpredictable way. She must have weighed three hundred pounds, and she was dressed in something resembling a tent made of samples from patchwork quilts. But the woman had a degree from Oxford, and another from Yale; she'd won a Nobel Prize in something to do with world nutrition, which she said was "merely a matter of intelligent Third World crises anticipation . . . any fool with half a brain and a whole conscience could do what I do."

But as much as Wallingford admired the big woman from Ghana, they didn't like her in New York. "Too fat," Dick told Patrick. "Black people will think we're making fun of her."

"But *we* didn't make her fat!" Patrick protested. "The point is, she's *smart*—she's actually got something to *say*!"

"You can find someone else with something to say, can't you? Jesus Christ, find someone smart who's *normal*-looking!" But as Wallingford would discover at the "Future of Women" conference in Tokyo, this was exceedingly hard to do—taking into account that, by "*normal*-looking," Dick no doubt meant not fat, not black, and not Japanese.

Patrick took one look at the Chinese geneticist, who had an elevated, hairy mole in the middle of her forehead; he wouldn't bother trying to interview her. He could already hear what that dick Dick in New York would say about her. "Talk about making fun of people—Jesus Christ! We might as well bomb a Chinese embassy in some asshole country and try calling it an *accident* or something!"

So Patrick talked to the Korean doctor of infectious diseases, who he thought was kind of cute. But she turned out to be camera-shy, which took the form of her staring obsessively at his stump. Nor could she name a single infectious disease without stuttering; the mere mention of a disease seemed to grip her in terror.

As for the Russian film director—"*No one* has seen her movies," the news editor in New York told Wallingford—Ludmilla (we'll leave it at that) was as ugly as a toad. Also, as Patrick would discover at two o'clock one morning when she came to his hotel room, she wanted to defect. She didn't mean to Japan. She wanted Wallingford to smuggle her into New York. In *what*? Wallingford would wonder. In his garment bag, now permanently reeking of Filipino dog piss?

Surely a Russian defector was news, even in New

York. So what if no one had seen her movies? "She wants to go to Sundance," Patrick told Dick. "For Christ's sake, Dick, she wants to *defect*! That's a story!" (No sensible news network would turn down a story on a Russian defector.)

But Dick was unimpressed. "We just did five minutes on a Cuban defector, Pat."

"You mean that no-good baseball player?" Wallingford asked.

"He's a halfway-decent shortstop, and the guy can hit," Dick said, and that was that.

Then came the rejection from the green-eyed Danish novelist; she turned out to be a touchy writer who refused to be interviewed by someone who hadn't read her books. Who did she think she was, anyway? Wallingford didn't have the time to read her books! At least he'd guessed right about how to pronounce her name—it was "bode *eel*," accent on the *eel*.

Those too-numerous Japanese women in the arts were eager to talk to him, and they were fond, when they talked to him, of sympathetically touching his left forearm a little above where he'd lost his hand. But the news editor in New York was "sick of the arts." Dick further claimed that the Japanese women would give the television audience the false impression that the only participants in this conference were Japanese.

"Since when do we worry that we're giving our viewers a false impression?" Patrick plucked up the courage to ask.

"Listen, Pat," Dick said, "that runt poet with the facial tattoo would even put off other poets."

Wallingford had already been in Japan too long. He was so used to the people's mispronunciation of his mother tongue that he now misheard his news editor, too. He simply didn't hear "runt poet"; he heard "cunt poet" instead.

"No, *you* listen, Dick," Wallingford retorted, with an uncharacteristic display of something less than his usually sweet-dispositioned self. "I'm not a woman, but even I take offense at that word."

"*What* word?" Dick asked. "Tattoo?"

"You know what word!" Patrick shouted. "Cunt!"

"I said 'runt,' not 'cunt,' Pat," the news editor informed Wallingford. "I guess you just hear what you think about all the time."

Patrick had no recourse. He had to interview Jane Brown, the English economist who'd threatened to undress, or he had to talk to Evelyn Arbuthnot, the presumed lesbian who loathed him and was ashamed that, if only for a moment, she'd been attracted to him.

The English economist was a dingbat of a distinctly English kind. It didn't matter—Americans are suckers for an English accent. Jane Brown screeched like an unattended tea kettle, not about world economy but on the subject of threatening to take off her clothes in front of men. "I know from experience that the men will never allow me to finish undressing," Ms. Brown told Patrick Wallingford on-camera, in that overenunciated manner of a character actress of a certain age and background on the English stage. "I never even get down to my undergarments before the men have fled the room—it happens every time! Men are very reliable. By that I mean only that they can be counted on to flee from me!"

Dick in New York loved it. He said that the Jane Brown interview "contrasted nicely" with the earlier footage of her throwing a fit about rape on the first day of the conference. The twenty-four-hour international channel had its story. The "Future of Women" conference in Tokyo had been covered—better to say, it had been covered in the all-news network's way, which was to marginalize more than Patrick Wallingford; it was also to marginalize the news. A women's conference in Japan had been reduced to a story about a matronly and histrionic Englishwoman threatening to take off her clothes at a panel discussion on rape—in Tokyo, of all places.

"Well, wasn't *that* cute?" Evelyn Arbuthnot would say, when she saw the minute-and-a-half story on the TV in her hotel room. She was still in Tokyo—it was the closing day of the conference. Wallingford's cheap-shot channel hadn't even waited for the conference to be over.

Patrick was still in bed when Ms. Arbuthnot called him. "Solly," was all Wallingford could manage to say. "I'm not the news editor; I'm just a field reporter."

"You were just following orders—is that what you mean?" Ms. Arbuthnot asked him.

Evelyn Arbuthnot was much too tough for Patrick Wallingford, especially because Wallingford had not recovered from a night on the town with his Japanese hosts. He thought even his soul must smell like sake. Nor could Patrick remember which of his favorite Japanese newspapermen had given him tickets for two on the high-speed train to and from Kyoto—"the bullet train," either Yoshi or Fumi had called it. A visit to a traditional inn in Kyoto could be very restorative, they'd told him; he remembered that. "But better go before the weekend." Regrettably, Wallingford would forget that part of their advice.

Ah, Kyoto—city of temples, city of prayer. Someplace more meditative than Tokyo *would* do Wallingford a world of good. It was high time he did a little meditating, he explained to Evelyn Arbuthnot, who continued to berate him about the fiasco of the coverage given to the women's conference by his "lousy *not*-the-news network."

"I know, I know . . ." Patrick kept repeating. (What else could he say?)

"And now you're going to Kyoto? To do what? *Pray?* Just what will you pray for?" she asked him. "The most publicly humiliating demise imaginable of your disaster-and-comedy-news network—that's what *I* pray for!"

"I'm still hopeful that something nice might happen to me in this country," Wallingford replied with as much dignity as he could summon, which wasn't much.

There was a thoughtful pause on Evelyn Arbuthnot's end of the phone. Patrick guessed that she was giving new consideration to an old idea.

"You want something nice to happen to you in Japan?" Ms. Arbuthnot asked. "Well . . . you can take me to Kyoto with you. I'll show you something *nice.*"

He was Patrick Wallingford, after all. He acquiesced. He did what women wanted; he generally did what he was told. But he'd thought Evelyn Arbuthnot was a lesbian! Patrick was confused.

"Uh . . . I thought . . . I mean from your remark to me about that Danish novelist, I took it to mean that . . . well, that you were *gay,* Ms. Arbuthnot."

"That's a trick I play all the time," she told him. "I didn't think you'd fallen for it."

"Oh," Wallingford said.

"I am not gay, but I'm old enough to be your mother. If you want to think about that and get back to me, I won't be offended."

"Surely you couldn't be my mother—"

"Biologically speaking, I surely could be," Ms. Arbuthnot said. "I could have had you when I was sixteen—when I looked eighteen, by the way. How's your math?"

"You're fifty-something?" he asked her.

"That's close enough," she said. "And I can't leave for Kyoto today. I won't skip the last day of this pathetic but well-intentioned conference. If you can wait until tomorrow, I'll go to Kyoto with you for the weekend."

"Okay," Wallingford agreed. He didn't tell her that he already had two tickets on "the bullet train." He could ask the concierge at the hotel to change his reservations for the train and inn.

"You sure you want to do this?" Evelyn Arbuthnot asked. She didn't sound too sure herself.

"Yes, I'm sure. I like you," Wallingford told Ms. Arbuthnot. "Even if I *am* an asshole."

"Don't be too hard on yourself for being an asshole," she told him. It was the closest her voice had come to a sexual purr. In terms of speed—most of all, in regard to how quickly she could change her mind—Evelyn was a kind of bullet train herself. Patrick began to have second thoughts about going anywhere with her.

It was as if she'd read his mind. "I won't be too demanding," she suddenly said. "Besides, you should have some experience with a woman my age. One day, when you're in your seventies, women my age are going to be as young as you can get."

Over the course of the rest of that day and night, while Wallingford waited to take the bullet train to Kyoto with Evelyn Arbuthnot, his hangover gradually subsided; when he went to bed, he could taste the sake only when he yawned.

The next day dawned bright and fair in the land of the rising sun—a false promise, as it turned out.

Wallingford rode on a two-hundred-mile-an-hour train with a woman old enough to be his mother, and with about five hundred screaming schoolchildren, all girls, because—as far as Patrick and Evelyn could understand the tortuous English of the train's conductor—it was something called National Prayer Weekend for Girls and every schoolgirl in Japan was going to Kyoto, or so it seemed.

It rained the entire weekend. Kyoto was overrun with Japanese schoolgirls, praying. Well, they must have prayed *some* of the time that they overran the city, although Patrick and Evelyn never saw them actually do so. When they weren't praying, they did what schoolgirls everywhere do. They laughed, they shrieked, they burst into hysterical sobs—all for no apparent reason.

"Wretched hormones," Evelyn said, as if she knew.

The schoolgirls also played the worst Western music imaginable, and they took a surfeit of baths—so many baths that the traditional inn where Wallingford and Evelyn Arbuthnot stayed was repeatedly running out of hot water.

"Too many not-praying girls!" the apologetic innkeeper told Patrick and Evelyn, not that they really cared about the lack of hot water; a tepid bath or two would do. They were fucking nonstop, all weekend long, with only occasional visits to the temples for which Kyoto (unlike Patrick Wallingford) was justly famous.

It turned out that Evelyn Arbuthnot liked to have a lot of sex. In forty-eight hours . . . no, never mind. It would be boorish to count the number of times they did it. Suffice it to say that Wallingford was completely worn out at the end of the weekend, and by the time he and Evelyn were riding the two-hundred-mile-an-hour train back to Tokyo, Patrick's cock was so sore that he felt like a teenager who'd wanked himself raw.

He loved what he'd seen of the wet temples. Standing inside the huge wooden shrines with the rain beating down was like being held captive in a primitive, drumlike wooden instrument with the prevailing, high-pitched yammer of rampant schoolgirls surrounding you.

Many of the girls wore their school uniforms, which lent to their presence the monotony of a military band. Some were pretty, but most were not; besides, on that particular National Prayer Weekend for Girls, which was probably not what the weekend was officially called, Wallingford had eyes only for Evelyn Arbuthnot.

He liked making love to her, no small part of the reason being that she so clearly enjoyed herself with him. He found her body, which was by no means beautiful, nonetheless astutely purposeful. Evelyn used her body as if it were a well-designed tool. But on one of her small breasts was a fairly large scar—not from an accident, clearly. (It was too straight and thin; it had to be a surgical scar.) "I had a lump re-moved," she told Patrick, when he asked her about it.

"It must have been a pretty big lump," he said.

"It turned out to be nothing. I'm fine," she replied.

Only on the return trip to Tokyo had she begun to mother him a little. "What are you going to do with yourself, Patrick?" she'd asked, holding his one hand.

"Do with myself?"

"You're a mess," she told him. He saw in her face the genuineness of her concern for him.

"I'm a mess," he repeated to Evelyn.

"Yes, you are, and you know it," she told him. "Your career is unsatisfying, but what's more impor-tant is you don't have a *life*. You might as well be lost at sea, dear." (The "dear" was something new and unappealing.)

Patrick began to babble about Dr. Zajac and the prospect of having hand-transplant surgery—of actu-ally, after these five long years, getting back a left hand.

"That's not what I mean," Evelyn interrupted him. "Who cares about your left hand? It's been five years! You can do without it. You can always find someone to help you slice a tomato, or you can just do without the tomato. You're not a good-looking joke *because of* your missing hand. It's partly be-cause of your job, but, chiefly, it's because of how you live your *life*!"

"Oh," Wallingford said. He tried to take his hand out of her motherly grasp, but Ms. Arbuthnot wouldn't let him; after all, she had two hands and she firmly held his one hand between them.

"Listen to me, Patrick," Evelyn said. "It's great that Dr. Sayzac wants to give you a new left hand—"

"Dr. *Zajac*," Wallingford corrected her petulantly.

"Dr. Zajac, then," Ms. Arbuthnot continued. "I don't mean to take anything away from the courage involved in subjecting yourself to such a risky experiment—"

"It would be only the *second* such surgery *ever,*" Patrick, again petulantly, informed her. "The first one didn't work."

"Yes, yes—you've told me," Ms. Arbuthnot reminded him. "But do you have the courage to change your *life?*" Then she fell asleep, her grip on his hand relaxing as she did so. Wallingford probably could have pulled his hand away without waking her, but he didn't want to risk it.

Evelyn would be flying to San Francisco; Wallingford was on his way back to New York. There was another women-related conference in San Francisco, she'd told him.

He hadn't asked her what her "message" was, nor would he ever finish one of her books. The only one he tried to read would be disappointing to him. Evelyn Arbuthnot was more interesting as a person than she was as a writer. Like many smart, motivated people who've had busy and informed lives, she didn't write especially well.

In bed, where personal history is most unself-consciously forthcoming, Ms. Arbuthnot had told Patrick that she'd been married twice—the first time when she was very young. She'd divorced her first husband; her second, the one she'd truly loved, had died. She was a widow with grown children and several young grandchildren. Her children and grandchildren, she'd told Wallingford, were her life; her writing and traveling were only her message. But in what little Wallingford managed to read of Evelyn Arbuthnot's writing, her "message" eluded him. Yet whenever he thought of her, he had to admit that she'd taught him quite a lot about himself.

On the bullet train, just before their arrival in Tokyo, some Japanese schoolgirls and their accompanying teacher recognized him. They seemed to be gathering their courage to send one of the girls the length of the passenger car to ask the lion guy for his autograph. Patrick hoped not—giving the girls his signature would require extricating his right hand from Evelyn's sleeping fingers.

Finally none of the schoolgirls could summon the courage to approach him; their teacher came down the aisle of the bullet train instead. She was wearing a uniform that closely resembled those of her young charges, and although she was young herself, she conveyed both the severity and formality of a much older woman when she spoke to him. She was also exceedingly polite; she made such an effort to keep her voice low and soft, so as not to wake Evelyn, that Wallingford had to lean a little into the aisle in order to hear her above the clatter of the speeding train.

"The girls wanted me to tell you that they think you're very handsome, and that you must be very brave," she told Patrick. "I have something to say to you, too," she whispered. "When I first saw you, with the lion, I regret that I didn't think you would be such a *nice* man. But seeing you as you are—you know, just traveling and talking with your mother—I now realize that you are a *very* nice man."

"Thank you," Wallingford whispered back, although her misunderstanding pained him, and when the young teacher had returned to her seat, Evelyn gave his hand a squeeze—just to let him know she'd been awake. When Wallingford looked at her, her eyes were open wide and she was smiling at him.

Less than a year later, when he heard of her death— "The breast cancer returned," one of her daughters told Wallingford when he called to give Evelyn's children and grandchildren his condolences—Patrick would remember her smile on the bullet train. The lump, which Evelyn had told him was nothing, had been something after all. Given how long a scar it had been, maybe she'd already known that.

There was something entirely too fragile about Patrick Wallingford. Women—his ex-wife, Marilyn, excepted—were always trying to spare him things, although that hardly had been Evelyn Arbuthnot's style.

Wallingford would remember, too, that he could have asked the Japanese schoolteacher what the official name for National Prayer Weekend for Girls was, but he hadn't. Incredibly, especially for a journalist, he'd spent six days in Japan and learned absolutely nothing about the country.

Like the young schoolteacher, the Japanese he'd met had been extremely civilized and courteous, including the Japanese newspapermen who'd been Wallingford's hosts—they'd been a lot more respectful and well mannered than most of the journalists Patrick worked with in New York. But he'd asked them nothing; he'd been too consumed studying himself. All he'd half-learned was how to mock their accents, which he imitated incorrectly.

Fault Marilyn, Wallingford's ex-wife, all you want. She was right about at least one thing—Patrick was permanently a boy. Yet he was capable of growing up, or so he hoped.

There is often a defining experience that marks any significant change in the course of a person's life. Patrick Wallingford's defining experience was *not* losing his left hand, nor was it adjusting to life without that hand. The experience that truly changed him was a largely squandered trip to Japan.

"Tell us about Japan, Pat. How was it?" those fast-talking women in the New York newsroom would ask him in their ever-flirtatious, always-baiting voices.

(They'd already learned from Dick how Wallingford had heard "cunt" when Dick had said "runt.")

But when Wallingford was asked about Japan, he would duck the question. "Japan is a novel," Patrick would say, and leave it at that.

He already believed that the trip to Japan had made him sincerely want to change his life. He would risk everything to change it. He knew it wouldn't be easy, but he believed he had the willpower to try. To his credit, the first moment he was alone with Mary whatever-her-name-was in the newsroom, Wallingford said, "I'm very sorry, Mary. I am truly, deeply sorry for what I said, for upsetting you so—"

She interrupted him. "It wasn't what you said that upset me—it's my *marriage*. It's not working out very well, and I'm pregnant."

"I'm sorry," Patrick said again.

Calling Dr. Zajac and confirming that he wanted to undergo the transplant surgery had been relatively easy.

The next time Patrick had a minute alone with Mary, he made a blunder of the well-intentioned kind. "When are you expecting, Mary?" (She wasn't showing yet.)

"I lost the baby!" Mary blurted out; she burst into tears.

"I'm sorry," Patrick repeated.

"It's my second miscarriage," the miserable young woman told him. She sobbed against his chest, wetting his shirt. When some of those savvy New York newsroom women saw them, they shot one another their most knowing glances. But they were wrong— that is, they were wrong this time. Wallingford *was* trying to change.

"I *should* have gone to Japan with you," Mary whatever-her-name-was whispered in Patrick's ear.

"No, Mary—no, no," Wallingford said. "You should *not* have gone to Japan with me, and I was wrong to propose it." But the young woman cried all the harder.

In the company of crying women, Patrick Wallingford did what many men do—he thought of other things. For example, how exactly do you *wait* for a hand when you've been without one for five years?

His recent experience with sake notwithstanding, he was not a drinker; but he grew strangely fond of sitting alone in an unfamiliar bar—always a different bar—in the late afternoon. A kind of lassitude compelled him to play this game. As the cocktail hour came, and the place filled with people intent on becoming more and more companionable, Patrick Wallingford sat sipping a beer; his objective was to project an aura of such unapproachable sadness that no one would intrude on his solitude.

They would all recognize him, of course; possibly he would overhear a whispered "lion guy" or "disaster man," but no one would speak to him. That was the game—it was an actor's exercise in finding the right look. (*Pity me,* the look said. *Pity me, but leave me alone.*) It was a game at which he became pretty good.

Then, one late afternoon—shortly before the cocktail hour—Wallingford went to a bar in his old New York neighborhood. It was too early for the night doorman in Patrick's former apartment building to start his shift, but Wallingford was surprised to see the doorman in the bar—all the more so because he wasn't wearing his doorman's uniform.

"Hi, Mr. O'Neill," Vlad or Vlade or Lewis greeted him. "I saw you was in Japan. They play pretty good baseball over there, don't they? I suppose it's an alternative for you, if things don't work out here."

"How are you, Lewis?" Wallingford asked.

"It's Vlade," Vlad said gloomily. "This here's my brother. We're just killin' some time before I go to work. I don't enjoy the night shift no more."

Patrick nodded to the nice-looking young man standing at the bar with the depressed-looking doorman. His name was Loren or Goran, or possibly Zorbid; the brother was shy and he'd mumbled his name.

But when Vlad or Vlade or Lewis went off to the men's room—he'd been drinking glass after glass of cranberry juice and soda—the shy brother confided to Patrick, "He doesn't mean any harm, Mr. Wallingford. He's just a little confused about things. He doesn't know you're not Paul O'Neill, even though he *does* know it. I honestly believed that, after the lion thing, he would finally get it. But he doesn't. Most of the time, you're just Paul O'Neill to him. I'm sorry. It must be a nuisance."

"Please don't apologize," Patrick said. "I like your brother. If I'm Paul O'Neill to him, that's fine. At least I've left Cincinnati."

They both looked a little guilty, just sitting there at the bar, when Vlad or Vlade or Lewis returned from the men's room. Patrick regretted that he hadn't asked the normal brother what the confused doorman's real name was, but the moment had passed. Now the three-named doorman was back; he looked more like his old self because he'd changed into his uniform in the men's room.

The doorman handed his regular clothes to his brother, who put them in a backpack resting against the footrail at the bar. Patrick hadn't seen the backpack until now, but he realized that this was part of a routine with the brothers. Probably the normal brother came back in the morning to take Vlad or Vlade or Lewis home; he looked like that kind of good brother.

Suddenly the doorman put his head down on the bar as if he wanted to go to sleep on the spot. "Hey, come on—don't do that," his brother said affectionately to him. "You don't want to do that, especially not in front of Mr. O'Neill."

The doorman lifted his head. "I just get tired of workin' so late, sometimes," he said. "No more night shifts, please. No more night shifts."

"Look—you have a job, don't you?" the brother said, trying to cheer him up.

Miraculously—that quickly!—Vlad or Vlade or Lewis broke into a grin. "Gosh, look at me," he said. "I'm feelin' sorry for myself while I'm sittin' with the best right fielder I can think of, and he's got no left hand! And he bats left and throws left, too. I'm very sorry, Mr. O'Neill. I got no business feelin' sorry for myself in front of *you*."

Naturally Wallingford felt sorry for himself, too, but he wanted to be Paul O'Neill for a little while longer. It was the beginning of getting away from being the *old* Patrick Wallingford.

Here he was, disaster man, cultivating a look for the cocktail hour. The look was just an act, the lion guy knew, but the *pity-me* part was true.

CHAPTER FIVE

An Accident on Super Bowl Sunday

ALTHOUGH MRS. CLAUSEN had written to Schatzman, Gingeleskie, Mengerink & Associates that she was from Appleton, Wisconsin, she meant only that she'd been born there. By the time of her marriage to Otto Clausen, she was living in Green Bay, the home of the celebrated professional football team. Otto Clausen was a Packer fan; he drove a beer truck for a living, and the only bumper sticker he permitted was in Green Bay green on a field of gold.

PROUD TO BE A CHEESEHEAD!

Otto and his wife had made plans to go to their favorite sports bar in Green Bay on Sunday night, January 25, 1998. It was the night of Super Bowl XXXII, and the Packers were playing the Denver Broncos in

San Diego. But Mrs. Clausen had felt sick to her stomach all day; she would say to her husband, as she often did, that she hoped she was pregnant. She wasn't—she had the flu. She quickly developed a fever and threw up twice before kickoff. Both the Clausens were disappointed that it wasn't morning sickness. (Even if she were pregnant, she'd had her period only two weeks ago; it would have been too soon for her to have had morning sickness.)

Mrs. Clausen's moods were very readable—at least Otto believed that he usually knew what his wife was thinking. She wanted to have a baby more than anything in the world. Her husband wanted her to have one, too—she couldn't fault him for that. She just felt awful about having no children, and she knew that Otto felt awful about it, too.

Regarding this particular case of the flu, Otto had never seen his wife so sick; he volunteered to stay home and take care of her. They could watch the game on the TV in the bedroom. But Mrs. Clausen was so ill that she couldn't imagine watching the game, and she was a virtual cheesehead, too; that she'd been a Packer fan all her life was a principal bond between her and Otto. She even worked for the Green Bay Packers. She and Otto could have had tickets to the game in San Diego, but Otto hated to fly.

Now it touched her deeply: Otto loved her so much that he would give up seeing the Super Bowl at the sports bar. Mrs. Clausen wouldn't hear of his staying home. Although she felt too nauseated to talk, she summoned her strength and declared, in a complete sentence, one of those oft-repeated truths of the sports world that render football fans mute with agreement (at the same time striking everyone indifferent to football as a colossal stupidity). "There's no guarantee of returning to the Super Bowl," Mrs. Clausen stated.

Otto was childishly moved. Even on her sickbed, his wife wanted him to have fun. But one of their two cars was in the body shop, the result of a fender-bender in a supermarket parking lot. Otto didn't want to leave his wife home sick without a car.

"I'll take the beer truck," he told her. The truck was empty, and Otto was friends with everyone at the sports bar; they would let him park the truck at the delivery entrance. There weren't going to be any deliveries on a Super Bowl Sunday.

"Go, Packers!" his wife said weakly—she was already falling asleep. In a gesture of unspoken physical tenderness that she would long remember, Otto put the TV remote on the bed beside her and made sure that the television was on the correct channel.

Then he was off to the game. The beer truck was lighter than he was used to; he kept checking his speed while he maneuvered the big vehicle through the near-empty Sunday streets. Not since he was six or seven had Otto Clausen missed the kickoff of a

Packer game, and he wouldn't miss this one. He may have been only thirty-nine, but he'd seen all thirty-one previous Super Bowls. He would see Super Bowl XXXII from the opening kickoff to the bitter end.

Most sportswriters would concede that the thirty-second Super Bowl was among the best ever played— a close, exciting game that the underdog won. It is common knowledge that most Americans love underdogs, but not in Green Bay, Wisconsin, in the case of Super Bowl XXXII, where the upstart Denver Broncos beat the Packers, rendering all cheeseheads despondent.

Green Bay fans were borderline suicidal by the end of the fourth quarter—not necessarily Otto, who was despondent but also very drunk. He'd fallen sound asleep at the bar during a beer commercial in the final two minutes of the game, and while he woke up the moment play resumed, he had suffered another unabridged edition of his worst recurring dream, which seemed to be hours longer than the commercial.

He was in a delivery room, and a man who was just a pair of eyes above a surgical mask was standing in a corner. A female obstetrician was delivering his wife's baby, and a nurse whom he was certain he'd never seen before was helping. The obstetrician was Mrs. Clausen's regular OB-GYN; the Clausens had been to see her together, many times.

Although Otto hadn't recognized the man in the corner the first time he'd had the dream, he now knew in advance who the man was, thus giving him a sense of foreboding.

When the baby was born, the joy on his wife's face was so overwhelming that Otto always cried in his sleep. That was when the other man removed his mask. It was that playboy TV reporter—the lion guy, disaster man. What the fuck was his name? Anyway, the joy in Mrs. Clausen's expression was directed at him, not at Otto; it was as if Otto weren't really in the delivery room, or as if only Otto knew he was there.

What was wrong with the dream was that the lion guy had two hands and was holding the newborn baby in both of them. Suddenly Otto's wife reached up and stroked the back of his left hand.

Then Otto saw himself. He was staring at his own body, looking for his hands. The left one was gone—his own left hand was gone!

That was when he woke up, sobbing. This time, at the sports bar in Green Bay, with under two minutes remaining in the Super Bowl, a fellow Packer fan misunderstood his anguish and patted Otto on the shoulder. "Lousy game," he said with gruff sympathy.

Drunk as he was, Otto had to make a concerted effort not to doze off again. It wasn't that he didn't want to miss the end of the game; he didn't want to have that dream again, not if he could help it.

Naturally he knew where the dream came from, and he was so ashamed of its source that he'd never told his wife about the dream.

As a beer-truck driver, Otto believed himself to be a role model for Green Bay's youth—not once had he been a drunk driver. Otto hardly drank at all; and when he drank, he drank nothing stronger than beer. He was instantly as ashamed of his own inebriation as he was of his dream and the outcome of the game.

"I'm too drunk to drive," Otto confessed to the bartender, who was a decent man and a trusted friend. The bartender wished that there were more drunks like Otto Clausen, meaning responsible ones.

They quickly agreed on the best way for Otto to get himself home, which was *not* by accepting a ride with any of several drunken and despondent friends. Otto could easily move the beer truck the mere fifty yards from the delivery entrance to the bar's main parking lot so that it would not be in the way of any Monday-morning deliveries. Since the parking lot and the delivery entrance were adjacent to each other, he wouldn't even have to cross a public side-walk or a street. The bartender would then call Otto a taxi to take him home.

No, no, no—the phone call wasn't necessary, Otto had mumbled. He had a cell phone in his truck. He would move the beer truck first and call the taxi him-self. He would wait in his truck for the taxi. Besides, he wanted to call his wife—just to see how she was feeling and to commiserate with her about Green

Bay's tragic loss. Furthermore, the cold air would do him good.

He may have been less certain about the effect of the cold air than he was about the rest of his plan, but Otto also wanted to escape the televised postgame show. The sight of those lunatic Denver fans in the multiple frenzies of their celebrations would be truly revolting, as would the replays of Terrell Davis slicing through the Packers' secondary. The Broncos' running back had made the Green Bay defense look as soft as . . . well, yes, *cheese.*

The thought of those Denver running plays made Otto feel like throwing up, or else he was coming down with his wife's flu. He'd not felt as awful since he'd seen that pretty-boy journalist have his hand eaten by lions. What *was* the peckerhead's name?

Mrs. Clausen knew the unfortunate reporter's name. "I wonder how that poor Patrick Wallingford is doing," she would say, apropos of nothing, and Otto would shake his head and feel like throwing up.

After a reverential pause, his wife would add: "I'd give that poor man my own hand, if I knew I was dying. Wouldn't you, Otto?"

"I don't know—I don't even *know* him," Otto had replied. "It's not like giving a stranger one of your organs. They're just organs. Who ever sees them? But your *hand* . . . well, gee, it's a recognizable part of you, if you know what I mean."

"When you're dead, you're dead," Mrs. Clausen had said.

Otto remembered the paternity suit against Patrick Wallingford—it had been on TV, and in all the magazines and newspapers. Mrs. Clausen had been riveted to the case; she'd been noticeably disappointed when the DNA test proved that Wallingford wasn't the father.

"What do you care who the father is?" Otto had asked.

"He just looked like he was the father," Mrs. Clausen answered. "He looks like he *should* be, I mean."

"He's good-looking enough—is that what you're saying?" Otto asked.

"He looks like a paternity suit waiting to happen."

"Is that the reason you want me to give him my hand?"

"I didn't say that, Otto. I just said, 'When you're dead, you're dead.' "

"I got that part," Otto had told her. "But why *my* hand? Why *him*?"

Now, there's something you should know about Mrs. Clausen, even before you know what she looks like: when she wanted to, there was something about her tone of voice that could give her husband a hard-on. It didn't take long, either.

"Why *your* hand?" she'd asked him, in that tone of voice. "Why . . . because I love you, and I'll never love anyone else. Not in the same way." This had weakened Otto to the degree that he felt too near death to speak; all the blood from his brain, his heart, and his lungs was going to his erection. It happened that way every time.

"Why *him*?" Mrs. Clausen had continued, knowing that Otto was entirely hers from this point on. "Why . . . because he clearly needs a hand. Nothing could be plainer."

It had taken all of Otto's strength to summon a weak response to her. "I suppose there's other guys who've lost their hands."

"But we don't know them."

"We don't know *him,* either."

"He's on TV, Otto. *Everyone* knows him. Besides, he looks nice."

"You said he looked like a paternity suit waiting to happen!"

"That doesn't mean he isn't nice," Mrs. Clausen replied.

"Oh."

The "Oh" exhausted the last of his failing power. Otto knew what was coming next. Once more it was her tone of voice that killed him.

"What are you doing right now?" she'd asked him. "Want to make a baby?"

Otto could scarcely nod his head.

But there was still no baby. When Mrs. Clausen wrote to Schatzman, Gingeleskie, Mengerink & Associates, she included a typed statement, which she'd asked Otto to sign. He hadn't protested. He felt that his fingers had lost all circulation and that he was watching another man's hand sign his name. "What are you doing right now?" she'd asked him that time, too.

Then the dreams had begun. Now, on that miserable Super Bowl Sunday, Otto was not only stupendously drunk; he was also burdened by the weight of an implausible jealousy. And moving the beer truck a mere fifty yards was not as simple as it had seemed. Otto's clumsy efforts to engage the ignition with the key convinced him; he was not only too drunk to drive—he might be too drunk to start the truck. It took a while, as it did for the truck's defroster to melt the ice under the snow on the windshield. It had snowed only another two inches since the kickoff.

Otto may have skinned the knuckles of his left hand while brushing the snow off the side-view mirrors. (This is a guess. We'll never know how he skinned the knuckles of that hand, just that they were skinned.) And by the time he'd slowly turned and backed the beer truck the short distance between the delivery entrance and the parking lot, most of the bar's Super Bowl patrons had gone home. It wasn't even nine-thirty, but not more than four or five cars shared the lot with him. He had the feeling that their owners had done what he was doing—called for a taxi to take them home. All the other drunks, lamentably, had driven themselves.

Then Otto remembered that he hadn't yet called a cab. At first the number, which the bartender had written out for him, was busy. (On that Super Bowl Sunday night in Green Bay, how many people must have been calling for taxis to take them home?) When Otto finally got through, the dispatcher warned him that there would be a wait of at least half an hour. "Maybe forty-five minutes." The dispatcher was an honest man.

What did Otto care? It was a seasonably mild twenty-five degrees outside, and running the defroster had partially heated the cab of the truck. Although it would soon get cold in there, what was twenty-five degrees with light snow falling to a guy who'd downed eight or nine beers in under four hours?

Otto called his wife. He could tell he'd woken her up. She'd seen the fourth quarter; then, because she was both depressed and sick, she'd fallen back to sleep.

"I couldn't watch the postgame stuff, either," he admitted.

"Poor baby," his wife said. It was what they said to console each other, but lately—given Mrs. Clausen's as-yet-unsuccessful struggle to get pregnant—they'd been considering a new endearment. The phrase stuck like a dagger in Otto's inebriated heart.

"It'll happen, honey," Otto suddenly promised her, because the dear man, even drunk and despondent, was sensitive enough to know that his wife's principal distress was that she had the flu when she wanted morning sickness. The meaningless postgame stuff, even the Packers' heartbreaking defeat, wasn't what was really bothering her.

It made perfect sense that Mrs. Clausen's regular OB-GYN had found her way into Otto's dream; she was not only the physician whom Mrs. Clausen regularly consulted about her difficulties in getting pregnant, but she'd also told Otto and his wife that he should have himself "checked." (She meant the sperm-count thing, as Otto unspokenly thought of it.) Both the doctor and Mrs. Clausen suspected that Otto was the problem, but his wife loved him to such a degree that she'd been afraid to find out. Otto had been afraid to find out, too—he'd not had himself "checked."

Their complicity had drawn the Clausens even closer than they already were, but now there was something complicitous in the silences between them. Otto couldn't stop thinking about the first time they'd made love. This was not merely romantic of him, although he was a deeply romantic man. In the Clausens' case, that first act of lovemaking had itself been the proposal.

Otto's family had a summer cottage on a lake. There are lots of small lakes in northern Wisconsin, and the Clausens owned a quarter of the shoreline of one of them. When Mrs. Clausen first went there, the misnamed "cottage" turned out to be a cluster of cabins, with a nearby boathouse bigger than any of them. There was room for a small apartment in the unfinished space above the boats, and although there was no electricity on the property, there was a fridge (actually two) and a stove and hot-water heaters (all propane) for the main cabin.

The water for the plumbing came from the lake; the Clausens didn't drink the water, but they could take a hot bath, and there were two flush toilets. They pumped the water out of the lake by means of a gasoline engine of the kind that can run a lawn mower, and they had their own septic tank—quite a large one. (The Clausens were religious about not polluting their little lake.)

One weekend when his mom and dad weren't able to go there, Otto brought his future wife to the lake. They swam off the dock just before sunset, and their wet bathing suits leaked through the planks. It was so quiet, except for the loons, and they sat so still that the water dripping off their bathing suits sounded as if someone had not quite shut off a faucet. The sun, which had departed only minutes before, had warmed the wooden planks all day; Otto and his bride-to-be could feel its warmth when they took off their wet bathing suits. They lay down on a dry towel together. The towel smelled like the sun, and the water drying on their bodies smelled like the lake and the sun, too.

There was no "I love you," no "Will you marry me?" In each other's arms on the towel on the warm dock, with their skin still wet and cool, it was a moment that called for more of a commitment than that. This was the first time the future Mrs. Clausen let

Otto hear her special tone of voice, and her arousing question: "What are you doing right now?" This was the first time Otto discovered he was too weak to speak. "Do you want to make a baby?" she'd asked. That was the first time they'd tried.

That had been the marriage proposal. He'd said "yes" with his hard-on, an erection with the blood of a thousand words.

After the wedding, Otto had built two separate rooms off a shared hallway above the boats in the boathouse. They were two unusually long, thin rooms—"like bowling alleys," Mrs. Clausen had teased him—but he'd done it that way so that the occupants of both rooms could see the lakefront. One was their room—their bed took up almost its entire width and was elevated to window level to give them the optimum view. The other room had twin beds; it was for the baby.

It made Otto cry to think of that unoccupied room above the gently rocking boats. The sound he had loved most at night, which was the barely heard sound of the water lapping against the boats in the boathouse and the dock where they'd first made love, now only reminded him of the emptiness of that unused room.

The feeling, at the end of the day—of a wet bathing suit, and of taking it off; the smell of the sun and the lake on his wife's wet skin—now seemed ruined by unfulfilled expectations. The Clausens had been married for more than a decade, but in the last two or three summers they'd all but stopped going to the cottage on the lake. Their life together in Green Bay had grown busier; it seemed harder and harder to get away. Or so they said. But in truth, it was even harder for them both to accept that the smell of pine trees was a thing of the past.

Then the Packers had to lose to the fucking Broncos! Otto grieved. The unhappy, drunken man could scarcely remember what had started him crying in the cold, parked beer truck. Oh, yes, it had been his wife saying, "Poor baby." Lately those words had a devastating effect on him. And when she said them in that tone of voice of hers . . . well, what a merciless world! What had possessed her to do that when they were not physically together, when they were only talking on the phone? Now Otto was crying *and* he had a hard-on. He was further frustrated that he couldn't remember how the phone call with his wife had ended, or when.

It had already been half an hour since he'd told the taxi dispatcher to have the driver look for him in the parking lot behind the bar. ("I'll be in the beer truck—you can't miss it.") Otto stretched to reach the glove compartment, where he had put his cell phone—carefully, so as not to disturb the beer coasters and stickers, which he also kept there. He handed them out to the kids who surrounded him when he made his deliveries. In Otto's neighborhood, the kids called him "Coaster Man" or "Sticker Man," but what they really sought were the beer posters. Otto kept the posters in the back of the truck, with the beer.

He saw nothing wrong in these boys displaying beer posters in their bedrooms, years before they were old enough to drink. Otto would have been wounded to his core if anyone had accused him of leading young men down the road to alcoholism; he simply liked to make the kids happy, and he handed out the coasters and stickers and posters with the same concern for their welfare as he expressed by not driving when he was drunk.

But how had he managed to fall asleep while reaching for the glove compartment? That he was too drunk to have dreams was a blessing, or so he thought. Otto *had been* dreaming—he was just too drunk to know it. Also the dream was a new one, too new for him to know it was a dream.

He felt the warm, sweat-slick back of his wife's neck in the crook of his right arm; he was kissing her, his tongue deep inside her mouth, while with his left hand—Otto was left-handed—he touched her again and again. She was very wet, her abdomen pressing upward against the heel of his hand. His fingers touched her as lightly as possible; he was trying his best to touch her barely at all. (She'd had to teach him how to do that.)

Suddenly, in the dream that Otto didn't know was a dream, Mrs. Clausen seized her husband's left hand and brought it to her lips; she took his fingers into her mouth, where he was kissing her, and they both tasted her sex as he rolled on top and entered her. As he held her head lightly against his throat, the fingers of his left hand, in her hair, were close enough for him to smell. On the bed, by her left shoulder, was Otto's right hand; it was gripping the bedsheet. Only Otto didn't recognize it—it was not his hand! It was too small, too fine-boned; it was almost delicate. Yet the *left* hand had been his—he would know it anywhere.

Then he saw his wife under him, but from a distance. It wasn't Otto she was under; the man's legs were too long, his shoulders too narrow. Otto recognized the lion guy's face in profile—Patrick Wallingford was fucking his wife!

Only seconds later, and in reality not more than a couple of minutes after he'd passed out in his truck, Otto woke up lying on his right side. His body was bent across the gear box, the stick shift nudging his ribs; his head rested on his right arm, his nose touching the cold passenger seat. As for his erection, for quite naturally his dream had given him a hard-on, he had a firm hold of it with his left hand. In a parking lot! he thought, ashamed. He quickly tucked in his shirt and cinched his belt.

Otto stared into the open glove compartment. There was his cell phone—also there, in the far right corner, was his snub-nosed .38 revolver, a Smith & Wesson, which he kept fully loaded with the barrel pointed in the general direction of the truck's right front tire.

Otto must have propped himself up on his right elbow, or else he came nearly to a sitting position, before he heard the sound of the teenagers breaking into the back of his truck. They were just kids, but they were a little older than the neighborhood boys to whom Otto Clausen gave the beer coasters, stickers, and posters—and these teenagers were up to no good. One of them had positioned himself near the entrance to the sports bar; if a patron had emerged and made his (or her) way to the parking lot, the lookout could have warned the two boys breaking into the back of the truck.

Otto Clausen didn't carry a loaded .38 in his glove compartment *because* he was a beer-truck driver and beer trucks were commonly broken into. Otto wouldn't have dreamed of shooting anyone, not even in defense of beer. But Otto was a gun guy, as many of the good people of Wisconsin are. He liked all kinds of guns. He was also a deer hunter and a duck hunter. He was even a bow hunter, in the bow season for deer, and although he'd never killed a deer with a bow and arrow, he had killed many deer with a rifle—most of them in the vicinity of the Clausens' cottage.

Otto was a fisherman, too—he was an all-around outdoorsman. And while it was illegal for him to keep a loaded .38 in his glove compartment, not a single beer-truck driver would have faulted him for this; in all probability, the brewery he worked for would have applauded his spirit, at least privately.

Otto would have needed to take the gun from the glove compartment with his right hand—because he couldn't have reached into the compartment, from behind the steering wheel, with his left—and, because he was left-handed, he almost certainly would have transferred the weapon from his right to his left hand before investigating the burglary-in-progress at the rear of his truck.

Otto was still very drunk, and the subfreezing coldness of the Smith & Wesson might have made the gun a little unfamiliar to his touch. (And he'd been startled out of a dream as disturbing as death itself—his wife having sex with disaster man, who'd been touching her with Otto's left hand!) Whether he cocked the revolver with his right hand before attempting to transfer it to his left, or whether he'd cocked the weapon inadvertently when he removed it from the glove compartment, we'll never know.

The gun fired—we know that much—and the bullet entered Otto's throat an inch under his chin. It followed an undeviating path, exiting the good man's head at the crown of his skull, taking with it flecks of blood and bone and a briefly blinding bit of brain matter, the evidence of which would be found on the upholstered ceiling of the truck's cab. The bullet itself also exited the roof. Otto was dead in an instant.

The gunshot scared the bejesus out of the young thieves at the back of the truck. A patron leaving the sports bar heard the gunshot and the plaintive appeals for mercy by the frightened teenagers, even the clang of the crowbar they dropped in the parking lot as they raced into the night. The police would soon find them, and they would confess everything—their entire life stories, up to the moment of that earsplitting gunshot. Upon their capture, they didn't know where the shot had come from or that anyone had actually been shot.

While the alarmed patron returned to the sports bar, and the bartender called the police—reporting only that there'd been a gunshot, and someone had seen teenagers running away—the taxi driver arrived in the parking lot. He had no difficulty spotting the beer truck, but when he approached the cab, knocked on the driver's-side window, and opened the door, there was Otto Clausen slumped against the steering wheel, the .38 in his lap.

Even before the police notified Mrs. Clausen, who was sound asleep when they called, they already felt sure that Otto's death wasn't a suicide—at least it wasn't what the cops called a "planned suicide." Clearly, to the police, the beer-truck driver hadn't meant to kill himself.

"He wasn't that kind of guy," the bartender said.

Granted, the bartender had no idea that Otto Clausen had been trying to get his wife pregnant for more than a decade; the bartender didn't know diddly-squat about Otto's wife wanting Otto to bequeath his left hand to Patrick Wallingford, the lion guy, either. The bartender only knew that Otto Clausen would never have killed himself because the Packers lost the Super Bowl.

It's anybody's guess how Mrs. Clausen was composed enough to make the call to Schatzman, Gingeleskie, Mengerink & Associates that same Super Bowl Sunday night. The answering service reported her call to Dr. Zajac, who happened to be at home.

Zajac was a Broncos fan. Just to clarify that: Dr. Zajac was a New England Patriots fan, God help him, but he'd been rooting for the Broncos in the Super Bowl because Denver was in the same conference as New England. In fact, at the time of the phone call from his answering service, Zajac had been trying to explain the tortured logic of why he'd wanted the Broncos to win to his six-year-old son. In Rudy's opinion, if the Patriots weren't in the Super Bowl, and they weren't, what did it matter who won?

They'd had a reasonably healthy snack during the game—chilled celery stalks and carrot sticks, dipped in peanut butter. Irma had suggested to Dr. Zajac that he try the "peanut-butter trick," as she called it, to get Rudy to eat more raw vegetables. Zajac was making a mental note to thank Irma for her suggestion when the phone rang.

The phone startled Medea, who was in the kitchen. The dog had just eaten a roll of duct tape. She was not yet feeling sick, but she was feeling guilty, and the phone call must have convinced her that she'd been caught in the act of eating the duct tape, although Rudy and his father wouldn't know she'd eaten it until she threw it up on Rudy's bed after everyone had gone to sleep.

The duct tape had been left behind by the man who'd come to install the new DogWatch system, an underground electric barrier designed to keep Medea in her yard. The invisible electric fence meant that Zajac (or Rudy or Irma) didn't have to be outside with the dog. But *because* no one had been outside with her, Medea had found and eaten the duct tape.

Medea now wore a new collar with two metal prods turned inward against her throat. (There was a battery in the collar.) If the dog strayed across the invisible electric barrier in her yard, these prods would zap her a good one. But before Medea could get shocked, she would be warned; when she got too close to the unseen fence, her collar made a sound.

"What does it sound like?" Rudy had asked.

"We can't hear it," Dr. Zajac explained. "Only dogs can."

"What does the zap feel like?"

"Oh, nothing much—it doesn't really hurt Medea," the hand surgeon lied.

"Would it hurt *me,* if I put the collar around my neck and walked out of the yard?"

"Don't you *ever* do that, Rudy! Do you understand?" Dr. Zajac asked a little too aggressively, as was his fashion.

"So it hurts," the boy said.

"It doesn't hurt *Medea,*" the doctor insisted.

"Have you tried it around *your* neck?"

"Rudy, the collar isn't for people—it's for dogs!"

Then their conversation turned to the Super Bowl, and why Zajac had wanted Denver to win.

When the phone rang, Medea scurried under the kitchen table, but the message from Dr. Zajac's answering service—"Mrs. Clausen called from Wisconsin"—caused Zajac to forget all about the stupid dog. The eager surgeon called the new widow back immediately. Mrs. Clausen wasn't yet sure of the condition of the donor hand, but Dr. Zajac was nonetheless impressed by her composure.

Mrs. Clausen had been a little less composed in her dealings with the Green Bay police and the examining physician. While she seemed to grasp the particulars of her husband's "presumably accidental death by gunshot," there was almost immediately the expression of a new doubt upon her tear-streaked face.

"He's really dead?" she asked. Her strangely futuristic look was nothing the police or the examining physician had ever seen before. Upon establishing that her husband was "really dead," Mrs. Clausen paused only briefly before inquiring, "But how is Otto's *hand*? The left one."

CHAPTER SIX

The Strings Attached

IN BOTH THE *Green Bay Press-Gazette* and *The Green Bay News-Chronicle,* Otto Clausen's post-game, self-inflicted shooting was relegated to the trivial end of Super Bowl coverage. One Wisconsin sportscaster was gauche enough to say, "Hey, there are a lot of Packer fans who probably considered shooting themselves after Sunday's Super Bowl, but Otto Clausen of Green Bay actually pulled the trigger." Yet even the most tactless, insensitive reporting of Otto's death did not seriously label it a suicide.

When Patrick Wallingford first heard about Otto Clausen—he saw the minute-and-a-half story on his very own international channel in his hotel room in Mexico City—he vaguely wondered why that dick Dick hadn't sent him to interview the widow. It was the kind of story he was usually assigned.

But the all-news network had sent Stubby Farrell, their old sports hack, who'd been at the Super Bowl in San Diego, to cover the event. Stubby had been in Green Bay many times before, and Patrick Wallingford had never even watched a Super Bowl on TV.

When Wallingford saw the news that Monday morning, he was already rushing to leave his hotel to catch his flight to New York. He scarcely noticed that the beer-truck driver had a widow. "Mrs. Clausen couldn't be reached for comment," the ancient sports hack reported.

Dick would have made *me* reach her, Wallingford thought, as he bolted his coffee; yet his mind registered the ten-second image of the beer truck in the near-empty parking lot, the light snow covering the abandoned vehicle like a gauzy shroud.

"Where the party ended, for this Packer fan," Stubby intoned. Cheesy, Patrick Wallingford thought. (No pun intended—he as yet had no idea what a cheesehead was.)

Patrick Ωwas almost out the door when the phone rang in his hotel room; he very nearly let it ring, worried as he was about catching his plane. It was Dr. Zajac, all the way from Massachusetts. "Mr. Wallingford, this is your lucky day," the hand surgeon began.

As he awaited his subsequent flight to Boston, Wallingford watched himself on the twenty-four-hour news; he saw what remained of the story he'd been sent to Mexico City to cover. On Super Bowl

Sunday, not everyone in Mexico had been watching the Super Bowl.

The family and friends of renowned sword-swallower José Guerrero were gathered at Mary of Magdala Hospital to pray for his recovery; during a performance at a tourist hotel in Acapulco, Guerrero had tripped and fallen onstage, lancing his liver. They'd risked flying him from Acapulco to Mexico City, where he was now in the hands of a specialist— liver stab wounds bleed very slowly. More than a hundred friends and family members had assembled at the tiny private hospital, which was surrounded by hundreds more well-wishers.

Wallingford felt as if he'd interviewed them all. But now, about to leave for Boston to meet his new left hand, Patrick was glad that his three-minute report had been edited to a minute and a half. He was impatient to see the rerun of Stubby Farrell's story; he would pay closer attention this time.

Dr. Zajac had told him that Otto Clausen was left-handed, but what did that mean, exactly? Wallingford was right-handed. Until the lion, he'd always held the microphone in his left hand so that he would be free to shake hands with his right. Now that he had only one hand in which to hold the microphone, Wallingford had largely dispensed with shaking hands.

What would it be like to be right-handed and then get a left-handed man's left hand? Hadn't the left-handedness been a function of Clausen's brain? Surely the predetermination to left-handedness was not in the hand. Patrick kept thinking of a hundred such questions he wanted to ask Dr. Zajac.

On the telephone, all the doctor had said was that the medical authorities in Wisconsin had acted quickly enough to preserve the hand because of the "prompt consideration of Mrs. Clausen." Dr. Zajac had been mumbling. Normally he didn't mumble, but the doctor had been up most of the night, administering to the vomiting dog, and then—with Rudy's overzealous assistance—he had attempted to analyze the peculiar-looking substance (in her vomit) that had made Medea sick. Rudy's opinion was that the partially digested duct tape looked like the remains of a seagull. If so, Zajac thought to himself, the bird had been long dead and sticky when the dog ate it. But the analytically minded father and son wouldn't really get to the bottom of what Medea had eaten until the DogWatch man called on Monday morning to inquire how the invisible barrier was working, and to apologize for leaving behind his roll of duct tape.

"You were my last job on Friday," the DogWatch man said, as if he were a detective. "I must have left my duct tape at your place. I don't suppose you've seen it around."

"In a manner of speaking, yes—we have," was all Dr. Zajac could manage to say.

The doctor was still recovering from the sight

of Irma, fresh from her morning shower. The girl had been naked and toweling dry her hair in the kitchen. She'd come back from the weekend early Monday morning, gone for a run, and then taken a shower. She was naked in the kitchen because she'd assumed she was alone in the house—but don't forget that she *wanted* Zajac to see her naked, anyway.

Normally at that time Monday morning, Dr. Zajac had already returned Rudy to his mother's house—in time for Hildred to take the boy to school. But Zajac and Rudy had both overslept, the result of their being up most of the night with Medea. Only after Dr. Zajac's ex-wife called and accused him of kidnapping Rudy did Zajac stumble into the kitchen to make some coffee. Hildred went on yelling after he put Rudy on the phone.

Irma didn't see Dr. Zajac, but he saw her—everything but her head, which was largely hidden from view because she was toweling dry her hair. Great abs! the doctor thought, retreating.

Later he found he couldn't speak to Irma, except in an uncustomary stammer. He haltingly tried to thank her for her peanut-butter idea, but she couldn't understand him. (Nor did she meet Rudy.) And as Dr. Zajac drove Rudy to his angry mother's house, he noticed that there was a special spirit of camaraderie between him and his little boy—they had *both* been yelled at by Rudy's mother.

Zajac was euphoric when he called Wallingford in Mexico, and much more than Otto Clausen's suddenly available left hand was exciting him—the doctor had spent a terrific weekend with his son. Nor had his view of Irma, naked, been unexciting, although it was typical of Zajac to notice her abs. Was it only Irma's abs that had reduced him to stammering? Thus the "prompt consideration of Mrs. Clausen" and similar formalities were all the soon-to-be-celebrated hand surgeon could manage to impart to Patrick Wallingford over the phone.

What Dr. Zajac didn't tell Patrick was that Otto Clausen's widow had demonstrated unheard-of zeal on behalf of the donor hand. Mrs. Clausen had not only accompanied her husband's body from Green Bay to Milwaukee, where (in addition to most of his organs) Otto's left hand was removed; she'd also insisted on accompanying the hand, which was packed in ice, on the flight from Milwaukee to Boston.

Wallingford, of course, had no idea that he was going to meet more than his new hand in Boston; he was also going to meet his new hand's widow.

This development was less upsetting to Dr. Zajac and the other members of the Boston team than a more unusual but no less spur-of-the-moment request of Mrs. Clausen's. Yes, there were some strings attached to the donor hand, and Dr. Zajac was only now learning of them. He had probably been wise in not telling Patrick about the new demands.

With time, everyone at Schatzman, Gingeleskie, Mengerink & Associates hoped, Wallingford might warm to the widow's seemingly last-minute ideas. Apparently not one to beat around the bush, she had requested visitation rights with the hand after the transplant surgery.

How could the one-handed reporter refuse?

"She just wants to see it, I suppose," Dr. Zajac suggested to Wallingford in the doctor's office in Boston.

"Just *see* it?" Patrick asked. There was a disconcerting pause. "Not *touch* it, I hope—not hold hands or anything."

"*Nobody* can touch it! Not for a considerable period of time after the surgery," Dr. Zajac answered protectively.

"But does she mean one visit? Two? For a *year*?"

Zajac shrugged. "Indefinitely—those are her terms."

"Is she crazy?" Patrick asked. "Is she morbid, grief-stricken, deranged?"

"You'll see," Dr. Zajac said. "She wants to meet you."

"Before the surgery?"

"Yes, now. That's part of her request. She needs to be sure that she wants you to have it."

"But I thought her *husband* wanted me to have it!" Wallingford cried. "It was *his* hand!"

"Look—all I can tell you is, the widow's in the driver's seat," Dr. Zajac said. "Have you ever had to deal with a medical ethicist?" (Mrs. Clausen had been quick to call a medical ethicist, too.)

"But *why* does she want to meet me?" Patrick wanted to know. "I mean before I get the hand."

This part of the request *and* the visitation rights struck Dr. Zajac as the kind of thing only a medical ethicist could have thought up. Zajac didn't trust medical ethicists; he believed that they should keep out of the area of experimental surgery. They were always meddling—doing their best to make surgery "more human."

Medical ethicists complained that hands were not necessary to live, and that the anti-rejection drugs posed many risks and had to be taken for life. They argued that the first recipients should be those who had lost *both* hands; after all, double-hand amputees had more to gain than recipients who'd lost only one hand.

Unaccountably, the medical ethicists *loved* Mrs. Clausen's request—not just the creepy visitation rights, but also that she insisted on meeting Patrick Wallingford and deciding if she liked him before permitting the surgery. (You can't get "more human" than that.)

"She just wants to see if you're . . . nice," Zajac tried to explain.

This new affront struck Wallingford as both an insult and a dare; he felt simultaneously offended and challenged. Was he nice? He didn't know. He hoped he was, but how many of us truly know?

As for Dr. Zajac, the doctor knew he himself wasn't especially nice. He was cautiously optimistic that Rudy loved him, and of course he knew that he loved his little boy. But the hand specialist had no illusions concerning himself in the niceness department; Dr. Zajac, except to his son, had never been very lovable.

With a pang, Zajac recalled his brief glimpse of Irma's abs. She must do sit-ups and crunches all day!

"I'll leave you alone with Mrs. Clausen now," Dr. Zajac said, uncharacteristically putting his hand on Patrick's shoulder.

"I'm going to be alone with her?" Wallingford asked. He wanted more time to get ready, to test expressions of nice. But he needed only a second to imagine Otto's hand; maybe the ice was melting.

"Okay, okay, okay," Patrick repeated.

Dr. Zajac and Mrs. Clausen, as if choreographed, changed places in the doctor's office. By the third "okay," Wallingford realized that he was alone with the brand-new widow. Seeing her gave him a sudden chill—what he would think of later as a kind of cold-lake feeling.

Don't forget, she had the flu. When she dragged herself out of bed on Super Bowl Sunday night, she was still feverish. She put on clean underwear and the pair of jeans that were on the bedside chair, and also the faded green sweatshirt—Green Bay green, with the lettering in gold. She'd been wearing the jeans and the sweatshirt when she started to feel ill. She put on her old parka, too.

Mrs. Clausen had owned that faded Green Bay Packers sweatshirt for as long as she could remember going with Otto to the cottage. The old sweatshirt was the color of the fir trees and white pines on the far shore of the lake at sunset. There had been nights in the boathouse bedroom when she'd used the sweatshirt as a pillowcase, because laundry at the cottage could be done only in the lake.

Even now, when she stood in Dr. Zajac's office with her arms crossed on her chest—as if she were cold, or concealing from Patrick Wallingford any impression he might have been able to have of her breasts—Mrs. Clausen could almost smell the pine needles, and she sensed Otto's presence as strongly as if he were right there with her in Zajac's office.

Given the hand surgeon's photo gallery of famous patients, it's a wonder that neither Patrick Wallingford nor Mrs. Clausen paid much attention to the surrounding walls. The two of them were too engaged in noticing each other, although, in the beginning, there was no eye contact between them.

Mrs. Clausen's running shoes had got wet in the snow back in Wisconsin, and they still looked wet to Wallingford, who found himself staring at her feet.

Mrs. Clausen took her parka off and sat in the chair beside Patrick. It was Wallingford's impression that, when she spoke, she addressed his surviving hand.

"Otto felt awful about your hand—the other one, I mean," she began, never taking her eyes from the hand that remained. Patrick Wallingford listened to her with the concealed disbelief of a veteran journalist who usually knows when an interviewee is lying, which Mrs. Clausen was.

"But," the widow went on, "I tried not to think about it, to tell you the truth. And when they showed the lions eating you up, I had trouble watching it. It still makes me sick to think about it."

"Me, too," Wallingford said; he didn't believe she was lying now.

It's hard to tell much about a woman in a sweatshirt, but she seemed fairly compact. Her dark-brown hair needed washing, but Patrick sensed that she was generally a clean person who maintained a neat appearance.

The overhead fluorescent light was harsh to her face. She wore no makeup, not even lipstick, and her lower lip was dry and split—probably from biting it. The circles under her brown eyes exaggerated their darkness, and the crow's-feet at the corners indicated that she was roughly Patrick's age. (Wallingford was only a few years younger than Otto Clausen, who'd been only a little older than his wife.)

"I suppose you think I'm crazy," Mrs. Clausen said.

"No! Not at all! I can't imagine how you must feel—I mean beyond how sad you must be." In truth, she looked like so many emotionally drained women he'd interviewed—most recently, the sword-swallower's wife in Mexico City—that Patrick felt he'd met her before.

Mrs. Clausen surprised him by nodding and then pointing in the general direction of his lap. "May I see it?" she asked. In the awkward pause that followed, Wallingford stopped breathing. "Your *hand* . . . please. The one you still have."

He held out his right hand to her, as if it had been newly transplanted. She reached out to take it but stopped herself, leaving his hand extended in a life-less-looking way.

"It's just a little small," she said. "Otto's is bigger."

He took back his hand, feeling unworthy.

"Otto cried when he saw how you lost your other hand. He actually cried!" We know, of course, that Otto had felt like throwing up; it had been Mrs. Clausen who'd cried, yet she managed to make Wallingford think that her husband's compassionate tears were a source of wonder to her still. (So much for a veteran journalist knowing when someone was lying. Wallingford was completely taken in by Mrs. Clausen's account of Otto's crying.)

"You loved him very much. I can see that," Patrick said.

The widow bit her lower lip and nodded fiercely, tears welling in her eyes. "We were trying to have a baby. We just kept trying and trying. I don't know why it wasn't working." She dropped her chin to her

chest. She held her parka to her face and sobbed quietly into it. Although it was not as faded, the parka
was the same Green Bay green as her sweatshirt,
with the Packers' logo (the gold helmet with the
white *G*) emblazoned on the back.

"It will always be Otto's hand to me," Mrs.
Clausen said with unexpected volume, pushing the
parka away. For the first time, she leveled her gaze at
Patrick's face; she looked as if she'd changed her
mind about something. "How old are you, anyway?"
she asked. Perhaps from seeing Patrick Wallingford
only on television, she'd expected someone older or
younger.

"I'm thirty-four," Wallingford answered, defen-
sively.

"You're my age exactly," she told him. He detected the faintest trace of a smile, as if—either in
spite of her grief or because of it—she were genuinely mad.

"I won't be a nuisance—I mean after the operation," she continued. "But to see his hand . . . later, to
feel it . . . well, that shouldn't be very much of a burden to you, should it? If you respect me, I'll respect
you."

"Certainly!" Patrick said, but he failed to see what
was coming.

"I still want to have Otto's baby."

Wallingford still didn't get it. "Do you mean you
might be pregnant?" he cried excitedly. "Why didn't

you say so? That's wonderful! When will you know?"

That same trace of an insane smile crossed her face again. Patrick hadn't noticed that she'd kicked off her running shoes. Now she unzipped her jeans; she pulled them down, together with her panties, but she hesitated before taking off her sweatshirt.

It was additionally disarming to Patrick that he'd never seen a woman undress this way—that is, bottom first, leaving the top until last. To Wallingford, Mrs. Clausen seemed sexually inexperienced to an embarrassing degree. Then he heard her voice; something had changed in it, and not just the volume. To his surprise, he had an erection, not because Mrs. Clausen was half naked but because of her new tone of voice.

"There's no other time," she told him. "If I'm going to have Otto's baby, I should already be pregnant. After the surgery, you'll be in no shape to do this. You'll be in the hospital, you'll be taking a zillion drugs, you'll be in pain—"

"Mrs. Clausen!" Patrick Wallingford said. He quickly stood up—and as quickly he sat back down. Until he'd tried to stand, he hadn't realized how much of a hard-on he had; it was as obvious as what Wallingford said next.

"This would be *my* baby, not your husband's, wouldn't it?"

But she'd already taken off the sweatshirt. Al-

though she'd left her bra on, he could nonetheless
see that her breasts were more special than he'd
imagined. There was the glint of something in her
navel; the body-piercing was also unexpected. Patrick didn't look at the ornament closely—he was
afraid it might have something to do with the Green
Bay Packers.

"His hand is the closest to him I can get," Mrs.
Clausen said with unflagging determination. The ferocity of her will could easily have been mistaken for
desire. But what worked, meaning what was irresistible, was her voice.

She held Wallingford down in the straight-backed
chair. She knelt to undo his belt buckle, then she
yanked down his pants. By the time Patrick leaned
forward, to stop her from removing his undershorts,
she'd already removed them. Before he could stand
up again, or even sit up straight, she had straddled his
lap; her breasts brushed his face. She moved so
quickly, he'd somehow missed the moment when
she'd taken off her bra.

"I don't have his hand yet!" Wallingford protested,
but when had he ever said no?

"Please respect me," she begged him in a whisper.
What a whisper it was!

Her small, firm buttocks were warm and smooth
against his thighs, and his fleeting glimpse of the
doohickey in her navel—even more than the appeal
of her breasts—had instantly given Wallingford what
felt like an erection on top of his erection. He was

aware of her tears against his neck as her hand guided him inside her.

It was not his right hand that she clutched in hers and pulled to her breast—it was his stump. She murmured something that sounded like, "What were you going to do right now, anyway—nothing this important, right?" Then she asked him, "Don't you want to make a baby?"

"I respect you, Mrs. Clausen," he stammered, but he abandoned all hope of resisting her. It was clear to them both that he'd already given in.

"Please call me Doris," Mrs. Clausen said through her tears.

"Doris?"

"Respect me, respect me. That's all I ask." She was sobbing.

"I do, I *do* respect you . . . Doris," Patrick said.

His one hand had instinctively found the small of her back, as if he'd slept beside her every night for years and even in the dark he could reach out and touch exactly that part of her he wanted to hold. At that moment, he could have sworn that her hair was wet—wet and cold, as if she'd just been swimming.

Of course, he would think later, she must have known she was ovulating; a woman who's been trying and trying to get pregnant surely knows. Doris Clausen must also have known that her difficulty in getting pregnant had been entirely Otto's problem.

"Are you nice?" Mrs. Clausen was whispering to him, while her hips moved relentlessly against the downward pressure of his one hand. "Are you a good man?"

Although Patrick had been forewarned that this was what she wanted to know, he never expected she would ask him directly—no more than he'd anticipated a sexual encounter with her. Speaking strictly as an erotic experience, having sex with Doris Clausen was more charged with longing and desire than any other sexual encounter Wallingford had ever had. He wasn't counting the wet dream induced by that cobalt-blue capsule he'd been given in Junagadh, but that extraordinary painkiller was no longer available—not even in India—and it should never be considered in the same category as actual sex.

As for actual sex, Patrick's encounter with Otto Clausen's widow, singular and brief though it was, put his entire weekend in Kyoto with Evelyn Arbuthnot to shame. Having sex with Mrs. Clausen even eclipsed Wallingford's tumultuous relationship with the tall blond sound technician who'd witnessed the lion attack in Junagadh.

That unfortunate German girl, who was back home in Hamburg, was still in therapy because of those lions, although Wallingford suspected she'd been more profoundly traumatized by fainting and then waking up in one of the meat carts than by seeing poor Patrick lose his left wrist and hand.

"Are you *nice*? Are you a good man?" Doris repeated, her tears wetting Patrick's face. Her small, strong body drew him farther and farther inside her, so that Wallingford could scarcely hear himself answer. Surely Dr. Zajac, as well as some other members of the surgical team who were presently assembling in the waiting room, must have heard Patrick's plaintive cries.

"Yes! Yes! I *am* nice! I *am* a good man!" Wallingford wailed.

"Is that a promise?" Doris asked him in a whisper. It was that whisper again—what a killer!

Once more Wallingford answered her so loudly that Dr. Zajac and his colleagues could hear. "Yes! Yes! I promise! I *do,* I really do!"

The knock on the hand surgeon's office door came a little later, after it had been quiet for a while. "Are we all right in there?" asked the head of the Boston team.

At first Zajac thought they looked all right. Patrick Wallingford was dressed again and still sitting in the straight-backed chair. Mrs. Clausen, fully dressed, lay on her back on Dr. Zajac's office rug. The fingers of her hands were clasped behind her head, and her elevated feet rested on the seat of the empty chair beside Wallingford.

"I have a bad back," Doris explained. She didn't, of course. It was a recommended position in several of the many books she'd read about how to get pregnant. "Gravity," was all she'd said in way of explanation to Patrick, as he'd smiled enchantedly at her.

They're both crazy, thought Dr. Zajac, who could smell sex in the room. A medical ethicist might not have approved of this new development, but Zajac was a hand surgeon, and his surgical team was raring to go.

"If we're feeling pretty comfy about this," Zajac said—looking first at Mrs. Clausen, who looked *very* comfortable, and then at Patrick Wallingford, who looked stupefyingly drunk or stoned—"how about it? Do we have a green light?"

"Everything's okay with me!" Doris Clausen said loudly, as if she were calling to someone over an expanse of water.

"Everything's fine with me," Patrick replied. "I guess we have a green light."

It was the degree of sexual satisfaction in Wallingford's expression that rang a bell with Dr. Zajac. Where had he seen that expression before? Oh, yes, he'd been in Bombay, where he'd been performing a number of exceedingly delicate hand surgeries on children in front of a selective audience of Indian pediatric surgeons. Zajac remembered one surgical procedure from there especially well—it involved a three-year-old girl who'd got her hand caught and mangled in the gears of some farm machinery.

Zajac was sitting with the Indian anesthesiologist when the little girl started to wake up. Children are always cold, often disoriented, and usually frightened when they awaken from general anesthesia. On occasion, they're sick to their stomachs.

Dr. Zajac remembered that he'd excused himself in order to miss seeing the unhappy child. He would have a look at how her hand was doing, of course, but that could be later on, when she was feeling better.

"Wait—you have to see this," the Indian anesthesiologist told Zajac. "Just have a quick look at her."

On the child's innocent face was the expression of a sexually satisfied woman. Dr. Zajac was shocked. (The sad truth was that Zajac had never, personally, seen the face of a woman as sexually satisfied as that before.)

"My God, man," Dr. Zajac said to the Indian anesthesiologist, "what did you give her?"

"Just a little something extra in her I.V.—not very much of it, either!" the anesthesiologist replied.

"But what is it? What's it called?"

"I'm not supposed to tell you," said the Indian anesthesiologist. "It's not available in your country, and it never will be. It's about to become unavailable here, too. The ministry of health intends to ban it."

"I should hope so," Dr. Zajac remarked—he abruptly left the recovery room.

But the girl hadn't been in any pain; and when Zajac examined her hand later, it was fine, and she was resting comfortably.

"How's the pain?" he asked the child. A nurse had to translate for him.

"She says 'everything's okay.' She has no pain," the nurse interpreted. The girl went on babbling.

"What's she saying now?" Dr. Zajac asked, and the nurse became suddenly shy or embarrassed.

"I wish they wouldn't put that painkiller in the anesthesia," the nurse told him. The child appeared to be relating a long story.

"What's she telling you?" Zajac asked.

"Her dream," the nurse answered, evasively. "She believes she's seen her future. She's going to be very happy and have lots of children. Too many, in my opinion."

The little girl just smiled at him; for a three-year-old, there'd been something inappropriately seductive in her eyes.

Now, in Dr. Zajac's Boston office, Patrick Wallingford was grinning in the same shameless fashion.

What an absolutely cuckoo coincidence! Dr. Zajac decided, as he looked at Wallingford's sexually besotted expression.

"The tiger patient," he'd called that little girl in Bombay, because the child had explained to her doctors and nurses that, when her hand had been caught in the farm machinery, the gears had growled at her like a tiger.

Cuckoo or not, something about the way Wallingford looked gave Dr. Zajac pause. "The lion patient," as Zajac had long thought of Patrick Wallingford, was possibly in need of more than a new left hand.

What Dr. Zajac didn't know was that Wallingford had finally found what he needed—he'd found Doris Clausen.

CHAPTER SEVEN

The Twinge

$\mathcal{A}$s DR. ZAJAC EXPLAINED in his first press conference following the fifteen-hour operation, the patient was "at risk." Patrick Wallingford was sleepy but in stable condition after awakening from general anesthesia. Of course the patient was taking "a combination of immunosuppressant drugs"—Zajac neglected to say how many or for how long. (He didn't mention the steroids, either.)

The hand surgeon, at the very moment national attention turned to him, was noticeably short-tempered. In the words of one colleague—that moron Mengerink, the cuckolding cretin—Zajac was also "as beady-eyed as the proverbial mad scientist."

Before the historic procedure, Dr. Zajac had been running in the predawn darkness in the gray slush along the banks of the Charles. To his dismay, a young woman had passed him in the ghostly mist as if he'd been standing still. Her taut buttocks in spandex tights, moving resolutely away from Zajac, tightened and released like the fingers of a hand making a fist and then relaxing, and then making a fist again. What a fist it was!

It was Irma. Dr. Zajac, only hours before he would attach Otto Clausen's left hand and wrist to the waiting stump of Patrick Wallingford's left forearm, felt his heart constrict; his lungs seemed to cease expanding and he experienced a stomach cramp that was as crippling to his forward progress as being hit by, let's say, a beer truck. Zajac was doubled over in the slush when Irma came sprinting back to him.

He was speechless with pain, gratitude, shame, adoration, lust—you name it. Irma led him back to Brattle Street as if he were a runaway child. "You're dehydrated—you need to replenish your fluids," she scolded. She'd read volumes on the subject of dehydration and the various "walls" that serious runners supposedly "hit," which they must train themselves to "run through."

Irma was what they call "maxed out" on the vocabulary of extreme sports; the adjectives of maniacal stamina in the face of grueling tests of endurance had become her primary modifiers. ("Gnarly," for example.) Irma was no less steeped in eat-to-run theory—from conventional carbo-loading to ginseng enemas, from green tea and bananas before the run to cranberry-juice shakes after.

"I'm gonna make you an egg-white omelet as soon as we get home," she told Dr. Zajac, whose shin splints were killing him; he hobbled beside her like a crippled racehorse. This lent nothing newly attractive to his appearance, which had already been likened (by one of his colleagues) to that of a feral dog.

On the biggest day of his professional career, Dr. Zajac had breathlessly fallen in love with his housekeeper/assistant–turned–personal trainer. But he couldn't tell her—he couldn't talk. As Zajac gasped for breath in hopes of quieting the radiating pain in his solar plexus, he noticed that Irma was holding his hand. Her grip was strong; her fingernails were cut shorter than most men's, but she was not a nail-biter. A woman's hands mattered a lot to Dr. Zajac. To put in ascending order of importance how he'd fallen for Irma seems crass, but here it is: her abs, her buttocks, her hands.

"You got Rudy to eat more raw vegetables," was all the hand surgeon managed to say, between gasps.

"It was just the peanut butter," Irma said. She easily supported half his weight. She felt she could have carried him home—she was that exhilarated. He'd complimented her; she knew he'd noticed her, at last. As if for the first time, he was really seeing who she was.

"The next weekend Rudy is with me," Zajac choked, "perhaps you'll stay here? I'd like you to meet him."

This invitation seemed as conclusive to Irma as his hand on her breast, which she'd only imagined. Suddenly she staggered, yet she was still bearing only half his weight; the unpredictable timing of her triumph had made her weak.

"I like shaved carrots and a little tofu in my egg-white omelets, don't you?" she asked, as they neared the house on Brattle Street.

There was Medea, taking a dump in the yard. Seeing them, the craven dog furtively eyed her own shit; then she sprinted away from it, as if to say, "Who can stand to be near that stuff? Not me!"

"That dog is very dumb," Irma observed matter-of-factly. "But I love her, somewhat," she added.

"I do, too!" Zajac croaked, his heart aching. It was the "somewhat" that sent him over the edge for Irma; he had the exact same feelings for the dog.

The doctor was too excited to eat his egg-white omelet with shaved carrots and tofu, although he tried. Nor could he finish the tall shake Irma made him—cranberry juice, mashed banana, frozen yogurt, protein powder, and something grainy (possibly a pear). He poured half of it down the toilet, together with the uneaten omelet, before he took a shower.

It was in the shower that Zajac noticed his hard-on. His erection had Irma's name written all over it, although there'd been nothing physical between them—discounting Irma's assistance in getting him home. Fifteen hours of surgery beckoned. This was no time for sex.

At the postoperative press conference, even the most envious of his colleagues—the ones who secretly wanted him to fail—were disappointed on Dr. Zajac's behalf. His remarks were too trenchant; they suggested that hand-transplant surgery would one day soon be in the no-big-deal category of a tonsillectomy. The journalists were bored; they couldn't wait to hear from the medical ethicist, whom all the surgeons at Schatzman, Gingeleskie, Mengerink & Associates despised. And before the medical ethicist could finish, the media's attention shifted restlessly to Mrs. Clausen. Who could blame them? She was the epitome of human interest.

Someone had got her clean, more feminine clothes, free of Green Bay logos. She'd washed her hair and put on a little lipstick. She looked especially small and demure in the TV lights, and she'd not let the makeup girl touch the circles under her eyes; it was as if she knew that what was fleeting about her beauty was also the only permanent thing about it. She was pretty in a kind of damaged way.

"If Otto's hand survives," Mrs. Clausen began, in her soft but strangely arresting voice—as if her late husband's hand, not Patrick Wallingford, were the principal patient—"I guess I will feel a little better, one day. You know, just being assured that a part of him is where I can see him . . . touch him . . ." Her voice trailed away. She'd already stolen the press conference from Dr. Zajac and the medical ethicist, and she was not done—she was just getting started.

The journalists crowded around her. Doris Clausen's sadness was spilling into homes and hotel rooms and airport bars around the world. She seemed not to hear all the questions the reporters were asking her. Later Dr. Zajac and Patrick Wallingford would realize that Mrs. Clausen had been following her own script—with no TelePrompTer, either.

"If I only knew . . ." She trailed away again; undoubtedly the pause was deliberate.

"If you only knew *what?*" one of the journalists cried.

"If I'm pregnant," Mrs. Clausen answered. Even Dr. Zajac held his breath, waiting for her next words. "Otto and I were trying to have a baby. So maybe I'm pregnant, or maybe I'm not. I just don't know."

Every man at the press conference must have had a hard-on, even the medical ethicist. (Only Zajac was confused as to his erection's source—he thought it was Irma's lingering influence.) Every man in the aforementioned homes and hotel rooms and airport bars around the world was feeling the effects of Doris Clausen's arousing tone of voice. As surely as water loves to lap a dock, as surely as pine trees sprout new needles at the tips of their branches, Mrs. Clausen's voice was at that moment giving a hard-on to every heterosexual male transfixed by the news.

The next day, as Patrick Wallingford lay in his hospital bed beside the enormous, foreign-looking bandage, which was almost all he could see of his new left hand, he watched Mrs. Clausen on the all-news network (his own channel of employment) while the actual Mrs. Clausen sat possessively at his bedside.

Doris was riveted by what she could see of Otto's index, middle, and ring fingers—only their tips—and the tip of her late husband's thumb. The pinky of Patrick's new left hand was lost in all the gauze. Under the bandage was a brace that immobilized Wallingford's new wrist. The bandage was so extensive that you couldn't tell where Otto's hand and wrist, and part of his forearm, had been attached.

The coverage of the hand transplant on the all-news network, which was repeated hourly, began with an edited version of the lion episode in Junagadh. The snatching and eating took only about fifteen seconds in this version, which should have forewarned Wallingford that he would also be assigned a lesser role in the footage to come.

He'd foolishly hoped that the surgery itself would be so fascinating that the television audience would soon think of him as "the transplant guy," or even "transplant man," and that these revised or repaired versions of himself would replace "the lion guy" and "disaster man" as the new but enduring labels of his life. In the footage, there were some grisly goings-on of an unclear but surgical nature at the Boston hospital, and a shot of Patrick's gurney disappearing down a corridor; yet the gurney and Wallingford were soon lost from view because they were surrounded by seventeen frantic-looking doctors and nurses and anesthesiologists—the Boston team.

Then there was a clip of Dr. Zajac speaking tersely to the press. Naturally Zajac's "at risk" comment was taken out of context, which made it appear that the patient was already in the gravest trouble, and the part about the combination of immunosuppressant drugs sounded blatantly evasive, which it was. While those drugs have improved the success rate of organ transplants, an arm is composed of several different tissues—meaning different degrees of rejection reactions are possible. Hence the steroids, which (together with the immunosuppressant drugs) Wallingford would be required to take every day for the rest of his life, or for as long as he had Otto's hand.

There was a shot of Otto's abandoned beer truck in the snowy parking lot in Green Bay, but Mrs. Clausen never flinched at Patrick's bedside; she kept herself focused on Otto's three fingertips and the tip of his thumb. Moreover, Doris was as close to her husband's former hand as she could get; if Wallingford had had any feeling in those fingertips and the tip of that thumb, he would have felt the widow breathing on them.

Those fingers were numb. That they would remain numb for months would become a matter of some concern to Wallingford, although Dr. Zajac was dismissive of his fears. It would be almost eight months before the hand could distinguish between hot and cold—a sign that the nerves were regenerating—and close to a year before Patrick felt confident enough in his grip on a steering wheel to drive a car. (It would also be close to a year, and only after hours of physical therapy, before he would be able to tie his own shoes.)

But from a journalistic point of view, it was there, in his hospital bed, that Patrick Wallingford saw the writing on the wall—his full recovery, or lack thereof, would never be the main story.

The medical ethicist spoke for longer, on-camera, than the twenty-four-hour international channel had given Dr. Zajac. "In cases like these," the ethicist intoned, "candor like Mrs. Clausen's is rare, and her ongoing connection to the donor hand is invaluable."

In *what* "cases like these"? Zajac must have been thinking, while he fumed off-camera. This was only the *second* hand transplant *ever,* and the first one had been a failure!

While the ethicist was still speaking, Wallingford saw the cameras move in on Mrs. Clausen. Patrick felt a flood of desire and longing for her. He feared he would never attain her again; he foresaw that she wouldn't encourage it. He watched her shift the entire press conference from his hand transplant to her late husband's hand itself, and then to the baby she hoped she carried inside her. There was even a close-up of Mrs. Clausen's hands holding her flat stomach.

She had spread the palm of her right hand on her belly; her left hand, already without a wedding ring, overlapped her right.

As a journalist, Patrick Wallingford knew in an instant what had happened: Doris Clausen, and the child she and Otto had wanted, had usurped Patrick's story. Wallingford was aware that such a substitution happened sometimes in his irresponsible profession— not that television journalism is the *only* irresponsible profession.

But Wallingford didn't really care, and this surprised him. Let her usurp me, Patrick thought, simultaneously realizing that he was in love with Doris Clausen. (There's no telling what the all-news network, or a medical ethicist, might have made of that.)

But a part of the improbability of Wallingford falling in love with Mrs. Clausen was his recognition of the unlikelihood of her ever loving him. It had previously been Patrick's experience that women were easily smitten with him, at least initially; it had also been his experience that women got over him easily, too.

His ex-wife had likened him to the flu. "When you were with me, Patrick, every hour I thought I was going to die," Marilyn told him. "But when you were gone, it was as if you'd never existed."

"Thanks," said Wallingford, whose feelings, until now, had never been as easily hurt as most women assumed.

What affected him about Doris Clausen was that

her unusual determination had a sexual component; what she wanted was brightly marked, at every phase, with unconcealed sexual overtones. What began in the slight alterations in her tone of voice was continued in the intensity of her small, compact body, which was wound as tightly as a spring, coiled for sex.

Her mouth was soft-looking, her lips perfectly parted; and in the general tiredness around her eyes, there was a seductive acceptance of the world as it was. Mrs. Clausen would never ask you to change who you were—maybe only your habits. She expected no miracles. What you saw in her was what you got, a loyalty that knew no bounds. And it appeared that she would never get over Otto—she'd been smitten for life.

Doris had used Patrick Wallingford for the one job Otto couldn't finish; that she'd somehow chosen him for the job gave Patrick the slimmest hope that she would one day fall in love with him.

The first time Wallingford even slightly wiggled Otto Clausen's fingers, Doris cried. The nurses had been told to speak sternly to Mrs. Clausen if she tried to kiss the fingertips. It made Patrick happy, in a bitter kind of way, when some of her kisses managed to get through.

And long after the bandages came off, he remembered the first time he felt her tears on the back of that hand; it was about five months after the surgery. Wallingford had successfully passed the most vulnerable period, which was said to be from the end of the first week to the end of the first three months. The feeling of her tears made him weep. (By then he'd regained an astonishing twenty-two centimeters of nerve regeneration, from the place of attachment to the beginnings of the palm.)

Albeit very gradually, his need for the various painkillers went away, but he remembered the dream he'd often had, shortly after the painkillers had kicked in. Someone was taking his photograph. Occasionally, even when Wallingford had stopped using any painkillers, the sound of a camera's shutter (in his sleep) was very real. The flash seemed far away and incomplete, like heat lightning—not the real thing— but the sound of the shutter was so clear that he almost woke up.

While it was the nature of the painkillers that Wallingford wouldn't remember for how long he'd taken them—maybe four or five months?—it was also the nature of the dream that he had no recollection of ever seeing the photographs that were being taken or the photographer. And there were times he didn't think it *was* a dream, or he wasn't sure.

In six months, more concretely, he could actually feel Doris Clausen's face when she pressed it into his left palm. Mrs. Clausen never touched his other hand, nor did he once try to touch her with it. She'd made her feelings for him plain. When he so much as said her name a certain way, she blushed and shook her head. She would not discuss the one time they'd had sex. She'd *had* to do it—that was all she would say. ("It was the only way.")

Yet for Patrick there endured the hope, however scant, that she might one day consider doing it again—notwithstanding that she was pregnant, and she revered her pregnancy the way women who've waited a long time to get pregnant do. Nor was there any doubt in Mrs. Clausen's mind that this would be an only child.

Her most inviting tone of voice, which Doris Clausen could call upon when she wanted to, and which had the effect of sunlight after rain—the power to open flowers—was only a memory now; yet Wallingford believed he could wait. He hugged that memory like a pillow in his sleep, not unlike the way he was doomed to remember that blue-capsule dream.

Patrick Wallingford had never loved a woman so unselfishly. It was enough for him that Mrs. Clausen loved his left hand. She loved to put it on her swollen abdomen, to let the hand feel the fetus move.

Wallingford hadn't noticed when Mrs. Clausen stopped wearing the ornament in her navel; he'd not seen it since their moment of mutual abandonment in Dr. Zajac's office. Perhaps the body-piercing had been Otto's idea, or the doohickey itself had been a gift from him (hence she was loath to wear it now). Or else the unidentified metal object had become uncomfortable in the course of Mrs. Clausen's pregnancy.

Then, at seven months, when Patrick felt an unfamiliar twinge in his new wrist—one especially strong kick from the unborn child—he tried to conceal his pain. Naturally Doris saw him wince; he couldn't hide anything from her.

"What is it?" she asked. She instinctively moved the hand to her heart—to her *breast,* was what registered with Wallingford. He recalled, as if it were yesterday, how she had held his stump there while she'd mounted him.

"It was just a twinge," Patrick replied.

"Call Zajac," Mrs. Clausen demanded. "Don't fool around."

But there was nothing wrong. Dr. Zajac seemed miffed at the apparently easy success of the hand transplant. There'd been an early problem with the thumb and index finger, which Wallingford could not get his muscles to move on command. But that was because he'd been without a hand and wrist for five years—his muscles had to relearn a few things.

There'd been no crises for Zajac to avert; the hand's progress had been as relentless as Mrs. Clausen's plans for the hand. Perhaps the true cause of Dr. Zajac's disappointment was that the hand seemed more like *her* triumph than his. The principal news was that the donor's widow was pregnant, and that she still maintained a relationship with her late husband's hand. And the labels for Wallingford were never "the transplant guy" or "transplant man"—he was still and would remain "the lion guy" and "disaster man."

And then, in September 1998, there was a successful hand-and-forearm transplant in Lyon, France. Clint Hallam, a New Zealander living in Australia, was the recipient. Zajac seemed miffed about that, too. He had reason to be. Hallam had lied. He'd told his doctors that he lost his hand in an industrial accident on a building site, but it turned out that his hand had been severed by a circular saw in a New Zealand prison, where he'd been serving a two-and-a-half-year sentence for fraud. (Dr. Zajac, of course, thought that giving a new hand to an ex-convict was a decision only a medical ethicist could have made.)

For now, Clint Hallam was taking more than thirty pills a day and showing no signs of rejection. In Wallingford's case, eight months after his attachment surgery, he was still popping more than thirty pills a day, and if he dropped his pocket change, he couldn't pick it up with Otto's hand. More encouraging to the Boston team was the fact that his left hand, despite the absence of sensation at the extremities, was almost as strong as his right; at least Patrick could turn a doorknob enough to open the door. Doris had told him that Otto had been fairly strong. (From lifting all those cases of beer, no doubt.)

Occasionally Mrs. Clausen and Wallingford would sleep together—without sex, even without nakedness. Doris would just sleep beside him—at his left side, naturally. Patrick didn't sleep well, to a large degree because he was comfortable sleeping only on his back. The hand ached when he lay on his side or his stomach; not even Dr. Zajac could tell him why. Maybe it had something to do with a reduced blood supply to the hand, but the muscles and tendons and nerves were obviously getting a good supply of blood.

"I would never say you were home free," Zajac told Wallingford, "but that hand is looking more and more like a keeper to me."

It was hard to understand Zajac's newfound casualness, let alone his love of Irma's vernacular. Mrs. Clausen and her fetus had usurped Dr. Zajac's three minutes in the limelight, but Zajac seemed relatively undepressed. (That a criminal was Wallingford's only competition in hand-transplant surgery made Zajac more pissed-off than depressed.) And, as a result of Irma's cooking, he'd actually put on a little weight; healthy food, in decent quantities, still adds up. The hand surgeon had given in to his appetites. He was famished because he was getting laid every day.

That Irma and her former employer were now happily married was no business of Wallingford's, but it was all the talk at Schatzman, Gingeleskie, Mengerink, *Zajac* & Associates. And if the best surgeon among them was looking less and less like a feral dog, his once-undernourished son, Rudy, had also gained a few pounds. Even to the envious souls who stood at the periphery of Dr. Zajac's life and cravenly mocked him, the little boy whose father loved him now struck nearly everyone as happy and normal.

No less surprising, Dr. Mengerink confessed to Zajac that he'd had an affair with the vengeful Hildred, Dr. Zajac's now-overweight first wife. Hildred was seething about Irma, although Zajac had increased her alimony—the cost to Hildred was straightforward: she would accept dual, which was to say *equal,* custody of Rudy.

Instead of becoming overwrought at Dr. Mengerink's startling confession, Dr. Zajac was a portrait of sensitivity and compassion. "With Hildred? You poor man . . ." was all Zajac had said, putting his arm around Mengerink's stooped shoulders.

"It's a wonder what a little nooky will do for you," the surviving Gingeleskie brother remarked enviously.

Had the shit-eating dog also turned a corner? In a way, she had. Medea was *almost* a good dog; she still experienced what Irma called "lapses," but dogshit and its effects no longer dominated Dr. Zajac's life. Dog-turd lacrosse had become just a game. And while the doctor had tried a glass of red wine every day for the sake of his heart, his heart was in good hands with Irma and Rudy. (Zajac's growing fondness for red Bordeaux quite exceeded the parsimonious allotment that was deemed to be good for his ticker.)

The unexplained ache in Patrick Wallingford's new left hand continued to be of little concern to Dr. Zajac. But one night when Patrick was lying chastely in bed with Doris Clausen, she asked him, "What do you mean by an 'ache,' exactly? What kind of ache is it?"

"It's a kind of straining, only my fingers are barely moving, and it hurts in the tips of the fingers, where I still have no feeling. It's weird."

"It hurts where you have no feeling?" Doris asked.

"So it seems," Patrick explained.

"I know what's wrong," Mrs. Clausen said. Just because she wanted to lie next to his left hand, she should not have imposed the wrong side of the bed on Otto.

"On Otto?" Wallingford asked.

Otto had always slept at her left side, Doris explained. How this wrong-side-of-the-bed business had affected Patrick's new hand, he would soon see.

With Mrs. Clausen asleep beside him, at his *right* side, something that seemed utterly natural happened. He turned to her, and—as if ingrained in her, even in her sleep—she turned to him, her head nestling in the crook of his right arm, her breath against his throat. He didn't dare swallow, lest he wake her.

His left hand twitched, but there was no ache now. Wallingford lay still, waiting to see what his new hand would do next. He would remember later that the hand, entirely of its own accord, went under the hem of Doris Clausen's nightie—the unfeeling fingers moving up her thighs. At their touch, Mrs. Clausen's legs drew apart; her hips opened; her pubic hair brushed against the palm of Patrick's new left hand, as if lifted by an unfelt breeze.

Wallingford knew where his fingers went, although he couldn't feel them. The change in Doris's breathing was apparent. He couldn't help himself—he kissed her forehead, nuzzled her hair. Then she seized his probing hand and brought his fingers to her lips. He held his breath in anticipation of the pain, but there was none. With her other hand, she took hold of his penis; then she abruptly let it go.

Wrong penis! The spell was broken. Mrs. Clausen was wide awake. They could both smell the fingers of Otto's remarkable left hand—it rested on the pillow, touching their faces.

"Is the ache gone?" Doris asked him.

"Yes," Patrick answered. He meant only that it was gone from the *hand.* "But there's another ache, a *new* one . . ." he started to say.

"I can't help you with that one," Mrs. Clausen declared. But when she turned her back to him, she gently held his left hand against her big belly. "If you want to touch yourself—you know, while you hold me—maybe I can help you a *little.*"

Tears of love and gratitude sprang to Patrick's eyes.

What decorum was called for here? It seemed to Wallingford that it would be most proper if he could finish masturbating before he felt the baby kick, but Mrs. Clausen held his left hand tightly to her stomach—*not* to her breast—and before Patrick could come, which he managed with uncommon quickness, the unborn child kicked twice. The second time elicited that exact same twinge of pain he'd felt before, a pain sharp enough to make him flinch. This time Doris didn't notice, or else she confused it with the sudden shudder with which he came.

Best of all, Wallingford would think later, Mrs. Clausen had then rewarded him with that special voice of hers, which he hadn't heard in a long time.

"Ache all gone?" she'd asked. The hand, again of its own accord, slipped from her giant belly to her swollen breast, where she let it stay.

"Yes, thank you," Patrick whispered, and fell into a dream.

There was a smell he at first failed to recognize because it was so unfamiliar to him; it's not a smell one experiences in New York or Boston. Pine needles! he suddenly realized.

There was the sound of water, but not the ocean and not from a tap. It was water lapping against the bow of a boat—or maybe slapping against a dock—but whatever water it was, it was music to the hand, which moved as softly as water itself over the enlarged contour of Mrs. Clausen's breast.

The twinge (even his memory of the twinge) was gone, and in its aftermath floated the best night's sleep Wallingford would ever have, but for the disquieting thought, when he woke up, that the dream had seemed not quite his. It was also not as close to his cobalt-blue-capsule experience as he would have liked.

To begin with, there'd been no sex in the dream,

nor had Wallingford felt the heat of the sun in the planks of the dock, or the dock itself through what seemed to be a towel; instead there'd been only a far-off sense that there was a dock somewhere else.

That night he didn't hear the camera shutter in his sleep. You could have taken Patrick Wallingford's photograph a thousand times that night. He would never have known.

CHAPTER EIGHT

Rejection and Success

IT WAS ALL RIGHT with Wallingford when Doris talked about wanting her child to know his or her father's hand. What this meant to Patrick was that he could expect to go on seeing her. He loved her with slimmer and slimmer hope of her reciprocation, which was disquietingly unlike the way she loved the hand. She would hold it to her belly, against the unborn child's persistent kicks, and while she could occasionally feel Wallingford flinch in pain, she had ceased to find his twinges alarming.

"It's not really your hand," Mrs. Clausen reminded Patrick, not that he needed reminding. "Imagine what it must be like for Otto—to feel a child he's never going to see. Of course it hurts him!"

But wasn't it Wallingford's pain? In his former life, with Marilyn, Patrick might have responded sarcastically. ("Now that you put it that way, I'm not worried about the pain.") But with Doris . . . well, all he could do was adore her.

Moreover, there was strong support for Mrs. Clausen's argument. The new hand didn't look like Patrick's—it never would. Otto's left hand was not that much bigger, but we do a lot of looking at our hands—it's hard to get used to someone else's. There were times when Wallingford would stare at the hand intently, as if he expected it to speak; nor could he resist smelling the hand—it did not have his smell. He knew that from the way Mrs. Clausen closed her eyes, when *she* smelled the hand, it smelled like Otto.

There were welcome distractions. During his long recovery and rehabilitation, Patrick's career, which had been grounded in the Boston newsroom so that he could be close to Dr. Zajac and the Boston team, began to flourish. (Maybe "flourish" is too strong a word; let's just say that the network allowed him to branch out a bit.)

The twenty-four-hour international channel created a weekend-anchor slot for him following the evening news; this Saturday-night sidebar to the regular news show was telecast from Boston. While the producers still gave Wallingford all the stories about bizarre casualties, they permitted him to introduce and summarize these stories with a dignity that was surprising and newfound—both in Wallingford *and* in the all-news network. No one in Boston or

New York—not Patrick, not even Dick—could explain it.

Patrick Wallingford acted on-camera as if Otto Clausen's hand were truly his own, conveying a sympathy previously absent from the calamity channel and his own reporting. It was as if he knew he'd got more than a hand from Otto Clausen.

Of course, among serious reporters—meaning those journalists who reported the hard news in depth and in context—the very idea of a sidebar to what passed for the news on the disaster network was laughable. In the *real* news, there were refugee children whose mothers and aunts had been raped in front of them, although neither the women nor the children would usually admit to this. In the real news, the fathers and uncles of these refugee children had been murdered, although there was scant admitting to this, either. There were also stories of doctors and nurses being shot—deliberately, so that the refugee children would be without medical care. But tales of such willful evil in foreign countries were not reported in depth on the so-called international channel, nor would Patrick Wallingford ever get a field assignment to report them.

More likely, he would be expected to find improbable dignity in and sympathy for the victims of frankly stupid accidents, like his. If there was what could be called a thought behind this watered-down version of the news, the thought was as small as this: that even in what was gruesome, there was (or should be) something *uplifting,* provided that what was gruesome was idiotic enough.

So what if the all-news network would never send Patrick Wallingford to Yugoslavia? What was it the confused doorman's brother had said to Vlad or Vlade or Lewis? ("Look—you have a job, don't you?") Well, Wallingford had a job, didn't he?

And most Sundays he was free to fly to Green Bay. When the football season started, Mrs. Clausen was eight months pregnant; it was the first time in recent memory that she wouldn't see a single Packer home game at Lambeau Field. Doris joked that she didn't want to go into labor on the forty-yard line—not if it was a good game. (What she meant was that no one would have paid any attention to her.) Therefore, she and Wallingford watched the Packers on television. Absurdly, he flew to Green Bay just to watch TV.

But a Packer game, even on television, provided the longest sustained period of time that Mrs. Clausen would stroke the hand or permit the hand to touch her; and while she stared transfixed at the football game, Patrick could look at her the same way. He was conscious of memorizing her profile, or the way she bit her lower lip when it was third and long. (Doris had to explain to him that third and long was when Brett Favre, the Green Bay quarterback, had the greatest potential for getting sacked or throwing an interception.)

Occasionally she hurt Wallingford without meaning to. When Favre got sacked, or when he was intercepted—worse, whenever the other team scored—Mrs. Clausen would sharply squeeze her late husband's hand.

"Aaahhh!" Wallingford would cry out, shamelessly exaggerating his agony.

There would be kisses for the hand, even tears. It was worth the pain, which was quite different from those twinges caused by the kicking of the unborn child; those pins and needles were from another world.

Thus, bravely, Wallingford flew almost every week to Green Bay. He never found a hotel he liked, but Doris wouldn't allow him to stay in the house she'd shared with Otto. During these trips, Patrick met other Clausens—Otto had a huge, supportive family. Most of them weren't shy about demonstrating their affection for Otto's hand. While Otto's father and brothers had choked back sobs, Otto's mother, who was memorably large, had wept openly; and the only unmarried sister had clutched the hand to her breast, just before fainting. Wallingford had looked away, thereby failing to catch her when she fell. Patrick blamed himself that she'd chipped a tooth on a coffee table, and she was not a woman with the best of smiles to begin with.

While the Clausens were a clan whose outdoorsy good cheer contrasted sharply with Wallingford's reserve, he found himself strangely drawn to them. They had the loyal exuberance of season-ticket holders, and they'd all married people who looked like

Clausens. You couldn't tell the in-laws from the blood relatives, except for Doris, who stood apart.

Patrick could see how kind the Clausens were to her, and how protective. They'd accepted her, although she was clearly different; they loved her as one of their own. On television, those families who resembled the Clausens were nauseating, but the Clausens were not.

Wallingford had also traveled to Appleton to meet Doris's mother and father, who wanted to visit with the hand, too. It was from Mrs. Clausen's father that Wallingford learned more about Doris's job; he hadn't known that she'd had the job ever since her graduation from high school. For longer than Patrick Wallingford had been a journalist, Doris Clausen had worked in ticket sales for the Green Bay Packers. The Packers' organization had been very supportive of Mrs. Clausen—they'd even put her through college.

"Doris can get you tickets, you know," Mrs. Clausen's father told Patrick. "And tickets are wicked hard to come by around here."

Green Bay would have a rough season following their loss to Denver in Super Bowl XXXII. As Doris had said so movingly to Otto, the last day the unlucky man was alive, "There's no guarantee of returning to the Super Bowl."

The Packers wouldn't get past the wild-card game, losing what Mrs. Clausen called a heartbreaker in the first round of the playoffs to San Francisco. "Otto thought we had the 49ers' number," Doris said. But by then she had a new baby to take care of. She was more philosophical now about Green Bay's losses than she and Otto had ever been before.

It was a big baby, a boy—nine pounds, eight ounces—and he was so long overdue that they'd wanted to induce labor. Mrs. Clausen wouldn't hear of it; she was one to let nature take its course. Wallingford missed the delivery. The baby was almost a month old before Patrick could get away from Boston. He should never have flown on Thanksgiving Day—his flight was late getting into Green Bay. Even so, he arrived in time to watch the fourth quarter of the Minnesota Vikings' game with the Dallas Cowboys, which Minnesota won. (A good omen, Doris declared—Otto had hated the Cowboys.) Perhaps because her mother was staying with her, to help with Otto junior, Mrs. Clausen was relaxed about inviting Wallingford to visit her and the new baby at home.

Patrick did his best to forget the details of that house—all the pictures of Otto senior, for example. It was no surprise to see photographic evidence that Otto senior and Doris had been sweethearts—she'd already told Wallingford about that—but the photos of the Clausens' marriage were more than Patrick could bear. There was in their photographs not only their obvious pleasure, which was always of the moment, but also their anticipated happiness—their unwavering expectations of a future together, and of a baby in that future.

And what was the setting of the pictures that so seized Wallingford's attention? It was neither Appleton nor Green Bay. It was the cottage on the lake, of course! The weathered dock; the lonely, dark water; the dark, abiding pines.

There was also a photo of the boathouse apartment under construction, and there were Otto's and Doris's wet bathing suits, drying in the sunlight on the dock. Surely the water had lapped against the rocking boats, and—especially before a storm—it must have slapped against the dock. Patrick had heard it many times.

Wallingford recognized in the photographs the source of the recurrent dream that wasn't quite his. And always underlying that dream was the *other* one, the one the prescience pill had inspired—that wettest of all wet dreams brought on by the unnamed Indian painkiller, now banned.

Looking at the photographs, Wallingford began to realize that it was not the "unmanly" loss of his hand that had conclusively turned his ex-wife against him; instead, in refusing to have children, he'd already lost her. Patrick could see how the paternity suit, even though it proved to be false, had been the bitterest pill for Marilyn to swallow. She'd wanted children. How had he underestimated the urgency of that?

Now, as he held Otto junior, Wallingford wondered how he could not have wanted one of these. His own baby in his arms!

He cried. Doris and her mother cried with him. Then they shut off the tears because the twenty-four-hour international news team was there. Although he was not the reporter assigned to this story, Wallingford could have predicted all the shots.

"Get a close-up of the hand, maybe the baby with the hand," Patrick heard one of his colleagues say. "Get the mother and the hand and the baby together." And later, in a sharply spoken aside to the cameraman: "I don't care if Pat's *head* is in the frame, just so his *hand* is there!"

On the plane back to Boston, Wallingford remembered how happy Doris had looked; although he rarely prayed, he prayed for the health of Otto junior. He hadn't realized that a hand transplant would make him so emotional, but he knew it wasn't just the hand.

Dr. Zajac had warned him that any decline in his slowly acquired dexterity could be a sign of a rejection reaction. Also, rejection reactions could occur in the skin. Patrick had been surprised to hear this. He'd always known that his own immune system could destroy the new hand, but why *skin*? There seemed to be so many more important, internal functions that could go wrong. "Skin is a bugger," Dr. Zajac had said.

No doubt "bugger" was an Irma-ism. She and

Zajac, whom she called Nicky, were in the habit of renting videos and watching them in bed at night. But being in bed led to other things—Irma was pregnant, for example—and in the last video they'd watched, many of the characters had called one another *buggers.*

That skin could be a bugger would be imparted to Patrick soon enough. On the first Monday in January, the day after the Packers dropped that wild-card game in San Francisco, Wallingford flew to Green Bay. The town was in mourning; the lobby of his hotel was like a funeral home. He checked into his room, he showered, he shaved. When he called Doris, her mother answered the phone. Both the baby and Doris were napping; she'd have Doris call him at his hotel when she woke up. Patrick was considerate enough to ask her to pass along his condolences to Doris's father. "About the 49ers, I mean."

Wallingford was still napping—dreaming of the cottage on the lake—when Mrs. Clausen came to his hotel room. She hadn't called first. Her mother was watching the baby. She'd brought the car and would drive Patrick to her house to see Otto junior a little later.

Wallingford didn't know what this meant. Was she seeking a moment to be alone with him? Did she want some contact, if only with the hand, that she didn't want her mother to see? But when Patrick touched her face with the palm of his hand—being careful to touch her with his *left* hand, of course—

Mrs. Clausen abruptly turned her face away. And when he thought about touching her breasts, he could see that she'd read his mind and was repulsed.

Doris didn't even take off her coat. She'd had no ulterior motive for coming to his hotel. She must have felt like taking a drive—that was all.

This time, when Wallingford saw the baby, little Otto appeared to recognize him. This was highly unlikely; nevertheless, it further broke Patrick's heart. He got back on the plane to Boston with a disturbing premonition. Not only had Doris permitted no contact with the hand—she'd barely looked at it! Had Otto junior stolen all her affection and attention?

Wallingford had a bad week or more in Boston, pondering the signals Mrs. Clausen might be sending him. She'd said something about how, when little Otto was older, he might like seeing and holding his father's hand from time to time. What did she mean by "older"—how much older? What had she meant, "from time to time"? Was Doris trying to tell Patrick that she intended to see him *less*? Her recent coldness to the hand caused Wallingford his worst insomnia since the pain immediately following his surgery. Something was wrong.

Now when Wallingford dreamed of the lake, he felt cold—a wet-bathing-suit-after-the-sun-has-gone-down kind of cold. While this had been one of several sensations he'd experienced in the Indian painkiller dream, in this new version his wet bathing suit never led to sex. It led nowhere. All Patrick felt was cold, a kind of up-north cold.

Then, not long after his Green Bay visit, he woke up unusually early one morning with a fever—he thought it was the flu. He had a good look at his left hand in the bathroom mirror. (He'd been training the hand to brush his teeth; it was an excellent exercise, his physical therapist had told him.) The hand was green. The new color began about two inches above his wrist and darkened at his fingertips and the tip of his thumb. It was the mossy-green color of a well-shaded lake under a cloudy sky. It was the color of firs from a distance, or in the mist; it was the blackening dark green of pine trees reflected in water. Wallingford's temperature was 104.

He thought of calling Mrs. Clausen before he called Dr. Zajac, but there was an hour's time difference between Boston and Green Bay and he didn't want to wake up the new mother or her baby. When he phoned Zajac, the doctor said he'd meet him at the hospital—adding, "I told you skin was a bugger."

"But it's been a *year*!" Wallingford cried. "I can tie my shoes! I can drive! I can *almost* pick up a quarter. I've come close to picking up a *dime*!"

"You're in uncharted water," Zajac replied. The doctor and Irma had seen a video with that lamentable title, *Uncharted Water,* the night before. "All we know is, you're still in the fifty-percent-probability range."

"Fifty percent probability of *what*?" Patrick asked.

"Of rejection *or* acceptance, pal," Zajac said. "Pal" was Irma's new name for Medea.

They had to remove the hand before Mrs. Clausen could get to Boston, bringing her baby and her mother with her. There would be no last looks, Dr. Zajac had to tell Mrs. Clausen—the hand was too ugly.

Wallingford was resting fairly comfortably when Doris came to his bedside in the hospital. He was in some pain, but there was nothing comparable to what he'd felt after the attachment. Nor was Wallingford mourning the loss of his hand, again—it was losing Mrs. Clausen that he feared.

"But you can still come see me, *and* little Otto," Doris assured him. "We'd enjoy a visit, from time to time. You *tried* to give Otto's hand a life!" she cried. "You did your best. I'm proud of you, Patrick."

This time, she paid no attention to the whopping bandage, which was so big that it looked as if there might still be a hand under it. While it pleased Wallingford that Mrs. Clausen took his right hand and held it to her heart, albeit briefly, he was suffering from the near-certain foreknowledge that she might not clutch this remaining hand to her bosom ever again.

"I'm proud of *you* . . . of what you've done," Wallingford told her; he began to cry.

"With your help," she whispered, blushing. She let his hand go.

"I love you, Doris," Patrick said.

"But you can't," she replied, not unkindly. "You just can't."

Dr. Zajac had no explanation for the suddenness of the rejection—that is, he had nothing to say beyond the strictly pathological.

Wallingford could only guess what had happened. Had the hand felt Mrs. Clausen's love shift from it to the child? Otto might have known that his hand would give his wife the baby they'd tried and tried to have together, but how much had his *hand* known? Probably nothing.

As it turned out, Wallingford needed only a little time to accept the end result of the fifty-percent-probability range. After all, he knew divorce—he'd been rejected before. Physically *and* psychologically speaking, losing the first hand had been harder than losing Otto's. No doubt Mrs. Clausen had helped Wallingford feel that Otto's hand was never quite his. (We can only guess what a medical ethicist might have thought of that.)

Now when Wallingford tried to dream of the cottage on the lake, nothing was there. Not the smell of the pine needles, which he'd first struggled to imagine but had since grown used to; not the lap of the water, not the cries of the loons.

It is true, as they say, that you can feel pain in an amputated limb long after the limb is gone, but this came as no surprise to Patrick Wallingford. The fingertips of Otto's left hand, which had touched Mrs.

Clausen so lightly, had been without feeling; yet Patrick had truly felt Doris when the hand touched her. When, in his sleep, he would raise his bandaged stump to his face, Wallingford believed he could still smell Mrs. Clausen's sex on his missing fingers.

"Ache all gone?" she'd asked him.

Now the ache wouldn't leave him; it seemed as permanently a part of him as his not having a left hand.

Patrick Wallingford was still in the hospital on January 24, 1999, when the first *successful* hand transplant in the United States was performed in Louisville, Kentucky. The recipient, Matthew David Scott, was a New Jersey man who'd lost his left hand in a fireworks accident thirteen years before the attachment surgery. According to *The New York Times,* "a donor hand suddenly became available."

A medical ethicist called the Louisville hand transplant "a justifiable experiment"; unremarkably, not every medical ethicist agreed. ("The hand is not essential for life," as the *Times* put it.)

The head of the surgical team for the Louisville operation made the now-familiar point about the transplanted hand: that there was only "a fifty-percent probability that it will survive a year, and after that we just really don't know." He was a hand surgeon, after all; like Dr. Zajac, of course he would talk about "it" surviving, meaning the hand.

Wallingford's all-news network, aware that Patrick was still recovering in a Boston hospital, interviewed a spokesperson for Schatzman, Gingeleskie, Mengerink, Zajac & Associates. Zajac thought the so-called spokesperson must have been Mengerink, because the statement, while correct, demonstrated a characteristic insensitivity to Wallingford's recent loss. The statement read: "Animal experiments have shown that rejection reactions rarely occur before seven days, and ninety percent of the reactions occur in the first three months," which meant that Patrick's rejection reaction was out of sync with the animals'.

But Wallingford wasn't offended by the statement. He wholeheartedly wished Matthew David Scott well. Of course he might have felt more affinity for the world's very first hand transplant, because it, like his, had failed. That one was performed in Ecuador in 1964; in two weeks, the recipient rejected the donor's hand. "At the time, only crude anti-rejection therapy was available," the *Times* pointed out. (In '64, we didn't have the immunosuppressant drugs that are in standard use in heart, liver, and kidney transplants today.)

Once out of the hospital, Patrick Wallingford moved quickly back to New York, where his career blossomed. He was made the anchor for the evening news; his popularity soared. He'd once been a faintly mocking commentator on the kind of calamity that had befallen him; he'd heretofore behaved as if there were less sympathy for the bizarre death, the bizarre loss, the bizarre grief, simply because they were bizarre. He knew now that the bizarre was commonplace, hence not bizarre at all. It was all death, all loss, all grief—no matter how stupid. Somehow, as an anchor, he conveyed this, and thereby made people feel cautiously better about what was indisputably bad.

But what Wallingford could do in front of a TV camera, he could not duplicate in what we call real life. This was most obvious with Mary whatever-her-name-was—Patrick utterly failed to make her feel even a little bit good. She'd gone through an acrimonious divorce without realizing that there was rarely any other kind. She was still childless. And while she'd become the smartest of the New York newsroom women, with whom Wallingford now worked again, Mary was not as nice as she'd once been. There was something edgy about her behavior; in her eyes, where Wallingford had formerly spotted only candor and an acute vulnerability, there was evidence of irritability, impatience, and cunning. These were all qualities that the other New York newsroom women had in spades. It saddened Wallingford to see Mary descending to their level—or growing up, as those other women would doubtless say.

Still Wallingford wanted to befriend her—that was truly *all* he wanted to do. To that end, he had dinner with her once a week. But she always drank too much and, when Mary drank, their dinner conversation turned to that topic between them which Wallingford vigilantly tried to avoid—namely, why he wouldn't sleep with her.

"Am I *that* unattractive to you?" she would usually begin.

"You're *not* unattractive to me, Mary. You're a very good-looking girl."

"Yeah, right."

"Please, Mary—"

"I'm not asking you to marry me," Mary would say. "Just a weekend away somewhere—just one night, for Christ's sake! Just *try* it! You might even be interested in more than one night."

"Mary, *please*—"

"Jesus, Pat—you used to fuck *any*one! How do you think it makes me feel . . . that you won't fuck *me*?"

"Mary, I want to be your friend. A good one."

"Okay, I'll be blunt—you've forced me," Mary told him. "I want you to make me pregnant. I want a baby. You'd produce a good-looking baby. Pat, I want your *sperm*. Is that okay? I want your *seed*."

We can imagine that Wallingford was a little reluctant to act on this proposition. It wasn't as if he didn't know what Mary meant; he just wasn't sure that he wanted to go through all that again. Yet, in one sense, Mary was right: Wallingford *would* produce a good-looking kid. He already had.

Patrick was tempted to tell Mary the truth: that he'd made a baby, and that he loved his baby very much; that he loved Doris Clausen, the beer-truck driver's widow, too. But as seemingly nice as Mary was, she still worked in the New York newsroom,

didn't she? She was a journalist, wasn't she? Wallingford would have been crazy to tell her the truth.

"What about a sperm bank?" Patrick asked Mary
one night. "I would be willing to consider making a
contribution to a sperm bank, if you really have your
heart set on having my child."

"You shit!" Mary cried. "You can't stand the
thought of fucking me, can you? Jesus, Pat—do you
need two hands just to get it up? What's the matter
with you? Or is it *me*?"

It was an outburst of the kind that would put an
end to their having dinner together on a weekly basis,
at least for a while. On that upsetting evening, when
Patrick had the taxi drop Mary at her apartment
building first, she wouldn't even say good night.

Wallingford, who was understandably distracted,
told the taxi driver the wrong address. By the time
Patrick realized his mistake, the cabbie had left him
outside his old apartment building on East Sixty-
second Street, where he'd lived with Marilyn. There
was nothing to do but walk half a block to Park Avenue and hail an uptown cab; he was too tired to walk
the twenty-plus blocks. But naturally the confused
doorman recognized him and came running out on
the sidewalk before Patrick could slip away.

"Mr. Wallingford!" Vlad or Vlade or Lewis said,
in surprise.

"Paul O'Neill," Patrick said, alarmed. He held
out his one and only hand. "Bats left, throws left—
remember?"

"Oh, Mr. Wallingford, Paul O'Neill couldn't hold a fuckin' Roman candle to you! That's a kinda firecracker," the doorman explained. "I *love* the new show! Your interview with the legless child . . . you know, that kid who fell or was pushed into the polar-bear tank."

"I know, Vlade," Patrick said.

"It's Lewis," Vlad said. "Anyway, I just *loved* it! And that miserable fuckin' woman who was given the results of her sister's *smear* test—I don't believe it!"

"I had trouble believing that one myself," Wallingford admitted. "It's called a Pap smear."

"Your wife's with someone," the doorman noted slyly. "I mean *tonight* she's with someone."

"She's my *ex*-wife," Patrick reminded him.

"Most nights she's alone."

"It's her life," Wallingford said.

"Yeah, I know. You're just payin' for it!" the doorman replied.

"I have no complaints about how she lives her life," Patrick said. "I live uptown now, on East Eighty-third Street."

"Don't worry, Mr. Wallingford," the doorman told him. "I won't tell anybody!"

As for the missing hand, Patrick had learned to enjoy waving his stump at the television camera; he happily demonstrated his repeated failures with a variety of prosthetic devices, too.

"Look here—there are people only a little better

coordinated than I am who have mastered this gizmo," Wallingford liked to begin. "The other day, I watched a guy cut his dog's toenails with one of these things. It was a frisky dog, too."

But the results were predictably the same: Patrick would spill his coffee in his lap, or he would get his prosthesis snagged in his microphone wire and pop the little mike off his lapel.

In the end he would be one-handed again, nothing artificial. "For twenty-four-hour international news, this is Patrick Wallingford. Good night, Doris," he would always sign off, waving his stump. "Good night, my little Otto."

Patrick would be a long time re-entering the dating scene. After he tried it, the pace disappointed him— it seemed either too fast or too slow. He felt out of step, so he stopped altogether. He occasionally got laid when he traveled, but now that he was an anchor, not a field reporter, he didn't travel as much as he used to. Besides, you can't call getting laid "dating"; Wallingford, typically, wouldn't have called it any-thing at all.

At least there was nothing comparable to the an-ticipation he'd felt when Mrs. Clausen would roll on her side, away from him, holding his (or was it Otto's?) hand at first against her side and then against her stomach, where the unborn child was waiting to kick him. There would be no matching that, or the taste of the back of her neck, or the smell of her hair.

Patrick Wallingford had lost his left hand twice,

but he'd gained a soul. It was both loving and losing Mrs. Clausen that had given Patrick his soul. It was both his longing for her and the sheer wishing her well; it was getting back his left hand and losing it again, too. It was wanting his child to be Otto Clausen's child, almost as much as Doris had wanted this; it was loving, even unrequited, both Otto junior and the little boy's mother. And such was the size of the ache in Patrick's soul that it was *visible*—even on television. Not even the confused doorman could mistake him for Paul O'Neill, not anymore.

He was still the lion guy, but something in him had risen above that image of his mutilation; he was still disaster man, but he anchored the evening news with a newfound authority. He had actually mastered the look he'd first practiced in bars at the cocktail hour, when he was feeling sorry for himself. The look still said, *Pity me,* only now his sadness seemed approachable.

But Wallingford was unimpressed by the progress of his soul. It may have been noticeable to others, but what did that matter? He didn't have Doris Clausen, did he?

CHAPTER NINE

Wallingford Meets a Fellow Traveler

MEANWHILE, AN ATTRACTIVE, photogenic woman with a limp had just turned sixty. As a teenager, and all her adult life, she'd worn long skirts or dresses to conceal her withered leg. She'd been the last person in her hometown to come down with poliomyelitis; the Salk vaccine was available too late for her. For almost as long as she'd had the deformity, she'd been writing a book with this provocative title: *How I Almost Missed Getting Polio.* She said that the end of the century struck her as "as good a time as any" to make multiple submissions to more than a dozen publishers, but they all turned her book down.

"Bad luck or not, polio or whatever, the book isn't very well written," the woman with the limp and the withered leg admitted to Patrick Wallingford, on-camera. She looked terrific when she was sitting down. "It's just that everything in my life happened because I didn't get that damn vaccine. I got polio instead."

Of course she quickly acquired a publisher after her interview with Wallingford, and almost overnight she had a new title: *I Got Polio Instead.* Someone rewrote the book for her, and someone else would make a movie of it—starring a woman who looked nothing at all like the woman with the limp and the withered leg, except that the actress was attractive and photogenic, too. That was what being on-camera with Wallingford could do for you.

Nor would Patrick miss the irony that when he'd lost his left hand the first time, the world had been watching. In those best-of-the-century moments that were positively made for television, the lion-eating-the-hand episode was always included. Yet when he'd lost his hand the second time—more to the point, when he'd lost Mrs. Clausen—the camera wasn't on him. What mattered most to Wallingford had gone unrecorded.

The new century, at least for a while, would remember Patrick as the lion guy. But it was neither news nor history that, if Wallingford were keeping score of his life, he wouldn't have started counting until he met Doris Clausen. So much for how the world keeps score.

In the category of transplant surgery, Patrick Wallingford would not be remembered. At the close of the century, one counts the successes, not the failures. Thus, in the field of hand-transplant surgery, Dr. Nicholas M. Zajac would remain unfamous, his moment of possible greatness surpassed by what truly became the first successful hand-transplant procedure in the United States, and only the second ever. "The fireworks guy," as Zajac crudely called Matthew David Scott, appeared to have what Dr. Zajac termed a keeper.

On April 12, 1999, less than three months after receiving a new left hand, Mr. Scott threw out the ceremonial first pitch at the Phillies' opening game in Philadelphia. Wallingford wasn't exactly jealous. (Envious . . . well, maybe. But not in the way you might think.) In fact, Patrick asked Dick, his news editor, if he could interview the evident "keeper." Wouldn't it be fitting, Wallingford suggested, to congratulate Mr. Scott for having what he (Wallingford) had lost? But Dick, of all people, thought the idea was "tacky." As a result, Dick was fired, though many would argue he was a news editor waiting to be fired.

Any euphoria among the New York newsroom women was short-lived. The new news editor was as much of a dick as Dick had ever been; anticlimactically, his name was Fred. As Mary whatever-her-name-was would say—Mary had developed a sharper tongue in the intervening years—"If I'm going to be dicked around, I think I'd rather be Dicked than *Fredded*."

In the new century, that same international team of surgeons who performed the *world*'s first successful hand transplant in Lyon, France, would try again, this time attempting the world's first *double* hand-and-forearm transplant. The recipient, whose name was not made public, would be a thirty-three-year-old Frenchman who'd lost both his hands in a fireworks accident (another one) in 1996, the donor a nineteen-year-old who had fallen off a bridge.

But Wallingford would be interested only in the fates of the first two recipients. The first, ex-convict Clint Hallam, would have his new hand amputated by one of the surgeons who performed the transplant operation. Two months prior to the amputation, Hallam had stopped taking the medication prescribed as part of his anti-rejection treatment. He was observed wearing a leather glove to hide the hand, which he described as "hideous." (Hallam would later deny failing to take his medication.) And he would continue his strained relationship with the law. Mr. Hallam had been seized by the French police for allegedly stealing money and an American Express card from a liver-transplant patient who'd befriended him in the hospital in Lyon. While he was eventually allowed to leave France—after he repaid some of the money—the police would issue warrants for Hallam's arrest in Australia concerning his possible role in a fuel scam. (It seems that Zajac was right about him.)

The second, Matthew David Scott of Absecon,

New Jersey, is the only successful recipient of a new hand whom Wallingford would admit to envying in an interesting way. It was never Mr. Scott's new hand that Patrick Wallingford envied. But in the media coverage of that Phillies game, where the fireworks guy threw out the first ball, Wallingford noted that Matthew David Scott had his son with him. What Patrick envied Mr. Scott was his *son.*

He'd had premonitions of what he would call the "fatherhood feeling" when he was still recovering from losing Otto senior's hand. The painkillers were nothing special, but they may have been what prompted Patrick to watch his first Super Bowl. Of course he didn't know how to watch a Super Bowl. You're not supposed to watch a game like that alone.

He kept wanting to call Mrs. Clausen and ask her to explain what was happening in the game, but Super Bowl XXXIII was the symbolic anniversary of Otto Clausen's accident (or suicide) in his beer truck; furthermore, the Packers weren't playing. Therefore, Doris had told Patrick that she intended to lock herself away from sight or sound of the game. He would be on his own.

Wallingford drank a beer or two, but what people liked about watching football eluded him. To be fair, it was a bad matchup; while the Broncos won their second straight Super Bowl, and their fans were no doubt delighted, it was not a close or even a competitive game. The Atlanta Falcons had no business being in the Super Bowl in the first place. (At least that was the opinion of everyone Wallingford would later talk to in Green Bay.)

Yet, even distractedly watching the Super Bowl, Patrick for the first time could imagine going to a Packer home game at Lambeau Field with Doris and Otto junior. Or just with little Otto, maybe when the boy was a bit older. The idea had surprised him, but that was January 1999. By April of that year, when Wallingford watched Matthew David Scott and his son at the Phillies game, the thought was no longer surprising; he'd had a couple more months of missing Otto junior and the boy's mother. Even if it was true that he'd lost Mrs. Clausen, Wallingford rightly feared that if he didn't make an effort to see more of little Otto now—meaning the summer of '99, when Otto junior was still only eight months old (he wasn't quite crawling)—there would simply be no relationship to build on when the boy was older.

The one person in New York to whom Wallingford confided his fears of the missed opportunity of fatherhood was Mary. Boy, was she a bad choice for a confidante! When Patrick said that he longed to be "more like a father" to Otto junior, Mary reminded him that he could knock her up anytime he felt like it and become the father of a child living in New York.

"You don't have to go to Green Bay, Wisconsin, to be a father, Pat," Mary told him.

How she'd gone from being such a nice girl to expressing her one-note wish to have Wallingford's *seed* was not a credit to the other women in the New

York newsroom, or so Patrick believed. He continued to overlook the fact that *men* had been a far greater influence on Mary. She'd had problems with men, or at least she thought she had. (Same difference.)

Every weeknight, when he concluded his telecast, Wallingford never knew if they were watching when he said, "Good night, Doris. Good night, my little Otto." Mrs. Clausen had not once called to say she'd seen the evening news.

It was July 1999. There was a heat wave in New York. It was a Friday. Most summer weekends, Wallingford went to Bridgehampton, where he'd rented a house. Except for the swimming pool—Patrick made a point of not swimming in the ocean with one hand—it was really like staying in the city. He saw all the same people at the same kinds of parties, which, in fact, was what Wallingford and a lot of other New Yorkers liked about being out there.

That weekend, friends had invited him to the Cape; he was supposed to fly to Martha's Vineyard. But even before he felt a slight prickling where his hand had been detached—some of the twinges seemed to extend to the empty space where his left hand used to be—he'd phoned his friends and canceled the trip with some bullshit excuse.

At the time, he didn't know how lucky he was, not to be flying to Martha's Vineyard that Friday night. Then he remembered that he'd lent his house in Bridgehampton for the weekend. A bunch of the New York newsroom women were having a weekend-long baby shower there. Or an orgy, Patrick cynically imagined. He passingly wondered if Mary would be there. (That was the old Patrick Wallingford wondering.) But Patrick didn't ask Mary if she was one of the women using his summer house that weekend. If he'd asked, she would have known he was free and offered to change her plans.

Wallingford was still undervaluing how sensitive and vulnerable women who have struggled to have a child were; a weekend-long baby shower for someone else would not likely have been Mary's choice.

So he was in New York on a Friday in mid-July with no weekend plans and nowhere to go. As he sat in makeup for the Friday-evening news, he thought of calling Mrs. Clausen. He had never invited himself to Green Bay; he'd always waited to be invited. Yet both Doris and Patrick were aware that the intervals between her invitations had grown longer. (The last time he'd been in Wisconsin, there was still snow on the ground.)

What if Wallingford simply called her and said, "Hi! What are you and little Otto doing this weekend? How about I come to Green Bay?" Remarkably, without second-guessing himself, he just did it; he called her out of the blue.

"Hello," said her voice on the answering machine. "Little Otto and I are up north for the weekend. No phone. Back Monday."

He didn't leave a message, but he did leave some makeup on the mouthpiece of the phone. He was so distracted by hearing Mrs. Clausen's voice on the answering machine, and even more distracted by that half-imagined, half-dreamed image of her at the cottage on the lake, that without thinking he attempted to wipe the makeup off the mouthpiece with his left hand. He was surprised when the stump of his left forearm made contact with the phone—that was the first twinge.

When he hung up, the prickling sensations continued. He kept looking at his stump, expecting to see ants, or some other small insects, crawling over the scar tissue. But there was nothing there. He knew there couldn't be bugs *under* the scar tissue, yet he felt them all through the telecast.

Later Mary would remark that there'd been something listless in the delivery of his usually cheerful good-night wishes to Doris and little Otto, but Wallingford knew that they couldn't have been watching. There was no electricity at the cottage on the lake— Mrs. Clausen had told him that. (For the most part, she seemed unwilling to talk about the place up north, and when she did talk about it, her voice was shy and hard to hear.)

The prickling sensations continued while Patrick had his makeup removed; his skin crawled. Because he was thinking about something Dr. Zajac had said to him, Wallingford was only vaguely mindful that the regular makeup girl was on vacation. He supposed she had a crush on him—he'd not yet been tempted. He thought it was the way she chewed her gum that he missed. Only now, in her absence, did he fleetingly imagine her in a new way—naked. But the supernatural twinges in his nonhand kept distracting him, as did his memory of Zajac's blunt advice.

"Don't mess around if you ever think you need me." Therefore, Patrick didn't mess around. He called Zajac at home, although he assumed that Boston's most renowned hand surgeon would be spending his summer weekends out of town.

Actually, Dr. Zajac had rented a place in Maine that summer, but only for the month of August, when he would have custody of Rudy. Medea, now more often called Pal, would eat a ton of raw clams and mussels, shells and all; but the dog had seemingly outgrown a taste for her own turds, and Rudy and Zajac played lacrosse with a lacrosse ball. The boy had even attended a lacrosse clinic in the first week of July. Rudy was with Zajac for the weekend, in Cambridge, when Wallingford called.

Irma answered the phone. "Yeah, what is it?" she said.

Wallingford contemplated the remote possibility that Dr. Zajac had an unruly teenage daughter. He knew only that Zajac had a younger child, a six- or seven-year-old boy—like Matthew David Scott's son. In his mind's eye, Patrick was forever seeing that unknown little boy in a baseball jersey, his hands raised like his father's—both of them celebrating that victory pitch in Philadelphia. (A "victory pitch" was how someone in the media had described it.)

"*Yeah?*" Irma said again. Was she a surly, over-sexed babysitter for Zajac's little boy? Perhaps she was the housekeeper, except she sounded too coarse to be Dr. Zajac's housekeeper.

"Is Dr. Zajac there?" Wallingford asked.

"This is *Mrs.* Zajac," Irma answered. "Who wants him?"

"This is Patrick Wallingford. Dr. Zajac operated on—"

"Nicky!" Patrick heard Irma yell, although she'd partly covered the mouthpiece of the phone with her hand. "It's the lion guy!"

Wallingford could identify some of the background noise: almost certainly a child, definitely a dog, and the unmistakable thudding of a ball. There was the scrape of a chair and the scrambling sound of the dog's claws slipping on a wood floor. It must have been some kind of game. Were they trying to keep the ball away from the dog? Zajac, out of breath, finally came to the phone.

When Wallingford finished describing his symptoms, he added hopefully, "Maybe it's just the weather."

"The weather?" Zajac asked.

"You know—the heat wave," Patrick explained.

"Aren't you indoors most of the time?" Zajac asked. "Don't they have air-conditioning in New York?"

"It's not always pain," Wallingford went on. "Some-times the sensation is like the start of something that doesn't go anywhere. I mean you think the twinge or the prickle is going to lead to pain, but it doesn't—it just stops as soon as it starts. Like something inter-rupted . . . something electrical."

"Precisely," Dr. Zajac told him. What did Walling-ford expect? Zajac reminded him that, only five months after the attachment surgery, he'd regained twenty-two centimeters of nerve regeneration.

"I remember," Patrick replied.

"Well, look at it this way," Zajac said. "Those nerves still have something to say."

"But why *now*?" Wallingford asked him. "It's been half a year since I lost it. I've felt something before, but nothing this *specific*. I actually feel like I'm *touching* something with my left middle finger or my left index finger, and I don't even have a left *hand*!"

"What's going on in the rest of your life?" Dr. Zajac responded. "I assume there's some stress at-tached to your line of work? I don't know how your love life is progressing, or *if* it's progressing, but I re-member that your love life seemed to be a matter of some concern to you—or so you said. Just remem-ber, there are other factors affecting nerves, includ-ing nerves that have been cut off."

"They don't feel 'cut off'—that's what I mean," Wallingford told him.

"That's what *I* mean," Zajac replied. "What you're feeling is known medically as 'paresthesia'—a wrong sensation, beyond perception. The nerve that used to make you feel pain or touch in your left middle finger, or in your left index finger, has been severed twice—first by a lion and then by me! That cut fiber is still sitting somewhere in the stump of your nerve bundle, accompanied by millions of other fibers coming from and going everywhere. If that neuron is stimulated at the tip of your nerve stump—by touch, by memory, by a *dream*—it sends the same old message it always did. The feelings that seem to come from where your left hand used to be are being registered by the same nerve fibers and pathways that *used to* come from your left hand. Do you get it?"

"Sort of," Wallingford replied. ("Not really," was what he should have said.) Patrick kept looking at his stump—the invisible ants were crawling there again. He'd forgotten to mention the sensation of crawling insects to Dr. Zajac, but the doctor didn't give him time.

Dr. Zajac could tell that his patient wasn't satisfied. "Look," Zajac continued, "if you're worried about it, fly up here. Stay in a nice hotel. I'll see you in the morning."

"Saturday morning?" Patrick said. "I don't want to ruin your weekend."

"I'm not going anywhere," Dr. Zajac told him. "I'll just have to find someone to unlock the building. I've done that before. I have my own keys to the office."

Wallingford wasn't really worried about his missing hand anymore, but what else was he going to do this weekend?

"Come on—take the shuttle up here," Zajac was telling him. "I'll see you in the morning, just to put your mind at ease."

"At what time?" Wallingford asked.

"Ten o'clock," Zajac told him. "Stay at the Charles—it's in Cambridge, on Bennett Street, near Harvard Square. They have a great gym, and a pool."

Wallingford acquiesced. "Okay. I'll see if I can get a reservation."

"I'll get you a reservation," Zajac said. "They know me, and Irma has a membership at their health club." Irma, Wallingford deduced, must be the wife—she of the less-than-golden tongue.

"Thank you," was all that Wallingford could say. In the background, he could hear the happy shrieks of Dr. Zajac's son, the growls and romping of the savage-sounding dog, the bouncing of the hard, heavy ball.

"Not on my stomach!" Irma shouted. Patrick heard that, too. Not *what* on her stomach? Wallingford had no way of knowing that Irma was pregnant, much less that she was expecting twins; while she wasn't due until mid-September, she was already as big around as the largest of the songbirds' cages. Obviously, she didn't want a child or a dog jumping on her stomach.

Patrick said good night to the gang in the news-room; he'd never been the last of the evening-news people to leave. Nor would he be tonight, for there was Mary waiting for him by the elevators. What she'd overheard of his telephone conversation had misled her. Her face was bathed in tears.

"Who is she?" Mary asked him.

"Who's *who*?" Wallingford said.

"She must be married, if you're seeing her on a Saturday morning."

"Mary, please—"

"Whose weekend are you afraid of ruining?" she asked. "Isn't that how you put it?"

"Mary, I'm going to Boston to see my hand surgeon."

"Alone?"

"Yes, alone."

"Take me with you," Mary said. "If you're alone, why not take me? How much time can you spend with your hand surgeon, anyway? You can spend the rest of the weekend with me!"

He took a chance, a big one, and told her the truth. "Mary, I can't take you. I don't want you to have my baby because I already *have* a baby, and I don't get to see enough of him. I don't want another baby that I don't get to see enough of."

"Oh," she said, as if he'd hit her. "I see. That was clarifying. You're not always clear, Pat. I appreciate you being so clear."

"I'm sorry, Mary."

"It's the Clausen kid, isn't it? I mean he's actually yours. Is that it, Pat?"

"Yes," Patrick replied. "But it's not news, Mary. Please, let's not make it news."

He could see she was angry. The air-conditioning was cool, even cold, but Mary was suddenly colder. "Who do you think I am?" she growled. "What do you take me for?"

"One of us," was all Wallingford could say.

As the elevator door closed, he could see her pacing; her arms were folded across her small, shapely breasts. She wore a summery, tan-colored skirt and a peach-colored cardigan, buttoned at her throat but otherwise open down the front—"an anti-air-conditioning sweater," he'd heard one of the newsroom women call such cardigans. Mary wore the sweater over a white silk T-shirt. She had a long neck, a nice figure, smooth skin, and Patrick especially liked her mouth, which had a way of making him question his principle of not sleeping with her.

At La Guardia, he was put on standby for the first available shuttle to Boston; there was a seat for him on the second flight. It was growing dark as his plane landed at Logan, and there was a little fog or light haze over Boston Harbor.

Patrick would think about this later, recalling that his flight landed in Boston about the same time John F. Kennedy, Jr., was trying to land his plane at the airport in Martha's Vineyard, not very far away. Or else young Kennedy was trying to *see* Martha's Vineyard through that same indeterminate light, in something similar to that haze.

Wallingford checked into the Charles before ten and went immediately to the indoor swimming pool, where he spent a restorative half hour by himself. He would have stayed longer, but they closed the pool at ten-thirty. Wallingford—with his one hand—enjoyed floating and treading water. In keeping with his personality, he was a good floater.

He'd planned to get dressed and walk around Harvard Square after his swim. Summer school was in session; there would be students to look at, to remind him of his misspent youth. He could probably find a place to have a decent dinner with a good bottle of wine. In one of the bookstores on the square, he might spot something more gripping to read than the book he'd brought with him, which was a biography of Byron the size of a cinder block. But even in the taxi from the airport, Wallingford had felt the oppressive heat getting to him; and when he went back to his room from the pool, he took off his wet bathing suit and lay down naked on the bed and closed his eyes for a minute or two. He must have been tired. When he woke up almost an hour later, the air-conditioning had chilled him. He put on a bathrobe and read the room-service menu. All he wanted was a beer and a hamburger—he no longer felt like going out.

True to himself, he would not turn on a television on the weekend. Given that the only alternative was the Byron biography, Patrick's resistance to the TV was all the more remarkable. But Wallingford fell asleep so quickly—Byron had barely been born, and the wee poet's feckless father was still alive—that the biography caused him no pain at all.

In the morning, he ate breakfast in the casual restaurant in the downstairs of the hotel. The dining room irritated him without his knowing why. It wasn't the children. Maybe there were too many grown-ups who seemed bothered by the very presence of children.

The previous night and this morning, while Wallingford was not watching television or even so much as glancing at a newspaper, the nation had been reliving one of TV's not-the-news images. JFK, Jr.'s plane was missing; it appeared that he had flown into the ocean. But there was nothing to see—hence what was shown on television, again and again, was that image of young Kennedy at his father's funeral procession. There was John junior, a three-year-old boy in shorts saluting his father's passing casket—exactly as his mother, whispering in the little boy's ear, had instructed him to do only seconds before. What Wallingford would later consider was that this image might stand as the representative moment of our country's most golden century, which has also died, although we are still marketing it.

His breakfast finished, Patrick sat at his table, trying to finish his coffee without returning the relentless stare of a middle-aged woman across the room. But she now made her way toward him. Her path was deliberate; while she pretended to be only passing by,

Wallingford knew she was going to say something to him. He could always tell. Often he could guess what the women were going to say, but not this time.

Her face had been pretty once. She wore no makeup, and her undyed brown hair was turning gray. In the crow's-feet at the corners of her dark-brown eyes there was something sad and tired that reminded Patrick of Mrs. Clausen grown older.

"Scum . . . despicable swine . . . how do you sleep at night?" the woman asked him in a harsh whisper; her teeth were clenched, her lips parted no wider than was necessary for her to spit out her words.

"Pardon me?" said Patrick Wallingford.

"It didn't take you long to get here, did it?" she asked. "Those poor families . . . the bodies not even recovered. But that doesn't stop you, does it? You thrive on other people's misfortune. You ought to call yourself the *death* network—no, the *grief* channel! Because you do more than invade people's privacy—you steal their grief! You make their private grief public before they even have a chance to grieve!"

Wallingford wrongly assumed that she was speaking generically of his TV newscasts past. He looked away from the woman's entrenched stare, but among his fellow breakfast-eaters, he saw that no assistance would be forthcoming; from their unanimously hostile expressions, they appeared to share the demented woman's view.

"I try to report what's happened with sympathy,"

Patrick began, but the near-violent woman cut him off.

"Sympathy!" she cried. "If you had an ounce of sympathy for those poor people, you'd leave them alone!"

Since the woman was clearly deranged, what could Wallingford do? He pinned his bill to the table with the stump of his left forearm, quickly adding a tip and his room number before signing his name. The woman watched him coldly. Patrick stood up from the table. As he nodded good-bye to the woman and started to leave the restaurant, he was aware of the children gaping at his missing hand.

An angry-looking sous-chef, all in white, stood glaring at Wallingford from behind a counter. "Hyena," the sous-chef said.

"Jackal!" cried an elderly man at an adjacent table.

The woman, Patrick's first attacker, said to his back: "Vulture . . . carrion feeder . . ."

Wallingford kept walking, but he could sense that the woman was following him; she accompanied him to the elevators, where he pushed the button and waited. He could hear her breathing, but he didn't look at her. When the elevator door opened, he stepped inside and allowed the door to close behind his back. Until he pushed the button for his floor and turned to face her, he didn't know that the woman was not there; he was surprised to find himself alone.

It must be Cambridge, Patrick thought—all those Harvard and M.I.T. intellectuals who loathed the crassness of the media. He brushed his teeth, right-handed, of course. He was ever-conscious of how he'd been learning to brush his teeth with his left hand when it had just up and died. Still clueless about the breaking news, he rode the elevator down to the lobby and took a taxi to Dr. Zajac's office.

It was deeply disconcerting to Patrick that Dr. Zajac—specifically, his face—smelled of sex. This evidence of a private life was not what Wallingford wanted to know about his hand surgeon, even while Zajac was reassuring him that there was nothing wrong with the sensations he was experiencing in the stump of his left forearm.

It turned out there was a word for the feeling that small, unseen insects were crawling over or under his skin. "Formication," Dr. Zajac said.

Naturally Wallingford misheard him. "Excuse me?" he asked.

"It means 'tactile hallucination.' *Formication*," the doctor repeated, "with an *m*."

"Oh."

"Think of nerves as having long memories," Zajac told him. "What's triggering those nerves isn't your missing hand. I mentioned your love life because *you* once mentioned it. As for stress, I can only imagine what a week you have ahead of you. I don't envy you the next few days. You know what I mean."

Wallingford *didn't* know what Dr. Zajac meant. What did the doctor imagine of the week Wallingford had ahead of him? But Zajac had always struck Wallingford as a little crazy. Maybe everyone in Cambridge was crazy, Patrick considered.

"It's true, I'm a little unhappy in the love-life department," Wallingford confessed, but there he paused—he had no memory of discussing his love life with Zajac. (Had the painkillers been more potent than he'd thought at the time?)

Wallingford was further confused by trying to decide what was different about Dr. Zajac's office. After all, that office was sacred ground; yet it had seemed a very different place when Mrs. Clausen was having her way with him in the exact chair in which he now sat, scanning the surrounding walls.

Of course! The photographs of Zajac's famous patients—they were gone! In their place were children's drawings. One child's drawings, actually—they were all Rudy's. Castles in heaven, Patrick would have guessed, and there were several of a large, sinking ship; doubtless the young artist had seen *Titanic*. (Both Rudy and Dr. Zajac had seen the movie twice, although Zajac had made Rudy shut his eyes during the sex scene in the car.)

As for the model in the series of photos of an increasingly pregnant young woman . . . well, not surprisingly, Wallingford felt drawn to her coarse sexuality. She must have been Irma, the self-described *Mrs.* Zajac, who'd spoken to Patrick on the phone. Wallingford learned that Irma was expecting twins only when he inquired about the empty picture frames that were hanging from the walls in half a dozen places, always in twos.

"They're for the twins, after they're born," Zajac told Patrick proudly.

No one at Schatzman, Gingeleskie, Mengerink, Zajac & Associates envied Zajac having twins, although that moron Mengerink opined that twins were what Zajac deserved for fucking Irma twice as much as Mengerink believed was "normal." Schatzman had no opinion of the upcoming birth of Dr. Zajac's twins, because Schatzman was more than retired— Schatzman had died. And Gingeleskie (the living one) had shifted his envy of Zajac to a more virulent envy of a younger colleague, someone Dr. Zajac had brought into the surgical association. Nathan Blaustein had been Zajac's best student in clinical surgery at Harvard. Dr. Zajac didn't envy young Blaustein at all. Zajac simply recognized Blaustein as his technical superior—"a physical genius."

When a ten-year-old in New Hampshire had lopped off his thumb in a snow blower, Dr. Zajac had insisted that Blaustein perform the reattachment surgery. The thumb was a mess, and it had been unevenly frozen. The boy's father had needed almost an hour to find the severed thumb in the snow; then the family had to drive two hours to Boston. But the surgery had been a success. Zajac was already lobbying his colleagues to have Blaustein's name added to the office name-

plate and letterhead—a request that caused Mengerink to seethe with resentment, and no doubt made
Schatzman and Gingeleskie (the dead one) roll in
their graves.

As for Dr. Zajac's ambitions in hand-transplant
surgery, Blaustein was now in charge of such procedures. (There would soon be many procedures of that
kind, Zajac had predicted.) While Zajac said he
would be happy to be part of the team, he believed
young Blaustein should head the operation because
Blaustein was now the best surgeon among them. No
envy or resentment there. Quite unexpectedly, even
to himself, Dr. Nicholas M. Zajac was a happy, relaxed man.

Ever since Wallingford had lost Otto Clausen's
hand, Zajac had contented himself with his inventions of prosthetic devices, which he designed and
assembled on his kitchen table while listening to
his songbirds. Patrick Wallingford was the perfect
guinea pig for Zajac's inventions, because he was
willing to model any new prosthesis on his evening
newscast—even though he chose not to wear a prosthesis himself. The publicity had been good for the
doctor.

A prosthesis of his invention—it was predictably
called "The Zajac"—was now manufactured in Germany and Japan. (The German model was mar-
ginally more expensive, but both were marketed
worldwide.) The success of "The Zajac" had permit-

ted Dr. Zajac to reduce his surgical practice to half-time. He still taught at the medical school, but he could devote more of himself to his inventions, and to Rudy and Irma and (soon) the twins.

"You should have children," Zajac was telling Patrick Wallingford, as the doctor turned out the lights in his office and the two men awkwardly bumped into each other in the dark. "Children change your life."

Wallingford hesitantly mentioned how much he wanted to construct a relationship with Otto junior. Did Dr. Zajac have any advice about the best way to connect with a young child, especially a child one saw infrequently?

"Reading aloud," Dr. Zajac replied. "There's nothing like it. Begin with *Stuart Little,* then try *Charlotte's Web.*"

"I remember those books!" Patrick cried. "I loved *Stuart Little,* and I can remember my mother weeping when she read me *Charlotte's Web.*"

"People who read *Charlotte's Web* without weeping should be lobotomized," Zajac responded. "But how old is little Otto?"

"Eight months," Wallingford answered.

"Oh, no, he's just started to crawl," Dr. Zajac said. "Wait until he's six or seven—I mean *years.* By the time he's eight or nine, he'll be reading *Stuart Little* and *Charlotte's Web* to himself, but he'll be old enough to listen to those stories when he's younger."

"Six or seven," Patrick repeated. How could he

wait that long to establish a relationship with Otto junior?

After Zajac locked his office, he and Patrick rode the elevator down to the ground floor. The doctor offered to drive his patient back to the Charles Hotel since it was on his way home, and Wallingford gladly accepted. It was on the car radio that the famous TV journalist finally learned of Kennedy's missing plane.

By now it was mostly old news to everyone but Wallingford. JFK, Jr., was, together with his wife and sister-in-law, lost at sea, presumed dead. Young Kennedy, a relatively new pilot, had been flying the plane. There was mention of the haze over Martha's Vineyard the previous night. Luggage tags had been found; later would come the luggage, then the debris from the plane itself.

"I guess it would be better if the bodies were found," Zajac remarked. "I mean better than the speculation if they're never found."

It was the speculation that Wallingford foresaw, regardless of finding or not finding the bodies. There would be at least a week of it. The coming week was the week Patrick had almost chosen for his vacation; now he wished he *had* chosen it. (He'd decided to ask for a week in the fall instead, preferably when the Green Bay Packers had a home game at Lambeau Field.)

Wallingford went back to the Charles like a man condemned. He knew what the news, which was *not* the news, would be all the next week; it was everything that was most hateful in Patrick's profession, and he would be part of it.

The *grief* channel, the woman at breakfast had said, but the deliberate stimulation of public mourning was hardly unique to the network where Wallingford worked. The overattention to death had become as commonplace on television as the coverage of bad weather; death and bad weather were what TV did best.

Whether they found the bodies or not, or regardless of how long it might take to find them—with or without what countless journalists would call "closure"—there would *be* no closure. Not until every Kennedy moment in recent history had been relived. Nor was the invasion of the Kennedy family's privacy the ugliest aspect of it. From Patrick's point of view, the principal evil was that it wasn't news—it was recycled melodrama.

Patrick's hotel room at the Charles was as silent and cool as a crypt; he lay on the bed trying to anticipate the worst before turning on the TV. Wallingford was thinking about JFK, Jr.'s older sister, Caroline. Patrick had always admired her for remaining aloof from the press. The summer house Wallingford was renting in Bridgehampton was near Sagaponack, where Caroline Kennedy Schlossberg was spending the summer with her husband and children. She had a plain but elegant kind of beauty; although she would be under intense media scrutiny now, Patrick believed that she would manage to keep her dignity intact.

In his room at the Charles, Wallingford felt too sick to his stomach to turn the TV on. If he went back to New York, not only would he have to answer the messages on his answering machine, but his phone would never stop ringing. If he stayed in his room at the Charles, he would eventually have to watch television, even though he already knew what he would see—his fellow journalists, our self-appointed moral arbiters, looking their most earnest and sounding their most sincere.

They would already have descended on Hyannisport. There would be a hedge, that ever-predictable barrier of privet, in the background of the frame. Behind the hedge, only the upstairs windows of the brilliantly white house would be visible. (They would be dormer windows, with their curtains drawn.) Yet, somehow, the journalist standing in the foreground of the shot would manage to look as if he or she had been invited.

Naturally there would be an analysis of the small plane's disappearance from the radar screen, and some sober commentary on the pilot's presumed error. Many of Patrick's fellow journalists would not pass up the opportunity to condemn JFK, Jr.'s judgment; indeed, the judgment of *all* Kennedys would be questioned. The issue of "genetic restlessness" among the male members of the family would surely be raised. And much later—say, near the end of the

following week—some of these same journalists
would declare that the coverage had been excessive.
They would then call for a halt to the process. That
was always the way.

Wallingford wondered how long it would take for
someone in the New York newsroom to ask Mary
where he was. Or was Mary herself trying to reach
him? She knew he was seeing his hand surgeon; at
the time of the procedure, Zajac's name had been in
the news. As he lay immobilized on the bed in the
cool room, Patrick found it strange that someone
from the all-news network hadn't already called him
at the Charles. Maybe Mary was also out of reach.

On an impulse, Wallingford picked up the phone
and dialed the number at his summer house in Bridgehampton. A hysterical-sounding woman answered
the phone. It was Crystal Pitney—that was her married name. Patrick couldn't remember what Crystal's
last name had been when he'd slept with her. He recalled that there was something unusual about her
lovemaking, but he couldn't think what it was.

"Patrick Wallingford is not here!" Crystal shouted
in lieu of the usual hello. "No one here knows where
he is!"

In the background, Patrick heard the television;
the familiar, self-serious droning was punctuated by
occasional outbursts from the newsroom women.

"Hello?" Crystal Pitney said into the phone. Wallingford hadn't said a word. "What are you, a creep?"

Crystal asked. "It's a *breather*—I can hear him breath-ing!" Mrs. Pitney announced to the other women.

That was it, Wallingford remembered. When he'd made love to her, Crystal had forewarned him that she had a rare respiratory condition. When she got out of breath and not enough oxygen went to her brain, she started seeing things and generally went a little crazy—an understatement, if there ever was one. Crystal had got out of breath in a hurry; before Wallingford knew what was happening, she'd bitten his nose and burned his back with the bedside lamp.

Patrick had never met Mr. Pitney, Crystal's hus-band, but he admired the man's fortitude. (By the standards of the New York newsroom women, the Pitneys had had a long marriage.)

"You pervert!" Crystal yelled. "If I could see you, I'd bite your face off!"

Patrick didn't doubt this; he hung up before Crys-tal got out of breath. He immediately put on his bathing suit and a bathrobe and went to the swim-ming pool, where no one could phone him.

The only other person in the pool besides Walling-ford was a woman swimming laps. She wore a black bathing cap, which made her head resemble the head of a seal, and she was churning up the water with choppy strokes and a flutter kick. To Patrick, she manifested the mindless intensity of a windup toy. Finding it unsettling to share the swimming pool with her, Wallingford retreated to the hot tub, where

he could be alone. He did not turn on the whirlpool
jets, preferring the water undisturbed. He gradually
grew accustomed to the heat, but no sooner had he
found a comfortable position, which was halfway between sitting and floating, than the lap-swimming
woman got out of the pool, turned on the timer for
the jets, and joined him in the bubbling hot tub.

She was a woman past the young side of middle
age. Wallingford quickly noted her unarousing body
and politely looked away.

The woman, who was disarmingly without vanity,
sat up in the roiling water so that her shoulders and
upper chest were above the surface; she pulled off
her bathing cap and shook out her flattened hair.
It was then that Patrick recognized her. She was
the woman who'd called him a "carrion feeder" at
breakfast—hounding him, with her burning eyes and
noticeable breathing, all the way to the elevators.
The woman could not now conceal her shock of
recognition, which was simultaneous to his.

She was the first to speak. "This is awkward." Her
voice had a softer edge than what Wallingford had
heard in her attack on him at breakfast.

"I don't want to antagonize you," Patrick told the
woman. "I'll just go to the swimming pool. I prefer
the pool to the hot tub, anyway." He rested the heel
of his right hand on the underwater ledge and pushed
himself to his feet. The stump of his left forearm
emerged from the water like a raw, dripping wound.

It was as if some creature below the hot tub's surface had eaten his hand. The hot water had turned the scar tissue blood-red.

The woman stood up when he did. Her wet bathing suit was not flattering—her breasts drooped; her stomach protruded like a small pouch. "Please stay a minute," the woman asked. "I want to explain."

"You don't need to apologize," Patrick replied. "In general, I agree with you. It's just that I didn't understand the context. I didn't come to Boston because JFK, Jr.'s plane was missing. I didn't even *know* about his plane when you spoke to me. I came to see my doctor, because of my hand." He instinctively lifted his stump, which he still spoke of as a hand. He quickly lowered it to his side, where it trailed in the hot tub, because he saw that, inadvertently, he'd pointed with his missing hand to her sagging breasts.

She encircled his left forearm with both her hands, pulling him into the churning hot tub with her. They sat beside each other on the underwater ledge, her hands holding him an inch or two above where he'd been dismembered. Only the lion had held him more firmly. Once again he had the sensation that the tips of his left middle and left index fingers were touching a woman's lower abdomen, although he knew those fingers were gone.

"Please listen to me," the woman said. She pulled his maimed arm into her lap. He felt the end of his

forearm tingle as his stump brushed the small bulge
of her stomach; his left elbow rested on her right
thigh.

"Okay," Wallingford said, in lieu of grabbing the
back of her neck in his right hand and forcing her
head underwater. Truly, short of half-drowning her in
the hot tub, what else could he have done?

"I was married twice, the first time when I was
very young," the woman began; her bright, excited
eyes held his attention as firmly as she held his arm.
"I lost them. The first one divorced me, the second
died. I actually loved them both."

Christ! Wallingford thought. Did every woman of
a certain age have a version of Evelyn Arbuthnot's
story? "I'm sorry," Patrick said, but the way she
squeezed his arm indicated that she didn't want to be
interrupted.

"I have two daughters, from my first marriage,"
the woman went on. "Throughout their childhood
and adolescence, I never slept. I was certain something terrible was going to happen to them, that I
would lose them, or one of them. I was afraid all the
time."

It sounded like a true story. (Wallingford couldn't
help judging the start of any story this way.)

"But they survived," the woman said, as if most
children didn't. "They're both married now and have
children of their own. I have four grandchildren. Three
girls, one boy. It kills me not to see more of them

than I do, but when I see them, I feel afraid for them. I start to worry again. I don't sleep."

Patrick felt the radiating twinges of mock pain where his left hand had been, but the woman had slightly relaxed her grip and there was an unanalyzed comfort in having his arm held so urgently in her lap, his stump pressing against the swell of her abdomen.

"Now I'm pregnant," the woman told him; his forearm didn't respond. "I'm fifty-one! I'm not supposed to get pregnant! I came to Boston to have an abortion—my doctor recommended it. But I called the clinic from the hotel this morning. I lied. I said my car had broken down and I had to reschedule the appointment. They told me they can see me next Saturday, a week from today. That gives me more time to think about it."

"Have you talked to your daughters?" Wallingford asked. Her lion's grip on his arm was there again.

"They'd try to convince me to have the baby," the woman replied, with renewed intensity. "They'd offer to raise the child with their children. But it would still be mine. I couldn't stop myself from loving it, I couldn't help but be involved. Yet I simply can't stand the fear. The mortality of children . . . it's more than I can bear."

"It's your choice," Patrick reminded her. "Whatever decision you make, I'm sure it will be the right one." The woman didn't look so sure.

Wallingford wondered who the unborn child's father was; whether or not this thought was conveyed by the tremble in his left forearm, the woman either felt it or she read his mind.

"The father doesn't know," she said. "I don't see him anymore. He was just a colleague."

Patrick had never heard the word "colleague" used so dismissively.

"I don't want my daughters to know I'm pregnant because I don't want them to know I have sex," the woman confessed. "That's also why I can't make up my mind. I don't think you should have an abortion because you're trying to keep the fact that you've had sex a secret. That's not a good enough reason."

"Who's to say what's a 'good enough' reason if it's *your* reason? It's your choice," Wallingford repeated. "It's not a decision anyone else can or should make for you."

"That's not hugely comforting," the woman told him. "I was all set to have the abortion until I saw you at breakfast. I don't understand what you triggered."

Wallingford had known from the beginning that all this would end up being his fault. He made the most tentative effort to retrieve his arm from the woman's grasp, but she was not about to let him go that easily.

"I don't know what got into me when I spoke to you. I've never spoken to anyone like that in my life!" the woman continued. "I shouldn't blame you, personally, for what the media does, or what I think they do. I was just so upset to hear about John junior, and I was even more upset by my first reaction. When I heard about his plane being lost, do you know what I thought?"

"No." Patrick shook his head; the hot water was making his forehead perspire, and he could see beads of sweat on the woman's upper lip.

"I was glad his mother was dead . . . that she didn't have to go through this. I was sorry for him, but I was glad for her that she was dead. Isn't that awful?"

"It's perfectly understandable," Wallingford replied. "You're a mother . . ." His instinct just to pat her on the knee, underwater, was sincere—that is, heartfelt without being in the least sexual. But because the instinct traveled down his left arm, there was no hand to pat her knee with. Unintentionally, he jerked his stump away from her; he'd felt the invisible crawling insects again.

For a pregnant fifty-one-year-old mother of two and a pregnant grandmother of four, the woman was undaunted by Wallingford's uncontrollable gesture. She calmly reached for his handless arm again. To Patrick's surprise, he willingly put his stump back in her lap. The woman took hold of his forearm without reproach, as if she'd only momentarily misplaced a cherished possession.

"I apologize for attacking you in public," she said sincerely. "It was uncalled for. I'm simply not myself." She gripped his forearm so tightly that an impossible pain was registered in Wallingford's missing left thumb. He flinched. "Oh, God! I've hurt you!" the woman cried, letting go of his arm. "And I haven't even asked you what your doctor said!"

"I'm okay," Patrick said. "It's principally the nerves that were regenerated when the new hand was attached. Those nerves are acting up. My doctor thought my love life was the problem, or just stress."

"Your love life," the woman repeated flatly, as if that were not a subject she cared to address. Wallingford didn't want to address it, either. "But why are you still here?" she suddenly asked.

Patrick thought she meant the hot tub. He was about to say that he was there because she'd *held* him there! Then he realized that she meant why hadn't he gone back to New York. Or, if not New York, shouldn't he be in Hyannisport or Martha's Vineyard?

Wallingford dreaded telling her that he was stalling his inevitable return to his questionable profession ("questionable" given the Kennedy spectacle, to which he would soon be contributing); yet he admitted this to the woman, however reluctantly, and further told her that he'd intended to walk to Harvard Square to pick up a couple of books that his doctor had recommended. He'd considered that he might spend what remained of the weekend reading them.

"But I was afraid someone in Harvard Square would recognize me and say something to me along the lines of what you said to me at breakfast." Patrick added: "It wouldn't have been undeserved."

"Oh, God!" the woman said again. "Tell me what

the books are. I'll go get them for you. No one ever recognizes *me*."

"That's very kind of you, but—"

"*Please* let me get the books for you! It would make me feel better!" She laughed nervously, pushing her damp hair away from her forehead.

Wallingford sheepishly told her the titles.

"Your *doctor* recommended them? Do you have children?"

"There's a little boy who's like a son to me, or I want him to be more like a son to me," Patrick explained. "But he's too young for me to read him *Stuart Little* or *Charlotte's Web*. I just want them so that I can imagine reading them to him in a few years."

"I read *Charlotte's Web* to my grandson only a few weeks ago," the woman told him. "I cried all over again—I cry every time."

"I don't remember the book very well, just my mother crying," Wallingford admitted.

"My name is Sarah Williams." There was an uncharacteristic hesitation in her voice when she said her name and held out her hand.

Patrick shook her hand, both their hands touching the foamy bubbles in the hot tub. At that moment, the whirlpool jets shut off and the water in the tub was instantly clear and still. It was a little startling and too obvious an omen, which elicited more nervous laughter from Sarah Williams, who stood up and stepped out of the tub.

Wallingford admired that way women have of getting out of the water in a wet bathing suit, a thumb or a finger automatically pulling down the back of the suit.

When she stood, her small belly looked almost flat—it was swollen ever so slightly. From his memory of Mrs. Clausen's pregnancy, Wallingford guessed that Sarah Williams couldn't have been more than two, at the most three, months pregnant. If she hadn't told him she was carrying a child, he would never have guessed. And maybe the pouch was always there, even when she wasn't pregnant.

"I'll bring the books to your room." Sarah was wrapping herself up in a towel. "What's your room number?"

He told her, grateful for the occasion to prolong his procrastination, but while he was waiting for her to bring him the children's books, he would still have to decide whether to go back to New York that night or not until Sunday morning.

Maybe Mary wouldn't have found him yet; that would buy Patrick a little more time. He might even discover that he had the willpower to delay turning the TV on, at least until Sarah Williams came to his room. Maybe she would watch the news with him; they seemed to agree that the coverage would be unbearable. It's always better not to watch a bad newscast by yourself—let alone a Super Bowl.

Yet as soon as he was back in his hotel room, he could summon no further resistance. He took off his wet bathing suit but kept the bathrobe on, and—

while noticing that the message light on his telephone was flashing—he found the remote control for the TV in the drawer, where he'd hidden it, and turned the television on.

He flipped through the channels until he found the all-news network, where he watched what he could have predicted (John F. Kennedy, Jr.'s Tribeca connection) come to life. There were the plain metal doors of the loft John junior had bought at 20 North Moore. The Kennedys' residence, which was across the street from an old warehouse, had already been turned into a shrine. JFK, Jr.'s neighbors—and probably utter strangers posing as his neighbors—had left candles and flowers; perversely, they'd also left what looked like get-well cards. While Patrick felt genuinely awful that the young couple and Mrs. Kennedy's sister had, in all likelihood, died, he detested those people groveling in their fantasy grief in Tribeca; they were what made the worst of television possible.

But as much as Wallingford hated the telecast, he also understood it. There were only two positions the media could take toward celebrities: worship them or trash them. And since mourning was the highest form of worship, the deaths of celebrities were understandably to be prized; furthermore, their deaths allowed the media to worship *and* trash them all at once. There was no beating it.

Wallingford turned off the TV and put the remote back in the drawer; he would be on television and a part of the spectacle soon enough. He was relieved when he called to inquire about his message light— only the hotel itself had called, to ask when he was checking out.

He told the hotel he would check out in the morning. Then he stretched out on the bed in the semidark room. (The curtains were still closed from the night before; the maids hadn't touched the room because Patrick had left the *do not disturb* sign on the door.) He lay waiting for Sarah Williams, a fellow traveler, and the wonderful books for children and world-weary adults by E. B. White.

Wallingford was a news anchor in hiding; he was deliberately making himself unavailable at the moment the story of Kennedy's missing plane was unfolding. What would management make of a journalist who wasn't dying to report this story? In fact, Wallingford was shrinking from it—he was a reporter who was putting off doing his *job*! (No sensible news network would have hesitated to fire him.)

And what else was Patrick Wallingford putting off? Wasn't he also hiding from what Evelyn Arbuthnot had disparagingly called his *life*?

When would he finally get it? Destiny is not imaginable, except in dreams or to those in love. Upon meeting Mrs. Clausen, Patrick could never have envisioned a future with her; upon falling in love with her, he couldn't imagine the future without her.

It was not sex that Wallingford wanted from Sarah Williams, although he tenderly touched her drooping breasts with his one hand. Sarah didn't want to have sex with Wallingford, either. She might have wanted to mother him, possibly because her daughters lived far away and had children of their own. More likely, Sarah Williams realized that Patrick Wallingford was in need of mothering, and—in addition to feeling guilty for having publicly abused him—she was feeling guilty for how little time she spent with her grandchildren.

There was also the problem that Sarah was pregnant, and that she believed she could not endure again the fear of one of her own children's mortality; nor did she want her grown daughters to know she was having sex.

She told Wallingford that she was an associate professor of English at Smith. She definitely sounded like an English teacher when she read aloud to Patrick in a clear, animated voice, first from *Stuart Little* and then from *Charlotte's Web,* "because that is the order in which they were written."

Sarah lay on her left side with her head on Patrick's pillow. The light on the night table was the only one on in the darkened room; although it was midday, they kept all the curtains closed.

Professor Williams read *Stuart Little* past lunchtime. They weren't hungry. Wallingford lay naked beside her, his chest in constant contact with her back, his thighs touching her buttocks, his right hand holding one, and then the other, of her breasts. Pressed between them, where they were both aware of it, was the stump of Patrick's left forearm. He could feel it against his bare stomach; she could feel it against the base of her spine.

The ending of *Stuart Little,* Wallingford thought, might be more gratifying to adults than to children—children have higher expectations of endings.

Still it was "a youthful ending," Sarah said, "full of the optimism of young adults."

She sounded like an English teacher, all right. Patrick would have described the ending of *Stuart Little* as a kind of second beginning. One has the sense that a new adventure is waiting for Stuart as he again sets forth on his travels.

"It's a boy's book," Sarah said.

Mice might enjoy it, too, Patrick guessed.

They were mutually disinclined to have sex; yet if one of them had been determined to make love, they would have. But Wallingford preferred to be read to, like a little boy, and Sarah Williams was feeling more motherly (at the moment) than sexual. Furthermore, how many naked adults—strangers in a darkened hotel room in the middle of the day—were reading E. B. White aloud? Even Wallingford would have admitted to a fondness for the uniqueness of the situation. It was surely more unique than having sex.

"Please don't stop," Wallingford told Ms. Williams, in the same way he might have spoken to someone who was making love to him. "Please keep reading. If you start *Charlotte's Web,* I'll finish it. I'll read the ending to you."

Sarah had shifted slightly in the bed, so that Patrick's penis now brushed the backs of her thighs; the stump of his left forearm grazed her buttocks. It might have crossed her mind to consider which was which, notwithstanding the size factor, but that thought would have led them both into an altogether more ordinary experience.

When the phone call came from Mary, it interrupted that scene in *Charlotte's Web* when Charlotte (the spider) is preparing Wilbur (the pig) for her imminent death.

"After all, what's a life, anyway?" Charlotte asks. "We're born, we live a little while, we die. A spider's life can't help being something of a mess, with all this trapping and eating flies."

Just then the phone rang. Wallingford increased his grip on one of Sarah's breasts. Sarah indicated her irritation with the call by picking up the receiver and asking sharply, "Who is it?"

"Who is *this*? Just who are *you*?" Mary cried into the phone. She spoke loudly enough for Patrick to hear her—he groaned.

"Tell her you're my mother," Wallingford whispered in Sarah's ear. (He was briefly ashamed to remember that the last time he'd used this line, his mother was still alive.)

"I'm Patrick Wallingford's mother, dear," Sarah Williams said into the phone. "Who are *you*?" The familiar "dear" made Wallingford think of Evelyn Arbuthnot again.

Mary hung up.

Ms. Williams went on reading from the penultimate chapter of *Charlotte's Web,* which concludes, "No one was with her when she died."

Sobbing, Sarah handed the book to Patrick. He'd promised to read her the last chapter, about Wilbur the pig, "And so Wilbur came home to his beloved manure pile . . ." the story of which Wallingford reported without emotion, as if it were the news. (It was *better* than the news, but that was another story.)

When Patrick finished, they dozed until it was dark outside; only half awake, Wallingford turned off the light on the night table so that it was dark inside the hotel room, too. He lay still. Sarah Williams was holding him, her breasts pressing into his shoulder blades. The firm but soft bulge of her stomach fitted the curve at the small of his back; one of her arms encircled his waist. With her hand, she gripped his penis a little more tightly than was comfortable. Even so, he fell asleep.

Probably they would have slept through the night. On the other hand, they might have woken up just before dawn and made intense love in the semidarkness, possibly because they both knew they would never see each other again. But it hardly matters what they would have done, because the phone rang again.

This time Wallingford answered it. He knew who it was; even asleep, he'd been expecting the call. He'd told Mary the story of how and when his mother had died. Patrick was surprised how long it had taken Mary to remember it.

"She's dead. Your mother's *dead*! You told me yourself! She died when you were in college!"

"That's right, Mary."

"You're in love with someone!" Mary was wailing. Naturally Sarah could hear her.

"That's right," Wallingford answered. Patrick saw no reason to explain to Mary that it wasn't Sarah Williams he was in love with. Mary had hit on him for too long.

"It's that same young woman, isn't it?" Sarah asked. The sound of Sarah's voice, whether or not Mary actually heard what she said, was enough to set Mary off again.

"She sounds *old* enough to be your mother!" Mary shrieked.

"Mary, please—"

"That dick Fred is looking for you, Pat. *Everyone's* looking for you! You're not supposed to go off for a weekend without leaving a number! You're not supposed to be *unreachable*! Are you trying to get fired or what?"

That was the first time Wallingford thought about trying to get fired; in the dark hotel room, the idea glowed as brightly as the digital alarm clock on the night table.

"You *do* know what's happened, don't you?" Mary asked. "Or have you been *fucking* so much that you've somehow managed to miss the news?"

"I have *not* been fucking." Patrick knew it was a provocative thing to say. After all, Mary was a journalist. That Wallingford had been fucking a woman in a hotel room all weekend was a fairly obvious conclusion to come to; like most journalists, Mary had learned to draw her own fairly obvious conclusions quickly.

"You don't expect me to believe you, do you?" she asked.

"I'm beginning not to care if you believe me, Mary."

"That dick Fred—"

"Please tell him I'll be back tomorrow, Mary."

"You *are* trying to get fired, aren't you?" Mary said. Once again, she hung up first.

For the second time, Wallingford considered the idea of trying to get fired—he didn't know why it seemed to be such a glow-in-the-dark idea.

"You didn't tell me you were married or something," Sarah Williams said. He could tell she was not in the bed; he could hear her, but only dimly see her, getting dressed in the dark room.

"I'm not married or anything," Patrick said.

"She's just a particularly possessive girlfriend, I suppose."

"She's not a girlfriend. We've never had sex. We're not involved in that way," Wallingford declared.

"Don't expect me to believe that," Sarah said.

(Journalists aren't the only people who draw their own fairly obvious conclusions quickly.)

"I've really enjoyed being with you," Patrick told her, trying to change the subject; he was also being sincere. But he could hear her sigh; even in the dark, he could tell she was doubting him.

"If I decide to have the abortion, maybe you'll be kind enough to go with me," Sarah Williams ventured. "It would mean coming back here a week from today." Perhaps she meant to give him more time to think about it, but Wallingford was thinking of the likelihood of his being recognized—LION GUY ESCORTS UNIDENTIFIED WOMAN TO ABORTION MILL, or a headline to that effect.

"I just hate the idea of doing it alone, but I guess it doesn't sound like a fun date," Sarah continued.

"Of course I'll go with you," he told her, but she'd noticed his hesitation. "If you want me to." He immediately hated how this sounded. Of course she wanted him to! She'd asked him, hadn't she? "Yes, definitely, I'll go with you," Patrick said, but he was only making it worse.

"No, that's all right. You don't even know me," Sarah said.

"I *want* to go with you," Patrick lied, but she was over it now.

"You didn't tell me you were in love with someone," she accused him.

"It doesn't matter. She doesn't love me." Wallingford knew that Sarah Williams wouldn't believe that, either.

She had finished dressing. He thought she was groping for the door. He turned on the light on the night table; it momentarily blinded him, but he was nonetheless aware of Sarah turning her face away from the light. She left the room without looking at him. He turned off the light and lay naked in bed, with the idea of trying to get himself fired glowing in the dark.

Wallingford knew that Sarah Williams had been upset about more than Mary's phone call. Sometimes it's easiest to confide the most intimate things to a stranger—Patrick himself had done it. And hadn't Sarah mothered him for a whole day? The least he could do was go with her to the abortion. So what if someone recognized him? Abortion was legal, and he believed it should be legal. He regretted his earlier hesitation.

Therefore, when Wallingford called the hotel operator to ask for a wake-up call, he also asked to be connected to Sarah's room—he didn't know the number. He wanted to propose a late bite to eat. Surely some place in Harvard Square would still be serving, especially on a Saturday night. Wallingford wanted to convince Sarah to let him go with her to the abortion; he felt it would be better to try to persuade her over dinner.

But the operator informed him that no one named Sarah Williams was registered in the hotel.

"She must have just checked out," Patrick said.

There was the indistinct sound of fingers on a computer keyboard, searching. In the new century, Wallingford imagined, it was probably the last sound we would hear before our deaths.

"I'm sorry, sir," the hotel operator told him. "There never *was* a Sarah Williams staying here."

Wallingford wasn't that surprised. Later he would call the English Department at Smith—he would be equally unsurprised to discover that no one named Sarah Williams taught there. She may have sounded like an associate professor of English when she was discussing *Stuart Little,* and she may have taught at Smith, but she was not a Sarah Williams.

Whoever she was, the thought that Patrick had been cheating on another woman—or that there was another woman in his life, one who felt wronged—had clearly upset her. Possibly *she* was cheating on someone; probably she had been cheated on. The abortion business had sounded true, as had her fear of her children and grandchildren dying. The only hesitation he'd heard in her voice had been when she'd told him her name.

Wallingford was upset that he had become a man to whom any decent woman would want to remain anonymous. He'd never thought of himself that way before.

When he'd had two hands, Patrick had experimented with anonymity—in particular, when he was with the kind of woman to whom any man would prefer to remain anonymous. But after the lion episode, he could no more have got away with *not* being Patrick Wallingford than he could have passed for Paul O'Neill—at least not to anyone with his or her faculties intact.

Rather than be left alone with these thoughts, Patrick made the mistake of turning on the television. A political commentator whose specialty had always struck Wallingford as intellectually inflated hindsight was speculating on a sizable "what if . . ." in the tragically abbreviated life of John F. Kennedy, Jr. The self-seriousness of the commentator was perfectly matched to the speciousness of his principal assertion, which was that JFK, Jr., would have been "better off" in every way if he'd gone against his mother's advice and become a movie star. (Would young Kennedy not have died in a plane crash if he'd been an actor?)

It was a fact that John junior's mom hadn't wanted him to be an actor, but the presumptuousness of the political commentator was enormous. The most egregious of his irresponsible speculations was that John junior's smoothest, most unalterable course to the presidency lay through Los Angeles! To Patrick, the fatuousness of such Hollywood-level theorizing was twofold: first, to declare that young Kennedy *should have* followed in Ronald Reagan's footsteps; second, to claim that JFK, Jr., had *wanted* to be president.

Preferring his other, more personal demons, Patrick turned off the TV. There in the dark, the new idea of trying to get fired greeted him as familiarly as an old friend. Yet that other new notion—that he was a man whose company a woman would accept only on the condition of anonymity—gave Patrick the shivers. It also precipitated a third new idea: What if he stopped resisting Mary and simply slept with her? (At least Mary wouldn't insist on protecting her anonymity.)

Thus there were three new ideas glowing in the dark, distracting Patrick Wallingford from the loneliness of a fifty-one-year-old woman who didn't want to have an abortion but who was terrified of having a child. Of course, it was none of his business if that woman had an abortion or not; it was nobody's business but hers.

And what if she wasn't even pregnant? She may simply have had a small potbelly. Maybe she liked to spend her weekends in a hotel with a stranger, just acting.

Patrick knew all about acting; he was always acting.

"Good night, Doris. Good night, my little Otto," Wallingford whispered in the dark hotel room. It was what he said when he wanted to be sure that he wasn't acting.

CHAPTER TEN

Trying to Get Fired

THERE'D BEEN NEARLY a week of rapturous mourning when Wallingford tried and failed to ready himself for an impromptu weekend in Wisconsin with Mrs. Clausen and Otto junior at the cottage on the lake. The Friday-evening telecast, one week after the crash of Kennedy's single-engine plane, would be Patrick's last before his trip up north, although he couldn't get a flight from New York with a connection to Green Bay until Saturday morning. There was no good way to get to Green Bay.

The Thursday-evening telecast was bad enough. Already they were running out of things to say, an obvious indication of which was Wallingford's interview with a widely disregarded feminist critic. (Even Evelyn Arbuthnot had intentionally ignored her.) The critic had written a book about the Kennedy family, in which she'd stated that all the men were misogynists. It was no surprise to her that a young Kennedy male had killed two women in his airplane.

Patrick asked to have the interview omitted, but Fred believed that the woman spoke for a lot of women. Judging from the abrasive response of the New York newsroom women, the feminist critic did not speak for them. Wallingford, always unfailingly polite as an interviewer, had to struggle to be barely civil.

The feminist critic kept referring to young Kennedy's "fatal decision," as if his life and death had been a novel. "They left late, it was dark, it was hazy, they were flying over water, and John-John had limited experience as a pilot."

These were not new points, Patrick was thinking, an unconvincing half-smile frozen on his handsome face. He also found it objectionable that the imperious woman kept calling the deceased "John-John."

"He was a victim of his own virile thinking, the Kennedy-male syndrome," she called it. "John-John was clearly testosterone-driven. They all are."

" 'They . . .' " was all Wallingford managed to say.

"You know who I mean," the critic snapped. "The men on his father's side of the family."

Patrick glanced at the TelePrompTer, where he recognized what were to be his next remarks; they were intended to lead his interviewee to the even more dubious assertion of the "culpability" of Lauren Bessette's bosses at Morgan Stanley. That her bosses had made her stay late on "that fatal Friday," as the feminist critic called it, was another reason that the small plane had crashed.

In the script meeting, Wallingford had objected to the word-for-word content of one of his questions being on the prompter. That was almost never done—it was always confusing. You can't put everything that's supposed to be spontaneous on the Tele-PrompTer.

But the critic had come with a publicist, and the publicist was someone whom Fred was sucking up to—for unknown reasons. The publicist wanted Wallingford to deliver the question exactly as it was written, the point being that the demonization of Morgan Stanley was the critic's next agenda and Wallingford (with feigned innocence) was supposed to lead her into it.

Instead he said: "It's not clear to me that John F. Kennedy, Jr., was 'testosterone-driven.' You're not the first person I've heard say that, of course, but I didn't know him. Neither did you. What *is* clear is that we've talked his death to death. I think that we should summon some dignity—we should just stop. It's time to move on."

Wallingford didn't wait for the insulted woman's response. There was over a minute remaining in the telecast, but there was ample montage footage on file. He abruptly brought the interview to a close, as was his habit every evening, by saying, "Good night, Doris. Good night, my little Otto." Then came the ubiquitous montage footage; it hardly mattered that the presentation was a little disorderly.

Viewers of the twenty-four-hour international channel, already suffering from grief fatigue, were treated to reruns of the mourning marathon: the hand-held camera on the rolling ship (a shot of the bodies being brought on board), a totally gratuitous shot of the St. Thomas More church, and another of a burial at sea, if not the actual burial. The last of the montage, as time expired, was of Jackie as a mom, holding John junior as a baby; her hand cupped the back of the newborn's neck, her thumb three times the size of his tiny ear. Jackie's hairdo was out of fashion, but the pearls were timeless and her signature smile was intact.

She looks so young, Wallingford thought. (She *was* young—it was 1961!)

Patrick was having his makeup removed when Fred confronted him. Fred was an old guy—he often spoke in dated terms.

"That was a no-no, Pat," Fred said. He didn't wait around for Wallingford's reply.

An anchor had to be free to have the last word. What was on the TelePrompTer was not sacrosanct. Fred must have had another bug up his ass; it hadn't dawned on Patrick that, among his fellow journalists, everything to do with young Kennedy's story was sacrosanct. His not *wanting* to report that story was an indication to management that Wallingford had lost his zest for being a journalist.

"I kinda liked what you said," the makeup girl told Patrick. "It sorta needed sayin'."

It was the girl he thought had a crush on him—she was back from her vacation. The scent of her chewing gum merged with her perfume; her smell and how close she was to his face reminded Wallingford of the commingled odors and the heat of a high-school dance. He hadn't felt so horny since the last time he'd been with Doris Clausen.

Patrick was unprepared for how the makeup girl thrilled him—suddenly, and without reservation, he desired her. But he went home with Mary instead. They went to her place, not even bothering to have dinner first.

"Well, this is a surprise!" Mary remarked, as she unlocked the first of her two door locks. Her small apartment had a partial view of the East River. Wallingford wasn't sure, but he thought they were on East Fifty-second Street. He'd been paying attention to Mary, not to her address. He had hoped to see something with her last name on it; it would have made him feel a little better to remember her last name. But she hadn't paused to open her mailbox, and there were no letters strewn about her apartment—not even on her messy desk.

Mary moved busily about, closing curtains, dimming lights. There was a paisley pattern to the upholstery in the living room, which was claustrophobic and festooned with Mary's clothes. It was one of those one-bedroom apartments with no closet space, and Mary evidently liked clothes.

In the bedroom, which was bursting with more clothes, Wallingford noted the floral pattern of the bedspread that was a tad little-girlish for Mary. Like the rubber-tree plant, which took up too much room in the tiny kitchen, the Lava lamp on top of the squat dresser drawers had to have come from her college days. There were no photographs; their absence signified everything from her divorce that had remained unpacked.

Mary invited him to use the bathroom first. She called to him through the closed door, so that there could be no doubt in his mind regarding the unflagging seriousness of her intentions. "I have to hand it to you, Pat—you've got great timing. I'm ovulating!"

He made some inarticulate response because he was smearing toothpaste on his teeth with his right index finger; of course it was her toothpaste. He'd opened her medicine cabinet in search of prescription drugs—anything with her last name on it—but there was nothing. How could a recently divorced woman who worked in New York City be drug-free?

There had always been something a little bionic about Mary; Patrick considered her skin, which was flawless, her unadulterated blondness, her sensible but sexy clothes, and her perfect little teeth. Even her niceness—if she had truly retained it, if she was still really nice. (Her *former* niceness, safer to say.) But no prescription drugs? Maybe, like the absent photographs, the drugs were as yet unpacked from her divorce.

Mary had opened her bed for him, the covers turned down as if by an unseen hotel maid. Later she left the bathroom light on, with the door ajar; the only other lights in the bedroom were the pink undulations of the Lava lamp, which cast moving shadows on the ceiling. Under the circumstances, it was hard for Patrick not to view the protozoan movements of the Lava lamp as indicative of Mary's striving fertility.

She suddenly made a point of telling him that she'd thrown out all her medicine—"This was months ago." Nowadays she took nothing—"Not even for cramps." The second she conceived, she was going to lay off the booze and cigarettes.

Wallingford scarcely had time to remind her that he was in love with someone else.

"I know. It doesn't matter," Mary said.

There was something so resolute about her lovemaking that Wallingford quickly succumbed; yet the experience bore no comparison to the intoxicating way Mrs. Clausen had mounted him. He didn't love Mary, and she loved only the life she imagined would follow from having his baby. Maybe now they could be friends.

Why Wallingford didn't feel that he was submitting to his old habits is evidence of his moral confusion. To have acted upon his sudden desire for the makeup girl, to have taken *her* to bed, would have meant reverting to his licentious self. But with Mary he had merely acquiesced. If his baby was what she wanted, why not give her a baby?

It comforted him to have located the one unbionic part of her—an area of blond down, near the small of her back. He kissed her there before she rolled over and fell asleep. She slept on her back, snoring slightly, her legs elevated by what Wallingford recognized were the paisley seat cushions from the living-room couch. (Like Mrs. Clausen, Mary wasn't taking any chances with gravity.)

Patrick didn't sleep. He lay listening to the traffic on the FDR Drive while rehearsing what he would say to Doris Clausen. He wanted to marry her, to be a real father to little Otto. Patrick planned to tell Doris that he had performed "for a friend" the same service he'd "performed" for her; however, he would tactfully say, he had not enjoyed the process of making Mary pregnant. And while he would try to be a not-too-absent father to Mary's child, he would make it very clear to Mary that he wanted to live with Mrs. Clausen and Otto junior. Of course he was crazy to think such an arrangement could work.

How had he imagined that Doris could entertain the possibility? Surely he didn't believe she would uproot herself and little Otto from Wisconsin, and Wallingford was clearly not a man who could make a long-distance relationship (if *any* relationship) work.

Should he tell Mrs. Clausen that he was trying to get fired? He hadn't rehearsed that part, nor was he trying nearly hard enough. Fred's feeble threat notwithstanding, Patrick feared that he might have become irreplaceable at the not-the-news network.

Oh, for his mild Thursday-evening rebellion, there might be a producer or two to deal with—some spineless CEO spouting off on the subject of how "rules of behavior apply to everyone," or running on about Wallingford's "lack of appreciation for team-work." But they wouldn't fire him for his deviation from the TelePrompTer, not as long as his ratings held.

In fact, as Patrick correctly anticipated—and according to the minute-by-minute ratings—upon his remarks, viewer interest had more than picked up; it had soared. Like the makeup girl, the very thought of whom gave Wallingford an unexpected boner in Mary's bed, the television audience also believed it was "time to move on." Wallingford's notion of him-self and his fellow journalists—that "we should sum-mon some dignity," that "we should just stop"—had immediately struck a public nerve. Quite the con-trary to getting himself fired, Patrick Wallingford had made himself more popular than he'd ever been.

He still had a hard-on at dawn, when a boat out on the East River tooted obscenely. (It was probably towing a garbage scow.) Patrick lay on his back in the pink-tinged bedroom, which was the color of scar tissue. His erection was holding up the bedcovers. How women seemed to sense such things, he'd never understood; he felt Mary kick the couch cushions off the bed. He held on to her hips while she sat on him, rocking away. As they moved, the daylight came striding into the room; the hideous pink began to pale.

"I'll show you 'testosterone-driven,' " Mary whispered to him, just before he came. It didn't matter that her breath was bad—they were friends. It was just sex, as frank and familiar as a handshake. A barrier that had long existed had been lifted. Sex was a burden that had stood between them; now it was no big deal.

Mary had nothing to eat in her apartment. She'd never cooked a meal or even eaten breakfast there. She would start looking for a bigger apartment, she declared, now that she was going to have a baby.

"I know I'm pregnant," she chirped. "I can feel it."

"Well, it's certainly possible," was all Patrick said.

They had a pillow fight and chased each other naked through the small apartment, until Wallingford whacked his shin against the stupid glass-topped coffee table in the paisley confusion of the living room. Then they took a shower together. Patrick burned himself on the hot-water faucet while they were soaping each other up and squirming all around, chest-to-chest.

They took a long walk to a coffee shop they both

liked—it was on Madison Avenue, somewhere in the Sixties or Seventies. Because of the competing noise on the street, they had to shout at each other the whole way. They walked into the coffee shop still shouting, like people who've been swimming and don't know that their ears are full of water.

"It's a pity we don't love each other," Mary was saying much too loudly. "Then you wouldn't have to go break your heart in Wisconsin, and I wouldn't have to have your baby all by myself."

Their fellow breakfast-eaters appeared to doubt the wisdom of this, but Wallingford foolishly agreed. He told Mary what he was rehearsing to say to Doris. Mary frowned. She worried that the part about trying to lose his job didn't sound sincere. (As to what she truly thought about the *other* part—his fathering a child with her just prior to declaring his eternal love for Doris Clausen—Mary didn't say.)

"Look," she said. "You've got what, eighteen months, remaining on your contract? If they fired you now, they'd try to negotiate you down. You'd probably settle for them owing you only a year's salary. If you're going to be in Wisconsin, maybe you'll need more than a year to find a new job—I mean one you like."

It was Patrick's turn to frown. He had *exactly* eighteen months remaining on his contract, but how had Mary known that?

"Furthermore," Mary went on, "they're going to be reluctant to fire you as long as you're the anchor.

They have to make it look as if whoever's in the anchor chair is *everybody's* first choice."

It only now occurred to Wallingford that Mary herself might be interested in what she called the anchor chair. He'd underestimated her before. The New York newsroom women were no dummies; Patrick had sensed some resentment of Mary among them. He'd thought it was because she was the youngest, the prettiest, the smartest, and the presumed nicest— he hadn't considered that she might also be the most ambitious.

"I see," he said, although he didn't quite. "Go on."

"Well, if I were you," Mary said, "I'd ask for a new contract. Ask for three years—no, make that five. But tell them you don't want to be the anchor anymore. Tell them you want your pick of field assignments. Say you'll take only the assignments you like."

"You mean *demote* myself?" Wallingford asked. "This is the way to get fired?"

"Wait! Let me finish!" Everyone in earshot in the coffee shop was listening. "What you do is you start to refuse your assignments. You just become too picky!"

" 'Too picky,' " Patrick repeated. "I see."

"Suddenly something big happens—I mean *major* heartache, devastation, terror, and accompanying sorrow. Are you with me, Pat?"

He was. He was beginning to see where some of the hyperbole on the TelePrompTer came from—not

all of it was Fred's work. Wallingford had never
spent time with Mary in the hard midmorning light;
even the blueness in her eyes was newly clarifying.

"Go on, Mary."

"Calamity strikes!" she said. In the coffee shop,
cups were poised, or resting quietly in their saucers.
"It's big-time breaking news—you know the kind of
story. We *have* to send you. You simply refuse to go."

"*Then* they fire me?" Wallingford asked.

"Then we *have* to, Pat."

He didn't let on, but he'd already noticed when
"they" had become "we." He had underestimated
her, indeed.

"You're going to have one smart little baby,
Mary," was all he said.

"But do you *see*?" she insisted. "Let's say there's
still four or four and a half years remaining on your
new contract. They fire you. They negotiate you
down, but down to *what*? Down to three years,
maybe. They end up paying you *three years' salary*
and you're home free! Well . . . home free in Wisconsin, anyway, if that's really where you want to
be."

"It's not my decision," he reminded her.

Mary took his hand. All the while, they'd been
consuming a huge breakfast; the fascinated patrons
of the coffee shop had been watching them eat and
eat throughout their eager shouting.

"I wish you all the luck in the world with Mrs.

Clausen," Mary told him earnestly. "She'd be a fool not to take you."

Wallingford perceived the disingenuousness of this, but he refrained from comment. He thought that an early-afternoon movie might help, although the matter of which film they should see would prove defeating. Patrick suggested *Arlington Road.* He knew that Mary liked Jeff Bridges. But political thrillers made her too tense.

"*Eyes Wide Shut?*" Wallingford proposed. He detected an atypical vacancy in her expression. "Kubrick's last—"

"He just died, right?"

"That's right."

"All the eulogizing has made me suspicious," Mary said.

A smart girl, all right. But Patrick nonetheless believed he might tempt her to see the film. "It's with Tom Cruise and Nicole Kidman."

"It ruins it for me that they're married," Mary said.

The lull in their conversation was so sudden, everyone who was in a position to stare at them in the coffee shop was doing so. This was partly because they knew he was Patrick Wallingford, the lion guy, with some pretty blonde, but it was even more because there had passed between them such a frenzy of words, which had now abruptly ceased. It was like watching two people fuck; all of a sudden, seemingly without orgasm, they'd simply stopped.

"Let's not go to a movie, Pat. Let's go to your place. I've never seen it. Let's just go there and fuck some more."

This was surely better raw material than any would-be writer in the coffee shop could have hoped to hear. "Okay, Mary," Wallingford said.

He believed she was oblivious to the scrutiny they were under. People who were not used to being out in public with Patrick Wallingford were unaccustomed to the fact that, especially in New York, *everyone* recognized disaster man. But when Patrick was paying the bill, he observed Mary confidently meeting the stares of the coffee shop's patrons, and out on the sidewalk she took his arm and told him: "A little episode like that does wonders for the ratings, Pat."

It was no surprise to him that she liked his apartment better than her own. "All this for you alone?" she asked.

"It's just a one-bedroom, like yours," Wallingford protested. But while this was strictly true, Patrick's apartment in the East Eighties had a kitchen big enough to have a table in it, and the living room could be a living-dining room, if he ever wanted to use it that way. Best of all, from Mary's point of view, was that his apartment's one bedroom was spacious and L-shaped; a baby's crib and paraphernalia could fit in the short end of the L.

"The baby could go there," as Mary put it, pointing to the nook from the vantage of the bed, "and I'd still have a little privacy."

"You'd like to trade your apartment for mine—is that it, Mary?"

"Well . . . if you're going to be in Wisconsin most of the time. Come on, Pat, it sounds like all you'll really need to have in New York is a *pied-à-terre*. My place would be *perfect* for you!"

They were naked, but Wallingford rested his head on her flat, almost boyish stomach with more resignation than sexual enthusiasm; he'd lost the heart to "fuck some more," as Mary had so engagingly put it in the coffee shop. He was trying not to imagine himself in her noisy apartment on East Fifty-something. He hated midtown—there was always such a racket there. By comparison, the Eighties amounted to a neighborhood.

"You'll get used to the noise," Mary told him, rubbing his neck and shoulders soothingly. She was reading his mind, smart girl that she was. Wallingford wrapped his arms around her hips; he kissed her small, soft belly, trying to envision the changes in her body in six, then seven, then eight months' time. "You've got to admit that your place would be better for the baby, Pat," she said. Her tongue darted in and out of his ear.

He had no capacity for long-range scheming; he could only admire Mary for everything he'd underestimated about her. Possibly he could learn from her. Maybe then he could get what he wanted—the imagined life with Mrs. Clausen and little Otto. Or was that really what he wanted? A sudden crisis of confidence, the lack thereof, overcame him. What if all he *really* wanted was to get out of television and out of New York?

"Poor penis," Mary was saying consolingly. She was holding it fondly, but it was unresponsive. "It must be tired," she went on. "Maybe it should rest up. It should probably save itself for Wisconsin."

"We better both hope that it works out for me in Wisconsin, Mary. I mean for *both* our plans." She kissed his penis lightly, almost indifferently, in the manner that so many New Yorkers might kiss the cheek of a mere acquaintance or a not-so-close friend.

"Smart boy, Pat. And you're basically a good guy, too—no matter what anybody else says."

"It would appear that I'm perceived to be swimming near the top of the gene pool," was all Wallingford said in reply.

He was trying to imagine the TelePrompTer for the Friday-evening telecast, anticipating what Fred might already have contributed to it. He tried to imagine what Mary would add to the script, too, because what Patrick Wallingford said on-camera was written by many unseen hands, and Patrick now understood that Mary had always been part of the bigger picture.

When it was evident that Wallingford wasn't up to having sex again, Mary said they might as well go to work a little early. "I know you like to have some input in regard to what goes on the TelePrompTer," was how she expressed it. "I have a few ideas," she added, but not until they were in the taxi heading downtown.

Her timing was almost magical. Patrick listened to her talk about "closure," about "wrapping up the Kennedy thing." She'd already written the script, he realized.

Almost as an afterthought—they'd cleared security and were taking the elevator up to the newsroom—Mary touched his left forearm, a little above his missing hand and wrist, in that sympathetic manner to which so many women seemed addicted. "If I were you, Pat," she confided, "I wouldn't worry about Fred. I wouldn't give him a second thought."

At first, Wallingford believed that the newsroom women were all abuzz because he and Mary had come in together; doubtless at least one of them had seen them leave together the previous night, too. Now they all knew. But Fred had been fired—that was the reason for the women's mercurial chatter. Wallingford was not surprised that Mary wasn't shocked at the news. (With the briefest of smiles, she ducked into a women's room.)

Patrick *was* surprised to be greeted by only one producer and one CEO. The latter was a moon-faced young man named Wharton who always looked as if he were suppressing the urge to vomit. Was Wharton more important than Wallingford had thought? Had he underestimated Wharton, too? Suddenly Wharton's innocuousness struck Patrick as potentially dangerous. The young man had a blank, insipid quality that could have concealed a latent authority to fire people—even Fred, even Patrick Wallingford. But Wharton's only reference to Wallingford's small rebellion on the Thursday-evening telecast and to Fred's subsequently being fired was to utter (twice) the word "unfortunate." Then he left Patrick alone with the producer.

Wallingford couldn't quite tell what it meant—why had they sent only one producer to talk to him? But the choice was predictable; they'd used her before when it struck them that Wallingford needed a pep talk, or some other form of instruction.

Her name was Sabina. She had worked her way up; years ago, she'd been one of the newsroom women. Patrick had slept with her, but only once—when she was much younger and still married to her first husband.

"I suppose there's an interim replacement for Fred. A new dick, so to speak? A *new* news editor . . ." Wallingford speculated.

"I wouldn't call the appointment an interim replacement, if I were you," Sabina cautioned him. (Her vocabulary, like Mary's, was big on "if I were you," Patrick noticed.) "I would say that the appointment has been a long time coming, and that there's nothing in the least 'interim' about it."

"Is it you, Sabina?" Wallingford asked. (Was it Wharton? he was thinking.)

"No, it's Shanahan." There was just a hint of bit-
terness in Sabina's voice.

"Shanahan?" The name didn't ring a bell with
Wallingford.

"Mary, to you," Sabina told him.

So *that* was her name! He didn't even remember it
now. Mary Shanahan! He should have known.

"Good luck, Pat. I'll see you at the script meeting," was all Sabina said. She left him alone with his
thoughts, but he wasn't alone for long.

When Wallingford arrived at the meeting, the
newsroom women were already there; they were as
alert and jumpy as small, nervous dogs. One of them
pushed a memo across the table to Patrick; the paper
fairly flew out of her hands. At first glance, he
thought it was a press release of the news he already
knew, but he soon saw that—in addition to her duties
as the new news editor—Mary Shanahan had been
made a producer of the show. That must have been
why Sabina had so little to say at their earlier meeting. Sabina was a producer, too, only now it seemed
she was not as important a producer as she'd been
before Mary was made one.

As for Wharton, the moon-faced CEO never said
anything at the script meetings. Wharton was one of
those guys who made all his remarks from the vantage point of hindsight—his comments were strictly
after the fact. He came to the script meetings only to
learn who was responsible for everything Patrick

Wallingford said on-camera. This made it impossible to know how important, or not, Wharton was.

First they reviewed the selected montage footage on file. There was not one image that wasn't already part of the public consciousness. The most shameless shot, with which the montage concluded by freezing to a still, was a stolen image of Caroline Kennedy Schlossberg. The image wasn't entirely clear, but she seemed to be caught in the act of trying to block the camera's view of her son. The boy was shooting baskets, maybe in the driveway of the Schlossberg summer home in Sagaponack. The cameraman had used a telephoto lens—you could tell by the out-of-focus branches (probably privet) in the foreground of the frame. (Someone must have snaked a camera through a hedge.) The boy was either oblivious or pretending to be oblivious to the camera.

Caroline Kennedy Schlossberg was caught in profile. She was still elegant and dignified, but either sleeplessness or the tragedy had made her face more gaunt. Her appearance refuted the comforting notion that one grew accustomed to grief.

"Why are we using this?" Patrick asked. "Aren't we ashamed, or at least a little embarrassed?"

"It just needs some voice-over, Pat," Mary Shanahan said.

"How about this, Mary? How about I say, 'We're New Yorkers. We have the good reputation of offering anonymity to the famous. Lately, however, that reputation is undeserved.' How about *that*?" Wallingford asked.

No one answered him. Mary's ice-blue eyes were as sparkling as her smile. The newsroom women were twitching with excitement; if they had all started biting one another, Patrick wouldn't have been surprised.

"Or this," Wallingford went on. "How about I say *this*? 'By all accounts, from those who knew him, John F. Kennedy, Jr., was a modest young man, a decent guy. Some comparable modesty and decency from *us* would be refreshing.' "

There was a pause that would have been polite, were it not for the newsroom women's exaggerated sighs.

"I've written a little something," Mary said almost shyly. The script was already there, on the Tele-PrompTer; she must have written it the previous day, or the day before that.

"There seem to be certain days, even weeks," the script read, "when we are cast in the unwelcome role of the terrible messenger."

"Bullshit!" Patrick said. "The role *isn't* 'unwelcome'—we *relish* it!"

Mary sat smiling demurely while the TelePrompTer kept rolling: "We would rather be comforting friends than terrible messengers, but this has been one of those weeks." A scripted pause followed.

"I like it," one of the newsroom women said.

They'd had a meeting before this meeting, Wallingford knew. (There was always a meeting before the
meeting.) They had no doubt agreed which of them
would say, "I like it."

Then another of the newsroom women touched
Patrick's left forearm, in the usual place. "I like it because it doesn't make you sound as if you're apolo-
gizing, not exactly, for what you said last night," she
told him. Her hand rested on his forearm a little
longer than was natural or necessary.

"By the way, the ratings for last night were terrific," Wharton said. Patrick knew that he'd better
not look at Wharton, whose round face was a bland
dot across the table.

"You were great last night, Pat," Mary added.

Her remark was so well timed that this had to have
been rehearsed at the meeting before the meeting,
too, because there was not one titter among the newsroom women; they were as straight-faced as a jury
that's made its decision. Wharton, of course, was the
only one at the script meeting who didn't know that
Patrick Wallingford had gone home with Mary
Shanahan the previous night, nor would Wharton
have cared.

Mary gave Patrick an appropriate amount of time
to respond—they all did. Everyone was quiet and respectful. Then, when Mary saw that no response
would be forthcoming, she said, "Well, if everything's perfectly clear . . ."

Wallingford was already on his way to makeup. Thinking back, there was now only one conversation he *didn't* regret having with Mary. The second time they'd had sex, with the dawn breaking, he'd told her about his sudden and unaccountable lust for the makeup girl. Mary had been full of condemnation.

"You don't mean Angie, do you, Pat?"

He'd not known the makeup girl's name. "The one who chews gum—"

"That's *Angie!*" Mary had cried. "That girl is a *mess!*"

"Well, she turns me on. I can't tell you why. Maybe it's the gum."

"Maybe you're just horny, Pat."

"Maybe."

That hadn't been the end of it. They'd been walking crosstown, to the coffee shop on Madison, when Mary had blurted out, apropos of nothing, "*Angie!* Jesus, Pat—the girl's a *joke!* She still lives with her parents. Her father's a transit cop or something. In Queens. She's from *Queens!*"

"Who cares where she's from?" Patrick had asked.

In retrospect, he found it curious that Mary wanted his baby, wanted his apartment, wanted to advise him on the most advantageous way to get fired; all things considered, she truly seemed (to a carefully calculated degree) to want to be his friend. She even wanted things to work out for him in Wisconsin— meaning that she'd manifested no jealousy of Mrs.

Clausen that Wallingford could detect. Yet Mary was borderline apoplectic that a makeup girl had given him a hard-on. Why?

He sat in the makeup chair, contemplating the arousal factor, as Angie went to work on his crow's-feet and (today, especially) the dark circles under his eyes. "Ya didn't get much sleep last night, huh?" the girl asked him between snaps. She'd changed her gum; last night she'd given off a minty smell— tonight she was chewing something fruity.

"Sadly, no. Another sleepless night," Patrick replied.

"Why can'cha sleep?" Angie asked.

Wallingford frowned; he was thinking. How far should he go?

"Unscrunch your forehead. Relax, relax!" Angie told him. She was patting the flesh-colored powder on his forehead with her soft little brush. "That's betta," she said. "So why can'cha sleep? Aren't ya gonna tell me?"

Oh, what the hell! Patrick thought. If Mrs. Clausen turned him down, all this would be only the rest of his life. So what if he'd just got his new boss pregnant? He'd already decided, sometime during the script meeting, not to trade apartments with her. And if Doris said yes, this would be his last night as a free man. Surely some of us are familiar with the fact that sexual anarchy can precede a commitment to the monogamous life. This was the old Patrick Wallingford—his licentiousness reasserting itself.

"I can't sleep because I can't stop thinking about you," Wallingford confessed. The makeup girl had just spread her hand, her thumb and index finger smoothing what she called the "smile lines" at the corners of his mouth. He could feel her fingers stop on his skin as if her hand had died there. Her jaw dropped; her mouth hung open, midsnap.

Angie wore a snug, short-sleeved sweater the color of orange sherbet. On a chain around her neck was a thick signet ring, obviously a man's, which was heavy enough to separate her breasts. Even her breasts stopped moving while she held her breath; everything had stopped.

Finally she breathed again—one long exhalation, redolent of the chewing gum. Patrick could see his face in the mirror, but not hers. He looked at the tensed muscles in her neck; a strand or two of her jet-black hair hung down. The shoulder straps of her bra showed through her orange sweater, which had ridden up above the waistband of her tight black skirt. She had olive-colored skin, and dark, downy-looking hair on her arms.

Angie was only twenty-something. Wallingford had hardly been shocked to hear that she still lived with her parents. Lots of New York working girls did. To have your own apartment was too expensive, and parents were generally more reliable than multiple roommates.

Patrick was beginning to believe that Angie would never respond, and her soft fingers were once again working the rouge into his skin. At last Angie took a deep breath and held it, as if she were thinking of what to say; then she released another long, fruity breath. She started chewing her gum again, rapidly— her breaths were short and sweet. Wallingford was uncomfortably aware that she was scrutinizing his face for more than blemishes and wrinkles.

"Are ya askin' me out or somethin'?" Angie whispered to him. She kept glancing at the open doorway of the makeup room, where she was alone with Patrick. The woman who did hair had taken the elevator down to street level; she was standing on the sidewalk somewhere, smoking a cigarette.

"Think of it this way, Angie," Wallingford whispered to the agitated, breathy girl. "This is definitely a case of sexual harassment, if you play your cards right."

Patrick was pleased with himself for imagining a way to get fired that Mary Shanahan had not thought of, but Angie didn't know he was serious; the makeup girl wrongly believed he was just fooling around. And as Wallingford had correctly guessed, she had a crush on him.

"Ha!" Angie said, flashing him a frisky smile. He could see the color of her gum for the first time— it was purple. (Grape, or some synthetic variation thereof.) She had her tweezers out and seemed to be staring at a spot between his eyes. As she bent more closely over him, he breathed her in—her perfume, her hair, the gum. She smelled wonderful, in a kind of department-store way.

In the mirror, he could see the fingers of his right hand; he spread them as purposefully on the narrow strip of flesh between the waistband of her skirt and her high-riding sweater as he might have touched the keyboard of a piano before he started to play. At that moment he had a shameless sense of himself as a semiretired maestro, long out of practice, who'd not lost his touch.

There wasn't a lawyer in New York who wouldn't happily represent her case. Wallingford only hoped she wouldn't gouge his face with the tweezers.

Instead, as he touched her warm skin, Angie arched her back in such a way that she was pressing—no, make that snuggling—against his hand. With the tweezers, she gently plucked an errant eyebrow-hair from the bridge of his nose. Then she kissed him on the lips with her mouth a little open; he could taste her gum.

He meant to say something along the lines of "Angie, for Christ's sake, you should *sue* me!" But he couldn't take his one hand off her. Instinctively, his fingers slipped under her sweater; they slid up her spine, all the way to the back strap of her bra. "I love the gum," he told her, his old self easily finding the right words. She kissed him again, this time parting his lips, then his teeth, with her forceful tongue.

Patrick was briefly taken aback when Angie inserted her slick wad of gum into his mouth; for an alarming moment, he imagined that he'd bitten off her tongue. It simply wasn't the sort of foreplay he was used to—he hadn't gone out with a lot of gum-chewers. Her bare back squirmed against his hand; her breasts in her soft sweater brushed his chest.

It was one of the newsroom women who cleared her throat in the doorway. This was almost exactly what Wallingford had wanted; he'd hoped that Mary Shanahan might have seen him kissing and feeling up Angie, but he had no doubt that the incident would be reported to Mary before he went on-camera. "You've got five minutes, Pat," the newsroom woman told him.

Angie, who'd left him with her gum, was still pulling her sweater down when the woman who did hair returned from her sidewalk smoke. She was a heavy black woman who smelled like cinnamon-raisin toast, and she always made a point of feigning exasperation when there was nothing Patrick's hair needed. Sometimes she squirted a little hair spray on him, or rubbed him with a dab of gel; this time she just patted him on the top of his head and left the room again.

"Ya sure ya know whatcha gettin' into?" Angie asked. "I gotta complicated sorta life," she warned him. "I'm a handful of problems, if ya know what I mean."

"What do you mean, Angie?"

"If we're gonna go out tonight, there's some stuff

I gotta blow off," she said. "I gotta buncha phone calls to make, for starters."

"I don't want to cause you any trouble, Angie."

The girl was searching through her purse—for phone numbers, Wallingford assumed. But, no, it was for more gum. "Look"—she was chewing again—"do ya wanna go out tonight or what? It's no trouble. I just gotta start makin' some calls."

"Yes, tonight," Patrick replied.

Why not yes, why not tonight? Not only was he not married to Mrs. Clausen, but she had given him no encouragement whatsoever. He had no reason to think he ever would be married to her; he knew only that he wanted to ask. Under the circumstances, sexual anarchy was both understandable and commendable. (To the *old* Patrick Wallingford, that is.)

"Ya gotta phone at your place, I guess," Angie was saying. "Betta gimme the numba. I won't give it to nobody unless I hafta."

He was writing out his phone number for her when the same newsroom woman reappeared in the doorway. She saw the piece of paper change hands. This gets better and better, Wallingford was thinking. "Two minutes, Pat," the observant woman told him.

Mary was waiting for him in the studio. She held out her hand to him, a tissue covering her open palm. "Lose the gum, asshole," was all she said. Patrick took no small amount of pleasure in depositing the slippery purple wad in her hand.

"Good evening," he began the Friday telecast,

more formally than usual. "Good evening" wasn't on the prompter, but Wallingford wanted to sound as insincerely somber as possible. After all, he knew the level of insincerity behind what he had to say next. "There seem to be certain days, even weeks, when we are cast in the unwelcome role of the terrible messenger. We would rather be comforting friends than terrible messengers," he went on, "but this has been one of those weeks."

He was aware that his words fell around him like wet clothes, as he'd intended. When the file footage began and Patrick knew he was off-camera, he looked for Mary, but she'd already left, as had Wharton. The montage dragged on and on—it had the tempo of an overlong church service. You didn't need to be a genius to read the ratings for this show in advance.

At last came that gratuitous image of Caroline Kennedy Schlossberg, shielding her son from the telephoto lens; when the image froze to a still, Patrick prepared himself for his closing remarks. There would be time to say the usual: "Good night, Doris. Good night, my little Otto." Or something of equivalent length.

While Wallingford hardly felt he was being unfaithful to Mrs. Clausen, since they were not a couple, it nonetheless seemed to him some slight betrayal of his devotion—that is, if he delivered his usual blessing to her and their son. Knowing what he'd done the night before with Mary, and thinking that he knew what the night ahead of him, with Angie, held, he felt disinclined even to speak Mrs. Clausen's name.

Furthermore, there was something else he wanted to say. When the montage footage finally ended, he looked straight at the camera and declared, "Let's hope that's the end of it." It was only one word shorter than his benediction to Doris and Otto junior, but there was no pause for a period—not to mention the two commas. In fact, it took only three seconds to say instead of four; Patrick knew because he'd timed it.

While Wallingford's concluding remark didn't save the ratings, there would be some good press for the evening news because of it. An Op-Ed piece in *The New York Times,* which amounted to a caustic review of the television coverage of JFK, Jr.'s death, praised Patrick for what the writer termed "three seconds of integrity in a week of sleaze." Despite himself, Wallingford was looking more irreplaceable than ever.

Naturally, Mary Shanahan was nowhere to be found at the conclusion of the Friday-evening telecast; also absent were Wharton and Sabina. They were no doubt having a meeting. Patrick made a public display of his physical affection for Angie during the makeup-removal process, so much so that the hairdresser left the room in disgust. Wallingford also made a point of not leaving with Angie until a small but highly communicative gathering of the newsroom women were whispering together by the elevators.

But was a night with Angie truly what he wanted? How could a sexual adventure with the twenty-something makeup girl be construed as progress in the journey to better himself? Wasn't this plainly the *old* Patrick Wallingford, up to his old tricks? How many times can a man repeat his sexual past before his past becomes who he is?

Yet without being able to explain the feeling, not even to himself, Wallingford felt like a new man, and one on the right track. He was a man on a mission, on his labyrinthine way to Wisconsin—notwithstanding the present detour he was taking. And what about the detour of the night before? Regardless, these detours were merely preparations for meeting Mrs. Clausen and winning her heart. Or so Patrick convinced himself.

He took Angie to a restaurant on Third Avenue in the Eighties. After a vinous dinner, they walked to Wallingford's apartment—Angie a little unsteadily. The excited girl gave him her gum again. The slippery exchange followed a long, tongue-thrusting kiss, only seconds after Patrick had at first unlocked and then relocked his apartment door.

The gum was a new flavor, something ultra-cool and silvery. When Wallingford breathed through his nose, his nostrils stung; when he breathed through his mouth, his tongue felt cold. As soon as Angie excused herself to use the bathroom, Patrick spit the gum into the palm of his one hand. Its shiny, metallic surface quivered like a puddle of mercury. He managed to throw the gum away and wash his hand in the kitchen sink before Angie emerged from the bathroom, wearing nothing but one of Wallingford's towels, and hurled herself into his arms. A forward girl, a strenuous night ahead. Patrick would be hard-pressed to find the time to pack for Wisconsin.

In addition, there were the phone calls, which were broadcast on his answering machine throughout the night. He was in favor of killing the volume, but Angie insisted on monitoring the calls; it had been in case of an emergency that she'd given Patrick's home phone number to various members of her family in the first place. But the initial phone call was from Patrick's new news editor, Mary Shanahan.

He heard the background cacophony of the newsroom women, the high hilarity of their celebration—including the contrasting baritone of a waiter reciting "tonight's specials"—before Mary uttered a word. Wallingford could imagine her hunched over her cell phone, as if it were something she intended to eat. One of her fine-boned hands would be cupping her ear—the other, her mouth. A strand of her blond hair would have fallen across her face, possibly concealing one of her sapphire-blue eyes. Of course the newsroom women would know she was calling him, whether she'd told them or not.

"That was a dirty trick, Pat," Mary's message on the answering machine began.

"It's Ms. Shanahan!" Angie whispered in a panic, as if Mary could hear her.

"Yes, it is," Patrick whispered back. The makeup girl was writhing on top of him, the luxurious mass of her jet-black hair entirely covering her face. All Wallingford could see was one of Angie's ears, but he deduced (from the smell) that her new gum was of a raspberry or strawberry persuasion.

"Not a word from you, not even 'Congratulations,' " Mary went on. "Well, I can live with that, but not that awful girl. You must *want* to humiliate me. Is that it, Pat?"

"Am I the awful girl?" Angie asked. She was beginning to pant. She was also emitting a low growling sound from the back of her throat; maybe it was caused by the gum.

"Yes, you are," Patrick replied, with some difficulty—the girl's hair kept getting in his mouth.

"What's Ms. Shanahan care about *me* for?" Angie asked; she sounded out of breath. Shades of Crystal Pitney? Wallingford hoped not.

"I slept with Mary last night. Maybe I got her pregnant," Patrick said. "She wanted me to."

"That kinda explains it," said the makeup girl.

"I know you're there! Answer me, you asshole!" Mary wailed.

"Boy . . ." Angie started to say. She seemed to be trying to roll Wallingford on top of her—apparently she'd had enough of being on top.

"You should be packing for Wisconsin! You should

be resting up for your trip!" Mary shouted. One of the newsroom women was trying to calm her down. The waiter could be overheard saying something about the truffle season.

Patrick recognized the waiter's voice. The restaurant was an Italian place on West Seventeenth. "What about Wisconsin?" Mary whined. "I wanted to spend the weekend in your apartment while you were in Wisconsin, just to try it out . . ." She began to cry.

"What about Wisconsin?" Angie panted.

"I'm going there first thing tomorrow," was all Wallingford said.

A different voice spoke up from the answering machine; one of the newsroom women had seized Mary's cell phone after Mary dissolved in tears. "You shit, Pat," the woman said. Wallingford could visualize her surgically slimmed-down face. It was the woman he'd been in Bangkok with, a long time ago; her face had been fuller then. That was the end of the call.

"Ha!" Angie cried. She'd twisted the two of them into a sideways position, which Wallingford was unfamiliar with. The position was a little painful for him, but the makeup girl was gathering momentum—her growl had become a moan.

When the answering machine picked up the second call, Angie dug one of her heels into the small of Patrick's back. They were still joined sideways, the girl grunting loudly, as a woman's voice asked mournfully, "Is my baby girl there? Oh, Angie, Angie—my dahlin', my dahlin'! Ya gotta stop whatcha doin', Angie. Ya breakin' my heart!"

"Mom, for Christ's sake . . ." Angie started to say, but she was gasping. Her moan had become a growl again—her growl, a roar.

She's probably a screamer, Wallingford considered—his neighbors would think he was murdering the girl. I *should* be packing for Wisconsin, Patrick thought, as Angie violently heaved herself onto her back. Somehow, although they were nonetheless deeply joined, one of her legs was flung over one of his shoulders; he tried to kiss her but her knee was in the way.

Angie's mother was weeping so rhythmically that the answering machine emitted a pre-orgasmic sound of its own. Wallingford never heard her hang up; the last of her sobs was drowned out by Angie's screams. Not even childbirth could be this loud, Patrick wrongly supposed—not even Joan of Arc, blazing at the stake. But Angie's screams abruptly ceased. For a second she lay as if paralyzed; then she began to thrash. Her hair whipped Wallingford's face, her body bucked against him, her nails raked his back.

Uh-oh, a screamer and a scratcher, Wallingford thought—the younger, unmarried Crystal Pitney not forgotten. He hid his face against Angie's throat so that she couldn't gouge his eyes. He was frankly afraid of the next phase of her orgasm; the girl seemed to possess superhuman strength. Without a sound, not even a groan, she was strong enough to arch her back and roll him off her—first on his side, then on his back. Miraculously, they'd not once become disconnected; it was as if they never could be. They felt permanently fastened together, a new species. He could feel her heart pounding; her whole chest was vibrating but not a sound came from her, not a breath.

Then he realized she wasn't breathing. Was she a screamer and a scratcher and a *fainter*? It took all his strength to straighten his arms. He pushed her chest off him—his one hand on one breast, his stump on the other. That was when he saw she was choking on her gum—her face was blue, her dark-brown eyes showing only the whites. Wallingford gripped her lolling jaw in his hand; he drove the stump of his forearm under her ribcage, a punch without a fist. The pain was reminiscent of the days following his attachment surgery, a sickening pain that shot up his forearm to his shoulder before it traveled to his neck. But Angie exhaled sharply, expelling the gum.

The phone rang while the frightened girl lay shaking on his chest, wracked with sobs, sucking huge gulps of air. "I was *dyin'*," she managed to gasp. Patrick, who'd thought she was coming, said nothing while the machine answered the call. "I was dyin' and comin' at the same time," the girl added. "It was weird."

From the answering machine, a voice spoke from the city's grim underground; there were metallic shrieks and the lurching rumble of a subway train,

over which Angie's father, a transit policeman, made
his message clear. "Angie, are ya tryin' to kill your
muthuh or what? She's not eatin', she's not sleepin',
she's not goin' to Mass . . ." Another train screeched
over the cop's lament.

"Daddy," was all Angie said to Wallingford. Her
hips were moving again. As a couple, they seemed
eternally joined—a minor god and goddess repre-
senting death by pleasure.

Angie was screaming again when the phone rang a
fourth time. What time is it? Patrick wondered, but
when he looked at his digital alarm clock, something
pink was covering the time. It had a ghastly anatomi-
cal appearance, like part of a lung, but it was only
Angie's gum—definitely some sort of berry flavor.
The way the light of the alarm clock shone through
the substance made the gum resemble living tissue.

"God . . ." he said, coming, just as the makeup girl
also came. Her teeth, doubtless missing the gum,
sank into Wallingford's left shoulder. Patrick could
tolerate the pain—he'd known worse. But Angie was
even more enthusiastic than he'd expected her to be.
She was a screamer, a choker, and a biter. She was in
midbite when she fainted dead away.

"Hey, cripple," said a strange man's voice on Patrick's answering machine. "Hey, Mista One Hand,
do ya know what? You're gonna lose more than your
hand, that's what. You're gonna end up with nothin'
between your legs but a fuckin' *draft*."

Wallingford tried to wake up Angie by kissing her, but the fainted girl just smiled. "There's a call for you," Patrick whispered in her ear. "You might want to take this one."

"Hey, fuck-face," the man in the answering machine said, "did ya know that even television personalities can just *disappear*?" He must have been calling from a moving car. The radio was playing Johnny Mathis—softly, but not softly enough. Wallingford thought of the signet ring Angie wore on the chain around her neck; it would slip over a knuckle the size of his big toe. But she had already taken off the ring, and she'd dismissed its owner as "a nobody"—some guy who was "overseas." So who was the guy on the phone?

"Angie, I think you ought to hear this," Patrick whispered. He gently pulled the sleeping girl into a sitting position; her hair fell forward, hiding her face, covering her pretty breasts. She smelled like a delectable concoction of fruits and flowers; her body was coated with a thin and glowing film of sweat.

"Listen to me, Mista One Hand," the answering machine said. "I'm gonna grind up your prick in a *blenda*. Then I'm gonna make ya *drink* it!" That was the end of the charmless call.

Wallingford was packing for Wisconsin when Angie woke up.

"Boy, have I gotta pee!" the girl said.

"There was another call—not your mother. Some

guy said he was going to grind up my penis in a blender."

"That would be my brother Vittorio—Vito, for short," Angie said. She left the door to the bathroom open while she peed. "Did he really say 'penis'?" she called from the toilet.

"No, he actually said 'prick,' " Patrick replied.

"Definitely Vito," the makeup girl said. "He's harmless. Vito don't even have a job." How did Vito's unemployment make him harmless? "So what's in Minnesota, anyway?" Angie asked.

"Wisconsin," he corrected her.

"So who's there?"

"A woman I'm going to ask to marry me," Patrick answered. "She'll probably say no."

"Hey, ya gotta real problem, do ya know that?" Angie asked. She pulled him back to the bed. "Come here, ya gotta have more confidence than that. Ya gotta believe she's gonna say yes. Otherwise, why botha?"

"I don't think she loves me."

"Sure she does! Ya just gotta practice," the makeup girl said. "Go on—ya can practice on me. Go on—*ask* me!"

He tried; after all, he'd been rehearsing. He told her what he wanted to say to Mrs. Clausen.

"Geez . . . that's terrible," Angie said. "To begin with, ya can't start out apologizin' all over the place— ya gotta come right out and say, 'I can't live wid-outcha!' That kind of thing. Go on—*say* it!"

"I can't live without you," Wallingford announced unconvincingly.

"Geez . . ."

"What's wrong?" Patrick asked.

"Ya gotta say it betta than *that*!"

The phone rang, the fifth call. It was Mary Shanahan again, presumably calling from the solitude of her apartment on East Fifty-something—Wallingford could almost hear the whoosh of cars passing on the FDR Drive. "I thought we were friends," Mary began. "Is this how you treat a friend? Someone who's having your *baby* . . ." Either her voice broke or her thought trailed away.

"She's gotta point," Angie said to Patrick. "Ya betta say somethin' to her." Wallingford thought of shaking his head, but he was lying with his face on Angie's breasts; he considered it rude to shake his head there.

"You can't *still* be fucking that girl!" Mary cried.

"If ya don't talk to her, *I'm* gonna talk to her. Someone's gotta," the compassionate makeup girl said.

"You talk to her, then," Wallingford replied. He buried his face lower, in Angie's belly; he tried to muffle his hearing there, while she picked up the phone.

"This is Angie, Ms. Shanahan," the good-hearted girl began. "Ya shouldn't be upset. It hasn't been all that great here, really. A while ago, I nearly choked to death. I almost died—I'm not kiddin'." Mary hung up. "Was that bad?" Angie asked Wallingford.

"No, that was good. That was just fine. I think you're great," he said truthfully.

"Ya just sayin' that," Angie told him. "Are ya tryin' to get laid again or what?"

So they had sex. What else were they going to do? This time, when Angie fainted again, Wallingford thoughtfully removed her old gum from the face of his clock before setting the alarm.

Angie's mother called once more—at least that was who Patrick assumed the caller was. Without saying a word, the woman wept on and on, almost melodiously, while Wallingford drifted in and out of sleep.

He woke up before the alarm went off. He lay looking at the sleeping girl—her untrammeled good-will was truly a thing of beauty. Patrick shut off the alarm before it sounded; he wanted to let Angie sleep. After he showered and shaved, he made a survey of his damaged body: the bruise on his shin from the glass-topped table at Mary's, the burn from the hot-water faucet in Mary's shower. His back was scratched from Angie's nails; on his left shoulder was a sizable blood blister, a purplish hematoma and some broken skin from her spontaneous bite.

Patrick Wallingford seemed in dubious condition for offering a marriage proposal in Wisconsin, or anywhere else. He made some coffee and brought the sleeping girl a glass of cold orange juice in bed.

"Look at this place . . ." she was soon saying, marching naked through his apartment. "It looks like ya been havin' sex!" She stripped the sheets and the pillowcases; she started gathering up the towels. "Ya gotta washin' machine, don'tcha? I know ya gotta plane to catch—I'll clean up here. What if that woman says yes? What if she comes back here with ya?"

"That's not likely. I mean it's not likely she'll come back here with me, even if she does say yes."

"Spare me 'not likely'—she *might*. That's all ya gotta know. Ya catch the plane. I'll fix the place. I'll rewind the answering machine before I leave. I promise."

"You don't have to do this," Patrick told her.

"I wanna help!" Angie said. "I know what it's like to have a messy life. Go *on*—ya betta get outta here! Ya don't wanna miss your plane."

"Thank you, Angie." He kissed her good-bye. She tasted so good, he almost didn't go. What was wrong with sexual anarchy, anyway?

The phone rang as he was leaving. He heard Vito's voice on the answering machine. "Hey, listen up, Mista One Hand . . . Mista No Prick," Vittorio was saying. There was a mechanical whirring, a terrifying sound.

"It's just a stupid blenda. Go *on*—don't miss your plane!" Angie told him. Wallingford was closing the door as she was picking up the phone.

"Hey, Vito," he heard Angie say. "Listen up, limp

dick." Patrick paused on the landing by the stairs; there was a brief but pointed silence. "That's the sound *your* prick would make in the blenda, Vito— *no* sound, 'cause ya got *nothin'* there!"

Wallingford's nearest neighbor was on the landing—a sleepless-looking man from the adjacent apartment, getting ready to walk his dog. Even the dog looked sleepless as it waited, shivering slightly, at the top of the stairs.

"I'm going to Wisconsin," Patrick said hopefully.

The man, who had a silver-gray goatee, looked dazed with general indifference and self-loathing.

"Why don'tcha get a fuckin' *magnifyin'* glass so ya can beat off?" Angie was screaming. The dog pricked up its ears. "Ya know whatcha do with a prick as small as yours, Vito?" Wallingford and his neighbor just stared at the dog. "Ya go to a pet shop. Ya buy a mouse. Ya beg it for a blow job."

The dog, with grave solemnity, seemed to be considering all this. It was some kind of miniature schnauzer with a silver-gray beard, like its master's.

"Have a safe trip," Wallingford's neighbor told him.

"Thank you," Patrick said.

They started down the stairs together—the schnauzer sneezing twice, the neighbor saying that he thought the dog had caught an "air-conditioning cold."

They'd reached the half-landing between floors when Angie shouted something mercifully indistinct. The girl's heroic loyalty was enough to make Wallingford want to go back to her; she was a safer bet than Mrs. Clausen.

But it was early on a summer Saturday morning; the day was brimming with hope. (Maybe not in Boston, where a woman whose name wasn't Sarah Williams either was or was not waiting for an abortion.)

There was no traffic on the way to the airport. Patrick got to the gate before boarding began. Since he'd packed in the dark while Angie slept, he thought it wise to check the contents of his carry-on: a T-shirt, a polo shirt, a sweatshirt, two bathing suits, two pair of underwear—he wore boxers—two pairs of white athletic socks, and a shaving kit, which included his toothbrush and toothpaste and some everhopeful condoms. He'd also packed a paperback edition of *Stuart Little,* recommended for ages eight through twelve.

He had not packed *Charlotte's Web,* because he doubted that Doris's attention span could accommodate two books in one weekend; after all, Otto junior was not yet walking but he was probably crawling. There wouldn't be much time for reading aloud.

Why *Stuart Little* instead of *Charlotte's Web*? one might ask. Only because Patrick Wallingford considered the ending to be more in tune with his own on-the-road-again way of life. And maybe the melancholy of it would be persuasive to Mrs. Clausen—it was certainly more romantic than the birth of all those baby spiders.

In the waiting area, the other passengers watched Wallingford unpack and repack his bag. He'd dressed that morning in a pair of jeans and running shoes and a Hawaiian shirt, and he carried a light jacket, a kind of Windbreaker, to drape over his left forearm to conceal the missing hand. But a one-handed man unpacking and repacking a bag would get anyone's attention. By the time Patrick stopped fussing over what he was bringing to Wisconsin, everyone in the waiting area knew who he was.

They observed the lion guy holding his cell phone in his lap, pinning it against his thigh with the stump of his left forearm while he dialed the number with his one hand; then he picked up the phone and held it to his ear and mouth. When his Windbreaker slipped off the empty seat beside him, his left forearm reached to pick it up, but Wallingford thought better of it and returned the useless stump to his lap.

His fellow passengers must have been surprised. After all these years of handlessness, his left arm still *thinks* it has a hand! But no one ventured to retrieve the fallen Windbreaker until a sympathetic couple, traveling with a young boy, whispered something to their son. The boy, who was perhaps seven or eight, cautiously approached Patrick's jacket; he picked it up and put it carefully on the empty seat beside Wallingford's bag. Patrick smiled and nodded to the boy, who self-consciously hurried back to his parents.

The cell phone rang and rang in Wallingford's ear.

He had meant to call his own apartment and either speak to Angie or leave a message on his answering machine, which he hoped she would hear. He wanted to tell her how wonderful and natural she was; he'd thought of saying something that began, "In another life . . ." That kind of thing. But he hadn't made that call; something about the girl's sheer goodness made him not want to risk hearing her voice. (And what bullshit it was to call someone you'd spent only one night with "natural.")

He called Mary Shanahan instead. Her phone rang so many times that Wallingford was composing a message to leave on her answering machine when Mary picked up the receiver.

"It could only be you, you asshole," she said.

"Mary, we're not married—we're not even going steady. And I'm not trading apartments with you."

"Didn't you have a good time with me, Pat?"

"There was a lot you didn't tell me," Wallingford pointed out.

"That's just the nature of the business."

"I see," he said. There was that distant, hollow sound—the kind of echoing silence Wallingford associated with transoceanic calls. "I guess this wouldn't be a good time to ask you about a new contract," he added. "You said to ask for five years—"

"We should discuss this after your weekend in Wisconsin," Mary replied. "Three years would be more realistic than five, I think."

"And should I . . . well, how did you put it? Should

I sort of phase myself out of the anchor chair—is that your suggestion?"

"If you want a new, extended contract—yes, that would be one way," Mary told him.

"I don't know the history of pregnant anchors," Wallingford admitted. "Has there ever been a pregnant anchor? I suppose it could work. Is that the idea? We would watch you get bigger and bigger. Of course there would be some homey commentary, and a shot or two of you in profile. It would be best to have a brief maternity leave, to suggest that having a baby in today's family-sensitive workplace is no big deal. Then, after what seemed no longer than a standard vacation, you'd be back on-camera, almost as svelte as before."

That transoceanic silence followed, the hollow sound of the distance between them. It was like his marriage, as Wallingford remembered it.

"Am I understanding 'the nature of the business' yet?" Patrick asked. "Am I getting it right?"

"I used to love you," Mary reminded him; then she hung up.

It pleased Wallingford that at least one phase of the office politics between them was over. He would find his own way to get fired, when he felt like it; if he decided to do it Mary's way, she would be the last to know when. And, if it turned out Mary was pregnant, he would be as responsible for the baby as she allowed him to be—he just wouldn't be dicked around by her.

Who was he kidding? If you have a baby with someone, of course you're going to be dicked around! And he had underestimated Mary Shanahan before. She could find a hundred ways to dick him around.

Yet Wallingford recognized what had changed in him—he was no longer acquiescing. Possibly he was the new or semi-new Patrick Wallingford, after all. Moreover, the coldness of Mary Shanahan's tone of voice had been encouraging; he'd sensed that his prospects for getting fired were improving.

On his way to the airport, Patrick had looked at the taxi driver's newspaper, just the weather page. The forecast for northern Wisconsin was warm and fair. Even the weather boded well.

Mrs. Clausen had expressed some anxiety about the weather, because they would be flying to the lake up north in a small plane; it was some kind of seaplane, or what Doris had called a floatplane. Green Bay itself was part of Lake Michigan, but where they were going was roughly between Lake Michigan and Lake Superior—the part of Wisconsin that is near Michigan's Upper Peninsula.

Since Wallingford couldn't get to Green Bay before Saturday and he had to be back in New York on Monday, Doris had determined they should take the little plane. It was too long a drive from Green Bay for such a short weekend; this way they would have two nights in the boathouse apartment at the cottage on the lake.

To get to Green Bay, Patrick had previously tried

two different Chicago connections and one connecting flight through Detroit; this time he'd opted for a change of planes in Cincinnati. Sitting in the waiting area, he was overcome by a moment of typically New York incomprehension. (This happened only seconds before the boarding call.) Why were so many people going to Cincinnati on a Saturday in July?

Of course Wallingford knew why *he* was going there—Cincinnati was simply the first leg of a journey in three parts—but what could possibly be attracting all these *other* people to the place? It would never have occurred to Patrick Wallingford that anyone knowing *his* reasons for the trip might have found Mrs. Clausen's lasting allure the most improbable excuse of all.

CHAPTER ELEVEN

Up North

*T*HERE WAS A MOMENT when the float-plane banked and Doris Clausen closed her eyes. Patrick Wallingford, eyes wide open, didn't want to miss the steep descent to the small, dark lake. Not even for a new left hand, a keeper, would Walling-ford have blinked or looked away from that sideslip-ping view of the dark-green trees and the suddenly tilted horizon. One wingtip must have been pointed at the lake; the window on the seaplane's downward side revealed nothing but the fast-approaching water.

At such a sharp angle, the pontoons shuddered and the plane shook so violently that Mrs. Clausen clutched little Otto to her breast. Her movement star-tled the sleeping child, who commenced to cry only seconds before the pilot leveled off and the small plane landed less than smoothly on the wind-ruffled water. The firs flew by and the white pines were a wall of green, a blur of jade where the blue sky had been.

Doris at last exhaled, but Wallingford hadn't been afraid. Although he'd never been to the lake up north before, nor had he ever flown in a floatplane, the water and the surrounding shore, as well as every frame of the descent and landing, were as familiar to him as that blue-capsule dream. All those years since he'd lost his hand the first time seemed shorter than a single night's sleep to him now; yet, during those years, he had wished continually for that pain-pill dream to come true. At long last, Patrick Wallingford had no doubt that he'd touched down in that blue-capsule dream.

Patrick took it as a good sign that the uncountable members of the Clausen family had not descended en masse on the various cabins and outbuildings. Was it out of respect for the delicacy of Doris's situation—a single parent, a widow with a possible suitor—that Otto senior's family had left the lakefront property unoccupied for the weekend? Had Mrs. Clausen asked them for this consideration? In which case, did she anticipate that the weekend had romantic potential?

If so, Doris gave no indication of it. She had a list of things to do, which she attended to matter-of-factly. Wallingford watched her start the pilot lights for the propane hot-water heaters, the gas refrigerators, and the stove. He carried the baby.

Patrick held little Otto in his left arm, without a hand, because at times he needed to shine the flashlight for Mrs. Clausen. The key to the main cabin was nailed to a beam under the sundeck; the key to the finished rooms above the boathouse was nailed to a two-by-four under the big dock.

It wasn't necessary to unlock and open all the cabins and outbuildings—they wouldn't be using them. The smaller shed, now used for tools, had been an outhouse before there was plumbing, before they pumped water from the lake. Mrs. Clausen expertly primed the pump and pulled the cord to start the gasoline engine that ran the pump.

Doris asked Patrick to dispose of a dead mouse. She held little Otto while Wallingford removed the mouse from the trap and loosely buried it under some leaves and pine needles. The mousetrap had been set in a kitchen cupboard; Mrs. Clausen discovered the dead rodent while she was putting the groceries away.

Doris didn't like mice—they were dirty. She was revolted by the turds they left in what she called "surprise places" throughout the kitchen. She asked Patrick to dispose of the mouse turds, too. And she disliked, even more than their turds, the suddenness with which mice moved. (Maybe I should have brought *Charlotte's Web* instead of *Stuart Little,* Wallingford worried.)

All the food in paper or plastic bags, or in cardboard boxes, had to be stored in tin containers because of the mice; over the winter, not even the canned food could be left unprotected. One winter something had gnawed through the cans—probably a rat, but maybe a mink or a weasel. Another winter, what was almost certainly a wolverine had broken into the main cabin and made the kitchen its lair; the animal had left a terrible mess.

Patrick understood that this was part of the summer-camp lore of the cottage. He could easily envision the life lived here, even without the other Clausens present. In the main cabin, where the kitchen and dining room were—also the biggest of the bathrooms—he saw the board games and puzzles stacked on shelves. There were no books to speak of, save a dictionary (doubtless for settling arguments in Scrabble) and the usual field guides that identify snakes and amphibians, insects and spiders, wildflowers, mammals, and birds.

In the main cabin, too, were the visualizations of the ghosts that had passed through or still visited there. These took the form of artless snapshots, curled at the edges. Some of these photos were badly faded from long exposure to sunlight; others were rust-spotted from the old tacks pinning them to the rough pine walls.

And there were other mementos that spoke of ghosts. The mounted heads of deer, or just their antlers; a crow's skull that revealed the perfect hole made by a .22-caliber bullet; some undistinguished fish, home-mounted on plaques of shellacked pine boards. (The fish looked as if they'd been crudely varnished, too.)

Most outstanding was a single talon of a large bird of prey. Mrs. Clausen told Wallingford it was an eagle's talon; it was not a trophy but a record of shame, displayed in a jewelry box as a warning to other Clausens. It was awful to shoot an eagle, yet one of the less disciplined Clausens had done the deed, for which he was harshly punished. He'd been a young boy at the time, and he'd been "grounded," Doris said—meaning he had missed two hunting seasons, back-to-back. If that wasn't lesson enough, the murdered eagle's talon remained as further evidence against him.

"Donny," Doris said, shaking her head as she uttered the eagle-killer's name. Attached to the plush lining of the jewelry box (by a safety pin) was a photo of Donny—he looked crazed. He was a grown man now, with children of his own; when his kids saw the talon, they were probably ashamed of their father all over again.

Mrs. Clausen's telling of the tale was sobering, and she related it in the manner that it had been told to her—a cautionary tale, a moral warning. DON'T SHOOT EAGLES!

"Donny was always a wild hair," Mrs. Clausen reported.

In his mind's eye, Wallingford could see them interacting—the ghosts in the photographs, the fishermen who had caught the shellacked fish, the hunters who'd shot the deer and the crow and the eagle. He imagined the men standing around the barbecue, which was covered with a tarp and stowed on the sundeck under an eave of the roof.

There was an indoor and an outdoor fridge, which Patrick imagined were full of beer. Mrs. Clausen later corrected this impression; only the outdoor refrigerator was full of beer. It was the designated beer fridge—nothing else was allowed in it.

While the men watched the barbecue and drank their beer, the women fed the children—at the picnic table on the deck in good weather, or at the long dining-room table when the weather was bad. The limitations of space in cottage life spoke to Wallingford of children and grown-ups eating separately. Mrs. Clausen, at first laughing at Patrick's question, confirmed that this was true.

There was a row of photographs of women in hospital gowns in beds, their newborns beside them; Doris's photo was not among them. Wallingford felt the conspicuousness of her and little Otto's absence. (*Big* Otto hadn't been there to take their picture.) There were men and boys in uniforms—all kinds of uniforms, military and athletic—and women and girls in formal dresses and bathing suits, most of them caught in the act of protesting that their pictures were being taken.

There was a wall for dogs—dogs swimming, dogs fetching sticks, some dogs forlornly dressed in children's clothes. And in a nook above the dresser drawers in one of the bedrooms, inserted by their edges into the frame of a pitted mirror, were photos of the elderly, probably now deceased. An old woman in a wheelchair with a cat in her lap; an old man without a paddle in the bow of a canoe. The old man had long white hair and was wrapped in a blanket like an Indian; he seemed to be waiting for someone to sit in the stern and paddle him away.

In the hall, opposite the bathroom door, was a cluster of photographs in the shape of a cross—a shrine to a young Clausen male declared missing-in-action in Vietnam. In the bathroom itself was another shrine, this one to the glory days of the Green Bay Packers—a hallowed gathering of old magazine photos picturing the "invincible ones."

Wallingford had great difficulty identifying these heroes; the pages torn from magazines were wrinkled and water-spotted, the captions barely legible. "In a locker room in Milwaukee," Wallingford struggled to read, "after clinching their second Western Division championship, December 1961." There were Bart Starr, Paul Hornung, and Coach Lombardi— the coach holding a bottle of Pepsi. Jim Taylor was bleeding from a gash on the bridge of his nose. Wallingford didn't recognize them, but he could identify with Taylor, who was missing several front teeth.

Who were Jerry Kramer and Fuzzy Thurston, and what was the "Packer sweep"? Who was that guy caked in mud? (It was Forrest Gregg.) Or Ray

Nitschke, muddy and bald and dazed and bleeding; sitting on the bench at a game in San Francisco, Nitschke held his helmet in his hands like a rock. Who are these people, or who *were* they? Wallingford wondered.

There was that famous photo of the fans at the Ice Bowl—Lambeau Field, December 31, 1967. They were dressed for the Arctic or the Antarctic; their breath obscured their faces in the cold. Some Clausens had to have been among them.

Wallingford would never know the meaning of that pile of bodies, or how the Dallas Cowboys must have felt to see Bart Starr lying in the end zone; not even his Green Bay teammates had known that Starr was going to improvise a quarterback sneak from the one-yard line. In the huddle, as every Clausen knew, the quarterback had called, "Brown right. Thirty-one wedge." The result was sports history—it just wasn't a history Wallingford knew.

To realize how little he knew Mrs. Clausen's world gave Patrick pause.

There were also the personal but unclear photos that required interpretation to outsiders. Doris tried to explain. That hulking rock in the wake off the stern of the speedboat—that was a black bear, discovered one summer swimming in the lake. That blurry shape, like a time-lapsed photograph of a cow grazing out-of-place among the evergreens, was a moose making its way to the swamp, which according to Mrs. Clausen was "not a quarter of a mile from here." And so on . . . the confrontations with nature and the crimes against nature, the local victories and the special occasions, the Green Bay Packers and the births in the family, the dogs and the weddings.

Wallingford noted, as quickly as he could, the photograph of Otto senior and Mrs. Clausen at their wedding. They were carving the cake; Otto's strong left hand covered Doris's smaller hand, which held the knife. Patrick experienced a pang of familiarity when he saw Otto's hand, although he'd not seen it with the wedding ring before. What had Mrs. Clausen done with Otto's ring? he wondered. What had she done with hers?

At the front of the well-wishers who surrounded the cutting of the cake, a young boy stood holding a plate and a fork. He was nine or ten; because he was formally dressed like the other members of the wedding party, Patrick assumed he'd been the ring bearer. He didn't recognize the kid, but since the ring bearer would be a young man now, Wallingford realized that he might have met him. (In all likelihood, given the boy's round face and determined cheerfulness, he was a Clausen.)

The maid of honor stood beside the boy, biting her lower lip; she was a pretty young woman who seemed easily distracted, a girl often swayed by caprice. Like Angie, maybe?

At a glance, Patrick knew he'd never met her before; that she was the kind of girl he was familiar with, he also knew. She was not as nice as Angie. Once upon a time, the maid of honor might have been Doris's best friend. But the choice could also have been political; possibly the wayward-looking girl was big Otto's kid sister. And whether or not she and Doris had ever been friends, Patrick doubted that they were friends now.

As for the sleeping arrangements, Wallingford's first look at the two finished rooms above the boat-house made the matter clear. Doris had set up the portable crib in the room with the twin beds, one of which she'd already used as a makeshift changing table—little Otto's diapers and clothes were arrayed there. Mrs. Clausen told Patrick that she would sleep in the other twin bed in that room, which left the second room above the boathouse to Wallingford; it had a queen-size bed, which looked bigger in the narrow room.

As Patrick unpacked his things, he noted that the left side of the bed was flush to the wall—that would have been Otto senior's side. Given the narrowness of the room, the only way into the bed was from Doris's side; even then, the passage was skinny. Maybe Otto senior had climbed in from the foot of the bed.

The walls of the room were the same rough pine as the interior of the main cabin, although the pine boards were lighter, almost blond—all but one large rectangle near the door, where perhaps a picture or a mirror had been hung. Sunlight had bleached the walls almost everywhere else. What had Mrs. Clausen taken down?

Thumbtacked to the wall, above Otto senior's side of the bed, were various photos of the restoration of the rooms above the boathouse. There was Otto senior, without a shirt, tanned and well muscled. (The carpenter's belt reminded Patrick of the tool belt Monika with a *k* had had stolen from her at the circus in Junagadh.) There was also a photo of Doris in a one-piece bathing suit—a purple tank, conservatively cut. She had her arms crossed over her breasts, which made Wallingford sad; he would have liked to have seen more of her breasts.

In the photograph, Mrs. Clausen was standing on the dock, watching Otto senior at work with a table saw. Since there was no electricity at the cottage on the lake, the gasoline generator on the dock must have supplied the power. The dark puddle at Doris's bare feet suggested that her bathing suit was wet. Quite possibly, she'd hugged her arms to her breasts because she was cold.

When Wallingford closed the bedroom door to change into his swim trunks, that same purple one-piece bathing suit was hanging on a nail on the back of the door. Patrick couldn't resist touching it. The purple bathing suit had spent much time in the water and in the sun; it's doubtful that even a trace of

Doris's scent was attached to it, although Wallingford held the suit to his face and imagined that he
could smell her.

In truth, the suit smelled more like Lycra, and like
the lake, and the wood of the boathouse; but Patrick
clutched the suit as tightly as he would have held fast
to Mrs. Clausen—had she been wet and cold and
shivering, the two of them taking off their wet
bathing suits together.

This was truly pathetic behavior to display in the
case of a no-nonsense, some would say frumpy, one-
piece tank suit, fully front-lined, with the shoulder
straps crossed in the back. The built-in shelf bra with
thin, soft cups was a practical choice for a large-
breasted but narrow-chested woman, which Doris
Clausen was.

Wallingford returned the purple bathing suit to
the nail on the back of the bedroom door; he hung
it, as she had done, by the shoulder straps. Beside it,
on another nail, was the only other article of Mrs.
Clausen's clothing in the bedroom—a once-white,
now somewhat grimy, terry-cloth robe. That this unexciting garment excited him was embarrassing.

He opened the dresser drawers as quietly as possible, looking for Doris's underwear. But the bottom
drawer held only sheets and pillowcases and an extra
blanket; the middle drawer was full of towels. The
top drawer rattled noisily with candles, flashlight
batteries, several boxes of wooden matches, an extra
flashlight, and a box of tacks.

In the rough pine boards above Mrs. Clausen's side of the bed, Patrick noticed the small holes that tacks had made. She'd once tacked photographs there, as many as a dozen. Of what, or of whom, Wallingford could only guess. Why Doris had apparently removed the photos was another unknown.

There came a knock on the bedroom door just as Patrick was tying the strings on his swim trunks, which he'd long ago learned to do with his right hand and his teeth. Mrs. Clausen wanted her bathing suit and the terry-cloth robe; she told Wallingford which drawer the towels were in, unaware that he already knew, and asked him to bring three towels to the dock.

When she'd changed, they met in the narrow hall and descended the steep stairs to the ground floor of the boathouse; the staircase was open, which would be hazardous to little Otto next summer. Otto senior had meant to enclose the staircase. "He just didn't get around to it," Mrs. Clausen commented.

There was a gangplank and a slender dock that separated the two boats tied up in the boathouse, the family speedboat and a smaller outboard. At the open end of the boathouse, a ladder went into the water from the dividing dock. Who would want to enter or climb out of the lake from inside the boathouse? But Patrick didn't mention the ladder because Mrs. Clausen was already making arrangements for the baby on the big outdoors dock.

She'd brought some toys and a quilt the size of a

picnic blanket. The child wasn't crawling as actively as Wallingford had expected. Otto junior could sit up by himself, until he seemed to forget where he was; then he'd roll over on his side. At eight months, the child could pull himself up to his feet—*if* there was a low table or some other sturdy thing for him to hang on to. But he often forgot he was standing; he would suddenly sit down or topple sideways.

And most of little Otto's crawling was backward—he could back up more easily than he could move forward. If he was surrounded by some interesting objects to handle and look at, he would sit in one spot quite contentedly—but not for long, Doris pointed out. "In a few weeks, we won't be able to sit on a dock with him. He'll be moving, on all fours, nonstop."

For now, because of the sun, the child wore a long-sleeved shirt, long pants, and a hat—also sunglasses, which he didn't pull off his face as frequently as Patrick would have predicted. "You swim. I'll watch him. Then you can watch him while I swim," Mrs. Clausen told Wallingford.

Patrick was impressed by the sheer amount of baby paraphernalia Mrs. Clausen had brought for the weekend; he was equally impressed by how calmly and effortlessly Doris seemed to have adjusted to being a mother. Or maybe motherhood did that to women who'd wanted to have a baby as badly and for as long as Mrs. Clausen had wanted one. Wallingford didn't really know.

The lake water felt cold, but only when you first went in. Off the deep end of the dock, the water was blue-gray; nearer shore, it took on a greener color from the reflected fir trees and white pines. The bottom was sandier, less muddy, than Patrick had anticipated, and there was a small beach of coarse sand, strewn with rocks, where Wallingford bathed little Otto in the lake. Initially the boy was shocked by the coldness of the water, but he never cried; he let Wallingford wade with him in his arms while Mrs. Clausen took their picture. (She seemed quite the expert with a camera.)

The grown-ups, as Patrick began to think of Doris and himself, took turns swimming off the dock. Mrs. Clausen was a good swimmer. Wallingford explained that, with one hand, he felt more comfortable just floating or treading water. Together they dried little Otto, and Doris let Patrick try to dress the child—his first attempt. She had to show him how to do the diaper.

Mrs. Clausen was deft at taking her bathing suit off under the terry-cloth robe. Wallingford, because of the one-hand problem, was less skillful at taking his suit off while wrapped in a towel. Finally Doris laughed and said she would look the other way while he managed it, out in the open. (She didn't tell him about the Peeping Tom with the telescope on the opposite shore of the lake—not yet.)

Together they carried the baby and his paraphernalia to the main cabin. There was a child's highchair already in place, and Wallingford drank a beer—he was still wearing just a towel—while Mrs. Clausen fed Otto junior. She told Patrick that they should feed the baby and make their own dinner, and be finished with everything they had to do in the main cabin—all before dark. After dark, the mosquitoes came. They should be settled into the boathouse apartment by then.

There was no bathroom in the boathouse. Doris reminded Wallingford that he should use the toilet in the main cabin, and brush his teeth in the bathroom sink there. If he had to get up and pee in the middle of the night, he could go outside with a flashlight and be quick about it. "Just get back to the boathouse before the mosquitoes find you," Mrs. Clausen warned.

Using her camera, Patrick took a picture of Doris and little Otto on the sundeck of the main cabin.

The grown-ups barbecued a steak for their dinner, which they ate with some green peas and rice. Mrs. Clausen had brought two bottles of red wine— they drank only one. While Doris did the dishes, Patrick took her camera down to the dock and took two pictures of their bathing suits side-by-side on the clothesline.

It seemed to him the height of privacy and domestic tranquillity that they had eaten their dinner together with Doris dressed in her old bathrobe and Wallingford wearing only a towel around his waist. He'd never lived like this, not with anyone.

Wallingford took another beer with him when they

went back to the boathouse. As they navigated the pine-needle path, they were aware that the west wind had dropped and the lake was dead-calm; the setting sun still struck the treetops on the eastern shore. In the windless evening, the mosquitoes had already risen—they hadn't waited till dark. Patrick and Doris were waving the mosquitoes away as they carried little Otto and the baby's paraphernalia into the boat-house apartment.

Wallingford watched the encroaching darkness from his bedroom window while he listened to Mrs. Clausen putting Otto junior to bed in the next room. She was singing him a nursery rhyme. Patrick's windows were open; he could hear the mosquitoes humming against the screens. The loons were the only other sound, save an outboard puttering on the lake, over which he could hear voices. Perhaps they were fishermen returning home, or teenagers. Then the outboard docked, far-off, and Mrs. Clausen was no longer singing to little Otto; it was quiet in the other bedroom. Now the loons and an occasional duck were the only sound, except for the mosquitoes.

Wallingford sensed a remoteness he'd never experienced, and it was not yet fully dark. Still wrapped in the towel, he lay on the bed and let the room grow darker. He tried to imagine the photographs that Doris had once tacked to the wall on her side of the bed.

He'd fallen sound asleep when Mrs. Clausen came and woke him with the flashlight. In her old white bathrobe, she stood at the foot of the bed like a ghost, the light pointed at herself. She kept blinking the flashlight on and off, as if she were trying to impress him with how dark it was, although there was nearly a full moon.

"Come on," she whispered. "Let's go swimming. We don't need suits for a night swim. Just bring your towel."

She went out into the hall and led him down the stairs, holding his one hand and pointing the flashlight at their bare feet. With his stump, Wallingford made a clumsy effort to keep the towel tight around his waist. The boathouse was very dark. Doris took him down the gangplank and out on the slender dividing dock between the moored boats. She shined the flashlight ahead of them, illuminating the ladder at the end of the dock.

So the ladder was for night swims. Patrick was being invited to take part in a ritual that Mrs. Clausen had enacted with her late husband. Their careful, single-file navigation of the thin, dark dock seemed a holy passage.

The flashlight caught a large spider moving quickly along a mooring line. The spider startled Wallingford, but not Mrs. Clausen. "It's just a spider," she said. "I like spiders. They're so industrious."

So she likes industriousness *and* spiders, Patrick thought. He hated himself for bringing *Stuart Little* instead of *Charlotte's Web.* Perhaps he wouldn't even mention to Doris that he had brought the stupid book with him, let alone that he'd imagined reading it first to her and then to little Otto.

At the ladder, Mrs. Clausen took off her robe. She'd clearly had some practice at arranging the flashlight on the robe so that it pointed out over the lake. The light would be a beacon for them to return to.

Wallingford took off his towel and stood naked beside her. She gave him no time to think about touching her; she went quickly down the ladder and slipped into the lake, making almost no sound. He followed her into the water, but not as gracefully or noiselessly as she had managed it. (You try going down a ladder with one hand.) The best Patrick could do was clutch the side rail in the crook of his left arm; his right hand and arm did most of the work.

They swam close together. Mrs. Clausen was careful not to swim too far ahead of him, or she treaded water or just floated until he caught up with her. They went out past the deep end of the big outdoors dock, where they could see the dark outline of the unlit main cabin and the smaller outbuildings; the rudimentary buildings resembled a wilderness colony, abandoned. Across the moonlit lake, the other summer cottages were unlit, too. The cottagers went to bed early and got up with the sun.

In addition to the flashlight aimed at the lake from the dock in the boathouse, there was another light visible—in Otto junior's bedroom. Doris had left the gas lamp on, in case the child woke up; she didn't want him to be frightened by the dark. With the windows open, she was sure she would hear the baby if he awakened and cried. Sound travels very clearly over water, especially at night, Mrs. Clausen explained.

She could easily talk while swimming—she didn't once sound out of breath. She talked and talked, explaining everything. How she and Otto senior could never swim at night by diving off the big outdoors dock, where the other Clausens (in the other cabins) would hear them. But by entering the lake from inside the boathouse, they'd discovered that they could reach the water undetected.

Wallingford could hear the ghosts of boisterous, fun-loving Clausens going back and forth to the beer fridge—a screen door whapping and someone calling, "Don't let the mosquitoes in!" Or a woman's voice: "That dog is all wet!" And the voice of a child: "Uncle Donny did it."

One of the dogs would come down to the lake and bark witlessly at Mrs. Clausen and Otto senior, swimming naked and undetected—except by the dog. "Someone shoot that damn dog!" an angry voice would call. Then someone else would say, "Maybe it's an otter or a mink." A third person, either opening or closing the door of the beer fridge, would comment: "No, it's just that brainless dog. That dog barks at anything, or at nothing at all."

Wallingford wasn't sure if he was really swimming naked with Doris Clausen, or if she was sleeplessly reliving her night swims with Otto senior. Patrick loved swimming beside her, despite the obvious melancholy attached to it.

When the mosquitoes found them, they swam underwater for a short distance, but Mrs. Clausen wanted to go back to the boathouse. If they swam underwater, even briefly, they wouldn't hear the baby if he cried or notice if the gaslight flickered.

There were the stars and the moon in the northern night sky; there was a loon calling, and another loon diving nearby. Just briefly, the swimmers thought they heard snatches of a song. Maybe someone in one of the dark cottages across the lake was playing a radio, but the swimmers didn't think it was a radio.

The song, which was a song they were both familiar with, was on their minds at that moment simultaneously. It was a popular song about missing someone, and clearly Mrs. Clausen was missing her late husband. Patrick missed Mrs. Clausen, although in truth they'd only ever been together in his imagination.

She went up the ladder first. Treading water, he saw her silhouette—the beam of the flashlight was behind her. She quickly put on her robe as he struggled one-handed up the ladder. She shined the flashlight down at the dock, where he could see his towel; while he picked it up and wrapped it around his waist, she waited with the light pointed at her feet. Then she reached back and took his one hand, and he followed her again.

They went to look at little Otto, sleeping. Wallingford was unprepared; he didn't know that watching a sleeping child was as good as a movie to some mothers. When Mrs. Clausen sat on one of the twin beds and commenced to stare at her sleeping son, Patrick sat down beside her. He had to—she'd not let go of his hand. It was as if the child were a drama, unfolding.

"Story time," Doris whispered, in a voice Wallingford had not heard before—she sounded ashamed. She gave a slight squeeze to Wallingford's one hand, just in case he was confused and had misunderstood her. The story was for him, not for little Otto.

"I tried to see someone, I mean someone else," she said. "I tried going out with him."

Did "going out" with someone mean what Wallingford thought it meant, even in Wisconsin?

"I slept with someone, someone I shouldn't have slept with," Mrs. Clausen explained.

"Oh . . ." Patrick couldn't help saying; it was an involuntary response. He listened for the breathing of the sleeping child, not hearing it above the sound the gaslight made, which was like a kind of breathing.

"He's someone I've known for a long time, but in another life," Doris went on. "He's a little younger than I am," she added. She still held Wallingford's one hand, although she'd stopped squeezing it. He wanted to squeeze her hand—to show her his sympathy, to support her—but his hand felt anesthetized. (He recognized the feeling.) "He used to be married to a friend of mine," Mrs. Clausen continued. "We all went out together when Otto was alive. We were always doing things, the four of us, the way couples do."

Patrick managed to squeeze her hand a little.

"But he broke up with his wife—this was after I lost Otto," Mrs. Clausen explained. "And when he called me and asked me out, I didn't say I would—not at first. I called my friend, just to be sure they were getting divorced and that our going out was all right with her. She said it was okay, but she didn't mean it. It *wasn't* okay with her, after the fact. And I *shouldn't* have. I didn't like him, anyway. Not in that way."

It was all Wallingford could do not to shout, "Good!"

"So I told him I wouldn't go out with him anymore. He took it okay, he's still friendly, but *she* won't talk to me. And she was the maid of honor at my wedding, if you can imagine that." Wallingford could, if only on the basis of a single photograph. "Well, that's all. I just wanted to tell you," Mrs. Clausen said.

"I'm glad you told me," Patrick managed to say, although "glad" didn't come close to what he felt—a devastating jealousy in tandem with an overwhelming relief. She'd slept with an old friend—that was all! That it hadn't worked out made Wallingford feel more than glad; he felt elated. He also felt naïve. Without being beautiful, Mrs. Clausen was one of the most sexually attractive women he'd ever met. Of course men would call her and ask her "out." Why hadn't he foreseen this?

He didn't know where to start. Possibly Patrick took too much encouragement from the fact that Mrs. Clausen now gripped his hand more tightly than before; she must have been relieved that he'd been a sympathetic listener.

"I love you," he began. He was pleased that Doris didn't take her hand away, although he felt her grip lessen. "I want to live with you and little Otto. I want to marry you." She was neutral now, just listening. He couldn't tell what she thought.

They didn't look at each other, not once. They continued to stare at Otto junior sleeping. The child's open mouth beckoned a story; therefore, Wallingford began one. It was the wrong story to begin, but he was a journalist—a fact guy, not a storyteller.

What he neglected was the very thing he deplored about his profession—he left out the context! He should have begun with Boston, with his trip to see Dr. Zajac because of the sensations of pain and crawling insects where Otto senior's hand had been. He should have told Mrs. Clausen about meeting the woman in the Charles Hotel—how they'd read E. B. White to each other, naked, but they'd *not* had sex;

how he'd been thinking of Mrs. Clausen the whole time. Really, he *had*!

All that was part of the context of how he'd acquiesced to Mary Shanahan's desire to have his baby. And while it might have gone better with Doris Clausen if Patrick had begun with Boston, it would have been better yet if he'd begun with Japan—how he'd first asked Mary, then a young married woman who was *pregnant,* to come to Tokyo with him; how he'd felt guilty about that, and for so long had resisted her; how he'd tried so hard to be "just a friend."

Because wasn't it part of the context, too, that he'd finally slept with Mary Shanahan with no strings attached? Meaning wasn't he being "just a friend" to give her what she said she wanted? Just a baby, nothing more. That Mary wanted his apartment, too, or maybe she wanted to move in with him; that she also wanted his job, and she knew all along that she was about to become his boss ... well, shit, *that* was a surprise! But how could Patrick have predicted it?

Surely if any woman could sympathize with another woman wanting to have Patrick Wallingford's baby, wasn't it reasonable for Patrick to think that Doris Clausen would be the one? No, it *wasn't* reasonable! And how *could* she sympathize, given the half-assed manner in which Wallingford told the story?

He'd just plunged in. He was artless, in the worst sense of the word—meaning oafish and crude. He began with what amounted to a confession: "I don't really think of this as an illustration of why I might have trouble maintaining a monogamous relationship, but it is a little disturbing."

What a way to begin a proposal! Was it any wonder that Doris withdrew her hand from his and turned to look at him? Wallingford, who sensed from his misguided prologue that he was already in trouble, couldn't look at her while he talked. He stared instead at their sleeping child, as if the innocence of Otto junior might serve to shield Mrs. Clausen from all that was sexually incorrigible and morally reprehensible in his relationship with Mary Shanahan.

Mrs. Clausen was appalled. She wasn't, for once, even looking at her son; she couldn't take her eyes off Wallingford's handsome profile as he clumsily recounted the details of his shameful behavior. He was babbling now, out of nervousness, in part, but also because he feared that the impression he was making on Doris was the opposite of what he'd intended.

What had he been thinking? What an absolute *mess* it would be if Mary Shanahan was pregnant with his child!

Still in a confessional mode, he lifted the towel to show Mrs. Clausen the bruise on his shin from the glass-topped table in Mary's apartment; he also showed her the burn from the hot-water faucet in Mary's shower. She'd already noticed how his back was scratched. And the love-bite on his left shoulder— she'd noticed that, too.

"Oh, that wasn't Mary," Wallingford confessed.

This was not the best thing he could have said.

"Who else have you been seeing?" Doris asked.

This wasn't going as he'd hoped. But how much more trouble could Patrick get into by telling Mrs. Clausen about Angie? Surely Angie's was a simpler story.

"I was with the makeup girl, but it was only for one night," Wallingford began. "I was just horny."

What a way with words he had! (Talk about neglecting the context!)

He told Doris about the phone calls from various members of Angie's distraught family, but Mrs. Clausen was confused—she thought he meant that Angie was underage. (All the gum-chewing didn't help.) "Angie is a good-hearted girl," Patrick kept saying, which gave Doris the impression that the makeup girl might be mentally disabled. "No, no!" Wallingford protested. "Angie is neither underage nor mentally disabled, she's just . . . well . . ."

"A bimbo?" asked Mrs. Clausen.

"No, no! Not exactly," Patrick protested loyally.

"Maybe you were thinking that she might be the very last person you would sleep with—that is, if I accepted you," Doris speculated. "And since you didn't know whether I would accept you or reject you, there was no reason *not* to sleep with her."

"Yes, maybe," Wallingford replied weakly.

"Well, that's not so bad," Mrs. Clausen told him. "I can understand that. I can understand Angie, I mean." He dared to look at her for the first time, but she looked away—she stared at Otto junior, who was still blissfully asleep. "I have more trouble understanding Mary," Doris added. "I don't know how you could have been thinking of living with me and little Otto while you were trying to make that woman pregnant. If she *is* pregnant, and it's your baby, doesn't that complicate things for us? For you and me and Otto, I mean."

"Yes, it does," Patrick agreed. Again he thought: *What was I thinking?* Wasn't this also a context he had overlooked?

"I can understand what Mary was up to," Mrs. Clausen went on. She suddenly gripped his one hand in both of hers, looking at him so intently that he couldn't turn away. "Who *wouldn't* want your baby?" She bit her lower lip and shook her head; she was trying not to get loud and angry, at least not in the room with her sleeping child. "You're like a pretty girl who has no idea how pretty she is. You have no clue of your *effect.* It's not that you're dangerous because you're handsome—you're dangerous because you don't know how handsome you are! And you're thoughtless." The word stung him like a slap. "How *could* you have been thinking of me while you were consciously trying to knock up somebody else? You *weren't* thinking of me! Not then."

"But you seemed such a . . . remote possibility," was all Wallingford could say. He knew that what she'd said was true.

What a fool he was! He'd mistakenly believed that he could tell her the stories of his most recent sexual escapades and make them as understandable to her as her far more sympathetic story was to him. Because *her* relationship, although a mistake, had at least been real; she'd tried to date an old friend who was, at the time, as available as she was. And it hadn't worked out—that was all.

Alongside Mrs. Clausen's single misadventure, Wallingford's world was sexually lawless. The sheer sloppiness of his thinking made him ashamed.

Doris's disappointment in him was as noticeable as her hair, which was still wet and tangled from their night swim. Her disappointment was as plainly apparent as the dark crescents under her eyes, or what he'd noticed of her body in the purple bathing suit, and what he'd seen of her naked in the moonlight and in the lake. (She'd put on a little weight, or had not yet lost the weight she'd put on when she was pregnant.)

What Wallingford realized he loved most about her went far beyond her sexual frankness. She was serious about everything she said, and purposeful about everything she did. She was as unlike Mary Shanahan as a woman could be: she was forthright and practical, she was trusting and trustworthy; and when Mrs. Clausen gave you her attention, she gave you all of it.

Patrick Wallingford's world was one in which sexual anarchy ruled. Doris Clausen would permit no such anarchy in hers. What Wallingford also realized was that she had actually taken his proposal seriously; Mrs. Clausen considered *everything* seriously. In all likelihood, her acceptance had not been as remote a possibility as he'd once thought—he'd just blown it.

She sat apart from him on the small bed with her hands clasped in her lap. She looked neither at him nor at little Otto, but at some undefined and enormous tiredness, which she was long familiar with and had stared at—often at this hour of the night or early morning—many times before. "I should get some sleep," was all she said.

If her faraway gaze could have been measured, Patrick guessed that she might have been staring through the wall—at the darker rectangle on the wall of the other bedroom, at that place near the door where a picture or a mirror had once hung.

"Something used to hang on the wall . . . in the other bedroom," he conjectured, trying without hope to engage her. "What was it?"

"It was just a beer poster," Mrs. Clausen flatly informed him, an unbearable deadness in her voice.

"Oh." Again his utterance was involuntary, as if he were reacting to a punch. Naturally it would have been a beer poster; of course she wouldn't have wanted to go on looking at it.

He extended his one hand, not letting it fall in her lap but lightly brushing her stomach with the backs of his fingers. "You used to have a metal thing in

your belly button. It was an ornament of some kind,"
he ventured. "I saw it only once." He didn't add that
it was the time she'd mounted him in Dr. Zajac's office. Doris Clausen seemed so unlike a person who
would have a pierced navel!

She took his hand and held it in her lap. This was
not a gesture of encouragement; she just didn't want
him touching her anywhere else. "It was supposed to
be a good-luck charm," Doris explained. In the way
she said "supposed to be," Wallingford could detect
years of disbelief. "Otto bought it in a tattoo shop.
We were trying everything at the time, for fertility. It
was something I wore when I was trying to get pregnant. It didn't work, except with you, and you probably didn't need it."

"So you don't wear it anymore?"

"I'm not trying to get pregnant anymore," she told
him.

"Oh." He felt sick with the certainty that he had
lost her.

"I should get some sleep," she said again.

"There was something I wanted to read to you," he
told her, "but we can do it another time."

"What is it?" she asked him.

"Well, actually, it's something I want to read to little Otto—when he's older. I wanted to read it to you
now because I was thinking of reading it to him
later." Wallingford paused. Out of context, this made
no more sense than anything else he'd told her. He
felt ridiculous.

"What is it?" she asked again.

"Stuart Little," he answered, wishing he'd never brought it up.

"Oh, the children's book. It's about a mouse, isn't it?" He nodded, ashamed. "He has a special car," she added. "He goes off looking for a bird. It's a kind of *On the Road* about a mouse, isn't it?"

Wallingford wouldn't have put it that way, but he nodded. That Mrs. Clausen had read *On the Road,* or at least knew of it, surprised him.

"I need to sleep," Doris repeated. "And if I can't sleep, I brought my own book to read."

Patrick managed to restrain himself from saying anything, but barely. So much seemed lost now—all the more so because he hadn't known that it might have been possible *not* to lose her.

At least he had the good sense not to jump into the story of reading *Stuart Little* and *Charlotte's Web* aloud (and naked) with Sarah Williams, or whatever her name was. Out of context—possibly, in *any* context—that story would have served only to underline Wallingford's weirdness. The time he might have told her that story, to his advantage, was long gone; now wouldn't have been good.

Now he was just stalling because he didn't want to lose her. They both knew it. "What book did *you* bring to read?" he asked.

Mrs. Clausen took this opportunity to get up from where she sat beside him on the bed. She went to her open canvas bag, which resembled several other small bags containing the baby's things. It was the only bag she'd brought for herself, and she'd not yet bothered (or had not yet had the time) to unpack it.

She found the book beneath her underwear. Doris handed it to him as if she were too tired to talk about it. (She probably was.) It was *The English Patient,* a novel by Michael Ondaatje. Wallingford hadn't read it but he'd seen the movie.

"It was the last movie I saw with Otto before he died," Mrs. Clausen explained. "We both liked it. I liked it so much that I wanted to read the book. But I put off reading it until now. I didn't want to be reminded of the last movie I saw with Otto."

Patrick Wallingford looked down at *The English Patient.* She was reading a grown-up literary novel and he'd planned to read her *Stuart Little.* How many more ways would he find to underestimate her?

That she worked in ticket sales for the Green Bay Packers didn't exclude her from reading literary novels, although (to his shame) Patrick had made that assumption.

He remembered liking the movie of *The English Patient.* His ex-wife had said that the movie was better than the book. That he doubted Marilyn's judgment on just about everything was borne out when she made a comment about the novel that Wallingford remembered reading in a review. What she'd said about *The English Patient* was that the movie was better because the novel was "too well written." That a book could be too well written was a concept only a critic—and Marilyn—could have.

"I haven't read it," was all Wallingford said to Mrs. Clausen, who put the book back in her open bag on top of her underwear.

"It's good," Doris told him. "I'm reading it very slowly because I like it so much. I think I like it better than the movie, but I'm trying not to remember the movie." (Of course this meant that there wasn't a scene in the film she would ever forget.)

What else was there to say? Wallingford had to pee. Miraculously, he refrained from telling Mrs. Clausen this—he'd said quite enough for one night. She shined the flashlight into the hall for him, so that he didn't have to grope in the dark to find his room.

He was too tired to light the gas lamp. He took the flashlight he found on the dresser top and made his way down the steep stairs. The moon had set; it was much darker now. The first light of dawn couldn't be far off. Patrick chose a tree to pee behind, although there was no one who could have seen him. By the time he finished peeing, the mosquitoes had already found him. He quickly followed the beam of his flashlight back to the boathouse.

Mrs. Clausen and little Otto's room was dark when Wallingford quietly passed their open door. He remembered her saying that she never slept with the gaslight on. The propane lamps were probably safe enough, but a lighted lamp was still a fire—it made her too anxious to sleep.

Wallingford left the door to his room open, too. He wanted to hear when Otto junior woke up. Maybe he would offer to watch the child so that Doris could go back to sleep. How difficult could it be to entertain a baby? Wasn't a television audience tougher? That was as far as he thought it out.

He finally took off the towel from around his waist. He put on a pair of boxer shorts and crawled into bed, but before he turned the flashlight off, he made sure he'd memorized where it was in case he needed to find it in the dark. (He left it on the floor, by Mrs. Clausen's side of the bed.) Now that the moon had set, there was an almost total blackness that resembled his prospects with Mrs. Clausen.

Patrick forgot to close his curtains, although Doris had warned him that the sun rose directly in his windows. Later, when he was still asleep, Wallingford was supernaturally aware of a predawn light in the sky. This was when the crows started cawing; even in his sleep, he was more aware of the crows than he was of the loons. Without seeing it, he sensed the increasing light.

Then little Otto's crying woke him, and he lay listening to Mrs. Clausen soothe the child. The boy stopped crying fairly quickly, but he still fussed while his mother changed him. From Doris's tone of voice, and the varying baby noises that Otto made, Wallingford could guess what they were doing. He heard them go down the boathouse stairs; Mrs. Clausen kept talking as they went up the path to the main cabin. Patrick remembered that the baby formula had to be mixed with bottled water, which Mrs. Clausen heated on the stove.

He looked first in the area of his missing left hand and then at his right wrist. (He would never get used to wearing his watch on his right arm.) Just as the rising sun shot through his bedroom windows from across the lake, Patrick saw that it was only a little past five in the morning.

As a reporter, he'd traveled all over the world—he was familiar with sleep deprivation. But he was beginning to realize that Mrs. Clausen had had eight months of sleep deprivation; it had been criminal of Wallingford to keep her up most of the night. That Doris carried only one small bag for all her things, yet she'd brought half a dozen bags of paraphernalia for the baby, was more than symbolic—little Otto was her life.

What measure of madness was it that Wallingford had even imagined *he* could entertain little Otto while Mrs. Clausen caught up on her sleep? He didn't know how to feed the child; he'd only once (yesterday) seen Doris change a diaper. And he couldn't be trusted to burp the baby. (He didn't know that Mrs. Clausen had stopped burping Otto.)

I should summon the courage to jump in the lake and drown, Patrick was thinking, when Mrs. Clausen came into his room carrying Otto junior. The baby was wearing only a diaper. All Doris was wearing was an oversize T-shirt, which had probably belonged to Otto senior. The T-shirt was a faded Green Bay green with the familiar Packers' logo; it hung past midthigh, almost to her knees.

"We're wide awake now, aren't we?" Mrs. Clausen was saying to little Otto. "Let's make sure Daddy is wide awake, too."

Wallingford made room for them in the bed. He tried to remain calm. (This was the first time Doris had referred to him as "Daddy.")

Before dawn, it had been cool enough to sleep under a blanket, but now the room was flooded with sunlight. Mrs. Clausen and the baby slipped under the top sheet while Wallingford pushed the blanket off the foot of the bed to the floor.

"You should learn how to feed him," Doris said, handing the bottle of formula to Patrick. Otto junior was laid upon a pillow; his bright eyes followed the bottle as it passed between his parents.

Later Mrs. Clausen sat Otto upright between two pillows. Wallingford watched his son pick up a rattle and shake it and put it in his mouth—not exactly a fascinating chain of events, but the new father was spellbound.

"He's a very easy baby," Mrs. Clausen said.

Wallingford didn't know what to say.

"Why don't you try reading him some of that mouse book you brought?" she asked. "He doesn't have to understand you—it's the sound of your voice that matters. I'd like to hear it, too."

Patrick climbed out of bed and came back with the book.

"Nice boxers," Doris told him.

There were parts of *Stuart Little* that Wallingford had marked, thinking that they might have special significance for Mrs. Clausen. How Stuart's first date with Harriet Ames goes awry because Stuart is too upset about his canoe being vandalized to accept Harriet's invitation to the dance. Alas, Harriet says goodbye, "leaving Stuart alone with his broken dreams and his damaged canoe."

Patrick had once thought Doris would like that part—now he wasn't so sure. He decided he would skip ahead to the last chapter, "Heading North," and read only the bit about Stuart's philosophical conversation with the telephone repairman.

First they talk about the bird Stuart is looking for. The telephone repairman asks Stuart to describe the bird, then the repairman writes down the description. While Wallingford read this part, Mrs. Clausen lay on her side and watched him with their son. Otto, with only an occasional glance at his mother, appeared to be listening intently to his father. With both his mother and father near enough to touch, the child was getting sufficient attention.

Then Patrick reached the moment when the telephone repairman asks Stuart where he's headed. Wallingford read this excerpt with particular poignancy.

"North," said Stuart.

"North is nice," said the repairman. "I've always enjoyed going north. Of course, south-west is a fine direction, too."

"Yes, I suppose it is," said Stuart, thoughtfully.

"And there's east," continued the repairman. "I once had an interesting experience on an easterly course. Do you want me to tell you about it?"

"No, thanks," said Stuart.

The repairman seemed disappointed, but he kept right on talking. "There's something about north," he said, "something that sets it apart from all other directions. A person who is heading north is not making any mistake, in my opinion."

"That's the way I look at it," said Stuart. "I rather expect that from now on I shall be traveling north until the end of my days."

"Worse things than that could happen to a person," said the repairman.

"Yes, I know," answered Stuart.

Worse things than that had happened to Patrick Wallingford. He'd not been heading north when he met Mary Shanahan, or Angie, or Monika with a *k*—or his ex-wife, for that matter. He had met Marilyn in New Orleans, where he was doing a three-minute story on excessive partying at Mardi Gras; he'd been having a fling with a Fiona somebody, another makeup girl, but he dumped Fiona for Marilyn. (A long-acknowledged mistake.)

A trivial statistic, but Wallingford couldn't think of a woman he'd had sex with while traveling north. As for being up north, he'd only been there with Doris Clausen, with whom he wanted to remain—not necessarily up north but *anywhere*—until the end of his days.

Pausing for dramatic effect, Patrick repeated just that phrase—"until the end of my days." Then he looked at little Otto, afraid that the child might be bored, but the boy was as alert as a squirrel; his eyes flashed from his father's face to the colored picture on the book's cover. (Stuart in his birchbark canoe with SUMMER MEMORIES stamped on the bow.)

Wallingford was thrilled to have seized and kept his young son's attention, but when he glanced at Mrs. Clausen, upon whom he'd hoped to make a re-deeming impression, he realized that she'd fallen asleep—in all likelihood, before she fully compre-hended the relevancy of the "Heading North" chap-ter. Doris lay on her side, still turned toward Patrick and their baby boy, and although her hair partly cov-ered her face, Wallingford could see that she was smiling.

Well . . . if not exactly smiling, at least she wasn't frowning. Both in her expression and in the tranquil-lity of her repose, Mrs. Clausen seemed more at peace than Wallingford had ever known her to be. Or more deeply asleep—Patrick couldn't really tell.

Taking his new responsibility seriously, Walling-ford picked up Otto junior and inched out of the bed—carefully, so as not to wake the boy's mother. He carried the child into the other bedroom, where he did his best to imitate Doris's orderly routine. He boldly attempted to change the baby on the bed that was appointed as a changing table, but (to Patrick's dismay) the diaper was dry, little Otto was clean, and while Wallingford contemplated the astonishing smallness of his son's penis, Otto peed straight up in the air in his father's face. Now Patrick had grounds for changing the diaper—not easy to do one-handed.

That done, Wallingford wondered what he should do next. As Otto junior sat upright on the bed, virtually imprisoned by the pillows Patrick had securely piled around him, the inexperienced father searched through the bags of baby paraphernalia. He assembled the following items: a packet of formula, a clean baby bottle, two changes of diapers, a shirt, in case it was cool outside—if they went outside—and a pair of socks and shoes, in case Otto was happiest bouncing in the jumper-seat.

That contraption was in the main cabin, where Wallingford carried Otto next. The socks and shoes, Patrick thought—thereby revealing the precautionary instincts of a good father—would protect the baby's tiny toes and prevent him from getting splinters in his soft little feet. As an afterthought, just before he'd left the boathouse apartment with Otto and the bag of paraphernalia, Wallingford had added the baby's hat to the bag, along with Mrs. Clausen's copy of *The English Patient*. His one hand had lightly touched Doris's underwear as he'd reached for the book.

It was cooler in the main cabin, so Patrick put the shirt on Otto, and just for the challenge, also dressed the boy in his socks and shoes. He tried putting Otto in the jumper-seat, but the child cried. Patrick then put the little boy in the highchair, which Otto seemed to like better. (Only momentarily—there was nothing to eat.)

Finding a baby spoon in the dish drainer, Wallingford mashed a banana for Otto, who enjoyed spitting out some of the banana and rubbing his face with it before wiping his hands on his shirt.

Wallingford wondered what else he could feed the child. The kettle on the stove was still warm. He dissolved the powdered formula in about eight ounces of the heated water and mixed some of the formula with a little baby cereal, but Otto liked the banana better. Patrick tried mixing the baby cereal with a teaspoon of strained peaches from one of the jars of baby food. Otto cautiously liked this, but by then several globs of banana, and some of the peach-cereal mixture, had found their way into his hair.

It was evident to Wallingford that he'd managed to get more food on Otto than in him. He dampened a paper towel with warm water and wiped the baby clean, or almost clean; then he took Otto out of the highchair and put him in the jumper-seat again. The boy bounced all around for a couple of minutes before throwing up half his breakfast.

Wallingford took his son out of the jumper-seat and sat down in a rocking chair, holding the child in his lap. He tried giving him a bottle, but the besmeared little boy drank only an ounce or two before he spit up in Wallingford's lap. (Wallingford was wearing just his boxer shorts, so what did it matter?)

Patrick tried pacing back and forth with Otto in the crook of his left arm and Mrs. Clausen's copy of *The English Patient* held open, like a hymnal, in his right hand. But given Wallingford's handless left arm, Otto was too heavy to carry in this fashion for long. Patrick returned to the rocking chair. He sat Otto on his thigh and let the boy lean against him; the back of the child's head rested on Wallingford's chest and left shoulder, with Wallingford's left arm around him. They rocked back and forth for ten minutes or more, until Otto fell asleep.

Patrick slowed the rocker down; he held the sleeping boy on his lap while he attempted to read *The English Patient.* Holding the book open in his one hand was less difficult than turning the pages, which required an act of considerable manual dexterity— as challenging to Wallingford as some of his efforts with prosthetic devices—but the effort seemed suited to the early descriptions of the burned patient, who doesn't appear to remember who he is.

Patrick read only a few pages, stopping at a sentence Mrs. Clausen had underlined in red—the description of how the eponymous English patient drifts in and out of consciousness as the nurse reads to him.

So the books for the Englishman, as he listened intently or not, had gaps of plot like sections of a road washed out by storms, missing incidents as if locusts had consumed a section of tapestry, as if plaster loosened by the bombing had fallen away from a mural at night.

It was not only a passage to be reread and admired; it also reflected well on the reader who had marked it. Wallingford closed the book and placed it gently on the floor. Then he shut his eyes and concentrated on the soothing motion of the rocker. When Wallingford held his breath, he could hear his son breathing—a holy moment for many parents. And as he rocked, Patrick made a plan. He would go back to New York and read *The English Patient.* He would mark his favorite parts; he and Mrs. Clausen could compare and discuss their choices. He might even be able to persuade her to rent a video of the movie, which they could watch together.

Well, Wallingford thought, as he fell asleep in the rocking chair, holding his sleeping son . . . wouldn't this be a more promising subject between them than the travels of a mouse or the imaginative ardor of a doomed spider?

Mrs. Clausen found them sleeping in the rocker. Good mother that she was, she closely examined the

evidence of Otto's breakfast—including what remained of the baby's formula in his bottle, her son's
strikingly spattered shirt, his peach-stained hair and
banana-spotted socks and shoes, and the unmistakable indication that he had puked on Patrick's boxer
shorts. Mrs. Clausen must have found everything
to her liking, especially the sight of the two of them
asleep in the rocking chair, because she photographed
them twice with her camera.

Wallingford didn't wake up until Doris had already made coffee and was cooking bacon. (He remembered telling her that he liked bacon.) She was
wearing her purple bathing suit. Patrick imagined his
swimming trunks all alone on the clothesline, a self-
pitying symbol of Mrs. Clausen's probable rejection
of his proposal.

They spent the day lazily, if not entirely relaxed,
together. The underlying tension between them was
that Doris made no mention of Patrick's proposal.

They took turns swimming off the dock and
watching Otto. Wallingford once again went wading
with the baby in the shallow water by the sandy
beach. They took a boat ride together. Patrick sat
in the bow, with little Otto in his lap, while Mrs.
Clausen steered the boat—the outboard, because
Doris understood it better. The outboard didn't go as
fast as the speedboat, but it wouldn't have mattered
as much to the Clausens if she'd scratched it or
banged it up.

They ferried their trash to a Dumpster on a dock

at the far end of the lake. All the cottagers took their trash there. Whatever garbage—bottles, cans, paper trash, uneaten food, Otto's soiled diapers—they *didn't* take to the Dumpster on the dock, they would have to carry with them on the floatplane.

In the outboard with the motor running, they couldn't hear each other talk, but Wallingford looked at Mrs. Clausen and very carefully mouthed the words: "I love you." He knew she'd read his lips and had understood him, but he didn't grasp what she said to him in return. It was a longer sentence than "I love you"; he sensed she was saying something serious.

On the way back from dumping the trash, Otto junior fell asleep. Wallingford carried the sleeping boy up the stairs to his crib. Doris said that Otto usually took two naps during the day; it was the motion of the boat that had lulled the child to sleep so soundly. Mrs. Clausen speculated that she would have to wake him up to feed him.

It was past late afternoon, already early evening; the sun had started sinking. Wallingford said: "Don't wake up little Otto just yet. Come down to the dock with me, please." They were both in their bathing suits, and Patrick made sure that they took two towels with them.

"What are we doing?" Doris asked.

"We're going to get wet again," he told her. "Then we're going to sit on the dock, just for a minute."

It bothered Mrs. Clausen that they might not hear

Otto crying if he woke up from his nap, not even with the windows in the bedroom open. The windows faced out over the lake, not over the big outdoors dock, and the occasional passing motorboat made an interfering noise, but Patrick promised that he'd hear the baby.

They dove off the big dock and climbed quickly up the ladder; almost immediately, the dock was enveloped in shade. The sun had dropped below the treetops on their side of the lake, but the eastern shore was still in sunlight. They sat on the towels on the dock while Wallingford told Mrs. Clausen about the pills he'd taken for pain in India, and how (in the blue-capsule dream) he'd felt the heat of the sun in the wood of the dock, even though the dock was in shade.

"Like now," he said.

She just sat there, shivering slightly in her wet bathing suit.

Patrick persisted in telling her how he had heard the woman's voice but never seen her; how she'd had the sexiest voice in the world; how she'd said, "My bathing suit feels so *cold.* I'm going to take it off. Don't you want to take yours off, too?"

Mrs. Clausen kept looking at him—she was still shivering.

"Please say it," Wallingford asked.

"I don't feel like doing this," Doris told him.

He went on with the rest of the cobalt-blue dream—how he'd answered, "Yes." And the sound of the water dripping from their wet bathing suits, falling between the planks of the dock, returning to the lake. He told her how he and the unseen woman had been naked; then how he'd smelled the sunlight, which her shoulders had absorbed; and how he'd tasted the lake on his tongue, which had traced the contours of the woman's ear.

"You had sex with her, in the dream?" Mrs. Clausen asked.

"Yes."

"I can't do it," she said. "Not out here, not now. Anyway, there's a new cottage across the lake. The Clausens told me that the guy has a telescope and spies on people."

Patrick saw the place she meant. The cabin across the lake was a raw-looking color; the new wood stood out against the surrounding blue and green.

"I thought the dream was coming true," was all he said. (It *almost* came true, he wanted to tell her.)

Mrs. Clausen stood up, taking her towel with her. She took off her wet bathing suit, covering herself with her towel in the process. She hung her suit on the line and wrapped herself more tightly in her towel. "I'm going to wake up Otto," she said.

Wallingford took off his swim trunks and hung his suit on the line beside Doris's. Because she'd already gone to the boathouse, he was unconcerned about covering himself with his towel. In fact, he faced the lake naked for a moment, just to force the asshole with the telescope to take a good look at him. Then

Wallingford wrapped his towel around himself and climbed the stairs to his bedroom.

He changed into a dry bathing suit and a polo shirt. By the time he went to the other bedroom, Mrs. Clausen had changed, too; she was wearing an old tank top and some nylon running shorts. They were clothes a boy might wear in a gym, but she looked terrific.

"You know, dreams don't have to be *exactly* true-to-life in order to come true," she told him, without looking at him.

"I don't know if I have a chance with you," Patrick said to her.

She walked up the path to the main cabin, purposely ahead of him, while he carried little Otto. "I'm still thinking about it," she said, keeping her back to him.

Wallingford calculated what she'd said by counting the syllables in her words. He thought it was what she'd said to him in the boat when he couldn't hear her. ("I'm still thinking about it.") So he had a chance with her, though probably a slim one.

They ate a quiet dinner on the screened-in porch of the main cabin, which overlooked the darkening lake. The mosquitoes came to the surrounding screens and hummed to them. They drank the second bottle of red wine while Wallingford talked about his fledgling effort to get fired. This time he was smart enough to leave Mary Shanahan out of the story. He didn't tell Doris that he'd first got the idea from something Mary had said, or that Mary had a fairly developed plan concerning *how* he might get himself fired.

He talked about leaving New York, too, but Mrs. Clausen seemed to lose patience with what he was saying. "I wouldn't want you to quit your job because of *me,*" she told him. "If I can live with you, I can live with you anywhere. Where we live or what you do isn't the issue."

Patrick paced around with Otto in his arms while Doris washed the dishes.

"I just wish Mary wouldn't have your baby," Mrs. Clausen finally said, when they were fighting off the mosquitoes on the path back to the boathouse. He couldn't see her face; again she was ahead of him, carrying the flashlight and a bag of baby paraphernalia while he carried Otto junior. "I can't blame her . . . wanting to have your baby," Doris added, as they were climbing the stairs to the boathouse apartment. "I just hope she doesn't have it. Not that there's anything you can or should do about it. Not now."

It struck Wallingford as typical of himself that here was an essential element of his fate, which he'd unwittingly set in motion but over which he had no control; whether Mary Shanahan was pregnant or not was entirely an accident of conception.

Before leaving the main cabin—when he had used the bathroom, and after he'd brushed his teeth—he had taken a condom from his shaving kit. He'd held it in his hand all the way to the boathouse. Now, as he put Otto down on the bed that served as a changing table in the bedroom, Mrs. Clausen saw that the fist of Wallingford's one hand was closed around something.

"What have you got in your hand?" she asked.

He opened the palm of his hand and showed her the condom. Doris was bending over Otto junior, changing him. "You better go back and get another one. You're going to need at least two," she said.

He took a flashlight and braved the mosquitoes again; he returned to his bedroom above the boathouse with a second condom and a cold beer.

Wallingford lit the gas lamp in his room. While this is an easy job for two-handed people, Patrick found it challenging. He struck the wooden match on the box, then held the lit match in his teeth while he turned on the gas. When he took the match from his mouth and touched the flame to the lamp, it made a popping sound and flared brightly. He turned down the propane, but the light in the bedroom dimmed only a little. It was not very romantic, he thought, as he took off his clothes and got into bed naked.

Wallingford pulled just the top sheet over him, up to his waist; he lay on his stomach, propped on his elbows, with the two pillows hugged to his chest. He looked out the window at the moonlight on the lake—the moon was huge. In only two or three more nights, it would be an official full moon, but it looked full now.

He'd left the unopened bottle of beer on the dresser top; he hoped they might share the beer later. The two condoms, in their foil wrappers, were under the pillows.

Between the racket the loons were making and a squabble that broke out among some ducks near shore, Patrick didn't hear Doris come into his room, but when she lay down on top of him, with her bare breasts against his back, he knew she was naked.

"My bathing suit feels so *cold*," she whispered in his ear. "I'm going to take it off. Don't you want to take yours off, too?"

Her voice was so much like the woman's voice in the blue-capsule dream that Wallingford had some difficulty answering her. By the time he managed to say "yes," she'd already rolled him over onto his back and pulled the sheet down.

"You better give me one of those things," she said.

He was reaching behind his head and under the pillows with his only hand, but Mrs. Clausen was quicker. She found one of the condoms and tore open the wrapper in her teeth. "Let me do it. I want to put it on you," she told him. "I've never done this." She seemed a little puzzled by the appearance of the condom, but she didn't hesitate to put it on him; unfortunately, she tried putting it on inside out.

"It's rolled a certain way," Wallingford said.

Doris laughed at her mistake. She not only put the condom on the right way; she was in too much of a hurry for Patrick to talk to her. Mrs. Clausen may never have put a condom on anyone before, but Wallingford was familiar with the way that she straddled him. (Only this time he was lying on his back, not sitting up straight in a chair in Dr. Zajac's office.)

"Let me say something to you about being faithful to me," Doris was saying, as she moved up and down with her hands on Patrick's shoulders. "If you've got a problem with monogamy, you better say so right now—you better stop me."

Wallingford said nothing, nor did he do anything to stop her.

"Please don't make anyone else pregnant," Mrs. Clausen said, even more seriously. She bore down on him with all her weight; he lifted his hips to meet her.

"Okay," he told her.

In the harsh light of the gas lamp, their moving shadows were cast against the wall where the darker rectangle had earlier caught Wallingford's attention—that empty place where Otto senior's beer poster had been. It was as if their coupling were a ghost portrait, their future together still undecided.

When they finished making love, they drank the beer, draining the bottle in a matter of seconds. Then they went naked for a night swim, with Wallingford taking just one towel for the two of them and Mrs. Clausen carrying the flashlight. They walked single-

file to the end of the boathouse dock, but this time
Doris asked Patrick to climb down the ladder into the
lake ahead of her. He'd no sooner entered the water
than she told him to swim back to her, under the narrow dock.

"Just follow the flashlight," she instructed him.
She shined the light through the planks in the dock,
illuminating one of the support posts that disappeared into the dark water. The post was bigger
around than Wallingford's thigh. Several inches
above the waterline, just under the planks of the dock
and alongside a horizontal two-by-four, something
gold caught Patrick's eye. He swam closer until he
was looking straight up at it. He had to keep treading
water to see it.

A tenpenny nail had been driven into the post; two
gold wedding bands were looped on the nail, which
had been hammered over, into a bent position, with
its head driven into the post. Patrick realized that
Mrs. Clausen would have needed to tread water
while she pounded in the nail, and then attached the
rings, and then bent the nail over with her hammer. It
hadn't been an easy job, even for a good swimmer
who was fairly strong and two-handed.

"Are they still there? Do you see them?" Doris
asked.

"Yes," he answered.

She once again positioned the flashlight so that the
beam was cast out over the lake. He swam out from

under the dock, into the beam of light, where he found her waiting for him; she was floating on her back with her breasts above the surface.

Mrs. Clausen didn't say anything. Wallingford remained silent with her. He speculated that, one winter, the ice could be especially thick; it might grind against the boathouse dock and the rings might be lost. Or a winter storm could sweep the boathouse away. Whatever, the wedding rings were where they belonged—that was what Mrs. Clausen had wanted to show him.

Across the lake, the newly arrived Peeping Tom had the lights on in his cabin. His radio was playing; he was listening to a baseball game, but Patrick couldn't tell which teams were playing.

They swam back to the boathouse, with both the flashlight on the dock and the gas lamps shining from the two bedroom windows to guide them. This time Wallingford remembered to pee in the lake so that later he wouldn't have to go in the woods, with the mosquitoes.

They both kissed Otto junior good night, and Doris extinguished the gaslight in the boy's room and closed his curtains. Then she turned off the lamp in the other bedroom, where she lay naked and cool from the lake, under just the top sheet, with her and Wallingford's hair still wet and cold in the moonlight. She'd not closed their curtains on purpose; she wanted to wake up early, before the baby. Both she and Patrick fell instantly asleep in the moonlit room. That night, the moon didn't set until almost three in the morning.

The sunrise was a little after five on Monday, but Mrs. Clausen was up well before then. When Wallingford woke, the room was a pearl-gray or pewter color and he was aware of being aroused; it was not unlike one of the more erotic moments in the blue-capsule dream.

Mrs. Clausen was putting the second condom on him. She had found what was, even for Wallingford, a novel way to do it—she was unrolling it on his penis with her teeth. For someone with no previous experience with condoms, she was surpassingly innovative, but Doris confessed that she had read about this method in a book.

"Was it a novel?" Wallingford wanted to know. (Of course it was!)

"Give me your hand," Mrs. Clausen commanded.

He naturally thought that she meant the right one—it was his only hand. But when he extended his right hand to her, she said, "No, the fourth one."

Patrick thought he'd misheard her. Surely she'd said, "No, the other one"—the no-hand or the non-hand, as almost everyone called it.

"The what?" Wallingford asked, just to be sure.

"Give me your hand, the fourth one," Doris said. She seized his stump and gripped it tightly between her thighs, where he could feel his missing fingers come to life.

"There were the two you were born with," Mrs. Clausen explained. "You lost one. Otto's was your third. As for *this* one," she said, clenching her thighs for emphasis, "this is the one that will never forget me. This one is mine. It's your fourth."

"Oh." Perhaps that was why he could feel it, as if it were real.

They swam naked again after they made love, but this time one of them stood at the window in little Otto's bedroom, watching the other swim. It was during Mrs. Clausen's turn that Otto junior woke up with the sunrise.

Then they were busy packing up; Doris did all the things that were necessary to close the cottage. She even found the time to take the last of their trash across the lake to the Dumpster on the dock. Wallingford stayed with Otto. Doris drove the boat a lot faster when the baby wasn't with her.

They had all their bags and the baby gear assembled on the big dock when the floatplane arrived. While the pilot and Mrs. Clausen loaded the small plane, Wallingford held Otto junior in his right arm and waved no-handed across the lake to the Peeping Tom. Every so often, they could see the sun reflected in the lens of his telescope.

When the floatplane took off, the pilot made a point of passing low over the newcomer's dock. The Peeping Tom was pretending that his telescope was a fishing pole and he was fishing off his dock; the silly asshole kept making imaginary casts. The tripod for the telescope stood incriminatingly in the middle of the dock, like the mounting for a crude kind of artillery.

There was too much noise in the cabin for Wallingford and Mrs. Clausen to talk without shouting. But they looked at each other constantly, and at the baby, whom they passed back and forth between them. As the floatplane was descending for its landing, Patrick told her again—without a sound, just by moving his lips—"I love you."

Doris did not at first respond, and when she did so—also without actually saying the words, but by letting him read her lips—it was that same sentence, longer than "I love you," which she had spoken before. ("I'm still thinking about it.")

Wallingford could only wait and see.

From where the seaplane docked, they drove to Austin Straubel Airport in Green Bay. Otto junior fussed in his car seat while Wallingford made an effort to amuse him. Doris drove. Now that they could hear each other talk, it seemed they had nothing to say.

At the airport, where he kissed Mrs. Clausen goodbye, and then little Otto, Patrick felt Mrs. Clausen put something in his right front pocket. "Please don't look at it now. Please wait until later," she asked him. "Just think about this: my skin has grown back together, the hole has closed. I couldn't wear that again if I wanted to. And besides, if I end up with you, I know I don't need it. I know *you* don't need it. Please give it away."

Wallingford knew what it was without looking at it—the fertility doohickey he'd once seen in her navel, the body ornament that had pierced her belly button. He was dying to see it.

He didn't have to wait long. He was thinking about the ambiguity of Mrs. Clausen's parting words—"if I end up with you"—when the thing she'd put in his pocket set off the metal-detection device in the airport. He had to take it out of his pocket and look at it then. An airport security guard took a good look at it, too; in fact, the guard had the first long look at it.

It was surprisingly heavy for something so small; the grayish-white, metallic color gleamed like gold. "It's platinum," the security guard said. She was a dark-skinned Native American woman with jet-black hair, heavyset and sad-looking. The way she handled the belly-button ornament indicated she knew something about jewelry. "This must have been expensive," she said, handing the doohickey back to him.

"I don't know—I didn't buy it," Wallingford replied. "It's a body-piercing item, for a woman's navel."

"I know," the security guard told him. "They usually set the metal detector off when they're in someone's belly button."

"Oh," Patrick said. He was only beginning to grasp what the good-luck charm was. A tiny hand—a left one.

In the body-piercing trade, it was what they called a barbell—a rod with a ball that screws on and off one end, just to keep the ornament from falling off, not unlike an earring post. But at the other end of the rod, which served the design as a slender wrist, was the most delicate, most exquisite little hand that Patrick Wallingford had ever seen. The middle finger was crossed over the index finger in that near-universal symbol of good luck. Patrick had expected a more specific fertility symbol—maybe a miniature god or something tribal.

Another security guard came over to the table where Wallingford and the first security guard were standing. He was a small, lean black man with a perfectly trimmed mustache. "What is it?" he asked his colleague.

"A body ornament, for your belly button," she explained.

"Not for mine!" the man said, grinning.

Patrick handed him the good-luck charm. That was when the Windbreaker slipped off Wallingford's left forearm and the guards saw that his left hand was gone.

"Hey, you're the lion guy!" the male guard said. He'd scarcely glanced at the small platinum hand with the crossed fingers, resting in the palm of his bigger hand.

The female guard instinctively reached out and touched Patrick's left forearm. "I'm sorry I didn't recognize you, Mr. Wallingford," she said.

What kind of sadness was it that showed in her

face? Wallingford had instantly known she was sad, but he'd not (until now) considered the possible reasons. There was a small, fishhook-shaped scar on her throat; it could have come from anything, from a childhood accident with a pair of scissors to a bad marriage or a violent rape.

Her colleague—the small, lean black man—was now looking at the body ornament with new interest. "Well, it's a hand. A left one. I get it!" he said excitedly. "I guess that *would* be your good-luck charm, wouldn't it?"

"Actually, it's for fertility. Or so I was told."

"It *is?*" the Native American woman asked. She took the doohickey out of her fellow guard's hand. "Let me see that again. Does it work?" she asked Patrick. He could tell she was serious.

"It worked once," Wallingford replied.

It was tempting to guess what her sadness was. The female security guard was in her late thirties or early forties; she was wearing a wedding ring on her left ring finger and a turquoise ring on the ring finger of her right hand. Her ears were pierced—more turquoise. Perhaps her belly button was pierced, too. Maybe she couldn't get pregnant.

"Do you want it?" Wallingford asked her. "I have no further use for it."

The black man laughed. He walked away with a wave of his hand. "Oooh-oooh! You don't want to go there!" he said to Patrick, shaking his head. Maybe the poor woman had a dozen children; she'd been begging to get her tubes tied, but her no-good hus-band wouldn't let her.

"You be quiet!" the female guard called after her departing colleague. He was still laughing, but she was not amused.

"You can have it, if you want it," Wallingford told her. After all, Mrs. Clausen had asked him to give it away.

The woman closed her dark hand over the fertility charm. "I would very much like to have it, but I'm sure I can't afford it."

"No, no! It's free! I'm giving it to you. It's already yours," Patrick said. "I hope it works, if you want it to." He couldn't tell if the woman guard wanted it for herself or for a friend, or if she just knew somewhere to sell it.

At some distance from the security checkpoint, Wallingford turned and looked at the Native Ameri-can woman. She was back at work—to all other eyes, she was just a security guard—but when she glanced in Patrick's direction, she waved to him and gave him a warm smile. She also held up the tiny hand. Wallingford was too far away to see the crossed fin-gers, but the ornament winked in the bright airport light; the platinum gleamed again like gold.

It reminded Patrick of Doris's and Otto Clausen's wedding rings, shining in the flashlight's beam be-tween the dark water and the underside of the boat-house dock. How many times since she'd nailed the rings there had Doris swum under the dock to look at them, treading water with a flashlight in her hand?

Or had she never looked? Did she only see them— as Wallingford now would—in dreams or in the imagination, where the gold was always brighter and the rings' reflection in the lake more everlasting?

If he had a chance with Mrs. Clausen, it was not really a matter that would be decided upon the discovery of whether or not Mary Shanahan was pregnant. More important was how brightly those wedding rings under the dock still shone in Doris Clausen's dreams, and in her imagination.

When his plane took off for Cincinnati, Wallingford was—at that moment, literally—as up in the air as Doris Clausen's thoughts about him. He would have to wait and see.

That was Monday, July 26, 1999. Wallingford would long remember the date; he wouldn't see Mrs. Clausen again for ninety-eight days.

CHAPTER TWELVE

Lambeau Field

$\mathcal{H}$E WOULD HAVE TIME to heal. The
bruise on his shin (the glass-topped table in Mary's
apartment) first turned yellow and then light brown;
one day it was gone. Likewise the burn (the hot-water
faucet in Mary's shower) soon disappeared. Where
his back had been scratched (Angie's nails), there
was suddenly no evidence of Patrick's thrashing encounter with the makeup girl from Queens; even the
sizable blood blister on his left shoulder (Angie's
love-bite) went away. Where there'd been a purplish
hematoma (the love-bite again), there was nothing
but Wallingford's new skin, as innocent-looking as
little Otto's shoulder—that bare, that unmarked.

Patrick remembered rubbing sunscreen on his
son's smooth skin; he missed touching and holding

his little boy. He missed Mrs. Clausen, too, but Wallingford knew better than to press her for an answer.

He also knew that it was too soon to ask Mary Shanahan if she was pregnant. All he said to her, as soon as he got back from Green Bay, was that he wanted to take her up on her suggestion to renegotiate his contract. There were, as Mary had pointed out, eighteen months remaining on Patrick's present contract. Hadn't it been her idea that he ask for three years, or even five?

Yes, it had. (She'd said, "Ask for three years— no, make that five.") But Mary seemed to have no memory of their earlier conversation. "I think three years would be a lot to ask for, Pat," was all she said.

"I see," Wallingford replied. "Then I suppose I might as well keep the anchor job."

"But are you sure you *want* the job, Pat?"

He believed that Mary wasn't being cautious just because Wharton and Sabina were there in her office. (The moon-faced CEO and the bitter Sabina sat listening with seeming indifference, not saying a word.) What Wallingford understood about Mary was that she didn't really know what he wanted, and this made her nervous.

"It depends," Patrick replied. "It's hard to imagine trading an anchor chair for field assignments, even if I get to pick my own assignments. You know what they say: 'Been there, done that.' It's hard to look forward to going backward. I guess you'd have to make me an offer, so I have a better idea of what you have in mind."

Mary looked at him, smiling brightly. "How was Wisconsin?" she asked.

Wharton, whose frozen blandness would begin to blend in with the furniture if he didn't say something (or at least twitch) in the next thirty seconds, coughed minimally into his cupped palm. The unbelievable blankness of his expression called to mind the vacuity of a masked executioner; even Wharton's cough was underexpressed.

Sabina, whom Wallingford could barely remember sleeping with—now that he thought of it, she'd whimpered in her sleep like a dog having a dream—cleared her throat as if she'd swallowed a pubic hair.

"Wisconsin was fine."

Wallingford spoke as neutrally as possible, but Mary correctly deduced that nothing had been decided between him and Doris Clausen. He couldn't have waited to tell her if he and Mrs. Clausen were really a couple. Just as, the second Mary knew she was pregnant, she wouldn't wait to tell him.

And they both knew it had been necessary to enact this standoff in the presence of Wharton and Sabina, who both knew it, too. Under the circumstances, it wouldn't have been advisable for Patrick Wallingford and Mary Shanahan to be alone together.

"Boy, is it ever *frosty* around here!" was what

Angie told Wallingford, when she got him alone in the makeup chair.

"Is it *ever!*" Patrick admitted. He was glad to see the good-hearted girl, who'd left his apartment the cleanest it had been since the day he moved in.

"So . . . are ya gonna tell me about Wisconsin or what?" Angie asked.

"It's too soon to say," Wallingford confessed. "I've got my fingers crossed," he added—an unfortunate choice of words because he was reminded of Mrs. Clausen's fertility charm.

"My fingers are crossed for ya, too," Angie said. She had stopped flirting with him, but she was no less sincere and no less friendly.

Wallingford would throw away his digital alarm clock and replace it with a new one, because whenever he looked at the old one he would remember Angie's piece of gum stuck there—as well as the near-death gyrations that had caused her gum to be expectorated with such force. He didn't want to lie in bed thinking about Angie unless Doris Clausen said no.

For now, Doris was being vague. Wallingford had to acknowledge that it was hard to know what to make of the photographs she sent him, although her accompanying comments, if not cryptic, struck him as more mischievous than romantic.

She hadn't sent him a copy of every picture on the roll; missing, Patrick saw, were two he'd taken himself. Her purple bathing suit on the clothesline, alongside his swimming trunks—he'd taken two shots in case she wanted to keep one of the photos for herself. She had kept them both.

The first two photos Mrs. Clausen sent were unsurprising, beginning with that one of Wallingford wading in the shallow water near the lakeshore with little Otto naked in his arms. The second picture was the one that Patrick took of Doris and Otto junior on the sundeck of the main cabin. It was Wallingford's first night at the cottage on the lake, and nothing had happened yet between him and Mrs. Clausen. As if she weren't even thinking that anything *might* happen between them, her expression was totally relaxed, free of any expectation.

The only surprise was the third photograph, which Wallingford didn't know Doris had taken; it was the one of him sleeping in the rocking chair with his son.

Patrick did not know how to interpret Mrs. Clausen's remarks in the note that accompanied the photographs—especially how matter-of-factly she reported that she'd taken two shots of little Otto asleep in his father's arms and had kept one for herself. The tone of her note, which Wallingford had at first found mischievous, was also ambiguous. Doris had written: *On the evidence of the enclosed, you have the potential to be a good father.*

Only *the potential*? Patrick's feelings were hurt. Nevertheless, he read *The English Patient* in the fervent hope he would find a passage to bring to her attention—maybe one she had marked, one they both liked.

When Wallingford called Mrs. Clausen to thank her for the photographs, he thought he might have found such a passage. "I loved that part about the 'list of wounds,' especially when she stabs him with the fork. Do you remember that? 'The fork that entered the back of his shoulder, leaving its bite marks the doctor suspected were caused by a fox.' "

Doris was silent on her end of the phone.

"You didn't like that part?" Patrick asked.

"I'd just as soon not be reminded of *your* bite marks, and your other wounds," she told him.

"Oh."

Wallingford would keep reading *The English Patient.* It was merely a matter of reading the novel more carefully; yet he threw caution to the wind when he came upon Almásy saying of Katharine, "She was hungrier to change than I expected."

This was surely true of Patrick's impression of Mrs. Clausen as a lover—she'd been voracious in ways that had astonished him. He called her immediately, forgetting that it was very late at night in New York; in Green Bay, it was only an hour earlier. Given little Otto's schedule, Doris usually went to bed early.

She didn't sound like herself when she answered the phone. Patrick was instantly apologetic.

"I'm sorry. You were asleep."

"That's okay. What is it?"

"It's a passage in *The English Patient,* but I can tell you what it is another time. You can call me in the morning, as early as you want. Please wake me up!" he begged her.

"Read me the passage."

"It's just something Almásy says about Katharine—"

"Go on. Read it."

He read: " 'She was hungrier to change than I expected.' " Out of context, the passage suddenly struck Wallingford as pornographic, but he trusted Mrs. Clausen to remember the context.

"Yes, I know that part," she said, without emotion. Maybe she was still half asleep.

"Well . . ." Wallingford started to say.

"I suppose *I* was hungrier than *you* expected. Is that it?" Doris asked. (The way she said it, she might as well have asked, "Is that *all*?")

"Yes," Patrick answered. He could hear her sigh.

"Well . . ." Mrs. Clausen began. Then she seemed to change her mind about what she was going to say. "It really is too late to call," was her only comment.

Which left Wallingford with nothing to say but "I'm sorry." He would have to keep reading and hoping.

Meanwhile, Mary Shanahan summoned him to her office—*not* for the purpose, Patrick soon realized, of telling him that she was or wasn't pregnant. Mary had something else on her mind. While Wallingford's idea of a renegotiated contract of at least three years' duration was not to the all-news network's liking—not even if Wallingford was willing to give up the anchor chair and return to reporting from the field—the twenty-four-hour international channel was interested to know if Wallingford would accept "occasional" field assignments.

"Do you mean that they want me to begin the process of phasing myself out of the anchor job?" Patrick asked.

"Were you to accept, we would renegotiate your contract," Mary went on, without answering his question. "Naturally you'd get to keep your present salary." She made the issue of not offering him a raise sound like a positive thing. "I believe we're talking about a two-year contract." She wasn't exactly committing herself to it, and a twoyear contract was superior to his present agreement by a scant six months.

What a piece of work she is! Wallingford was thinking, but what he said was, "If the intention is to replace me as the anchor, why not bring me into the discussion? Why not ask me how I'd like to be replaced? Maybe gradually would be best, but maybe not. I'd at least like to know the long-range plan."

Mary Shanahan just smiled. Patrick had to marvel at how quickly she'd adjusted to her new and undefined power. Surely she was not authorized to make decisions of this kind on her own, and she probably hadn't yet learned just how many other people were part of the decision-making process, but of course she conveyed none of this to Wallingford. At the same time, she was smart enough not to lie directly; she would never claim that there was *no* long-range plan, nor would she ever admit that there *was* one and that not even she knew what it was.

"I know you've always wanted to do something about Germany, Pat," was what she told him, seemingly out of the blue—but nothing with Mary was out of the blue.

Wallingford had asked to do a piece about German reunification—nine years after the fact. Among other things, he'd suggested exploring how the language for reunification—now "unification" in most of the official press—had changed. Even *The New York Times* had subscribed to "unification." Yet Germany, which had been one country, had been divided; then it was made one again. Why wasn't that *re*unification? Most Americans thought of Germany as *re*unified, surely.

What were the politics of that not-so-little change in the language? And what differences of opinion *among Germans* remained about reunification or unification?

But the all-news network hadn't been interested. "Who cares about Germans?" Dick had asked. Fred had felt the same way. (In the New York newsroom, they were always saying they were "sick of" something— sick of religion, sick of the arts, sick of children, sick of Germans.)

Now here was Mary, the new news editor, holding

out Germany as the dubious carrot before the reluctant donkey.

"What about Germany?" Wallingford asked suspiciously. Naturally Mary wouldn't have raised the
issue of him accepting "occasional" field assignments if the network hadn't had one such assignment
already in mind. What was it?

"Actually there are two items," Mary answered,
making it sound as if two were a plus.

But she'd called the stories "items," which forewarned Patrick. German reunification was no *item*—
that subject was too big to be called an item. "Items"
in the newsroom were trivial stories, freakish amuse-
ments of the kind Wallingford knew all too well.
Otto senior blowing his brains out in a beer truck
after the Super Bowl—that was an item. The lion guy
himself was an item. If the network had two "items"
for Patrick Wallingford to cover, Wallingford knew
they would be sensationally stupid stories, or trivial
in the extreme—or both.

"What are they, Mary?" Patrick asked. He was trying not to lose his temper, because he sensed that
these field assignments were not of Mary's choosing;
something about her hesitancy told him that she already knew how he would respond to the proposals.

"You'll probably think they're just silly," she said.
"But they *are* in Germany."

"What are they, Mary?"

The channel had already aired a minute and a half
of the first item—everyone had seen it. A forty-two-

year-old German had managed to kill himself while watching the solar eclipse that August. He'd been driving his car near Kaiserslautern when a witness observed him weaving from one side of the road to the other; then his car had accelerated and struck a bridge abutment, or some kind of pier. It was discovered that he'd been wearing his solar viewers—he didn't want to miss the eclipse. The lenses had been sufficiently dark to obscure everything but the partially occluded sun.

"We already ran that item," was Wallingford's only response.

"Well, we were thinking of a follow-up. Something more in-depth," Mary told him.

What "follow-up" could there be to such lunacy? How "in-depth" could such an absurd incident be? Had the man had a family? If so, they would no doubt be upset. But how long an interview could Wallingford possibly sustain with the witness? And for what purpose? To what end?

"What's the other item?"

He'd heard about the other story, too—it had been on one of the wire services. A fifty-one-year-old German, a hunter from Bad-somewhere, had been found shot dead beside his parked car in the Black Forest. The hunter's gun was pointed out the window of his car; inside the car was the dead hunter's frantic dog. The police concluded that the dog had shot him. (Unintentionally, of course—the dog had not been charged.)

Would they want Wallingford to interview the dog?

They were the kind of not-the-news stories that would end up as jokes on the Internet—they were already jokes. They were also business as usual, the bizarre-as-commonplace lowlights of the twenty-four-hour international news. Even Mary Shanahan was embarrassed to have brought them up.

"I was thinking of something *about* Germany, Mary," Patrick said.

"I know," she sympathized, touching him in that fondly felt area of his left forearm.

"Was there anything else, Mary?" he asked.

"There was an item in Australia," she said hesitantly. "But I know you've never expressed any interest in going there."

He knew the item she meant; no doubt there was a plan to follow up this pointless death, too. In this instance, a thirty-three-year-old computer technician had drunk himself to death in a drinking competition at a hotel bar in Sydney. The competition had the regrettable name of Feral Friday, and the deceased had allegedly downed four whiskeys, seventeen shots of tequila, and thirty-four beers—all in an hour and forty minutes. He died with a blood-alcohol level of 0.42.

"I know the story," was all Wallingford said.

Mary once more touched his arm. "I'm sorry I don't have better news for you, Pat."

What further depressed Wallingford was that these

silly items weren't even *new* news. They were in-significant snippets on the theme of the world being ridiculous; their punch lines had already been told.

The twenty-four-hour international channel had a summer intern program—in lieu of a salary, college kids were promised an "authentic experience." But even for free, couldn't the interns manage to do more than collect these stories of stupid and funny deaths? Somewhere down south, a young soldier had died of injuries sustained in a three-story fall; he had been engaged in a spitting contest at the time. (A true story.) A British farmer's wife had been charged by sheep and driven off a cliff in the north of England. (Also true.)

The all-news network had long indulged a col-legiate sense of humor, which was synonymous with a collegiate sense of death. In short, no context. Life was a joke; death was the final gag. In meeting after meeting, Wallingford could imagine Wharton or Sabina saying: "Let the lion guy do it."

As for what better news Wallingford wanted to hear from Mary Shanahan, it was simply that she wasn't pregnant. For that news, or its opposite, Wall-ingford understood that he would have to wait.

He wasn't good at waiting, which in this case pro-duced some good results. He decided to inquire about other jobs in journalism. People said that the so-called educational network (they meant PBS) was boring, but—especially when it comes to the news—boring isn't the worst thing you can be.

The PBS affiliate for Green Bay was in Madison, Wisconsin, where the university was. Wallingford wrote to Wisconsin Public Television and told them what he had in mind—he wanted to create a news-analysis show. He proposed examining the lack of context in the news that was reported, especially on television. He said he would demonstrate that often there was more interesting news *behind* the news; and that the news that was reported was not necessarily the news that *should* have been reported.

Wallingford wrote: "It takes time to develop a complex or complicated story; what works best on TV are stories that don't take a lot of time. Disasters are not only sensational—they happen immediately. Especially on television, immediacy works best. I mean 'best' from a marketing point of view, which is not necessarily good for the news."

He sent his curriculum vitae and a similar proposal for a news-analysis show to the public-television stations in Milwaukee and St. Paul, as well as the two public-television stations in Chicago. But why did he focus on the Midwest, when Mrs. Clausen had said that she would live anywhere with him—*if* she chose to live with him at all?

He had taped the photo of her and little Otto to the mirror in his office dressing room. When Mary Shanahan saw it, she looked closely at both the child and his mother, but more closely at Doris, and cattily observed: "Nice mustache."

It was true that Doris Clausen had the faintest,

softest down on her upper lip. Wallingford was in-
dignant that Mary had called this super-soft place a
mustache! Because of his own warped sensibilities,
and his overfamiliarity with a certain kind of New
Yorker, Patrick decided that Doris Clausen should
not be moved too far from Wisconsin. There was
something about the Midwest in her that Wallingford
loved.

If Mrs. Clausen moved to New York, one of those
newsroom women would persuade her to get a wax
job on her upper lip! Something that Patrick adored
about Doris would be lost. Therefore, Wallingford
wrote only to a very few PBS affiliates in the Midwest; he stayed as close to Green Bay as he could.

While he was at it, he didn't stop with noncom-
mercial television stations. The only radio he ever
listened to was public radio. He loved NPR, and
there were NPR stations everywhere. There were
two in Green Bay and two in Madison; he sent his
proposal for a news-analysis show to all four of
them, in addition to NPR affiliates in Milwaukee,
Chicago, and St. Paul. (There was even an NPR sta-
tion in Appleton, Wisconsin, Doris Clausen's hometown, but Patrick resisted applying for a job there.)

As August came and went—it was now nearly
gone—Wallingford had another idea. All the Big Ten
universities, or most of them, had to have graduate
programs in journalism. The Medill School of Journalism, at Northwestern, was famous. He sent his
proposal for a news-analysis course there, as well as

to the University of Wisconsin in Madison, the University of Minnesota in Minneapolis, and the University of Iowa in Iowa City.

Wallingford was on a roll about the unreported context of the news. He ranted, but effectively, on how trivializing to the real news the news that was reported had become. It was not only his subject; Patrick Wallingford was his argument's best-known example. Who better than the lion guy to address the sensationalizing of petty sorrows, while the underlying context, which was the terminal illness of the world, remained unrevealed?

And the best way to lose a job was not to wait to be fired. Wasn't the best way to be offered another job and then *quit*? Wallingford was overlooking the fact that, if they fired him, they would have to renegotiate the remainder of his contract. Regardless, it surprised Mary Shanahan when Patrick popped his head—*just* his head—into her office and cheerfully said to her: "Okay. I accept."

"Accept what, Pat?"

"Two years, same salary, *occasional* reporting from the field—per my approval of the field assignment, of course. I accept."

"You *do*?"

"Have a nice day, Mary," Patrick told her.

Just let them *try* to find a field assignment he'd accept! Wallingford not only intended to make them fire him; he fully expected to have a new job lined up and waiting for him when they pulled the fucking trigger. (And to think he'd once had no capacity for long-range scheming.)

They didn't wait long to suggest the next field assignment. You could just see them thinking: How could the lion guy resist *this* one? They wanted Wallingford to go to Jerusalem. Talk about disaster-man territory! Journalists love Jerusalem—no shortage of the bizarre-as-commonplace there.

There'd been a double car bombing. At around 5:30 P.M. Israeli time on Sunday, September 5, two coordinated car bombs exploded in different cities, killing the terrorists who were transporting the bombs to their designated targets. The bombs exploded because the terrorists had set them on daylight-saving time; three weeks before, Israel had prematurely switched to standard time. The terrorists, who must have assembled the bombs in a Palestinian-controlled area, were the victims of the Palestinians refusing to accept what they called "Zionist time." The drivers of the cars carrying the bombs had changed their watches, but not the bombs, to Israeli time.

While the all-news network found it funny that such self-serious madmen had been detonated by their own dumb mistake, Wallingford did not. The madmen may have deserved to die, but terrorism in Israel was no joke; it trivialized the gravity of the tensions in that country to call this klutzy accident *news*. More people would die in other car bombings, which wouldn't be funny. And once again the context of the story was missing—that is, *why* the Israelis had switched from daylight-saving to standard time prematurely.

The change had been intended to accommodate the period of penitential prayers. The *Selihoth* (literally, pardons) are prayers for forgiveness; the prayer-poems of repentance are a continuation of the Psalms. (The suffering of Israel in the various lands of the Dispersion is their principal theme.) These prayers have been incorporated into the liturgy to be recited on special occasions, and on the days preceding Rosh Hashanah; they give utterance to the feelings of the worshiper who has repented and now pleads for mercy.

While in Israel the time of day had been changed to accommodate these prayers of atonement, the enemies of the Jews had nonetheless conspired to kill them. *That* was the context, which made the double car bombing more than a comedy of errors; it was not a comedy at all. In Jerusalem, this was an almost ordinary vignette, both recalling and foreshadowing a tableau of bombings. But to Mary and the all-news network, it was a tale of terrorists getting their just deserts—nothing more.

"You must *want* me to turn this down. Is that it, Mary?" Patrick asked. "And if I turn down enough items like these, then you can fire me with impunity."

"We thought it was an interesting story. Right up your alley," was all Mary would say.

He was burning bridges faster than they could build new ones; it was an exciting but unresolved time. When he wasn't actively engaged in trying to lose his job, he was reading *The English Patient* and dreaming of Doris Clausen.

Surely she would have been enchanted, as he was, by Almásy's inquiring of Madox about "the name of that hollow at the base of a woman's neck." Almásy asks: "What is it, does it have an official name?" To which Madox mutters, "Pull yourself together." Later, pointing his finger at a spot near his own Adam's apple, Madox tells Almásy that it's called "the vascular sizood."

Wallingford called Mrs. Clausen with the heartfelt conviction that she would have liked the incident as much as he did, but she had her doubts about it.

"It was called something different in the movie," Doris told him.

"It was?"

He hadn't seen the film in how long? He rented the video and watched it immediately. But when he got to that scene, he couldn't quite catch what that part of a woman's neck was called. Mrs. Clausen had been right, however; it was not called "the vascular sizood."

Wallingford rewound the video and watched the scene again. Almásy and Madox are saying goodbye. (Madox is going home, to kill himself.) Almásy says, "There is no God." Adding: "But I hope someone looks after you."

Madox seems to remember something and points to his own throat. "In case you're still wondering—

this is called the suprasternal notch." Patrick caught the line the second time. Did that part of a woman's neck have two names?

And when he'd watched the film again, and after he'd finished reading the novel, Wallingford would declare to Mrs. Clausen how much he loved the part where Katharine says to Almásy, "I want you to ravish me."

"In the book, you mean," Mrs. Clausen said.

"In the book *and* in the movie," Patrick replied.

"It wasn't in the movie," Doris told him. (He'd just watched it—he felt certain that the line was there!) "You just thought you heard that line because of how much you liked it."

"You didn't like it?"

"It's a guy thing to like," she said. "I never believed she would say it to him."

Had Patrick believed so wholeheartedly in Katharine saying "I want you to ravish me" that, in his easily manipulated memory, he'd simply inserted the line into the film? Or had Doris found the line so unbelievable that she'd blanked it out of the movie? And what did it matter whether the line was or wasn't in the film? The point was that Patrick liked it and Mrs. Clausen did not.

Once again Wallingford felt like a fool. He'd tried to invade a book Doris Clausen had loved, and a movie that had (at least for her) some painful memories attached to it. But books, and sometimes movies, are more personal than that; they can be mutually appreciated, but the specific reasons for loving them cannot satisfactorily be shared.

Good novels and films are not like the news, or what passes for the news—they are more than items. They are comprised of the whole range of moods you are in when you read them or see them. You can never exactly imitate someone else's love of a movie or a book, Patrick now believed.

But Doris Clausen must have sensed his disheartenment and taken pity on him. She sent him two more photographs from their time together at the cottage on the lake. He'd been hoping that she would send him the one of their bathing suits side-by-side on the clothesline. How happy he was to have that picture! He taped it to the mirror in his office dressing room. (Let Mary Shanahan make some catty remark about *that*! Just let her try.)

It was the second photo that shocked him. He'd still been asleep when Mrs. Clausen had taken it, a self-portrait, with the camera held crookedly in her hand. No matter—you could see well enough what was going on. Doris was ripping the wrapper off the second condom with her teeth. She was smiling at the camera, as if Wallingford were the camera and he already knew how she was going to put the condom on his penis.

Patrick didn't stick that photograph on his office dressing-room mirror; he kept it in his apartment, on his bedside table, next to the telephone, so that he could look at it when Mrs. Clausen called him or when he called her.

Late one night, after he'd gone to bed but had not yet fallen asleep, the phone rang and Wallingford turned on the light on his night table so that he could look at her picture when he spoke to her. But it wasn't Doris.

"Hey, Mista One Hand . . . Mista No Prick," Angie's brother Vito said. "I hope I'm interruptin' somethin' . . ." (Vito called often, always with nothing to say.)

When Wallingford hung up, he did so with a decided sadness that was not quite nostalgia. In the at-home hours of his life, since he'd come back to New York from Wisconsin, he not only missed Doris Clausen; he missed that wild, gum-chewing night with Angie, too. At these times, he even occasionally missed Mary Shanahan—the *old* Mary, before she acquired the certitude of a last name and the uncomfortable authority she now held over him.

Patrick turned out the light. As he drifted into sleep, he tried to think forgivingly of Mary. The past litany of her most positive features returned to him: her flawless skin, her unadulterated blondness, her sensible but sexy clothes, her perfect little teeth. And, Wallingford assumed—since Mary was still hoping she was pregnant—her commitment to no prescription drugs. She'd been a bitch to him at times, but people are not only what they seem to be.

After all, he had dumped her. There were women who would have been more bitter about it than Mary was.

Speak of the devil! The phone rang and it was Mary Shanahan; she was crying into the phone. She'd got her period. It had come a month and a half late—late enough to have given her hope that she was pregnant—but her period had arrived just the same.

"I'm sorry, Mary," Wallingford said, and he genuinely was sorry—for her. For himself, he felt unearned jubilation; he'd dodged another bullet.

"Imagine you, of all people—shooting blanks!" Mary told him, between sobs. "I'll give you another chance, Pat. We've got to try it again, as soon as I'm ovulating."

"I'm sorry, Mary," he repeated. "I'm not your man. Blanks or no blanks, I've had my chance."

"What?"

"You heard me. I'm saying no. We're not having sex again, not for any reason."

Mary called him a number of colorful names before she hung up. But Mary's disappointment in him did not interfere with Patrick's sleep; on the contrary, he had the best night's sleep since he'd drifted off in Mrs. Clausen's arms and awakened to the feeling of her teeth unrolling a condom on his penis.

Wallingford was still sound asleep when Mrs. Clausen called. It may have been an hour earlier in Green Bay, but little Otto routinely woke up his mother a couple of hours before Wallingford was awake.

"Mary isn't pregnant. She just got her period," Patrick announced.

"She's going to ask you to do it again. That's what I would do," Mrs. Clausen said.

"She already asked. I already said no."

"Good," Doris told him.

"I'm looking at your picture," Wallingford said.

"I can guess which one," she replied.

Little Otto was talking baby-talk somewhere near the phone. Wallingford didn't say anything for a moment—just imagining the two of them was enough. Then he asked her, "What are you wearing? Have you got any clothes on?"

"I've got two tickets to a Monday-night game, if you want to go," was her answer.

"I want to go."

"It's *Monday Night Football,* the Seahawks and the Packers at Lambeau Field." Mrs. Clausen spoke with a reverence that was wasted on Wallingford. "Mike Holmgren's coming home. I wouldn't want to miss it."

"Me neither!" Patrick replied. He didn't know who Mike Holmgren was. He would have to do a little research.

"It's November first. Are you sure you're free?"

"I'll be free!" he promised. Wallingford was trying to sound joyful while, in truth, he was heartbroken that he would have to wait until November to see her.

It was only the middle of September! "Maybe you could come to New York before then?" he asked.

"No. I want to see you at the game," she told him. "I can't explain."

"You don't have to explain!" Patrick quickly replied.

"I'm glad you like the picture," was the way she changed the subject.

"I *love* it! I love what you did to me."

"Okay. I'll see you before too long," was the way Mrs. Clausen closed the conversation—she didn't even say good-bye.

The next morning, at the script meeting, Wallingford tried not to think that Mary Shanahan was behaving like a woman who was having a bad period, only more so, but that was his impression. Mary began the meeting by abusing one of the newsroom women. Her name was Eleanor and, for whatever reason, she'd slept with one of the summer interns; now that the boy had gone back to college, Mary accused Eleanor of robbing the cradle.

Only Wallingford knew that, before he'd stupidly agreed to try to make Mary pregnant, Mary had propositioned the intern. He was a good-looking boy, and he was smarter than Wallingford—he'd rejected Mary's proposal. Patrick not only liked Eleanor for sleeping with the boy; he had also liked the boy, whose summer internship had not entirely lacked an authentic experience. (Eleanor was one of the oldest of the married women in the newsroom.)

Only Wallingford knew that Mary didn't really give a damn that Eleanor had slept with the boy—she was just angry because she had her period.

Suddenly the idea of taking a field assignment, *any* assignment, attracted Patrick. It would at least get him out of the newsroom, and out of New York. He told Mary that she would find him open to a field assignment, next time, provided that she not try to accompany him where he was being sent. (Mary had volunteered to travel with him the next time she was ovulating.)

There was, in the near future, Wallingford informed Mary, only one day and night when he would *not* be available for a field assignment *or* to anchor the evening news. He was attending a *Monday Night Football* game in Green Bay, Wisconsin, on November 1, 1999—no matter what.

Someone (probably Mary) leaked it to ABC Sports that Patrick Wallingford would be at the game that night, and ABC immediately asked the lion guy to stop by the booth during the telecast. (Why say no to a two-minute appearance before how many million viewers? Mary would say to Patrick.) Maybe disaster man could even call a play or two. Did Wallingford know, someone from ABC asked, that his hand-eating episode had sold almost as many videos as the annual NFL highlights film?

Yes, Wallingford knew. He respectfully declined the offer to visit the ABC commentators. As he put it, he was attending the game with "a special friend"; he didn't use Doris's name. This might mean that a TV camera would be on him during the game, but so what? Patrick didn't mind waving once or twice, just to show them what they wanted to see—the no-hand, or what Mrs. Clausen called his fourth hand. Even the sports hacks wanted to see it.

That may have been why Wallingford got a more enthusiastic response to his letters of inquiry to public-television stations than he received from public radio or the Big Ten journalism schools. *All* the PBS affiliates were interested in him. In general, Patrick was heartened by the collective response; he would have a job to go to, possibly even an interesting one.

Naturally he breathed not a word of this to Mary, while he tried to anticipate what field assignments she might offer him. A war wouldn't have surprised him; an *E. coli* bacteria outbreak would have suited Mary's mood.

Wallingford longed to learn why Mrs. Clausen insisted on waiting to see him until a *Monday Night Football* game in Green Bay. He phoned her on Saturday night, October 30, although he knew he would see her the coming Monday, but Doris remained noncommittal on the subject of the game's curious importance to her. "I just get anxious when the Packers are favored," was all she said.

Wallingford went to bed fairly early that Saturday night. Vito called once, around midnight, but Patrick quickly fell back to sleep. When the phone rang on Sunday morning—it was still dark outside—Wallingford assumed it was Vito again; he almost didn't answer. But it was Mary Shanahan, and she was all business.

"I'll give you a choice," she told him, without bothering to say hello or so much as his name. "You can cover the scene at Kennedy, or we'll get you a plane to Boston and a helicopter will take you to Otis Air Force Base."

"Where's that?" Wallingford asked.

"Cape Cod. Do you know what's happened, Pat?"

"I was asleep, Mary."

"Well, turn on the fucking news! I'll call you back in five minutes. You can forget about going to Wisconsin."

"I'm going to Green Bay, no matter what," he told her, but she'd already hung up. Not even the brevity of her call or the harshness of her message could dispel from Patrick's memory the little-girlish and excessively floral pattern of Mary's bedspread, or the pink undulations of her Lava lamp and their protozoan movements across her bedroom ceiling—the shadows racing like sperm.

Wallingford turned on the news. An Egyptian jetliner carrying 217 people had taken off from Kennedy, an overnight flight bound for Cairo. It had disappeared from radar screens only thirty-three minutes after take-off. Cruising at 33,000 feet in good weather, the plane had suddenly plummeted into the Atlantic about sixty miles southeast of Nantucket Island. There'd been no distress call from the cockpit. Radar sweeps indicated that the jet's rate of descent was more than 23,000 feet per minute—"like a rock," an aviation expert put it. The water was fifty-nine degrees and more than 250 feet deep; there was little hope that anyone had survived the crash.

It was the kind of crash that opened itself up to media speculation—the reports would *all* be speculative. Human-interest stories would abound. A businessman who preferred to be unnamed had arrived late at the airport and been turned away at the ticket counter. When they'd told him the flight was closed, he'd screamed at them. He went home and woke up in the morning, alive. That kind of thing would go on for days.

One of the airport hotels at Kennedy, the Ramada Plaza, had been turned into an information and counseling center for grieving family members—not that there was much information. Nevertheless, Wallingford went there. He chose Kennedy over Otis Air Force Base on the Cape—the reason being that the media would have limited access to the Coast Guard crews who'd been searching the debris field. By dawn that Sunday, they'd reportedly found only a small flotsam of wreckage and the remains of one body. On the choppy sea, there was nothing adrift that looked burned, which suggested there'd been no explosion.

Patrick first spoke to the relatives of a young Egyptian woman who'd collapsed outside the Ramada Plaza. She'd fallen in a heap, in view of the television cameras surrounding the entrance to the hotel; police officers carried her into the lobby. Her relatives told Wallingford that her brother had been on the plane.

Naturally the mayor was there, giving what solace he could. Wallingford could always count on a comment from the mayor. Giuliani seemed to like the lion guy more than he liked most reporters. Maybe he saw Patrick as a kind of police officer who'd been wounded in the line of duty; more likely, the mayor remembered Wallingford because Wallingford had only one hand.

"If there's anything the City of New York can do to help, that's what we're trying to do," Giuliani told the press. He looked a little tired when he turned to Patrick Wallingford and said: "Sometimes, if the mayor asks, it happens a little faster."

An Egyptian man was using the lobby of the Ramada as a makeshift mosque: "We belong to God and to God we return," he kept praying, in Arabic. Wallingford had to ask someone for a translation.

At the script meeting before the Sunday-evening telecast, Patrick was told point-blank of the network's plans. "Either you're our anchor tomorrow evening or we've got you on a Coast Guard cutter," Mary Shanahan informed him.

"I'm in Green Bay tomorrow and tomorrow night, Mary," Wallingford said.

"They're going to call off the search for survivors

tomorrow, Pat. We want you there, at sea. Or here, in New York. Not in Green Bay."

"I'm going to the football game," Wallingford told her. He looked at Wharton, who looked away; then he looked at Sabina, who stared with feigned neutrality back at him. He didn't so much as glance at Mary.

"Then we'll fire you, Pat," Mary said.

"Then fire me."

He didn't even have to think about it. With or without a job at PBS or NPR, he'd made quite a lot of money; besides, they couldn't fire him without making some kind of salary settlement. Patrick didn't really *need* a job, at least for a couple of years.

Wallingford looked at Mary for some response, then at Sabina.

"Okay, if that's how it is, you're fired," Wharton announced.

Everyone seemed surprised that it was Wharton who said it, including Wharton. Before the script meeting, they'd had another meeting, to which Patrick had not been invited. Probably they'd decided that Sabina would be the one to fire Wallingford. At least Sabina looked at Wharton with an exasperated sense of surprise. Mary Shanahan had got over how surprised she was pretty quickly.

For once, maybe Wharton had felt something unfamiliar and exciting taking charge inside him. But everything that was eternally insipid about him had instantly returned to his flushed face; he was again as vapid as he'd ever been. Being fired by Wharton was like being slapped by a tentative hand in the dark.

"When I get back from Wisconsin, we can work out what you owe me," was all Wallingford told them.

"Please clear out your office and your dressing room before you go," Mary said. This was standard procedure, but it irritated him.

They sent someone from security to help him pack up his things and to carry the boxes down to a limo. No one came to say good-bye to him, which was also standard procedure, although if Angie had been working that Sunday night, she probably would have.

Wallingford was back in his apartment when Mrs. Clausen called. He hadn't seen his piece at the Ramada Plaza, but Doris had watched the whole story.

"Are you still coming?" she asked.

"Yes, and I can stay as long as you want me to," Patrick told her. "I just got fired."

"That's very interesting," Mrs. Clausen commented. "Have a safe flight."

This time he had a Chicago connection, which got him into his hotel room in Green Bay in time to see the evening telecast from New York. He wasn't surprised that Mary Shanahan was the new anchor. Once again Wallingford had to admire her. She wasn't pregnant, but Mary had wound up with at least one of the babies she wanted.

"Patrick Wallingford is no longer with us," Mary began cheerfully. "Good night, Patrick, wherever you are!"

There was in her voice something both perky and consoling. Her manner reminded Wallingford of that time in his apartment when he'd been unable to get it up and she'd sympathized by saying, "Poor penis." As he'd understood only belatedly, Mary had always been part of the bigger picture.

It was a good thing he was getting out of the business. He wasn't smart enough to be in it anymore. Maybe he'd never been smart enough.

And what an evening it was for news! Naturally no survivors had been found. The mourning for the victims on EgyptAir 990 had just begun. There was the footage of the usual calamity-driven crowd that had gathered on a gray Nantucket beach—the "body-spotters," Mary had once called them. The "death-watchers," which was Wharton's term for them, were warmly dressed.

That close-up from the deck of a Merchant Marine Academy ship—the pile of passengers' belongings retrieved from the Atlantic—must have been Wharton's work. After floods, tornadoes, earthquakes, train wrecks, plane crashes, school shootings, or other massacres, Wharton always chose the shots of articles of clothing, especially the shoes. And of course there were children's toys; dismembered dolls and wet teddy bears were among Wharton's favorite disaster items.

Fortunately for the all-news network, the first vessel to arrive at the crash site was a Merchant Marine Academy training ship with seventeen cadets aboard. These young novices at sea were great for the human-interest angle—they were about the age of college upperclassmen. There they were in the spreading pool of jet fuel with the fragments of the plane's wreckage, plus people's shopping bags and body parts, bobbing to the oily surface around them. All of them wore gloves as they plucked this and that from the sea. Their expressions were what Sabina termed "priceless."

Mary milked her end lines for all they were worth. "The big questions remain unanswered," Ms. Shanahan said crisply. She was wearing a suit Patrick had never seen before, something navy blue. The jacket was strategically opened, as were the top two buttons of her pale-blue blouse, which closely resembled a man's dress shirt, only silkier. This would become her signature costume, Wallingford supposed.

"Was the crash of the Egyptian jetliner an act of terrorism, a mechanical failure, or pilot error?" Mary pointedly asked.

I would have reversed the order, Patrick thought—clearly "an act of terrorism" should have come last.

In the last shot, the camera was not on Mary but on the grieving families in the lobby of the Ramada Plaza; the camera singled out small groups among them as Mary Shanahan's voice-over concluded, "So many people want to know." All in all, the ratings would be good; Wallingford knew that Wharton would be happy, not that Wharton would know how to express his happiness.

When Mrs. Clausen called, Patrick had just stepped out of the shower.

"Wear something warm," she warned him. To Wallingford's surprise, she was calling from the lobby. There would be time for him to see little Otto in the morning, Doris said. Right now it was time to go to the game; he should hurry up and get dressed. Therefore, not knowing what to expect, he did.

It seemed too soon to leave for the game, but maybe Mrs. Clausen liked to get there early. When Wallingford left his hotel room and took the elevator to the lobby to meet her, his sense of pride was only slightly hurt that not one of his colleagues in the media had tracked him down and asked him what Mary Shanahan had meant when she'd announced, to millions, "Patrick Wallingford is no longer with us."

There'd doubtless been calls to the network already; Wallingford could only wonder how Wharton was handling it, or maybe they had put Sabina in charge. They didn't like to say they'd fired someone— they didn't like to admit that someone had quit, either. They usually found some bullshit way to say it, so that no one knew exactly what had happened.

Mrs. Clausen had seen the telecast. She asked Patrick: "Is that the Mary who isn't pregnant?"

"That's her."

"I thought so."

Doris was wearing her old Green Bay Packers parka, the one she'd been wearing when Wallingford first met her. Mrs. Clausen was not wearing its hood as she drove the car, but Patrick could imagine her small, pretty face peering out from it like the face of a child. And she had on jeans and running shoes, which was how she'd dressed that night when the police informed her that her husband was dead. She was probably wearing her old Packers sweatshirt, too, although Wallingford couldn't see what was under her parka.

Mrs. Clausen was a good driver. She never once looked at Patrick—she just talked about the game. "With a couple of four-two teams, anything can happen," she explained. "We've lost the last three in a row on Monday night. I don't believe what they say. It doesn't matter that Seattle hasn't played a Monday-night game in seven years, or that there's a bunch of Seahawks who've never played at Lambeau Field before. Their coach knows Lambeau—he knows our quarterback, too."

The Green Bay quarterback would be Brett Favre. Wallingford had read a paper (just the sports pages) on the plane. That's how he'd learned who Mike Holmgren was—formerly the Packers' coach, now the coach of the Seattle Seahawks. The game was a homecoming for Holmgren, who'd been very popular in Green Bay.

"Favre will be trying too hard. We can count on

that," Doris told Patrick. As she spoke, the passing headlights flashed on and off her face, which remained in profile to him.

He kept staring at her—he'd never missed anyone so much. He would have liked to think she'd worn these old clothes for him, but he knew the clothes were just her game uniform. When she'd seduced him in Dr. Zajac's office, she must have had no idea what she was wearing, and she probably had no memory of the order in which she'd taken off her clothes. Wallingford would never forget the clothes and the order.

They drove west out of downtown Green Bay, which didn't have much of a downtown to speak of—nothing but bars and churches and a haggard-looking riverside mall. There weren't many buildings over three stories high; and the one hill of note, which hugged the river with its ships loading and unloading—until the bay froze in December—was a huge coal stack. It was a virtual mountain of coal.

"I would not want to be Mike Holmgren, coming back here with his four-two Seattle Seahawks," Wallingford ventured. (It was a version of something he'd read in the sports pages.)

"You sound like you've been reading the newspapers or watching TV," Mrs. Clausen said. "Holmgren knows the Packers better than the Packers know themselves. And Seattle's got a good defense. We haven't been scoring a lot of points against good defenses this year."

"Oh." Wallingford decided to shut up about the game. He changed the subject. "I've missed you and little Otto."

Mrs. Clausen just smiled. She knew exactly where she was going. There was a special parking sticker on her car; she was waved into a lane with no other cars in it, from which she entered a reserved area of the parking lot.

They parked very near the stadium and took an elevator to the press box, where Doris didn't even bother showing her tickets to an official-looking older man who instantly recognized her. He gave her a friendly hug and a kiss, and she said, with a nod to Wallingford, "He's with me, Bill. Patrick, this is Bill."

Wallingford shook the older man's hand, expecting to be recognized, but there was no sign of recognition. It must have been the ski hat Mrs. Clausen had handed to him when they got out of the car. He'd told her that his ears never got cold, but she'd said, "Here they will. Besides, it's not just to keep your ears warm. I want you to wear it."

It wasn't that she didn't want him to be recognized, although the hat would keep him from being spotted by an ABC cameraman—for once, Wallingford wouldn't be on-camera. Doris had insisted on the hat to make him look as if he belonged at the game. Patrick was wearing a black topcoat over a tweed jacket over a turtleneck, and gray flannel trousers. Almost no one wore such a dressy overcoat to a Packer game.

The ski hat was Green Bay green with a yellow headband that could be pulled down over your ears; it had the unmistakable Packers' logo, of course. It was an old hat, and it had been stretched by a head bigger than Wallingford's. Patrick didn't need to ask Mrs. Clausen whose hat it was. Clearly the hat had belonged to her late husband.

They passed through the press box, where Doris said hi to a few other official-looking people before entering the bleacher-style seats, high up. It wasn't the way most of the fans entered the stadium, but everybody seemed to know Mrs. Clausen. She was, after all, a Green Bay Packers employee.

They went down the aisle toward the dazzling field. It was natural grass, 87,000 square feet of it— what they called an "athletic blue blend." Tonight was its debut game.

"Wow," was all Wallingford said under his breath. Although they were early, Lambeau Field was already more than half full.

The stadium is a pure bowl, with no breaks and no upper deck; there is only one deck at Lambeau, and all the outdoor seats are of the bleacher type. The stands were a primordial scene during the pregame warm-ups: the faces painted green and gold, the yellow plastic-foam things that looked like big flexible penises, and the lunatics with huge wedges of cheese for hats—the *cheeseheads*! Wallingford knew he was not in New York.

Down the long, steep aisle they went. They had

seats at about midstadium level on the forty-yard
line; they were still on the press-box side of the field.
Patrick followed Doris, past the stout knees turned
sideways, to their seats. He grew aware that they
were seated among people who knew them—not just
Mrs. Clausen, but Wallingford, too. And it wasn't
that they knew him because he was famous, not in
Otto's hat; it was that they were *expecting* him. Patrick suddenly realized that he'd met more than half
of the closest surrounding fans before. They were
Clausens! He recognized their faces from the countless photos tacked to the walls of the main cabin at
the cottage on the lake.

The men patted his shoulders; the women touched
his arm, the left one. "Hey, how ya doing?" Wallingford recognized the speaker from his crazed look in
the photograph that was safety-pinned to the lining
of the jewelry box. It was Donny, the eagle-killer;
one side of his face was painted the color of corn, the
other the too-vivid green of an impossible illness.

"I missed seein' ya on the news tonight," a friendly
woman said. Patrick remembered her from a photograph, too; she'd been one of the new mothers, in a
hospital bed with her newborn child.

"I just didn't want to miss the game," Wallingford
told her.

He felt Doris squeeze his hand; until then, he'd not
realized she was holding it. In front of all of them!
But they knew already—long before Wallingford.
She'd already told them. She had accepted him!

He tried to look at her, but she'd put up the hood of her parka. It wasn't that cold; she was just hiding her face from him.

He sat down beside Mrs. Clausen, still holding her hand. His handless arm was seized by an older woman on his left. She was another Mrs. Clausen, a much larger Mrs. Clausen—the late Otto's mother, little Otto's grandmother, Doris's former mother-in-law. (Probably one shouldn't say "former," Patrick was thinking.) He smiled at the large woman. She was as tall as he was, sitting down, and she pulled him to her by his arm so that she could kiss his cheek.

"All of us are very happy to see you," she said. "Doris has informed us." She smiled approvingly.

Doris might have informed *me*! Wallingford was thinking, but when he looked at Doris, her face was hidden in the hood. It was only by the ferocity of her grip on his hand that he knew for certain she'd accepted him. To Patrick's astonishment, they *all* had.

There was a moment of silence before the game, which Wallingford assumed was for the 217 dead on EgyptAir 990, but he hadn't been paying attention. The moment of silence was for Walter Payton, who'd died of complications from liver disease at the age of forty-five. Payton had run for the most yards in NFL history.

The temperature was forty-five degrees at kickoff. The night sky was clear. The wind was from the west at seventeen miles per hour, with gusts to thirty. Maybe it was the gusts that got to Favre. In the first half, he threw two interceptions; by the end of the game, he'd thrown four. "I told you he'd be trying too hard," Doris would say four times, all the while hiding under her hood.

During the pregame introductions, the crowd at Lambeau had cheered the Packers' former coach, Mike Holmgren. Favre and Holmgren had embraced on the field. (Even Patrick Wallingford had noticed that Lambeau Field was located at the intersection of Mike Holmgren Way and Vince Lombardi Avenue.)

Holmgren had come home prepared. In addition to the interceptions, Favre lost two fumbles. There were even some boos—a rarity at Lambeau.

"Green Bay fans don't usually boo," Donny Clausen said, making it clear that *he* didn't boo. Donny leaned close to Patrick; his yellow-and-green face added an extra dementia to his already demented reputation as an eagle-killer. "We all want Doris to be happy," he whispered menacingly in Wallingford's ear, which was warm under Otto's old hat.

"So do I," Patrick told him.

But what if Otto *had* killed himself because he couldn't make Mrs. Clausen happy? What if she'd driven him to do it, had even suggested it in some way? Was it just a case of the bridal jitters that gave Wallingford these terrible thoughts? There was no question that Doris Clausen could drive Patrick Wallingford to kill himself if he ever disappointed her.

Patrick wrapped his right arm around Doris's

small shoulders, pulling her closer to him; with his right hand, he eased the hood of her parka slightly away from her face. He meant only to kiss her cheek, but she turned and kissed him on the lips. He could feel the tears on her cold face before she hid herself in the hood again.

Favre was pulled from the game, in favor of backup quarterback Matt Hasselbeck, with a little more than six minutes remaining in the fourth quarter. Mrs. Clausen faced Wallingford and said, "We're leaving. I'm not staying to watch the rookie."

Some of the Clausens grumbled at their going, but the grumbles were good-natured; even Donny's crazily painted face revealed a smile.

Doris led Patrick by his right hand. They climbed back up to the press box again; someone a little over-friendly let them in. He was a young-looking guy with an athletic build—sturdy enough to be one of the players, or a former player. Doris paid no attention to him, other than to point back in the young man's direction after she and Wallingford had left him standing at the side door to the press box. They were almost at the elevator when Mrs. Clausen asked, "Did you see that guy?"

"Yes," Patrick said. The young man was still smiling at them in his overfriendly fashion, although Mrs. Clausen had not once turned to look at him herself.

"Well, that's the guy I shouldn't have slept with,"

Doris told Wallingford. "Now you know everything about me."

The elevator was packed with sportswriters, mostly guys. The sports hacks always left the game a little early, to assure themselves of prime spots at the postgame press conference. Most of them knew Mrs. Clausen; although she worked principally in sales, Doris was often the one who issued the press passes. The hacks instantly made room for her. She'd pulled the hood back on her parka because it was warm and close in the elevator.

The sportswriters were spouting stats and clichés about the game. "Costly fumbles . . . Holmgren has Favre's number . . . Dotson getting thrown out didn't help . . . only the second Green Bay loss in the last thirty-six games at Lambeau . . . the fewest points the Packers have scored in a game since that twenty-one-to-six loss in Dallas in '96 . . ."

"So what did *that* game matter?" Mrs. Clausen asked. "That was the year we won the Super Bowl!"

"Are you coming to the press conference, Doris?" one of the hacks asked.

"Not tonight," she said. "I've got a date."

The sportswriters ooohed and aaahed; someone whistled. With his missing hand hidden in the sleeve of his topcoat, and still wearing Otto Clausen's hat, Patrick Wallingford felt confident that he was unrecognizable. But old Stubby Farrell, the ancient sports hack from the all-news network, recognized him.

"Hey, lion guy!" Stubby said. Wallingford nodded, at last taking off Otto's hat. "Did you get the ax or what?"

Suddenly it was quiet; all the sportswriters wanted to know. Mrs. Clausen squeezed his hand again, and Patrick repeated what he'd told the Clausen family. "I just didn't want to miss the game."

The hacks loved the line, Stubby especially, although Wallingford wasn't able to duck the question.

"Was it Wharton, that fuck?" Stubby Farrell asked.

"It was Mary Shanahan," Wallingford told Stubby, thus telling them all. "She wanted my job." Mrs. Clausen was smiling at him; she let him know that she knew what Mary had *really* wanted.

Wallingford was thinking that he might hear one of them (maybe Stubby) say that he was a good guy or a nice guy, or a good journalist, but all he caught of their conversation was more sports talk and the familiar nicknames that would follow him to his grave.

Then the elevator opened and the sports hacks trotted around the side of the stadium; they had to go out in the cold to get to either the home-team or the visiting-team locker rooms. Doris led Patrick out from under the stadium pillars and into the parking lot. The temperature had fallen, but the cold air felt good on Wallingford's bare head and ears as he walked to the car holding Mrs. Clausen's hand. The temperature might have been in the thirties, near freezing, but probably it was just the wind that made it feel that cold.

Doris turned the car radio on; from her comments, Patrick wondered why she wanted to hear the end of the game. The seven turnovers were the most by the Packers since they had committed seven against the Atlanta Falcons eleven years before. "Even Levens fumbled," Mrs. Clausen said in disbelief. "And Freeman—what did he catch? Maybe two passes all night. He might have got all of ten yards!"

Matt Hasselbeck, the Packers' rookie quarterback, completed his first NFL pass—he finished 2-of-6 for 32 yards. "Wow!" shouted Mrs. Clausen, derisively. "Holy cow!" The final score was Seattle 27, Green Bay 7.

"I had the best time," Wallingford said. "I loved every minute of it. I love being with you."

He took off his seat belt and lay down in the front seat beside her, resting his head in her lap. He turned his face toward the dashboard lights and cupped the palm of his right hand on her thigh. He could feel her thigh tighten when she accelerated or let up on the accelerator, and when she occasionally touched the brake. Her hand gently brushed his cheek; then she went back to holding the steering wheel with both her hands.

"I love you," Patrick told her.

"I'm going to try to love you, too," Mrs. Clausen said. "I'm really going to try."

Wallingford accepted that this was the most she could say. He felt one of her tears fall on his face, but he made no reference to her crying other than to offer to drive—an offer he knew she would refuse. (Who wants to be driven by a one-handed man?)

"I can drive," was all she said. Then she added: "We're going to your hotel for the night. My mom and dad are staying with little Otto. You'll see them in the morning, when you see Otto. They already know I'm going to marry you."

The beams from passing headlights streaked through the interior of the cold car. If Mrs. Clausen had turned the heat on, it wasn't working. She drove with the driver's-side window cracked open, too. There was little traffic; most of the fans were staying at Lambeau Field until the bitter end.

Patrick considered sitting up and putting his seat belt back on. He wanted to see that old mountain of coal on the west side of the river again. He wasn't sure what the coal stack signified to him—perseverance, maybe.

Wallingford also wanted to see the television sets glowing in the darkness, all along their route, on their way back downtown; surely every set was still turned on to the dying game, and would stay on for the postgame analysis, too. Yet Mrs. Clausen's lap was warm and comforting, and Patrick found it easier to feel her occasional tears on his face than to sit up beside her and see her crying.

As they were nearing the bridge, she spoke to him: "Please put your seat belt on. I don't want to lose you."

He sat up quickly and buckled his belt. In the dark car, he couldn't tell if she'd stopped crying or not.

"You can shut the radio off now," she told him. He did. They drove over the bridge in silence, the towering coal stack at first looming and then growing smaller behind them.

We never really know our future, Wallingford was thinking; nobody's future with anyone is certain. Yet he imagined that he could envision his future with Doris Clausen. He saw it with the unlikely and offsetting brightness with which her and her late husband's wedding rings had leapt out of the dark at him, under the boathouse dock. There was something golden in his future with Mrs. Clausen—maybe the more so because it struck him as so undeserved. He no more merited her than those two rings, with their kept and unkept promises, deserved to be nailed under a dock, only inches above the cold lake.

And for how long would he have Doris, or she him? It was fruitless to speculate—as fruitless as trying to guess how many Wisconsin winters it would take to bring the boathouse down and sink it in the unnamed lake.

"What's the name of the lake?" he asked Doris suddenly. "Where the cottage is . . . *that* lake."

"We don't like the name," Mrs. Clausen told him. "We never use the name. It's just the cottage on the lake."

Then, as if she knew he'd been thinking about her

and Otto's rings nailed under the dock, she said: "I've picked out our rings. I'll show them to you when we get to the hotel. I chose platinum this time. I'm going to wear mine on the ring finger of my right hand." (Where the lion guy, as everyone knew, would have to wear his, too.)

"You know what they say," Mrs. Clausen said. " 'Leave no regrets on the field.' "

Wallingford could guess the source. Even to him, the phrase smacked of football—and of a courage he heretofore had lacked. In fact, it was what the old sign said at the bottom of the stairwell at Lambeau Field, the sign above the doors that led to the Packers' locker room.

LEAVE

NO REGRETS

ON THE FIELD

"I get it," Patrick replied. In a men's room at Lambeau, he'd seen a man with his beard painted yellow and green, like Donny's face; the necessary degree of devotion was getting through to him. "I get it," he repeated.

"No, you don't," Mrs. Clausen contradicted him. "Not yet, not quite." He looked closely at her—she'd stopped crying. "Open the glove compartment," Doris said. He hesitated; it occurred to him that Otto Clausen's gun was in there, and that it was loaded. "Go on—open it."

In the glove compartment was an open envelope with photographs protruding from it. He could see the holes the tacks had made in the photos—the occasional rust spot, too. Of course he knew where the photos were from before he saw what they were of. They were the photographs, a dozen or more, that Doris had once tacked to the wall on her side of the bed—those pictures she'd taken down because she couldn't stand to see them in the boathouse anymore.

"Please look at them," Mrs. Clausen requested.

She'd stopped the car. They were in sight of the hotel. She had just pulled over and stopped with the motor running. Downtown Green Bay was almost deserted; everyone was at home or returning home from Lambeau Field.

The photographs were in no particular order, but Wallingford quickly grasped their theme. They all showed Otto Clausen's left hand. In some, the hand was still attached to Otto. There was the beer-truck driver's brawny arm; there was Otto's wedding ring, too. But in some of the pictures, Mrs. Clausen had removed the ring—from what Wallingford knew was the dead man's hand.

There were photos of Patrick Wallingford, too. Well, at least there were photos of Patrick's new left hand—just the hand. By the varying degrees of swelling in the hand and wrist, and in the forearm area of the surgical attachment, Wallingford could tell at what stages Doris had photographed him with Otto's hand—what she had called the third one.

So he hadn't dreamed that he was having his picture taken in his sleep. That was why the sound of the shutter had seemed so real. And with his eyes shut, naturally the flash would have struck him as faint and distant, as incomplete as heat lightning—just the way Wallingford remembered it.

"Please throw them away," Mrs. Clausen asked. "I've tried, but I can't make myself do it. Please just get rid of them."

"Okay," Patrick said.

She was crying again, and he reached out to her. He'd never initiated touching her breast with his stump before. Even through her parka, he could feel her breast; when she clasped his forearm tightly there, he could also feel her breathing.

"Just don't ever think I haven't lost something, too," Mrs. Clausen told him angrily.

Doris drove on to the hotel. After she'd handed Patrick the keys and had gone ahead of him into the lobby, he was left to park the car. (He decided to have someone from the hotel do it.)

Then he disposed of the photographs—he dropped them, and the envelope, in a public trash receptacle. They were quickly gone, but he'd not missed their message. Wallingford knew that Mrs. Clausen had just told him all she ever would about her obsession; showing him those photographs of the hand was the absolute end of what she had to say about it.

What had Dr. Zajac said? There was no *medical* reason why the hand-transplant surgery hadn't worked; Zajac couldn't explain the mystery. But it was no mystery to Patrick Wallingford, whose imagination didn't suffer the constraints of a scientific mind. The hand had finished with its business—that was all.

Interestingly, Dr. Zajac had little to say to his students at Harvard Medical School on the subject of "professional disappointment." Zajac was happy in his semiretirement with Irma and Rudy and the twins; he thought professional disappointment was as anticlimactic as professional success.

"Get your *lives* together," Zajac told his Harvard students. "If you've already come this far, your professions should take care of themselves." But what do medical-school students know about having *lives*? They haven't had time to have lives.

Wallingford went up to Doris Clausen, who was waiting for him in the lobby. They took the elevator to his hotel room without exchanging a word.

He let her use the bathroom first. For all her plans, Doris had brought nothing with her but a toothbrush, which she carried in her purse. And in her haste to get ready for bed, she forgot to show Patrick the platinum wedding rings, which were also in her purse. (She would show him the rings in the morning.)

While Mrs. Clausen was in the bathroom, Wallingford watched the late-night news—as a matter of principle, *not* on his old channel. One of the sports hacks had already leaked the story of Patrick's dismissal to another network; it made a good show-ender, a better-than-average kicker. "Lion Guy Gets Ax from Pretty Mary Shanahan." (That was who she would be from this time forth: "Pretty Mary.")

Mrs. Clausen had come out of the bathroom, naked, and was standing beside him.

Patrick quickly used the bathroom while Doris watched the wrap-up of the Green Bay game. She was surprised that Dorsey Levens had carried the ball twenty-four times for 104 yards, a solid performance for him in a losing cause.

When Wallingford, also naked, came out of the bathroom, Mrs. Clausen had already switched off the TV and was waiting for him in the big bed. Patrick turned out the lights and got into bed beside her. They held each other while they listened to the wind—it was blowing hard, in gusts, but they soon ceased to hear it.

"Give me your hand," Doris said. He knew which one she meant.

Wallingford began by holding Mrs. Clausen's neck in the crook of his right arm; with his right hand, he held fast to one of her breasts. She started by scissoring the stump of his left forearm between her thighs, where he could feel the lost fingers of his fourth hand touching her.

Outside their warm hotel, the cold wind was a harbinger of the coming winter, but they heard only their own harsh breathing. Like other lovers, they were oblivious to the swirling wind, which blew on and on in the wild, uncaring Wisconsin night.

ACKNOWLEDGMENTS

I AM INDEBTED TO Charles Gibson at ABC News and *Good Morning America* for his sixteen-page, single-spaced fax to me—the most detailed notes I received on the first draft of this (or any other) novel. Thank you, Charlie. I owe a similar debt to Dr. Martin Schwartz in Toronto; this isn't the first time that Dr. Schwartz has advised me on the medical verisimilitude in a work of fiction. Thank you again, Marty.

I am grateful to David Maraniss, whom I consulted on matters pertaining to Lambeau Field and the Green Bay Packers, and to Jane Mayer for her insightful article "Bad News," which was published in the August 14, 2000, *New Yorker.*

In *The New York Times* of November 1 and 2, 1999, the reporting of the crash of EgyptAir 990 was most informative to me—in particular, pieces by Francis X. Clines, John Kifner, Robert D. McFadden, Andrew C. Revkin, Susan Sachs, Matthew L. Wald, and Amy Waldman. Dr. Lawrence K. Altman's three stories on hand-transplant surgeries were especially enlightening; they appeared in the *Times* on January 26, 1999, January 15, 2000, and February 27, 2001.

As for the glut of commentary and opinion that followed the death of John F. Kennedy, Jr., my sources were largely undistinguished (and often indistinguishable from one another) and too numerous to cite. The same can be said for most of the television I watched on the subject.

Not least, I would like to thank the three assistants who worked for me in the period of time this novel was written: for their careful typing and proofreading of the manuscript, and their thoughtful criticism, my thanks to Chloe Bland, Edward McPherson, and Kelly Harper Berkson. More than ever, my editor, Harvey Ginsberg, has made me look better than I am. And, as always, to my friend David Calicchio and my wife, Janet, who both read this novel more than once—thanks again.

Janet gave me the idea for *The Fourth Hand*. One night we were watching the news on television before we went to bed. A story about the nation's first hand transplant got our attention. There were only brief views of the surgical procedure, and hardly a word about how the patient—the recipient, as I thought of him—lost his hand in the first place. There was nothing about the donor. The new hand had to have come from someone who'd died recently; probably he'd had a family.

Janet asked the inspiring question: "What if the donor's widow demands visitation rights with the hand?"

Dr. John C. Baldwin, the Dean of Dartmouth Medical School, has assured me that this probably wouldn't happen in what we call real life—not without the unlikely concurrence of enough lawyers and medical ethicists to start a small liberal-arts college. But I always listen to the storytelling possibilities. Every novel I've written has begun with a "What if . . ."

—J.I.

JOHN IRVING published his first novel at the age of twenty-six. He has received awards from the Rockefeller Foundation, the National Endowment for the Arts, and the Guggenheim Foundation; he has won an O. Henry Award, a National Book Award, and an Oscar.

In 1992, Mr. Irving was inducted into the National Wrestling Hall of Fame in Stillwater, Oklahoma. In January 2001, he was elected to the American Academy of Arts and Letters.